AFT

After Coffee

Abdelrashid Mahmoudi

Translated by
Nashwa Gowanlock

Hamad bin Khalifa University Press
P O Box 5825
Doha, Qatar

www.hbkupress.com

The author reviewed the translation

First published in Arabic as *Baad - AL - Qahwa*, in 2013
by Maktabat al-Dar al-Arabiyah lil-Kitab an imprint of AL Dar AL Masriah
AL Lubnaniah, Cairo, Egypt

Cover photo: TTstudio / Shutterstock.com
eFesenko / Shutterstock.com

ISBN: 978-9927118302

Qatar National Library Cataloging-in-Publication (CIP)

Maḥmūdī, ʻAbd al-Rashīd al-Ṣādiq, author.

After coffee / by Abdelrashid Mahmoudi, translated by Nashwa Gowanlock. – Doha : Hamad Bin Khalifa University Press , 2018.

Pages ; cm

ISBN: 978-9927-118-30-2

1. Arabic fiction – 20th century. I. Gowanlock, Nashwa, translator. II. Title.

PJ7846.A4862 A38 125 2018

892.736–dc23 2018 26680804

The Wolf Slayer

Khalil tossed and turned outside his shop, which overlooked the canal. He batted a fly that hovered over his nose, then dozed off again. The breeze toyed with the hem of his *jilbab,* as if it wanted to pick up the fabric and fly off. Nothing disrupted the serenity of this scene until a noise surfaced - a cacophony of screaming, laughter, and barking - from the direction of the canal. A group of boys was crossing over while a black dog protested over how they'd charged towards the water without him. The boys were fleeing from the Upper Egyptian locals with their loot: dates, prickly pears, and reeds. Khalil woke up when the boys' commotion reached him, and all traces of sleep disappeared once the afternoon call to prayer sounded from the farthest end of the village. It felt as if a firm hand was shaking him, urging Khalil to get up and go to the mosque to pray on time, but he didn't budge. Those little devils were still running riot, even though they usually panicked and scampered off to their hiding places once the blistering midday hour had passed. After the shame of what had happened with his sister, Khalil felt no desire to do his ablutions or pray. He wished he could sleep and never wake up. He didn't want to talk to anyone about anything. His customers no longer had anything to say to him, either. They each grabbed what they needed before hurrying off. No one would stay and sprawl out on the ground outside his shop anymore to play cards, drink tea, and smoke *muassel.* All that had ended, and anyway he didn't want to face them. He saw the question in people's eyes, which nobody dared to utter:

'Where did she go?' Every time a customer appeared, he lowered his head. He had transformed from an intimidating character to a man broken by the weight of shame and helplessness, all over what his sister Zakiya had done. *What's the use of having a shop and buying and selling when you can't talk to anyone? Wouldn't it be better to stay at home and let no one see your face?* He finally stood up to close the shop. *But what's the point of staying at home?* he wondered. There was only one person to turn to for help: Ibrahim Abu Zaid.

He walked past Nafisa's house. The old woman was outside chasing her chickens with a broomstick - a dried palm branch with its strands still intact - to bring them in for the night. She wouldn't usually do this before sunset, but had decided to bring them in early that day. As Khalil walked by, he turned his head to avoid greeting her. He had started to despise the old woman because his sister used to go to her house and work for free. 'I hope you're well, Khalil,' Nafisa called out to him, but he didn't reply.

'You bear a heavy burden, my boy,' she added, when he was further away. 'God help you, my dear.' Still, the fact that he'd ignored her had stung. She didn't deserve that. Whatever had happened had happened, and she was not to blame. Medhat had also passed by her house a short while ago with his dog and his friends, on their way back from the opposite bank of the canal, brandishing their reed sticks. 'Come here my darling,' she had called out to him. 'Give your nana a kiss, my love.' But the boy stopped to say with disdain, 'I don't kiss old people.' 'Come here boy, be kind,' she said. 'I'm your nana, your darling nana.' 'When you take off your nose ring,' he replied. *That scrawny kid is only five years old*, she thought as she shook her head. *You'd think he was spawned by devils. God rest the souls of your mother and father, Medhat.* Then she sighed. 'But then again, who does like old people?'

She was the last of the grandparents' generation. Back when she lived with her late brother's wife, Zainab, she was treated like a queen. But after Zainab died, she went to live with Fatima, Zainab's second cousin, until she grew weary of the way Fatima's daughters treated her. *The girls also don't like my nose ring, like Medhat,* she thought. 'What is that hanging from your nose, Nana?' they would say. 'No one wears those anymore.' They didn't like the tattoo on her chin, either. And they would never let her utter a single word without making fun of her. 'Nana never stops talking,' they would say, or - even worse - 'My nana's started spouting gibberish.'

They liked her food, sure, they would devour it - all the old recipes she carried in her heart - but they didn't want her to speak. Fatima had asked her to teach her eldest daughter the basics of cooking, in preparation for marriage, but could Saadiya endure her instructions and advice? 'Nana, you're driving me crazy with all this talk about how much water to add to the rice, because you say perfecting the rice is the stamp of a good cook. And the tomato sauce that has to be stewed just so... Do you think the man will be as bothered as you? Why can't he just be quiet and eat whatever I cook?' At first, Fatima would tell her daughters off, but she soon changed. After she got fed up with Nafisa's rambling about her missing son and her relentless, futile appeals to him, she gradually began to let their comments go. Whenever the memory of his absence became too painful, Nafisa would find somewhere private and start crying out, imploring him to come home. After Fatima gave up on her, she gathered her belongings and moved to this house that turned its back to the village, facing the country road instead. Here, no one had any right to complain about her, and she could see out her remaining years in peace. And here, she could wait for her absent loved one. Thirty years had passed since her son Hashem was whisked off to the provincial jail. It was said the police found him and the rest of the gang because one of them had left behind a sandal as he fled the scene, which is how the police dogs were able to trace them. She had seen one of them return - Musa Abu Mostafa. He had stepped out of the police van supported by two policemen because he couldn't walk on his own. After fifteen years in prison, he was back, but the happiness of his wife and children was short-lived. Shortly after reaching his house, he lay down and never got up again. He died after spending barely a week with his family. When she saw him clambering out of the police van, she knew he didn't have long. Having witnessed pangs of death in both the young and the old, she had come to recognise the meaning behind his pallor.

But her son Hashem never came home, not even after the end of his prison term. The rumour was that he had escaped prison and fled to Palestine. It was also said that he was spotted several times wandering the fields on the other side of the canal, near the Sa'ida, or Upper Egyptian, village. So why hadn't he returned? *Hashem, why won't you come back home?* She recalled his life from the day he was born, including the time she found him a fiancé, and how she had tried to hasten his wedding so she could become a grandmother, since he was her only son. She would return to her memories of each event as if it had happened yesterday, without skipping a single moment. She remembered the date, the season it fell in, what food she had prepared, and the colour of the chicken's feathers that she had slaughtered for the occasion. One of Fatima's daughters would interrupt her. 'Nana, do you have to go into so much detail? Do you really have to tell us about the rooster you slaughtered for the guests, how heavy it was, how its feathers were black and that its crest was large?' No one wanted to listen to her tales of sorrow.

Ever since she'd started living alone, the days had dragged and the nights even more so. Her visitors slowed to a trickle. Her family began to forget about her. Zaki no longer dropped in on her. He used to stop off after his afternoon nap, before the *asr* prayer, to see if she had anything he could snack on. She would bring him whatever he wanted - a hot loaf of bread, some crushed salt and chilli pepper. Zaki was the only one who was still faithful to the old days, and the only one whose heart still went out to everyone. But she didn't know what had happened to him lately. His visits had dwindled and, when they did happen, they were fleeting. His face seemed permanently strained.

Salama - *may God prolong his life and protect him from danger* - was the only one in her family who still cared about her. He farmed her land, was content with his share of the harvest - a quarter - and never refused her a single request. He also helped to sell her share and brought everything she needed from the Monday or Wednesday markets. 'The boy is gallant and chivalrous and has a kind heart, but what kind of a nightmare has he caught himself up in?' she wondered. There was no one left but Zakiya - the Baharwa girl - to help her with household chores like kneading the dough, baking, and washing. Guided by the Most Merciful One, she did it all for no wage, even though the Baharwa people were famous for being tightfisted. Then, the One and Only God ordained that this calamity would fall on her and Salama. Nafisa started to worry that Salama and Zakiya would end up as unlucky as Hashem - he, too, had been kind, chivalrous, and naïve. But still, God had brought a catastrophe down on him, great is His wisdom.

She worried they would end up doomed like Zainab's youngest and most handsome child. He was the one known as 'the star' and 'the neighbourhood heartthrob', before he was lured by some thugs, became addicted to 'snorting powder,' and ended up dying at one of those gatherings. Over the years, she had seen how misfortune only ever remembered the kind ones. Hashem, for example, didn't murder anyone, and none of that gang had any intention of killing a soul. *They were a bunch of misguided youths and the devil used them as his playthings. May God avenge them. That gang leader sent respectable kids to hell while he dozed at home so he could escape the consequences as smoothly as a strand of hair teased out of a lump of dough.* They had wanted to rob the home of a widow in the Nazlet Elwan village to steal her silver, but she woke up and confronted one of them, who stabbed her with a knife. It was an accidental blow. But Hashem didn't attack anyone; he didn't clash with anyone and hadn't even gone into the house. He'd been standing guard at the top of the road ready to whistle if he saw anyone approaching. 'Why did you do it, when you came from a good family?' she moaned. 'Did you need any gold or silver? Why then, when you're the one who always gives away everything you have? Why not come home, my son? My heart is tired of waiting, Hashem. They say you come to the other side of the canal at night. So take a little turn, my darling. Say, I'll go and see my mother whose tears have run dry. Hashem, there's nothing but a canal to separate us. You can cross the water by foot.... They are just a few short steps, my sweetheart.' When she had managed to usher in the last chicken, she fastened her door shut with a latch and key.

***

Hajj Zaki was the first to appear when the worshippers began arriving at the mosque in answer to the afternoon call to prayer. He circled the building to inspect its condition and reached the back door, pursing his lips with discontent. His brother still lifted water out of the mosque's well to fill the bathing basin, as well as the place for ablution and the latrines. He also raised the prayer call at the regular times with a booming voice that travelled across the canal and was heard at the Sa'ida's village - a beautiful sound that humbled people's hearts. But lately, it had started to cause a tightness in Zaki's chest. And the building was in a deplorable state; the wall by the well had large cracks in it that warned of imminent collapse. He appealed to the Muslims to rescue their mosque before it caved in, but none of the Qassimis or the Baharwa people were interested in his pleas. No one wanted to pull a piaster from their pocket to help repair the house of God. They wanted him to bear the burden on his own, as he had in the past, but he couldn't do it anymore. The mosque was old, built in his grandfather's time, and his father had taken charge of its upkeep throughout his whole life. As for the others, their hearts had toughened and their faith weakened. He sighed. The families of the neighbouring villages used to come for Friday prayers, but now their attendance was rare. He recalled painfully how he used to invite everyone after the prayers for lunch at the guesthouse they called the *seera*, serving them lentils in winter and rice pudding in summer. That was in the good old days. *An onion shared with a loved one is a lamb*, as the saying goes, but this loved one had neither lamb nor onions anymore.

He stopped to shoo away the boys who had gathered around the back door. They were carrying sticks made of reed, and some were as naked as the day they were born. The pack started to disperse but two lingered: Medhat and his black dog.

Medhat was rooted to his spot by the door and gazed out at the far corner of the mosque where a rectangular wooden box stood, tipped upright on four legs. They called it 'the coffin'. He would always see it there, in the same place, unless it had been removed by the village men as they hauled someone inside it to a distant place from which there was no return. This had happened when they carried his mother away and when they took his grandmother, covered in a white sheet that fluttered in the breeze. He may never have discovered what all this meant had he not wondered why neither his mother nor grandmother had come back from that faraway place. 'Where's my ma?' he had asked Na'sa, his wet-nurse. 'She went to the market to get you halva and a couple of loaves of special *bandar* bread,' she replied. 'And where's my nana?' he asked her. 'She went to visit her relatives in Hassiniya,' she said. Oh, how he'd waited for his mother to return with the halva and the special bread. And how he'd waited for his grandmother to come back from her family visit. But he now knew that Na'sa had lied and that anyone carried off in that box would not be back. That was the distant place they called 'death'.

One of his friends pulled at his arm and another struck him on the shoulder with a stick, but he didn't move. They were gesturing excitedly with their reed sticks because they were on their way to war…their mission at this hour was to attack the wasps that built their nests in the straw and firewood stored on the roofs of the houses. They were not deterred from battle by the fact that wasps defended their homes fiercely and were capable of inflicting serious injuries on the attackers - especially the naked ones. The child didn't budge until Hajj Zaki put his hand on his shoulder. 'Isn't it rude to walk around naked like that, Medhat?' 'We left our clothes by the canal,' Medhat replied. 'We sped off when the Sa'ida's dogs started chasing us'. 'All right, but hurry on along now please,' Zaki said. 'Goodbye.'

The two sheikhs, Hamed and Sayyid, approached, but stepped aside from leading the prayer when they saw Hajj Zaki. It wasn't because he was more educated than them, since he hadn't studied at al-Azhar Islamic University. And it wasn't because he was older, since he was actually younger than them both. It was because they recognised his stature. If he wasn't there, they would have ended up competing over who would lead the prayer and some of the congregation might have sided with one or the other, since they each had their own supporters. The first one, Sheikh Sayyid, had spent God knows how many years boarding at the revered University of al-Azhar without receiving a graduation certificate. As for the second sheikh, Hamed, he had spent only five years at the Religious Institute of Zagazig. Thus Sheikh Sayyid believed, along with his supporters, that it was his right, being the more educated, to lead the prayers. But Sheikh Hamed believed, and so did his supporters, that to pray behind Sheikh Sayyid was an arduous ordeal because he would forever stutter and stammer. And from time to time, he would emit a sound that resembled a cross between a sip and a slurp, and he would end up reciting the rebellious phrase or word over and over again until it obeyed him. Not only that, but these falterings that seemed to haunt Sheikh Sayyid would prompt the boys in the back rows to snigger and nudge each other, or worse. Sheikh Hamed, however, was characterised by his wit and eloquence. Most importantly, he would complete the prayer before the worshippers' patience had completely depleted, knowing that some of them wanted only to carry out the religious obligation in a slapdash manner. And so he would leave no room for the devil to penetrate the rows of worshippers and distract them from their state of submission as they stood in the hands of God.

If Hajj Zaki was present, it meant the end of the dispute; everyone would be in agreement, tranquillity would abound, and the prayer would be performed as it should be. Even Shabana, whose mockery no one could escape, would declare during his gatherings at the village's public *jurn* that 'Saad Pasha and Nahhas Pasha may be the elected leaders of the nation, but my cousin Zaki is the chief of the "sons of Qassim", without election or royal decree.' But this unelected leadership no longer pleased Zaki, since it had become too heavy a burden to bear. It had somehow been thrust upon him through neither his nor anyone else's will but God's. He was simply performing his duty, just as he had when his father was alive. Back then, he would receive guests generously and would sometimes act on his father's behalf in resolving conflicts. But he just couldn't keep doing it anymore; *God burdens not a person beyond his scope*, after all.

He called for the worshippers to straighten the rows as he led the congregational prayer so that 'God may have mercy on you', and everyone shuffled into position behind him. There was still some respect left. No one complained, no arguments erupted, and the boys didn't nudge each other in the back rows or snigger if the prayer dragged on. And so everyone was humble in the hands of the Sacred King. The crisis now was that he himself struggled to stay humble and focused. His mind would wander just as he started to recite a verse from the Quran, and he would try to remember the next one, but it would only come through arduous effort. Between one verse and another was a gap filled with silence, a gap mired in darkness. Between one verse and another, fear reared its head. And recently - since the quarrel with his brother - these gaps had been growing. If this continued, people would surely abandon him. Then there was Shabana at the *jurn* gatherings; if people found out about his situation, there was no way he would escape Shabana's ridicule. Fear resided deep inside him, and it surfaced during the prayers, or as soon as he laid his head on the pillow, or whenever he saw his brother. There was a phrase that was desperate to launch itself from the depths of his soul towards his lips in the shape of a scream, but it would always get lodged in his throat. And there were words he wished he could raise to the One from Whom Nothing is Concealed, but he found himself mute.

***

The village of the Qassimis, the descendants of the original settler, Qassim, was an odd kind of place, surrounded by secrets on every side. Most of the locals believed jinn inhabited the mosque's well, and it was said that a black, horned serpent guarded the bathing basin of the mosque. Sheikh Sayyid claimed that 'The Enemy' extended his hand and poked him on the right side of his body, trying to nullify his prayers, whenever he performed the voluntary, late-night *tahajjud*. Beyond the fields that extended south of the mosque was a stagnant pond with algae that rose above the water's surface. People would try to keep their distance as they walked past, because it was said to be deep, bottomless, and inhabited by various types of ghouls. Woe betide anyone who lost their footing and toppled in! The main road that split the village in two ended at the perpendicular country road that bordered the canal. Those were the northern borders of the village. But beyond those borders was the opposite bank of the canal, where the Sa'ida lived. There was some interaction between the Sa'ida people and the villagers, and they would sometimes visit each other. The village children would also cross to the other side on foot when the water was shallow - since the canal was four metres wide at most - or swim across during the periods of flooding. They would climb the Sa'ida's palm trees to steal their fruit in the date season. And they would chop up the reed branches they found floating on the surface of the water to use as spears that they would fling at wasps, or make reed pens to use at the Quranic school. Crossing to the opposite bank would fill the boys with fear and, to them, reaching the other side was an adventure to top all adventures.

At the western side of the village there was the waterwheel, shaded by the old sycamore tree whose branches extended over the path. The well at the waterwheel was inhabited and had its own tales of terror. It was said that a man called Abdulhadi had been mesmerised by a female jinn - one of the women of the underworld - while he watered his land one night. She had appeared to him from the well and forced him into an engagement, offering to take him to live down in the abundant bliss amongst her family. But he refused because he was faithful to his wife, the mother of his children. It was also said that he was strong and fought with her until she defeated him. She only managed to overcome him when she embraced him, pressing her breasts into his chest such that two nails protruding from her nipples hammered into him and pierced his heart. When was this? And to which past generation did Abdelhadi belong? And where was his wife whom he'd abandoned? And where were his remaining family? These were questions for which no one had answers. It wouldn't even cross anyone's mind in the village - apart from Shabana at the *jurn* gatherings - to ask them. There was another story about a young man called Abdelsalam who was enticed by a female jinn and disappeared with her to live together in her underground world, where they have remained ever since. Who were his mother and father? In which era did he live? These questions had no answer and no one except

Shabana thought to raise them, to ridicule the sons of Qassim and to highlight their foolishness. If ever the water buffalo's hoof slipped when it was in the vicinity of the waterwheel, causing it to topple into the well, it would be taken as an ominous sign and a harbinger of great catastrophe. The women's voices would then ring out as they screamed and wailed, and the men would rush from the outskirts of the village to the helpless animal to try and pull it out. If they failed to rescue it, they would bring a knife and slaughter the buffalo on the spot before it died.

The area around the waterwheel was inhabited, too. There was a spirit that appeared to passersby at night in the shape of a donkey whose back rose higher and higher until it was taller than the top of the sycamore tree and even reached the sky. If anyone approaching from the western side at night was destined to come across a spirit, then they would most likely spot it near the waterwheel and the sycamore tree. And it would be that satanic donkey they'd see.

This paranormal activity wasn't restricted to the western side of the country road, since the eastern side had its peculiar stories in turn. There, the spirits would not be limited to nocturnal appearances. Either 'Mother Ghoul' or 'The Summoner' might emerge in broad daylight, and especially during the siesta hour. Everyone would be asleep, and all the animals would appear stunned - the water buffalo, for example, would be powerless to bat the flies pinching at its tail - and the whole area around the *jurn* would be vacant. But people returning from the central market on Wednesday might be unfortunate enough to be heading back during the witching hour and could be half-asleep astride their donkeys when they would suddenly be woken up by the call of 'The Summoner'. Then woe betide those who responded, for the call was irresistible.

The world at large was divided into two: the countryside and the *bandar*. The *bandar* was the world of civilisation and luxury. The nearest town would not be considered *bandar*, nor would the capital of the province, or the provincial cities in general. Those areas were in between, only partially civilised. Cairo would be classified as *bandar,* and perhaps Alexandria too, since many of its residents were said to be foreigners.

But what was the secret of the spirits' fascination with donkeys? The question was once put to Shabana.

'Donkeys are easy to ride. If someone passing by obeys the devil and rides it, then they're doomed. It's the same with women. A woman entices you until you ride her and end up in hellfire. Ha ha ha!'

He laughed, and so did his audience. But his words seemed to carry a hint of cunning. Was he also alluding to what had happened to Salama and Zakariya?

***

Sheikh Hamed left the mosque, putting his hand out for his son to grab. He was with Sheikh Sayyid, who was swaying as usual as he walked, listening so as not to miss the sound of any invisible caller. Sheikh Sayyid was surprised when Sheikh Hamed invited him to drink tea at his house. How could that be? Hamed was not known for his generosity. So what did he want? *Oh, You who conceals benevolence, rescue us from what we fear.* He tried to evade him but failed, since Hamed insisted.

'Come on man, shame on you. How can you refuse a brother's invitation?'

Dear God, let it be good news. He sat down reluctantly, and then the reason became clear. All his astonishment disappeared when Hamed - before the tea had even arrived - floated his question. 'Sheikh Sayyid, I swear, this whole business with Salama is making me very unhappy. Is there any news? Has he turned up yet?' Sheikh Sayyid lowered his head for a long time, then took out a large thin needle from his turban, with which he started to darn his sandal. He never left his house unarmed. Tucked under his arm was Sheikh al-Bajouri's book of jurisprudence, and he had a large needle in his turban to mend his sandals, and a smaller one for the *jilbab* and such - oh, what a multitude of repairs! So the reason had become apparent: Sheikh Sayyid wanted to lure him into talking about his son, but he didn't want to broach that unstoppable evil. At first, he pretended he hadn't heard the question, until he was inspired, after one or two stitches, to distract Hamed from his goal.

'So here we are, with Ramadan at our door,' he said. 'What will you do?'

'Yes, you have touched on the wound now,' Hamed replied. 'What will I do in Ramadan? God only knows.' He shook his head sadly. 'God bless the good old days. They're over, Sheikh Sayyid. In the old days, as you know, Hajj Zaki - may God improve his lot - would invite me to celebrate the righteous month with him in the *seera*. At sunset, with the sounding of the *maghreb* call to prayer, the food would be served to break the fast. And what about the abundance: the poultry, the lamb, the stuffed vegetables and the *fatta*. Abundance followed by more abundance. And another feast would be prepared for the pre-dawn meal to prepare for fasting. Yes. Those were the days...'

'And between breaking the fast and the pre-dawn meal there would be stories, tales and poetry,' Sayyid said.

'Exactly,' Hamed replied. 'Stories, tales and poetry. I would recite a few pages of the Quran between the *maghreb* prayer and the early morning meal. And between one reading and another, we would tell stories and recite poetry. But as you can see, Zaki - may God help and support him - cannot arrange all of that anymore, not since his brother took his share of the land and separated from him. But what can I do? The fathers of the children I teach at the Quran school only give me a kilo of wheat or corn each. It's like pulling teeth. They want the kids to learn for free. I swear to God, have you ever seen anything as catastrophic as this?'

Sayyid was starting to enjoy the game, so he continued.

'By the way, I once heard you tell the story of the woman who married the caliph Muawiya ibn Abu Sufyan. Would you remind me again how the story goes?'

It pleased Hamed that his friend had asked him to recount one of the stories that were dear to his heart, and which he had told countless times at Ramadan night gatherings, so he cleared his throat.

'Do you mean Maysun bint Bahdal?' he replied. 'What a woman, Sheikh Sayyid! She was a beauty and the caliph Muawiya - may God be pleased with him - married her and installed her in a palace where she had everything she needed and more, but she longed for her old life in the desert. Can you believe how that respectable woman acted.... Then one day, the caliph walked in on her singing:

A rickety tent that the wind howls through
is dearer to me than a towering palace.
To wear a coarse abaya and a joyful soul
is dearer to me than some fine, sheer silk.
Nibbling crumbs of our homemade bread
is dearer to me than gorging a loaf.
The whistling of the wind along the mountain paths

is dearer to me than a tambourine's beat.
A dog who growls at a visitor in the night
is dearer to me than a friendly cat.
A kind-hearted thin man from my family
is dearer to me than some broad foreigner.
The rough life I lead as a desert Bedouin
is dearer to me than this opulent one.
Instead, all I want is my homeland,
that place of honour is enough for me.

So he pronounced her divorced, three times for confirmation, and sent her back to her family. Honestly, have you ever seen anything as marvellous, or more admirable behaviour than that of the prince of the believers, Muawiya, the companion of the prophet of God?'

'God bless you.' Sayyid said. 'There you have the moral in front of you, so you should heed it. Tell me, how can you recite this poem that advises self-restraint and moderation and, at the same time, mourn the days of poultry and stuffed vegetables? Would it not be more fitting for you, Hamed, to be content with whatever blessings God has given you, no matter how modest?'

Hamed paled. It took him a few moments to recover from the shock.

'Thank God for everything, but the little that is left is not enough to survive on. You don't realise. I swear to God Almighty, Sheikh Sayyid, even the mice at home are starving. Even the mice cannot find any food to eat. So what do they do? Human beings are the only things left for them. Last night, as I was sleeping, one of them - may God thwart his plans - was about to munch on my toe. I woke and found the bastard biting it. And I will not lie to you, I have no appetite for stories and poems. Ramadan is on its way and there will be nothing left but fasting during the day and hunger at night. But what can we say? Complaining to anyone but God is humiliating and one must…'

Hamed suddenly stopped when he realised how the conversation had strayed and that he hadn't reached his original goal.

'By the way, what is the latest news?' he asked. 'Has Salama still not appeared?'

'You're asking me about what has appeared and what hasn't appeared, so I will tell you what has appeared,' Sheikh Sayyid said. 'I was standing outside the mosque last night when I saw a light shining from the direction of the village of the Salehis. A torch directed towards us. And I knew that 'The Enemy' was waiting for us. Ibrahim Abu Zaid, that spawn of the devil, was aiming his torch at us, and danger was looming. I sought refuge in God from the accursed Satan and went into the mosque. While I was focused on the prayer, the accursed one put out his hand and poked me in the right side of my body.'

'But the devil lurks in the latrines and doesn't go near the prayer area,' Hamed said. 'What news is there of Salama?'

'That's true, but he has long arms, and he stretched his hand from the latrines to hurt me. Do you not see that even though Ibrahim Abu Zaid, that spawn of the devil, lives far away from us, he still reaches us with his torch?'

Sheikh Sayyid returned to the attack. 'I like the story of the Bedouin girl because she calls for moderation. Unlike the vulgar stories and poems you tell, Hamed.'

Sheikh Hamed was aghast. 'Me? You slanderer,' he said, reproachfully. 'I tell vulgar stories and poems?'

'I think you talk about the ghazal poets and their poetry of desire much more than is necessary, and a lot of that can corrupt the minds of the youth.'

'True, but I tell stories about chaste love.'

'Young people don't know the difference between what is chaste and what is not. The youth are made of fire. Tell them stories of lovers and love poetry, and they get enflamed. What do you think will happen to the girls if words like these reach them? You are opening up doors for the devil.'

'That is unfair!'

'I am not being unjust towards you. What about what happened to my son Salama with the Baharwa girl? Was it not love that allowed the devil to reach them? The story begins with chaste love then ends, as you know, in the cornfield and...'

Uh-oh... now he had gone and put his foot in it by talking about Salama and his scandals. Hamed decided to ignore the charges directed at him and take advantage of the opportunity that had inadvertently presented itself, delving into the subject.

'May God help you. Has the boy still not appeared?'

His question was never answered because when his friend reached that point in the conversation - the cornfield - he was afflicted by a severe agitation and began turning left and right.

'I can hear footsteps coming from there.'

He was pointing to the right. There were definitely footsteps, because he had seen the dust shift when he looked over. So 'The Enemy' had come. Here he was, crawling under the dirt, slithering like a serpent. Was last night's harassment not enough for him? He spat on the accursed devil and hurriedly slipped on his sandals and darted off. He left without hearing Hamed's objection. 'Wait, man. Be patient. God is with those who are patient. The tea is on its way.'

Hamed was always trying to overtake him, but what a preposterous idea! Hamed had spent several years at the Islamic institute, whereas he had spent thirteen years at al-Azhar

University. Thirteen or fourteen years? He didn't earn a university degree, but he was the authority in jurisprudence for the villagers and the people from neighbouring villages, and he would always refer to the accredited books. What did Sheikh Hamed offer them? He knew nothing about jurisprudence. He didn't refer to a single one of the imams' texts, and he would speak of things he didn't understand. All he had to offer was helping students memorize the Quran at his school (although he and his wife would exploit the pupils and ask them to do household chores, like gathering firewood, sweeping, and feeding the goat), he recited the Quran without perfecting his pronunciation, and told stories and recited poetry that distracted people from religious matters. Because of him, the boys and young men had become susceptible to corruption and were being preyed on by the devil. On the country road, he would spy them watching girls as they headed to the water. Some of them would walk along the road with their sleeves rolled up. He would advise them gently, telling them that when young men revealed their forearms, it created temptation, but none of them would ever heed his advice. And he would yell at the girls on their way to the water, because they wriggled as they walked with the buckets balanced on their heads. But he would get nothing from them but laughter and mockery. What would happen to this village whose elders turned a blind eye to this dreadful behaviour? And the worst of all the young men in the village was his own son, Salama. He had no idea about the meaning of modest dress. He would sometimes see Salama at the canal, turning the screw pump, dressed in his vest and baggy *sirwal*, which revealed his legs from the knees down. He would climb the palm tree without a long *jilbab,* and his *sirwal* would be the only thing covering his private parts. If anyone looked up and saw what they saw, a sin would have occurred. He had been in a panicked state ever since he saw his son watering the plants early one morning a few days ago. There was Salama, standing bare-chested, his feet sunk into the mud. This was during the time girls passed by on their way to fill up their buckets from the canal. What would happen if they were exposed to temptation? The boy never heeded his advice. His mother spoilt him, and he knew that she would always take his side and protect him in the face of any criticism. Then this scandal erupted, the news of which had spread far and wide. The people of the village consulted him on religious matters, but they hardly ever took his advice. Some of them made fun of him if his memory didn't come to his rescue with an answer to a question, when he would have to appeal for time to refer to the writings of the scholars. They were always in a rush to solve their problems, wanting a one-word answer instead of listening to all the text, commentary, and marginal glosses, as per the fundamental teachings he had studied at al-Azhar. And they didn't believe him when he tried to warn them about 'The Enemy'. 'Who is The Enemy, Sheikh Sayyid?' they would ask him slyly. They would pretend they didn't know who the enemy was or that he appeared in two forms, seeing as he resided in the mosque's well and its bathing area. Although he couldn't enter the courtyard of the mosque where the prayers were held and where the pulpit was, he had long arms. In his other form, he was personified as Ibrahim Abu Zaid from the village of the Salehis, who shone his torchlight on the village in order to see everything that was happening and to cast his evil over the victim of his choice. He must have had a hand in what happened to his son, Salama. He also told them about what he felt in his side, and what he saw when he left the mosque at night - yes, since he saw the torches locked on them - but they would just laugh. What would be the fate of this village whose people didn't pay attention to the dangers that surrounded it?

***

Zaki walked along the main road that extended from the mosque to the country road, splitting the village in half lengthwise. Every day, it was his habit to detour to the left when he reached the country road. He'd pass the waterwheel and then, when he reached the bridge leading to the Sa'ida's village on the opposite bank, he would walk back in the opposite direction, past Khalil's shop, until he reached another bridge leading to the mayor's village. During this walk, he would scrutinise the village and watch whatever was going on. But today he felt no desire to scrutinise or inspect. It was as though the reins had slipped from his hand. He noticed that Khalil's shop was closed and his aunt Nafisa had closed her door. There was no one by the canal. He stood for a long while under the sycamore tree that shaded the waterwheel and sighed. He'd been sixteen years old when his mother had said to him: 'My God, Zaki. You're all grown up. You're a man now. Why don't you want to make your mum happy?'

'It's still early for marriage, Ma.'

'What marriage, boy? Did I say anything about marriage? I'm talking about houseguests.'

'What houseguests, Ma?'

'Won't you man up a bit and bring back a visitor or two to the house?'

'We're blessed with my father for that, Ma.'

'What's this got to do with your old man? Where are your guests?'

'Are you asking me to pick up visitors from the country road?'

‘Why not? If anyone throws a greeting your way, grab hold of them and swear on your life that they’ve got to join you, then bring him to the house or to the *seera*. Tell him he’s welcome. Take his donkey, tether it, and bring it some fodder. Then come to your ma and tell her to “get up, Ma, and cook”. Even if this is at ten o’clock at night. That would be a happy day. If that happened, you would make me so glad, Zaki, and I would know that you’re a real man now.’

That was his first lesson in generous hospitality, and he tested his mother several times to see if she would keep to her word. She never disappointed him.

He walked back down to the village, passed three houses to the right, and reached the *seera*. He still cursed the day some ignorant folk decided to build their homes opposite the *seera*, thus shielding it from view. When he was young, it could be fully seen from the country road, as though to welcome people as they arrived. It used to be open day and night, welcoming visitors and travellers who wandered in the night and whose horses had run out of steam. How far we were from the good old days.... There was no one left who knew when the *seera* was built and why it was given that name, but it had been there since his childhood, and it had been there throughout the life of his father and his aunt Zainab and her husband, Hajj Mansur. It was said that it’d been built during the era of Qassim, when he and his family settled in this area and established the village. That meant the *seera* was as old as the village of the Qassimis, and that Qassim would only settle his family in that location if there was a place to receive visitors. The *seera* and the mosque were two landmarks that characterised the village and were dear to the district. The residents of the neighbouring villages would come to perform the Friday prayers and celebrate the two Eid festivals in the mosque. They'd then be hosted in the *seera*. And the blessed Friday would not be complete without the congregational prayer and lunch. There was no match to the *seera* in the district - the mayor's headquarters itself didn't compare - since it was a focal point for guests, strangers, and poets, both secular and religious. It was both a guesthouse and an events hall. Then, as it aged, it started to deteriorate, just as the wall of the mosque had started to crack. *Look what it had come to*. Who could he complain to of his ordeal? There were words deep inside him he wanted to raise to God, but they were wedged in his throat. *My Lord, help us and lift your hatred and anger from us.* Then he entered the *seera*.

***

Khalil cut through the fields towards the village of the Salehis, 'the sons of Saleh'. He could have walked on the country road along the canal, but the country road was never quiet, even at night, and he didn't want anyone to see him. The sky ahead lay flat and crammed with stars, but his eyes were focused on only one goal: Ibrahim Abu Zaid's house at the far edge of the village. He was a stranger who had come to the district before Khalil was born, heading straight to one corner of it, never visiting anyone nor being visited by anyone unless it was for a special purpose. The Salehis knew nothing of his family or background. But they knew, with the passing of time, that he was a drug dealer and a gang leader. Ever since he was a child, Khalil had heard that Ibrahim Abu Zaid was the one who masterminded the Nazlet Elwan incident. People said he was the one who gathered the members of the gang and delegated a role to each in the operation, while also ensuring he would emerge scot-free. When the police stormed his house and the investigation took its course, it was clear, based on definitive evidence, that the owner of the house had not left his home on the night of the incident. When Khalil first opened his shop, his father warned him firmly never to go to Ibrahim's home and not to deal with him unless it was for a lawful reason. 'The hashish and that other filth they snort is forbidden.' Yet here he was, despite his father's warnings, walking with his own two feet to Ibrahim to ask for help. Who else would he turn to? Where else could he seek help over what Salama had done? He had sullied the honour of Khalil's sister and ruined her. Salama's actions must have been calculated, relying on the fact that he was one of the Qassimis. The sons of Qassim thought they were the cream of the crop and that God had created them from a different dust from that of the Baharwa. Salama himself was poor and destitute - he had no land, cows or sheep - he earned his living as an agricultural labourer. Yet he would still strut around the village with his nose in the air because he was one of the Qassimis. How could he assault Khalil's sister? Why didn't she resist him? Why didn't she call for help? Had she done that, it would have proved that he'd wanted to rape her. But whatever happened passed without any fuss. No one would have found out about it had the news not spread. Could it be that his younger sister - a shy and inexperienced girl - brought this on herself? Salama - that poor and destitute guy - must have seen that she was a Baharwa girl whose honour wasn't worth preserving. His sight was set on Ibrahim's house, and he only wanted one thing: revenge. If only he could reach Salama, he would drink his blood. But how could he reach him? On the way to the village of the Salehis, he stopped several times, listening for a rustling between the corn reeds. 'Maybe a wolf or a fox,' he said to himself. Then he carried on walking, feeling for the darkened road with his staff.

***

Ibrahim Abu Zaid was about to start the night-time *esha* prayer. But when his daughter ran up crying, he stopped. 'What's wrong, Farida?' he asked. The girl was sobbing so intensely that she couldn't answer. Ibrahim - the man people called a 'murderous murderer', and who'd say of himself that his 'heart was hardened by the troubles hammered into it' - couldn't stand to see his daughter cry. He felt so sorry for the girl that his heart fluttered in his chest. His older children were grown men with moustaches. But this skinny girl, granted to him by God 'in his old age' from his second marriage, was the apple of his eye. 'Come sit next to me here,' he said. As she sobbed, Farida told him that her mother had smacked her with the broomstick because she was playing with boys. 'Never mind, my darling,' he said, patting the little girl's back. He called for the mother, who argued that the girl was growing up and it was high time she stopped playing with boys. Ibrahim patched things up between the two, but he winked at his wife before she left, giving her a look that meant, 'Don't be so strict. The girl is still a child'. Farida wiped her tears and told him that there was a man called Khalil Abu Radi waiting for him in the reception room, which made him smile. He was pleased with himself and his accurate assumptions. Khalil, the son of the Baharwa, had come to see him. Good. He had known, ever since the news had reached him, that the Baharwa people would have to seek his help. Who else would they ask to help them stand up to the sons of Qassim? The Baharwa were a peace-loving people who only cared about business and stacking up money and arable land. They never asked God for anything but protection, and they couldn't confront the sons of Qassim, 'the tyrants'. No one could dispense with his services - he was the stranger, the new arrival who had come to the district from afar. Some of his youth had been spent in Palestine, where he worked as a clothes presser for the Jews in Tel Aviv, and he'd had dealings with the British camps in the Suez Canal area, sometimes selling hashish to their soldiers and other times robbing their army. When he came to this district, everyone ignored him - the sons of Saleh and the sons of Qassim equally - yet they all sought his help. They couldn't live without him. He told Farida to ask the guest to wait until he finished the *esha* prayer. Just before she left, he stopped her. 'Offer him some tea, Farida.'

He received Khalil with a hug. 'What a pleasure. Your presence is cherished, Mister Khalil. Welcome, welcome.' Khalil started to talk. 'I'm coming to you, Uncle Ibrahim, to ask for a favour.' But Ibrahim interrupted him. 'There will be no chitchat before you drink tea,' he insisted. 'You can't come here and not drink our tea. Don't worry, you'll get what you want, God willing.' *What is he like, this guy?* Khalil thought. *This gang leader - he's such a soft touch.* He swallowed the hot tea before responding. 'Uncle Ibrahim, I'm coming to you to ask for a favour that will put me forever in your debt. That kid, Salama…' Ibrahim interrupted him again. 'I heard about what happened, and your request will be fulfilled, by the will of the One and Only.' 'It's the girl's honour, you know,' Khalil said. 'I mean, I don't know what to say.' Overcome by emotion, Khalil fell silent. Ibrahim patted his hand. 'I know,' he said. 'I swear to God, my heart goes out to you and your father. May God take revenge against the oppressor.' He paused, silently, for a moment. 'Look, Khalil. Do you see my daughter, Farida? I couldn't stand it if anyone touched a hair on her head. I know exactly what you mean.' He gave Khalil a piercing look. 'And your sister, Zakiya, is like my daughter.' Khalil felt a shiver run through his body - the man was now getting to the heart of the matter. 'I swear to God Almighty, I feel sorry for you and your father,' Ibrahim said. 'That righteous man who never hurt a soul. Then Salama Abu Sayyid goes and does something like that?' Relief washed over Khalil — the man understood completely. He asked him what he thought should be done. 'We can't go near Zakiya,' Ibrahim said. 'May God take revenge against the one who hurt her. As for Salama.... As for Salama, we'll need to deal with him in a different way.' 'You're quite right, uncle Ibrahim,' Khalil said. 'Let us focus on Salama. But we don't know where Salama went. He's been hiding out for a week now, but God knows where.' 'Where would he go?' Ibrahim replied. 'He must be with his relatives. He'll either be in Kafr Saqr or in al-Sharafa near Abu Kabir.' 'So how do we reach him?' Khalil asked. Ibrahim smiled. 'Leave that to your uncle Ibrahim.' Khalil became quiet and looked down, worried. 'But I'm afraid, Uncle Ibrahim,' he said. There was still a question inside him that he didn't dare utter. If Salama was killed in Kafr Saqr or in al-Sharafa or any other place, wouldn't the police eventually find out who was behind the crime? Wouldn't they be able to trace the matter straight to their front door? But Ibrahim reassured him. 'Don't worry about anything. We have our men in Kafr Saqr and in al-Sharafa. They'll do everything necessary, far from you or me. A fight will erupt, one way or another, and we won't have anything to do with it. Anyway, we're not going to kill him. The men there will give him the beating of a lifetime and leave him crippled. And by the way, he won't breathe a word himself about what happened to him or who beat him up. He won't dare. Do you think what he did was trivial?' There was a moment of silence before Ibrahim spoke again. 'But you know, Mr. Khalil, these men...we need to please them.' He stopped talking, but Khalil understood what he meant and put two pounds in the open palm. 'Here's a little something as a down payment.' Ibrahim smiled brightly. 'Whatever you see fit, Mr. Khalil. I would never haggle with you, I swear to God. For you, nothing is too dear to part with.' He walked Khalil to the front door. 'By the way, I want to tell you something about Zakiya. You should know that she hasn't left the village.' Khalil was stunned. 'How do you know that?' he asked. 'Where would a girl like that go?' Ibrahim told him. 'To the Sa'ida people? Really?' 'Okay, so where in the village?' Khalil asked. 'Whose house is she hiding at?' 'God knows,' Ibrahim replied. 'But she must be at one of the Qassimi homes.' Khalil was left speechless. After that, he didn't utter a single word.

On the way home, it felt as though his head would explode with worry. Gone was the comfort he had felt when he first heard Ibrahim's solution, about how Salama would receive the revenge he deserved, yet no blame would fall on him or his father. Ibrahim had unwittingly destroyed this sense of reassurance when he guessed - and it seemed he must be right - that Zakiya had not left the village. Which of the Qassimi homes could she be hiding at? He couldn't exactly go and inspect the houses of the Qassimi one by one in search of her. He didn't want to do that, and in any case he didn't want to find her. Finding her would be a huge disaster. What could he do with her, or for her? It would be better if she left and disappeared forever, without a trace. Salama could go to hell, but Zakiya? If she wasn't killed, what would they be able to do for her? No suitor would approach her, and no one would come near her. She would be disgraced... worse than a spinster, divorcee, or widow. Could she be locked up in the house so no one outside could see her? He had thought - and so had his parents - that she had run away, left the village completely. There was a solution in that - a kind of solution at least - to the problem. Until Ibrahim Abu Zaid, that cunning fox, had pointed out that she was hiding somewhere in the village. Khalil tapped on the ground with his staff. In this case, breaking Salama's bones would not be the end of the torment. He had defiled Khalil's sister, his own flesh and blood, and ruined her forever. Whenever the unbearable notion of his sister's fall from grace seized him, he wished he had insisted Ibrahim Abu Zaid kill the cowardly rascal.

***

Salama's heart pounded when he recognized Khalil Abu Radi in the dark. Salama was on his way back from his hiding place at his relatives' in Kafr Saqr, and he'd decided to take this roundabout route to his village, sneaking between the fields of the Salehis. But the Lord willed that he would end up bumping into Khalil right where he didn't expect to see him. Why was Khalil going to the village of the Salehis and taking this route in the dark of night? It was by chance that he had spotted Khalil from afar and had sunk down near the canal. If he'd hesitated for one moment, Khalil would have seen him, and he would have suffered the consequences. His heart raced when Khalil stopped. He must've heard him shuffling between the cotton reeds. Salama waited for a long time, crouched in his hiding place, holding his breath until he was sure that Khalil had moved far enough away. Now all that was left was to reach his village - and specifically the *seera* - without anyone seeing him. He didn't want anyone from his family to see him before he met his uncle Zaki in the *seera*. He needed to pass by Zaki first, before anything else. His uncle Zaki was the only one who could protect him, and he had to accept his judgment and punishment, whatever it would be. If he could get Zaki on his side, then it would be easier to convince everyone else, including Khalil, his father, and the rest of the

Baharwa clan. He could face everyone if Zaki supported him. When he reached the *seera*, he found Sheikh Zaki with his head buried between his arms and knees. He didn't notice the greeting that was called out to him. It seemed to Salama that his uncle was asleep, but in fact he was deep in thought.

Visitors and strangers would dismount from their horses before going down to the village, greeting anyone they found near the waterwheel. They might ask who the people of the village were, and they would be told, 'The Qassimis'. They would ask about the village chief, and they would be told, 'Hajj Zaki', to which they would reply, 'a blessed and gracious honour'. Whomever they found near the waterwheel - man or child - would accompany them to the *seera*. They would wait there for someone to come out to welcome them warmly and perform the duties of hospitality. The villagers knew that people arriving at the *seera* were everyone's guests, and that they should spare no effort in hosting them generously, and that the greatest responsibility fell on the head of the family. Originally, this was Zaki's uncle Mansur and then, after he died, his wife, Hajja Zainab, inherited the duty with the help of Zaki's father. When they were taken in turn into God's mercy, he became the one in charge to almost single-handedly cater to the arrivals, to organise events and delegate roles to those who could perform a function. Everyone accepted his leadership, but he was starting to struggle. Then a darkness appeared and settled deep within him. There were also strange sounds he heard whispering in his ears. The responsibility had been passed to him, but he could no longer carry out all these tasks. *God burdens not a person beyond his scope.* There was that phrase that never stopped tormenting him....

No one knew when Qassim or his family had first arrived in this district. And no one knew for certain where they'd come from. But the villagers had heard stories claiming that Qassim and his family were Arabs who had come from the East a long time ago, six or seven generations back. It was said that they had initially raised their tents and worked herding sheep and breeding horses, until eventually they settled in mud houses and worked in agriculture. When did this transformation take place? No one knew. Zaki himself didn't know, and his father hadn't known. These were nothing but titbits of stories shrouded in mystery. The old days were veiled in a mist of darkness.

Zaki had never met his uncle, but his father told him that Mansur had been extremely wealthy, and that the territory around his large house used to be full of stables and cattle sheds. He also said that the sons of Qassim, up until the era of Mansur, had held steadfast to their tradition of rearing precious Arab horses. As for Zainab, she was strong and very powerful. As the story goes, she woke one night when she heard a strange movement in the barn at the back of the house. It must have been a passing thief or a wolf hunting for its prey. When the intruding wolf saw her approaching with an axe in hand, he hid in a dark corner. She found him standing on his hind legs. But rather than panicking - she was braver than any man - she brought down the axe. According to the stories, she was stunning in her youth, having inherited her good looks from Saddina, a girl people knew very little about. Saddina was said to have been the daughter of Qassim, the eldest grandfather, who married her off to a man she didn't want. People were awestruck at the mere mention of her name. Whenever a pretty girl was born, they would say she was 'beautiful, like Saddina' and would feel sorrow over the injustice this beauty had suffered.

Time has no mercy. At the end of her life, Zainab was affected by that which afflicts the elderly. Her back hunched, she could walk only by leaning on a cane, and she lost her eyesight. But she didn't lose her prestige. No man would ride by her on horseback - even when she was blind - without dismounting. And if she walked past a group, leaning on her cane, they would all fall silent until one of them whispered, 'God is Glorious! She's the one who killed the wolf.' The *seera* remained prosperous in her care, as it had been once upon a time, a long time ago, and it didn't suffer from the decay that had afflicted the venerable lady. Poets used to turn up every year to perform in the village for two or three nights, chanting the epics. Zainab would cook meat in two large pots that would be placed by the doorway of the large house, and then thirty or more would gather around the dinner trays - men, women, and children. His father told him that the land had been filled with dovecotes, beehives, and a vegetable farm, extending from the front of the house to what they called the 'Gulf'. All of that was now gone. He also recalled that, when he was a child playing with his friends behind the mosque and the nearby houses, climbing plants had covered the backs of the houses, and there had been luxurious flowering thickets. Nothing was left of that, either. Or were those just visions he had seen in his dreams?

The minute he raised his head, Salama rushed over and fell at his uncle's feet. 'I seek your protection, uncle. I kiss your feet, I ask your forgiveness.' This wasn't a bad start, in Salama's eyes. He decided not to say a single word more and left it up to his uncle to take the lead. Then he suddenly stood up, as though he had remembered something, and began to prepare the tea in his usual, meticulous manner, as if nothing had happened. He set the dried corncobs on the stove, lit the fire, blew at it until the smoke cleared and the flames burnt right through and became transparent. Once they had settled, the teapot could be placed on the burning cobs. Salama was an artist at preparing tea. He boiled it until it was as black as ink, adding plenty of sugar so it became syrupy and delicious like honey. And when he poured it into the cups, he raised the teapot so that bubbles would form on the surface of the tea. This was the proper way.

Zaki had nothing to say. More than once, he tried to speak. 'What's going on, Salama?' he wanted to ask, but he couldn't, because he already knew the filthy story and didn't want to have to listen to it again. Instead of hearing it retold, it was more important to try and quench the flames of fury blazing in his chest, and to find the suitable punishment for the 'son of a bitch' who had brought shame on him and the rest of the Qassimis. Salama wished his uncle would start talking and question him if he liked, so that he could plead with him to hand down a punishment of his choosing that would eventually lead to his forgiveness. He wanted to weep between his hands, appeal to his kindness, and complain to him about the devil. 'The devil's cunning, uncle,' he wanted to say, but his uncle's terrible silence warned of danger. How could he explain the story to his uncle? He didn't dare, and the pious, righteous man wouldn't be able to understand love's madness in any case. And his uncle wouldn't allow him to wade in such shameful talk.

When had he fallen in love with Zakiya? God knows he wasn't to blame for what had happened at the start. The girl had still been a child who hadn't fully grown. She used to gather the cotton with the other labourers for five piasters a day. She was just like any of them, coming and going in the cotton field without drawing his attention. Just like the other labourers, she would use a rope as a belt and would bunch up the top of her dress to create a makeshift pocket where she would toss the cotton she gathered. Each time this pocket was full, she would go to the sack at the edge of the field to empty her stash. After that, the gathering and filling of the pocket would start again. Sometimes the labourers would work earnestly, especially when the girls sang to harness their energy. But then they would start slacking so, as foreman, he would wave a stick of firewood at them to prompt them to work faster. One time, he waved his stick at Zakiya - he waved it at her and God knows his intentions were pure and he had meant nothing untoward - so she turned towards him. 'Hit me, Salama,' she said. 'Hit me, Salama.' Why had the girl said that when he never used his stick to hit anyone? Her friend Suaad laughed cunningly. 'Hit her, Salama, *the smack of a loved one is as sweet as a sultana*.' Did love blossom that day? The girl was still a child, but he saw a strange look in her wide eyes as she spoke. Was she making fun of him, or telling him off? And what was all that about the smack of a loved one? Then he forgot about the whole thing. 'Child's play', he told himself.

But this child whose chest appeared flat at the neck of her dress was the same girl who would set his nerves alight years later, when he saw her sitting behind the washing tub at his nana Nafisa's house. Her body had matured into the figure of a woman. He saw her legs straddling the tub, and he noticed how her orange *sirwal* had ridden up on one side, revealing a shaded area that his eyes clung to ... not only that, but his soul too. As soon as she saw where his gaze was directed, she quickly pulled the hem of her *thawb* down to cover what had been showing. He thought he spotted a smile pass fleetingly over her face. After that, it was rare that he would sleep restfully. The image of the shadowy sighting would surprise him as he hoed, sowed seeds, or beat the water buffalo with a *farquilla* whip in the area around the waterwheel. And the girl would often come to him in his sleep and wouldn't leave until she had dragged him out of his bed so he could cleanse himself in the bathing basin of the mosque. He kept visiting his nana Nafisa's house, in the hopes that she would ask him to carry out a chore for her that would lead to him bumping into Zakiya there. And he would loiter if he found her, after exchanging greetings and chatter. He felt relaxed around her and wished he could prolong these moments.

She too would dawdle when she went to the fields carrying food that his nana sent him: two loaves of bread and a piece of cheese, or two loaves and two boiled eggs. She would sit and chat, the whole time looking over her shoulder, avoiding eye contact. Then she would suddenly get up and start rearranging her headscarf.

'Take care, Salama,' she would say. 'On your way back at the end of the day, don't forget to take the tray back to Hajja Nafisa,' she would sometimes add.

Hearing her say his name thrilled him. Then one day, he discovered that the eggs she brought him were not always from Nafisa. He found this out after once mentioning to Nafisa that the two eggs she'd sent were so big they looked like duck's eggs. Nafisa told him she had sent him only two loaves of bread, a piece of cheese, and an onion. 'What eggs are you talking about, son?' she said. 'Salama, my boy, what's happened to your mind?' It delighted him to hear this, and he smiled. The two eggs must have been a gift from Zakiya, who would have stolen them from her mother.

Then one day, he felt as though his heart would break when Nafisa told him the news. 'Zakiya's refusing to bring you food anymore,' Nafisa said. 'Come by and pick it up yourself.' Her visits cut off completely, and he would see her only from time to time, whenever he found her at Nafisa's house, or when she was with the other girls on their way to the canal to fill up their clay pots. He felt devastated when he noticed her avoiding him or looking the other way, even though her friends greeted him or talked to him as they passed. Why had she stopped talking to him? If only he could see her on her own, he would confront her and confess his feelings.

'Is love forbidden, Nana?' he asked Nafisa.

'Who has forbidden it, my boy?' she replied. 'Who do you love, apple of my eye?'

Salama didn't reply, so she repeated her question.

'Who is it, my darling, that you love? Tell me and we'll bring you together.'

When he raised the subject with his mother she screamed at him.

'Oh my God! God forbid. Marry one of the Baharwa? She's forbidden to you.'

'What does it matter if she's one of the Baharwa? Are the Baharwa not human beings?'

'Human beings or spawn of the devil! You are not going to marry Zakiya. Do you hear me?'

And all hell broke loose. His mother went to see the girl's mother and showered her with a string of insults, each more vulgar than the last, then ordered her to 'rein in her loose daughter'.

Then Zakiya disappeared completely, and he no longer saw her, not even with her friends when they filled their pots. Months passed this way, and he ran out of patience. People could tell what was troubling him when he walked in the direction of the homes of the Baharwa, then stopped in the middle of the road before reaching his goal.

That was until one day when he went to the well at the waterwheel to catch a catfish he saw wriggling in the water. The catfish had long whiskers and was large and elusive. Each time he was about to catch it, it would stab his hand and the blood would seep into the water. That happened three times before he was able to get a hold of the blasted thing. As he tried to climb back towards the light of day, he saw two wide eyes staring down at him. It was Zakiya! And she was whispering, 'Salama.' Was there any sound purer in the world than this voice whispering his name? When he reached the surface, he tossed the catfish to one side and didn't say a word. He took hold of the girl's hand, pulled her to his chest, and she leaned into him. Then he carried her in his arms and he was no longer aware of what was happening, as if in a trance, as if some kind of power had taken hold of him and pushed him to carry the girl and disappear with her between the corn reeds. He must have....

'The devil's cunning, uncle,' he finally said, his eyes brimming with tears.

'What devil, you son of a bitch?' Zaki replied, his eyes blazing with rage.

It was true. What have we got to do with the devil? *I was dying with longing,* he wanted to tell his uncle. *When the girl looked at me with those eyes, I lost my senses. I didn't know was happening to me. I lost my senses. I took the girl in my arms. But where could I go with her when everyone would be able to see us? I couldn't find anything but the cornfield to shield us. Uncle, am I not a human being, made of flesh and blood? I've been seeing her coming and going for years, knowing that we love each other. Since the day she said, 'Hit me, Salama.' It was love without any words, love from afar, God only knows. Zakiya, I love you, I wanted to say to her, I want to marry you. What have we got to do with the Qassimis and Baharwa? Between our house and yours are a few steps. No one is better than anyone else. They're accusing me of doing you wrong. They don't know that you're dearer to me than my own ... eyes, and that I could never harm you or let people gloat over you. All right, let's say I made a mistake. I made a mistake, forgive me. I've been seared by her love for years. I would crumble from one look from her eyes. I couldn't stand being deprived of her for months. Is it forbidden to look, or is it wrong to say hello? That's all I wanted. Am I not a human being?* But his uncle would never be able to understand. What love and what nonsense?

He cursed his miserable luck. When he carried the girl and disappeared with her between the cornstalks, he was trying to hide from people's eyes, and he'd checked all around him first. Who had managed to see them, when everything happened at lightning speed? Who had exposed them? And how had the news circulated around the village before morning had risen?

He didn't realise that his uncle didn't know what to do, that the worries had piled up on him until he couldn't find a way out. But what Zaki did know - especially when peace returned to him - was that if he wanted to survive, he would have to find solutions to these problems, and to handle them one by one. He felt grabbing hold of these problems with both hands - and he was gripping his palm at that moment - was the only way he could stop what was happening inside him. And what was happening inside him? After some soul-searching, he sensed that some kind of danger was looming, unless God quickly reached out to him with His mercy. It was something like the earth being cleaved in half over a bottomless void. And what were the dilemmas that he had to seize hold of? They were far too many for him to count. But the first that came to mind was the mosque's crumbling wall, the sorry situation of Sheikh Hamed, and the deterioration of the *seera*. Then there was his nephew, who had brought shame on his family. All these problems seemed intractable. There was no solution to some of them without money. And money wasn't available. But the biggest catastrophe was Salama assaulting the Baharwa girl. How could he confront that problem? Now darkness prevailed, and the world turned black in his eyes. If only Zainab were still alive! She would have said to him - as she always used to - 'Man up, Zaki' and he would man up. She had the strength of ten men. She looked after the mosque, the *seera,* and the Quran school. She looked after Hamed, and his sons, and would hire some of them to work for her as a way of helping their father. And she would claim she was only doing a fraction of what her husband Mansur used to do. She would say that he always quoted the holy verses: '*Did He not find you an orphan and give you a refuge? And He found you unaware and guided you? And He found you poor and made you rich?'* And in his mind, the idea became as clear as a lightning bolt followed by rumbling thunder - the idea of the eldest caring for the weak and needy - and the tears streamed from his eyes. Salama stood up when he heard the sound of his uncle reciting from the al-Duha chapter of the Quran. '*By the forenoon, And by the night when it is still, Your Lord has neither forsaken you nor hated you.'* He recited the verses humbly. Then a wail erupted from the man's belly in a harrowing sign of fear and bereavement.

'Don't leave me alone, don't abandon me.'

Salama turned around. There was no one in the *seera* but them. Who was his uncle addressing? But he didn't dare ask.

***

For Shabana, life was only ever sweet at the *jurn*, an open space at the edge of the village, which overlooked the country road and the canal. Most of the time, it seemed empty and dreary, day and night, except during harvest season, or when people were out playing games, or during one of Shabana's gatherings. When it was harvest season, the threshing machine would come alive - after having languished out of action for a long time - and an animal would pull it, like a donkey, cow, or camel, turning its sharp metal blades over the wheat stalks as it reaped. At night, it was delightful to stay up until the early hours of the morning and watch the winnowing machine devour the straw as it separated the seeds. Shabana also enjoyed watching *kahsha* matches, a rural version of hockey, from the sidelines. The eldest boys would be divided into two teams, each batting the ball with a thick stick into the goal of the opposite team, and a great deal of running would ensue, along with shouting and general commotion. On nights when the moon was fullest, the young children would play 'Hide the Hat in the Pocket', and would sit in single file, one behind the other, their legs extended until they touched the backside of the child in front. One would stand apart from the rest and guess who had hid the hat in the makeshift pocket of their *jilbab*. If he found it and pulled it out of the carrier's pocket, he would join the row of seated boys. The person who had hidden the hat last would have to guess next.

The happiest times in the *jurn* were when relief arrived in the form of a lump of opium. Its magic would only reveal itself after it was sucked with sips of bitter coffee. When the dose had its effect - and its effect was swift - the world would sparkle and nothing could stand in the way of the serenity it induced. This clear-headedness was a state Shabana called 'my peace and relaxation'. In that state, it made no difference to him whether the boys sat down beside him (when the latest gossip would be recounted and he would listen to them prattle on about futile matters) or not, since, once the dose had arrived, he would be happy enough to sit alone and drift through the 'kingdom'. His favourite time after the harvest season was the Coptic month of Amshir, at the tail end of winter. The days of Amshir were days of abundance, during which the earth would turn green with berseem clover, the beasts' appetites would be satisfied, and they would produce copious amounts of milk that would be stored in clay containers for a few days. After that, the women would remove a thick layer of cream from the top of each pot to reveal the clabbered milk. Cheese would be made by hanging a straw mat for the whey to ooze through until it turned to clabber. How Glorious God is. Clabber was his favourite food because, for some reason, it went well with opium.

But on that day, he hadn't been in a good mood. The *jurn* was deserted, bleak, and depressing. He had sent his son to the village of Nazlet Mandur to buy him the lump of opium he couldn't live without, and now the sun was sinking, little by little, behind the palm trees of the Sa'ida's village without there being any sign of the boy. A little while ago, he had passed the time by chatting to the boys, making fun of the Qassimis for still taking pride in their Arab origins and clinging to the glory of their ancestors, when God only knows how much truth there was in that. But the boys were distracted when they heard a rattling sound and started looking right and left. Then Ashur, the candyfloss seller, appeared on the country road. He was carrying a long stick around which he wrapped the candyfloss, and it was shielded from the flies beneath a gauze cover. He shook the stick and the rattle jangled again, putting an end to the conversation. One by one, the boys left, each rushing to their mothers to grab money for the candyfloss. Shabana tried in vain to stop them from going. 'Hey, kids! You little rascals,' Shabana cried. 'There's much more to hear. Who cares about candyfloss - it's nonsense! It's just a bit of sugar and lemon that the son of a bitch cooks so that it sticks together for the women to wax with.'

'We don't care,' one of the kids replied. 'We like candyfloss.' And they left. But what had happened to the boy who had gone to buy opium? Hadn't he found the dealer? Had the dealer snubbed the two and half piasters and started to mess around and haggle? Or had the donkey collapsed on the way, refusing to get up and not responding to shouts or kicks? Shabana couldn't lift his head without a dose of opium. His eyes would water, his nose would redden and start streaming, then the world would turn to black. Suddenly, Medhat appeared with his dog and sat in front of Shabana quietly as the black dog wagged his tail.

'*Aba* Shabana, shall I tell you a secret?' the boy whispered.

With difficulty, Shabana raised his head a little, since it felt like it was about to drop off his shoulders.

'No talking. Don't tell me anything.'

But that didn't deter Medhat.

'That guy, Salama, the rascal…'

Shabana hollered at him. 'For God's sake, I don't want to hear anything. My head is as heavy as lead.'

'It's your choice,' Medhat replied. 'You'll only have yourself to blame.'

Shabana was in such a state that he couldn't bear to listen to anything. His eyes watered so much he could hardly open them. 'They were veiled,' he would say at times like this. And his nose was red, swollen, and constantly dripping. As for the headache, it was like someone was hammering on his head. The time for the opium dose had come and gone (he needed it yesterday in fact, so it was well overdue). Now here he was, waiting for his son to come back with his medication. He had sent him before the afternoon call to prayer, and now the sun had almost set without any sign of him. He had sent him off on the back of the donkey, but he may as well have put him on the back of an ant.

Then relief finally hailed, and the weight on his chest lifted. The boy appeared on the back of the donkey, which was limping along the country road. The lump of opium was within an arm's reach, and as soon as the young boy dismounted and handed over the 'precious goods', his father told him to go home. '*Yalla*, hurry up, go home and tell your ma to get the coffee ready. And bring me the whole pot.' When the lump began to dissolve, Shabana could feel the first pangs of relaxation, followed by total tranquillity.

When Medhat came to him a second time with his dog, Shabana's eyes had dried and his cheeks were full of colour.

'What were you telling me before, Medhat? That kid, Salama the rascal, did what?'

'First you need to hand over the money for some candyfloss,' Medhat said, sitting down calmly.

Shabana tried in vain to elude him, but Medhat wouldn't reveal the secret until Shabana had given him a millieme coin.

Medhat cleared his throat. 'Pray for the prophet.'

Shabana prayed for the prophet.

'Listen, my dear man,' Medhat started. 'I was sleeping at the waterwheel, and when I woke up, I found Salama, the rascal, carrying the Baharwa girl in his arms.'

'Carrying who, kid?' Shabana asked, breathlessly.

'*Aba* Shabana,' the child shouted. 'Are you pretending to be dumb or what? Are you saying you don't know who the Baharwa girl is? Who else would it be but that hussy Zakiya? Basically, I saw the scoundrel carry the girl off in his arms and take her into the cornfield.'

'Oh, he's going to get it,' Shabana exclaimed. 'He went into the cornfield with her?!'

'Yes, I swear to God. He took her into the cornfield, and he must have ruined her.'

'God help us. How did you see him, you little kid, in the cornfield? Did you go in after them?'

Medhat didn't reply, but instead stood up quickly and set off with his dog.

'Hey, kid! Medhat!' Shabana called out to him. 'The secret's got to stay safe, kid. Swear you won't breathe a word of it to anyone.'

The boy walked back and made a solemn promise.

'I swear on my life I won't tell anyone. Here's Farid as my witness.'

He pointed at his dog and smiled. Then the five-year-old boy left, with his evil eye amulet dangling from his hat. Shabana let out a characteristic chuckle, long and exaggerated, with a hint of vulgarity. He thought about what had just happened. It occurred to him that Salama could be excused, and that the girl wasn't to blame, either. There was always a moment...a moment during which the inevitable happens. Maybe Zakiya saw him turning the screw pump or standing in the field planting rice seedlings, bare-chested in his *sirwal*. And maybe he saw the girl swaying her hips as she walked, balancing the clay pot on her head, the edge of her scarf hanging over her backside. That would be enough to ignite a spark, and the spark would charge - by the will of the Omnipotent One - in both directions, enflaming their hearts. The boy was excused and so was the girl. As for that little spawn of the devil, Medhat, you would think he was a circus monkey! Or look at the dog he'd named Farid! Who names a dog Farid, as if he were a real person?

***

Radi refused to eat when his wife asked if he wanted her to prepare dinner. He'd barely touched any food since Zakiya disappeared. 'My darling, how long will you keep fasting like this?' Sakina asked him. 'What good will hunger do?!' He asked her about Khalil, so she told him that he had gone out. 'Where did he go with the shop closed?' he asked. She didn't dare tell him that he'd gone to the village of the Salehis to meet Ibrahim Abu Zaid. 'I don't know where he went,' she replied, after hesitating for a while. If her husband knew where their son had gone, he would realize immediately that she was the one who had given Khalil the idea of taking revenge on Salama, and he would have been furious and spoilt the plan. She'd had a long talk with her husband and could not convince him to avenge his daughter's honour. His face was swollen, his eyes protruded from their sockets, and his chest heaved, as though he were about to have a heart attack. She quickly brought him the clay water pot. Sweat poured off him, so she helped him take off his turban and skullcap and lean his back against the wall.

'Is this the end of the road, Sakina?' he repeated.

It had been a long journey. When his grandfather brought his family to this district from the Buhaira province, they were destitute, and Mansur, the great landowner, had been kind to them. He put them up and hired Radi's grandfather and some of his sons to work his land. Radi was twelve years old when Mansur sent him to board at al-Azhar University with four others: his sons Fahmi and Rabi, his nephew Sayyid, and Fadel, the son of slaves whom Mansur had freed. There was an implicit understanding - accepted by Radi and his father - that in Cairo, he and Fadel would act as servants to the sons and nephew of the great landowner, Mansur. But none of the five young men succeeded in their studies, apart from Fadel, the son of slaves, and he was the only one who received the *alamiya* certificate and became a sharia lawyer. Fahmi, their eldest and the one with the highest status, had studied seriously for a few years until he lost interest. He then spent his time mixing with singers, actors, and dancers, going with them on tours in the rural regions. People said that he 'escorted' one of the singers until she ended up pulling him away from al-Azhar. Then he disappeared completely. It was said that he took part in the 1919 revolution and that there was a call for his arrest, so he fled to the Levant, never to return. As for Rabi, Sayyid, and Radi, they despaired of al-Azhar and the *alamiya*. They all returned to the village, one after the other. 'Stubborn,' Mansur said, surrendering his problem to God. Radi didn't grieve long over leaving al-Azhar and Cairo. He quickly settled amongst his family and eked out a living, first by reciting the Quran at funerals and agricultural work. This went on for several years, until he discovered that trade was the key to real wealth, so he started to rear cattle to sell in the district markets, and he traded in wheat. His wife began to sell chickens, eggs, and butter. On market day, she would stand alongside the country road from the early hours of the morning to sell her wares. They struggled for years, depriving themselves of their own produce so they could save up. Then a whole new world opened up to him once he started to trade in cotton. He earned enough money to buy arable land, starting off with kirats and then feddans. That was how the son of the penniless labourer rose to the level of the landowners. Not only that, but he became the richest man in the village and the surrounding area, as well as the most influential and prestigious. If a piece of land was offered for sale, he would be given first refusal.

The journey had been a long one. When he used to recite the Quran at graves, he would be paid in pastries that were baked as part of the mourning ritual. His voice wasn't melodic enough to compete with the other famous reciters who were paid handsomely. A long time had passed since he'd recited the Quran for money, just as Sakina had stopped selling her wares on the country road (although she carried on trading from home with customers who came to her door). Khalil now owned a shop on the main road. God had blessed them and immersed them in His grace, but now Zakiya had put an end to his journey and, from this day forward, he would be as good as finished.

He ached and groaned like a sick man. 'How can I show my face, Sakina?' A week had passed since the girl's disappearance, a week of being paralyzed, unable to do anything. Completely crippled, he couldn't go to the police with a case. What would he say to the chief officer - who knew him personally - about his daughter? He couldn't ask him, or anyone else, to look for her. And what would he do with her, or for her, if he found her? Even in her absence, there was nothing he could do to cover up her shameful disgrace. The girl had disappeared, but the scandal confronted him wherever he went. The people in the mosque looked at him with pity and compassion, so he stopped praying outside the house. Even if the girl disappeared, nothing would change. What had happened to her would remain in people's memories forever, because what had happened was unprecedented in the history of the village and the district. No man had ever attacked a virgin and been seen - since he must have been seen - as he carried her into the cornfield. Whenever Radi imagined his daughter being carried into the cornfield, he wrapped his head in his hands, because it felt as if it would explode.

'Get up and go talk to Zaki,' Sakina said, which prompted him to yell in astonishment: 'And say what to Zaki?' 'What do you mean, say what?' she replied. 'What kind of talk is that, Abu Khalil? Salama's their son, they're responsible for him, and he's the one who's ruined our daughter's life.' 'So you want me to go and grovel to Zaki, to beg him and kiss his feet?' he replied. 'What are you talking about, kiss his feet?' she said. 'Instead of kissing his feet, go and threaten him. Tell him either he sorts out his son or we take our revenge. We'll drink his blood.' Radi turned around in condemnation. 'What do you mean, drink his blood? You want us to kill Salama? Are we murderers, Sakina? The Qassimis can kill. They're Arabs. But us? We're simple people, living on God's grace. Have you forgotten how much we owe the Qassimis for their generosity, how kind Mansur was to us, and that I was only educated thanks to him? So you want me - who has memorized God's book by heart - to go and murder someone? And who should I murder? The son of Mansur. May God protect us from the accursed Satan.' The man was stunned by how his wife was acting, in a way he'd never seen before. She suddenly stood up to face him angrily. 'Enough of those outdated ideas. We are the children of today. The Qassimis are no better than us. They're not richer than us, and their daughters are not better than my daughter. So go and threaten him.' She had been smacking her chest with her fists as she raged, but then calmed down slightly and lowered her voice. 'If the threat doesn't work, we will kill. Why wouldn't we kill?' Her husband looked at her in bewilderment. Never in his life had he heard anything like this. The Baharwa were peaceful people who would never consider murder, no matter what happened. 'You want me to kill?' he asked, disdainfully. She replied immediately. 'Why would you do it? There are plenty who would kill on your behalf.' He didn't know that, when she said that, she had been considering commissioning Ibrahim Abu Zaid and that the idea had already reached Khalil. 'I want you to know,' she said. 'If you don't go to Zaki, then I'll go to him at the *seera* and make a huge scene.'

But when Zaki welcomed him with familiar affectionate greetings, he conveniently forgot what Sakina had said about threats and retaliation.

'Zaki, we are neighbours and brothers,' he said. 'And I can never forget the favours your uncle Mansur bestowed on us. So we have to solve the problem together, and I will accept whatever you say.'

Zaki was stunned and felt a deep desire to gloat. *I will accept whatever you say*, Radi had said! Glorious is the One who can turn the tables! Radi, who had refused to listen to him when he had grovelled and begged him not to buy his brother's land, was now coming to ask his opinion and humble himself at his feet? A thought kept turning over in his mind, a thought that had pursued him for years, about how deceitful Time was. Today, Radi came to him a broken man, when he had been as hard as a nail. But Time's treachery towards the people of Qassim had been tougher and more destructive. They had been the masters and landowners, and the Baharwa were their labourers. But the scales had tipped in favour of the impoverished ones. The ownership of the Qassimis' land gradually devolved to them. Zainab had held onto the reins of the situation after her husband died, and she had managed the land masterfully and decisively. None of her three sons had dared ask for their inheritance. So when she passed on into God's mercy, the inheritance was split between its beneficiaries and the ownership was scattered. The youngest of the three, Amin, died one night under the influence of drugs, and his share was passed on to his two sons. The other brothers, Fahmi and Rabi, sold their share and each moved with his respective wife to her part of the country, one going to Zagazig and the other to Minya al-Qamh. And all the land ended up in Radi's hands as he bought it, kirat after kirat, and feddan after feddan. He was neither satisfied nor thanked God for the blessings he was granted. Then the only thing left for Radi to buy was his brother Mahmud's share of the inheritance. How he had begged him to reject the deal and how he had begged his brother not to sell his land. 'Please, brother, no, let's stay together, and you're already getting everything you want,' he had pleaded. 'Have I ever kept anything from you, Mahmud? Have I ever refused one of your requests? Did I not help you get married and start a family, and do I not treat your children like my own? What you'll get for your bit of land won't be enough anyway. You'll sell it and spend the money. Fine, and then what?' But it was like talking to a brick wall. The piece of land was sold, and the buyer was none other than Radi.

Now here he was, coming to him in total submission, wanting to listen to his opinion. So be it, he would hear his opinion. After the tea had been drunk, the words of affection and brotherhood were over.

'Listen, Sheikh Radi,' Zaki said, firmly. 'Salama made a mistake, but he is our son and we will deal with him. As for your daughter....'

After a period of silence, he lifted his head proudly.

'If Zakiya was our daughter, we would have punished her. But she's your daughter and you're free to do with her as you please.'

His tone suggested that the Qassimis had no qualms over murdering someone in defence of their honour. But the Baharwa ... what could one of the Baharwa do in a situation like this? They were peaceful people who just wanted to live under God's protection, and they didn't have any proud heritage or glorious origins. They wanted nothing but security. But here they were, having been exposed in front of everyone. 'She is your daughter and you're free to do with her as you please.' That was how Zaki placed Radi between a rock and a hard place. It was either murder or the eternal stamp of shame. No, he couldn't murder or hire someone to murder her. And if he found her, she wouldn't be able to leave the house. Would he lock her up at home so that no one would see her until she died? Then wouldn't killing her be more merciful than this life sentence?

'What do you think, Sakina?'

Sakina didn't utter a single word. When she heard what her husband told her about his meeting with Zaki, she knew there was no use in talking. She had known the girl loved Salama; that was why she tried to prevent her from bumping into him. It was both to avoid a scandal and to make him understand that whoever wanted the girl had to come and ask for her hand. The truth of the matter was that, deep down, she held out hope in something she didn't dare express, which was for God to bless them with a marriage to one of the sons of Qassim, and let it be Salama. Then everyone would be equal and the barrier that separated them would be broken. An invisible barrier, even though no one had ever been able to cross it. And no one would be able to cross it after what had happened. What did she think? There was no point in talking. Men - she told herself - were sometimes more cowardly than women. She was determined to do what was necessary.

***

The Qassimis were Arabs who didn't approve of marrying peasants or strangers, unless they were from old, respectable, landowning families. And the Baharwa, who lived with them in the same village, were strangers and farm labourers, despite living amongst them for generations and becoming landowners in an ironic 'twist of fate'.... But in the long history of the Qassimis, there were two exceptions that people would cite. It was said that in the olden days, Saddina (said to be Qassim's daughter) married a man called Abu Jad. Little was known about this man except that he was a stranger and, according to the song handed down from generation to generation, he used to wear a cone-shaped *tartur* hat:

'Saddina, don't marry Abu Zad
whose tartur hat scares all the lads'

Everyone was opposed to the marriage between Abu Jad and this girl whose beauty people quoted in proverbs, but Qassim insisted that she marry the stranger. Why did he insist on it, even though the girl rejected him and her family objected? Why did he make his daughter a victim of a hateful marriage, which was still the subject of proverbs several generations later? That was what nobody could understand.

But Shabana had a theory that contradicted the Qassimis' beliefs, and which they denied because he used it to excuse Qassim's behaviour. 'I'm not convinced by this story about Saddina,' he would say. 'Could it be possible that Qassim, the sheikh of the Arabs, would marry his daughter to a peasant in a *tartur* hat? I think Abu Jad was one the great landowners in the district and Qassim was a shrewd political leader, meaning that this marriage was carried out for political reasons.' When people asked, 'What do you mean, for political reasons?' Shabana replied, 'Like the prophet, peace be upon him, married Maria the Copt. The king of the Christians sent her to him as a gift because he wanted to befriend him. And I think, and God only knows, that Qassim needed a piece of land - say a hundred acres - to build the village and farm the rest, and that Abu Jad sold him the land for little to nothing, as if it was a dowry for Saddina.' Then he would continue, addressing any Qassimi present. 'What else do you want? What should the man have done? If it weren't for that marriage, you wouldn't have been able to settle here and build homes instead of sleeping in tents, and to sow and reap. There wouldn't have been a village.' If he was asked: 'Okay, what about the *tartur* hat?' he would reply, 'Yes, didn't I tell you? The *tartur* was originally a long hat made of wool, like the ones your neighbours, the Salehis, still wear, and always will, to show off. But in the song, the hat became a *tartur*.'

But none of the Qassimis were convinced by Shabana's theory. They held on to their belief that what Qassim had done was an unforgivable injustice and that the girl had wilted and withered, the severity of her father's cruelty leading to her eventual death, three years after her wretched marriage. 'Her life was cut short,' they would say, and they still sang about her sorrowfully over the ages.

Saddina, with the pomegranate cheeks,
an angel of the Merciful deity.
Saddina, your eyes large and pearly,
turn him down, O honourable lady.
marrying the man with the tartur hat,
such cruelty would draw our Lord's fury

As for the second exception, it was the marriage of Fawziya, Hajja Zainab's daughter, to Hassan the camel driver, who was one of the Salehis. The village of the Qassimis was at most two kilometres from the village of the Salehis. Yet the fact that Zainab accepted her daughter's marriage to a man who was a peasant to his core was something no one had expected, and the sons of Saleh had never dreamed would happen. The two villages faced each other, and the only thing that separated them was a narrow road that overlooked the 'Gulf' - which was a narrow channel of water - and ran parallel to the Salehi properties and those of the sons of Qassim. It ran perpendicular to another 'Gulf' as well as another narrow road that defined the beginning of the Salehi properties. Despite that, between the two villages lay a huge social divide that both sides respected, for the Qassimis were Arabs and the Salehis peasants - a distance as far as the sky and the earth. The two clans exchanged visits and attended each other's weddings, funerals, and celebrations. And sometimes the Salehis would come for Friday prayers at the Qassimi mosque (since it served as the central mosque in the district), and the Qassimis carried out their duty as hosts, feeding the people coming to the *seera*. There were some trade relations too, since the Qassimis bought cucumbers and onions from the Salehis, to eat in their homes, and cotton because Sheikh Radi traded in it. And the Salehis brought their cows to the Qassimi village to mate with the stud bull, or 'the young man', as they called it. Then there was Ibrahim Abu Zaid - a stranger whose background was completely unknown, who had come to the village of the Salehis and settled amongst them. He connected the two villages through the services he offered the corrupt and reckless among the sons of Qassim. Marriage and the intermingling of blood between the peasant Salehi men and the Qassimi girls was hated, forbidden, and formed a red line between two worlds. The Qassimis believed they were more honourable and civilised than the Salehis - these were people who were attached to the land and knew nothing but hoeing, ploughing, and harvesting. They didn't understand horses - since they were camel owners - and they had never owned slaves. They also never sent any of their sons to al-Azhar University. And they didn't have a Quran school, so they sent their children to the school of the Qassimis. Most of them wore *jilbabs* with nothing underneath, and would sleep anywhere they wanted. In the summer, some of them slept on their rooftops or on the terraces outside their homes and, in the winter, some would sleep buried in piles of straw. And they had no history to cherish and had no illusions about their ancestors. They were people who had always lived 'hand to mouth', as they say. Their food was poor quality. Their bread was black, the white wheat flour - the sign of prosperity - mixed in with low grade flour like corn and fenugreek, and most of the time they ate nothing but camel meat and hedgehogs, if they found those. Despite the fact that most of the Qassimis had ended up poor, they still believed that poverty stopped at the sons of Saleh. And even though meat was rare in the lives of that majority, the Qassimis still poked fun at their neighbours because they cooked *kofta* with corn instead of minced meat. They also claimed that the Salehis were prone to strange illnesses, like favus, dropsy, and bladder cancer. So how had Hassan the camel driver broken through these barriers and married Fawziya, from a well-to-do family?

People say that when God Almighty puts forth His reasons, no one can prevent His judgement. Thus it was that early one morning Fawziya woke up to a clamour outside the house. Her mother was still sleeping, but she guessed that Hassan the camel driver must have come back early with the flour from the mill. For five years, he had been carrying their wheat to the mill, where he would spend the night in a long queue outside, waiting for his turn before returning with the flour the next morning. The girl got up, opened the door of the house, and discovered that she was right. Hassan urged his camel to kneel, and he unloaded it. At first, Fawziya didn't know what to do. When she told him that her mother was still asleep, he started to leave, so she invited him to stay until she brought him some breakfast, but he politely refused. He was shy by nature and did not dare raise his eyes to look directly at the girl's face. But the camel refused to get back up, and when Hassan tried to spur it with a strike of the stick on its neck, it only frothed and foamed. When he struck it again, it turned around angrily - and when a camel is angry it becomes brutal - and bit its owner on the forearm. Hassan's scream echoed, and Fawziya was shocked when she saw blood pouring from the young man's arm, so she hurried into the house to fetch any emergency supplies she could find. She disinfected the wound, stuffed it with ground coffee instead of the ash from the stove that they called the *sakan,* and wrapped it in a cloth bandage. 'Don't be so cruel, Hassan,' she said. 'The camel's hungry.' She brought the camel some water and fodder, and only then did Hassan accept the offer of breakfast. Zainab woke up and found him sitting on their low, mud-brick terrace outside the front door, drinking tea, with his head lowered. The young man was polite as a bashful girl and selfless. He accepted whatever fee she gave him without ever haggling. If she asked him, 'Are you happy, Hassan?' his answer would be, 'You're all kindness and blessings, Nana.' 'The boy has a sweet tongue,' she would always say. 'He's not vulgar like the rest of the sons of Saleh.' She was happy that her daughter had acted dutifully. The man of the house was the one who should carry out this task. If he wasn't there, then one of his children stood in for him. This would usually be the eldest son. If the son wasn't there, the wife would go out to welcome the guests and, if she wasn't there, then the daughter would go out to meet them, taking on the role of the men. Then she would truly be her father's daughter. This was the proper way of doing things, in accordance to that hierarchy.

When Hassan returned to his family, he told them that he wanted to marry Fawziya. His insane request left them all astounded. 'The boy is as foolish as his ancestors,' they said. They knew what Zainab thought of them. 'Couldn't you find anyone but Zainab's daughter?' his father said. 'There are girls all over the place.' His uncle took the same position. 'I swear to God,' Hassan vowed. 'I won't marry anyone else.' The conversation went on, and so did the shouting, until his grandfather woke up, lifting his head from underneath the thick woollen cover. 'What's all this racket? You people are giving me a headache. God bless the one who knows his own value. But Hassan, you know we're not good enough for them.' At this, Haniya, the wife of Hassan's uncle Saeed, intervened. 'Come on everyone, why do you want to put a damper on the man's hope? You're all sitting here, each of you pitching in with your opinion? Did any of you ask what Zainab thinks?' 'But we know what she thinks,' they replied. So Haniya addressed the grandfather. 'All you've been doing for ten years is falling asleep on the terrace and waking up again. You don't work or do anything to keep you occupied. All you do is eat and grumble: "I'm tired, I'm sick. Cook me a chicken so I can eat it with its soup. Take care of me in the few days left of my life. I'm on my way out of this world and you're on your way in."' 'What do you want someone of my age to do, Haniya?' he asked. 'Get up, lean on your cane, and go arrange for the boy to get married,' she replied. 'Maybe Zainab will feel sorry for you and be too embarrassed to turn you down.'

The grandfather covered his face with the woollen cover and muttered. 'Bitch...she has a loose tongue...tyrant.' But Haniya wasn't deterred. She suggested that she go to Zainab to gauge her reaction, an idea they immediately supported, so she might save them any potential embarrassment. When Haniya came back, she told them that Zainab had changed the subject as soon as she raised it. 'So you got the message then?' her husband asked. 'Good woman, didn't we warn you?' But Haniya had a different interpretation. 'I feel positive,' she said. 'Maybe silence is the sign of acceptance.'

The truth was that Zainab's silence was an expression of sadness and hesitation. She knew that, over the years, her daughter saw the young man whenever he came to them. So could there have been something going on between them? The boy was kind and courteous, but he was a peasant through and through. She decided to broach the subject with her daughter. 'I'm not happy with the idea of this marriage, Fawziya. And if your father were alive, he would refuse. What do you think?' She hoped her daughter would be wise enough to listen to her mother's advice and to reply with, 'As you see fit, Ma.' This is what Zainab thought would happen when Fawziya lowered her head and didn't say a word. But when the girl finally looked up, tears were streaming from her eyes, and she uttered a phrase that leapt to her mother's heart. 'You mean that, in the end, you want to marry me off to someone I want nothing to do with, like they married off Saddina?' Deeply perturbed, Zainab felt as if she'd just seen the ghost of Saddina sent back from the dead to complain about the injustice she had suffered. So the matter was settled. Barely two weeks had passed since the incident with the camel before Zainab found a delegation of Salehis at her door: the grandfather - who hadn't left his spot on the terrace for ten years - leaning on his cane, Hassan's father, and his uncle. She didn't hesitate for long before accepting. After the way things worked out, the news spread amongst the people. The storyteller would always conclude his story in the same way. 'If it weren't for the camel's bite, Hassan would never have managed to get Fawziya. But what can you say? It was early morning, the girl felt sorry for the boy, and Zainab's heart trembled for her only daughter. Your Lord prepared the reasons. Your Lord permitted it.' And the listeners would follow by saying: 'And how Magnificent is He.' All these sayings meant that Fawziya's marriage to Hassan was seen as an exception. Others couldn't measure against it, and it would never be repeated. That was why Salama's mother wasn't convinced of the merits of her son's marriage to a Baharwa girl. 'That might have been what Zainab did, and now she's gone,' she would say. 'But I'm not Zainab. And yes, Hassan was a peasant, but he's not one of the Baharwa. And Fawziya isn't Zakiya. Zakiya is a slut. She chased my son until she made him sin.'

***

From Na'sa's resonant ululations, Fawziya knew immediately that the baby was a boy. 'We'll call him Medhat,' she said. 'Why Medhat, my dear?' Na'sa asked. 'His pa won't allow it. Why don't we call him Ahmed or Abdelhamed? I hear people say *the best names are those where God is being worshipped or thanked*.' 'I don't care,' Fawziya said. 'We'll call him Medhat and that's that. The Turks call their children Medhat.' And Na'sa understood, since in the eyes of the sons of Qassim, the Turks, whose civilization had ended a long time ago, were still renowned for their fair skin, good looks, and leadership. But Fawziya's happiness with the baby would be only fleeting. She was so horrified when the midwife brought him in that she turned her head the other way. 'The boy is ugly, Na'sa,' she said. 'Give him a bit of time, dear,' Na'sa replied. 'The boy's just come out of your belly.' 'It's my miserable luck!' Fawziya wailed. 'The boy's dead, Na'sa!' Na'sa was shocked and speechless. Delivering the child had been laborious. It had been a troublesome labour that started after midnight, and now the midday prayer call had sounded, but the baby hadn't screamed or made a single sound or movement. It looked as though he really was dead, which would be God's will. Na'sa didn't know what else to do but wash the newborn and swaddle him carefully, covering him with a deep tray until his family decided to bury him. With a heavy heart, she left. 'May God help you, Fawziya.' As soon as Na'sa got home, she found her own son screaming from hunger, so she breastfed him until he was full and sleep overcame him. Then a thought suddenly leapt to her mind, 'What's going on with that baby who came out of his mother's belly without screaming or making a sound?' She pulled her son from her breast and hurried back to Fawziya's house, where she lifted the cover off the child, placed him in a small tub of warm water, and massaged his body and limbs. After doing this for a while, she spotted a vein pulsing in his stomach. This drew a second ululation from her, which was long and resounding. Everyone was happy to hear the joyful sound, but the father's happiness was destined to be brief. He died of bladder cancer a few months after the baby was born. And the mother continued to feel miserable about how ugly the child was until she died when he was three years old. Even when she was alive, she would leave him with her mother or Na'sa, who nursed him for the first two years with her son Ismail, the child who was mute and deaf. And when the boy was four years old, his grandmother passed away, and he was transferred fully to

Na'sa's care. But Medhat was never short of a carer since, in addition to his grandmother Zainab, for as long as she lived, and his wet nurse Na'sa, there was his uncle's wife, Haniya, who lived in the village of the Salehis. She paid Na'sa the wage Zainab had set and made sure the child was brought to her once a week so she could see him. She had several children - three boys and two girls - but Medhat was her 'son', too. Wasn't she the one who had arranged for his mother to marry his father, thereby quashing the ban on intermarriage between the two clans? If the boy ever felt hungry or tired, he could seek refuge in any of the homes of the sons of Qassim, and he would find someone there to feed him and look after him. These were the benefits he enjoyed because he was an orphan and because, at the end of the day, he was Zainab's boy.

Haniya had a large house and would keep her doors open - front and back - all day long, and anyone could enter from either side without having to ask permission. The house was also open to any young goats and sheep. But dogs weren't allowed inside to lick the dishes or go near anyone who lived in the house since, according to Sharia law, dogs are impure and touching them invalidates ablution and negates the prayer. The dogs here were generally stray and would mate secretly in the fields or wastelands. No one tamed dogs or coddled them unless they voluntarily performed some service. Sometimes a dog would impose itself on whoever was herding sheep, so the herder would take it in to guard the herd. This relationship would be limited to performing the service from a distance, and the guard would be fed with whatever could be spared. One day, a large black dog appeared and presented itself to Haniya's household. The family accepted the dog, up to a point. It wasn't allowed inside the house and, truth be told, the dog respected its limits. At meal times, it would appear, standing patiently near whoever was eating around the low, round table on the ground outside the house. It waited until someone shouted at it and sent it on its way or tossed some food towards it. The black dog kept coming and going like this until Medhat befriended him. Not only did the boy start to split his food with the dog or request that the dog get his own share, he also started to imitate some of the dog's behaviour, like crawling on all fours or sitting on his hind legs and barking. The child thought he was a breed of dog, which would make Haniya roar with laughter. Then one day, the boy decided to give his friend a human name, calling him Farid. That was the first time in the history of the village that a name would be given to a dog, let alone one usually reserved for humans. An animal might be called by a description, or a name with a unique characteristic, like Haniya's water buffalo, which was described during its pregnancy as al-Mabrouka, 'the blessed one' to shield it from the evil eye and protect the foetus. Or like her small newborn calf, which for a long time was called Rizq, 'blessing', both as a joke and because the calf was considered a blessing from God and a sign of good fortune. But for someone to give an animal a permanent name, transforming it into a distinct individual that people had to take into account, that was unheard of. And the first person to introduce this phenomenon was Medhat ibn Hassan.

The dog's luck in life changed in a flash the day Haniya gave Medhat a bowl of milk and a piece of bread.

'Where's Farid's share?' he asked.

Haniya turned to him. 'What are you talking about? Farid who?'

She couldn't believe it when Medhat pointed to the dog.

'But he's there, sitting right in front of you, isn't he.'

Haniya quickly grasped what he meant and burst out laughing. 'You mean the dog has a name now, Medhat?'

Haniya returned with the dog's share of the food. At first, she thought that Medhat's naming of the dog was a fleeting joke. But he was totally serious and always consistent in using the name Farid, until it was accepted by others. Farida, Ibrahim Abu Zaid's daughter, had no objections to the dog's name being so close to hers. She knew it was driven by Medhat's love for her. The dog began to accompany the child wherever he went and, like his owner, he would drift between the sons of Qassim and sons of Saleh. The families of the two villages welcomed him out of good will, because he was guarding the frail child - swarming around him 'like a locust' they would say - as he wandered the fields where foxes and wolves lurked. Even though Zainab was stricter than Haniya when it came to the impurity of dogs, she accepted this dog, approved of naming him, and began to treat him in a special way. He would get his own share of food, just like Medhat, so long as he didn't come into the house. She was happy because he became a personal bodyguard to the child, following him wherever he went. And Medhat's wanderings were frequent. He would go everywhere from the moment he was up on his feet. He hadn't wasted time in crawling and struggling to stand up - he stood up in one go, almost overnight, and started to walk. After that, nothing could stop him from walking every which way. He started roaming around with a group of boys who were older than him, crossing the canal together to the land of the Sa'ida, sneaking into the reed and cactus bushes to collect prickly pears and to steal the dates. He learnt how to get to the village of his paternal uncles, whether on his own or with others. Even his grandmother called him *barrawi* - comparing him to the wild, open country - or *gabalawy* - 'boy of the mountains'. Then

Farid appeared as a guardian to the child, and the grandmother breathed a sigh of relief. She could now feel reassured about the child's comings and goings through the fields.

She had more than one reason to worry about the wild *barrawi* child. He was the only son of her only daughter, and because he'd been prone to sickness since the day he was born, he would hardly eat and didn't get much attention from his mother. Unlike the other grandchildren, he started to get special treatment from his grandmother. She wouldn't be content for him to eat only with the other children, because she knew he couldn't compete with their 'ravenous appetites'. So she would take him to a room in the house and give him everything he wanted, like bananas and soft and chewy candies. One day, he fell ill with diphtheria, which was treated by cauterizing the lowest part of the armpit from behind. People said that 'cauterization is the last resort in medicine', because they had other types of folk medicine. The rural barber, for example, dealt with all their dental problems, circumcision, eye diseases, and packing of wounds. Then there were experts in bloodletting and bone-setting, as well as, naturally, practitioners of magic and writers of charms and spells. But diphtheria, the plague among children, exhausted the known medical treatments and had no treatment but cauterization, which, from a practical perspective, presented the only solution. The cauterization expert came, rolled up his sleeves, lit the fire, and heated a thick blacksmithing nail until it glowed and turned white. Then the man recited the name of God the Merciful as he prepared to apply the nail. Zainab watched what was going on patiently and intently until the doctor raised the blazing nail in order to bring it down on the child's body, when she screamed out. 'God forbid! My boy won't be cauterized with fire.' She stood between the man and the patient. 'So what should we do, Hajja?' the man asked. 'My boy will go to the doctor in Abu Kabir,' she replied. This would not have been the first time one of Zainab's grandchildren had been cauterized, and every other time she had agreed. But she couldn't stand to see her daughter's son receive this treatment. This became the first time a child was sent to a proper doctor in Abu Kabir.

***

Some of the women in Qassimi village objected to the friendship that tied Medhat to Farida.

'Couldn't he find anyone but that criminal's daughter to be friends with?'

'Leave the boy alone,' Zainab said. 'That poor kid...and he doesn't have a brother or sister.'

But although he had no siblings, Medhat was, like Haniya's water buffalo, protected from the world of the unseen. If he stumbled and fell, Na'sa would say, 'May the prophet's name guard and protect you.'

But Zainab would say, 'May God's name guard you; your sister protects you.'

This 'sister' was an invisible twin who lived underground and intervened to protect a child if he was ever in harm's way. But Farida was like a big sister, and she included Medhat in her gang of children. She was their eldest and bravest, and she was also the most skilled at certain activities, the leader in games, and would referee competitions and contests. She had many other qualities that Medhat noticed, because she would pay him special attention and sometimes play with him alone, introducing him to the facts of life he didn't know.

***

A delegation of Qassimis approached the *seera* one day: Sheikh Hamed; Salama's father, Sheikh Sayyid; his mother, Nawal; and his uncle, Shabana. Each offered their opinion on what had happened.

'I don't understand what the problem is,' Shabana started. 'Salama made a mistake. He should fix his mistake and marry the girl. God loves those who act kindly.'

'God forbid!' Nawal cried out. 'My son will not marry a Baharwa girl.'

'What's all this about the Qassimis and Baharwa?' Shabana replied. 'We're all Muslims. Prophet Mohamed said: '*Intermarry and reproduce so that I may be proud of you on Judgment Day*.'

'The girl is a hussy,' Nawal protested. 'She's the one who played with my son's mind, she—'

But Salama interrupted her. 'Don't be so harsh, Ma. It's not the girl's fault. I'm the one to blame.'

Sheikh Sayyid echoed his son's admission. 'Salama is to blame. It looks like he committed a sin, but it needs to be investigated. Did he kiss her, touch her thighs, or penetrate her? We need to call for any witnesses we can find.'

'Oh, come on. Don't land the boy in trouble!' his wife shouted at him. 'Let's have none of this penetrating or not penetrating. What kind of talk is that?'

'Nobody blames him for falling in love with Zakiya,' Sheikh Hamed intervened. 'He should have ignored the devil and stopped himself from committing a sin. Religion doesn't forbid chaste love. The prophet, peace be upon him, said, '*Whoever falls passionately in love and yet remains chaste and keeps his love secret until he dies, dies a martyr*.' And what the poet Abu Amr Jamil said was admirable:

Buthaina could please me so simply, it seems,
Would the tattler know, he would surely retire.
With 'no', 'I cannot' and some mere dreams,
With hope, where hope is only a futile desire.

'Is anything better than this?'

Zaki intervened firmly to settle the debate. 'I told Sheikh Radi that their daughter is not our responsibility...they can punish her their own way and we will punish our son, and we must punish him.'

Sheikh Sayyid returned to the attack. 'If it is proved that he sinned, either through a confession or by a witness, then the punishment of a hundred lashes must be applied.'

'No one touches my son,' Nawal replied. 'My son didn't do anything wrong.'

'We've never seen anyone whipped because he committed adultery or his hand cut off because he stole,' Shabana challenged his brother. 'Muslims stopped carrying out these traditions a long time ago.'

His brother called on God's protection from the accursed Satan. 'Don't you dare refute the religious limits or else you have become an infidel.'

Salama addressed Sheikh Zaki. 'I'm to blame, uncle, and I'll accept whatever punishment you choose.'

At that, Zaki stood up, took hold of one of his sandals and used it to pound Salama's neck and shoulders.

'Beat me, uncle... beat me,' Salama shouted. 'I deserve everything I get.'

Zaki beat him until his hand became weak, then he told everyone to leave.

'You haven't heard the last of this,' he said to Salama. 'You go with your mother and father, and don't leave the house until I give you a sign.'

He had asked everyone to go out of despair. Twenty or thirty strikes with his sandal wasn't enough, and he knew it wasn't the 'lesson' Salama deserved for the crime he'd committed. But he didn't know what else to do. Had he been in a better state - had he been in his normal state - maybe then he would've found a solution. But he felt muddled, deeply defeated, and helpless, as though his ability to resolve problems was out of reach. He sought the help of the family of the prophet whose tombs he visited in Cairo. 'Help me Hussain. I am seeking your protection, Zainab.'

Suddenly Nafisa appeared, but he didn't recognize her at first glance. He saw an old, stout woman wearing black and walking with difficulty.

'Good evening, Zaki,' she said.

He didn't reply and kept staring at her in astonishment, as if he had seen a ghost. It was only after she greeted him a second time that he realised who it was. He passed his palm over his face like someone ending their supplication.

'Good evening to you too, aunt. Welcome.'.

'Sakina came to me a little while ago in a terrible state,' she said. 'She told me godawful things that I don't want to repeat. She can say whatever she wants. She's excused. Zakiya is her daughter, and you know how a mother's heart is.'

'I know, aunt, but what has it got to do with us?' he replied. 'She's their daughter. They can do whatever they want.'

'What do you mean, Zaki? How can you talk like that? How can they do what they want, my dear? And what about you?'

'If you're after my opinion, the girl deserves to be killed.'

'Why? What did she do?'

'What do you mean, what did she do? You're asking me? Didn't you hear the talk that's going around in the village?'

'What talk, Zaki? Was anyone with Salama and the girl when they were in the cornfield? Did anyone see what they were doing apart from God?'

Zaki was taken aback by the question and hesitated before he finally replied.

'And were you with them, aunt? Did you see what they did?'

'No, I didn't see anything, but I know the girl well and I know Salama well. I want to tell you something: *Indeed, some suspicions are sins*. And do you think killing someone is a small matter, Zaki? You want to kill a girl in the prime of her youth just because you suspect something?'

Silence prevailed until Zaki spoke. 'How can disgrace be erased, aunt?'

Nafisa took hold of his hand. 'There's no need for that kind of talk, Zaki.'

'May God soften your heart, Zaki,' she said, starting to cry. 'Listen to me. I'm like your mother. I raised you, my love, and I carried you in these arms of mine many times. Salama is just like Hashem to me, and Zakiya is like my daughter.'

Zaki turned his head away. 'Now she's gone to hell.'

'The girl told me everything, and I believe her,' Nafisa said, drying her tears. 'Salama hugged her and kissed her. And so what? Did the world go to ruin? It's all child's play.'

'What's it got to do with us whether she deserves to be killed or not?' Zaki replied. 'Why are you burdening me with this problem, aunt? She's gone, let her go to hell.'

Nafisa prepared to leave. 'She hasn't gone or anything like it. The girl's at home with me.'

'What do you mean, she's with you?' Zaki replied, looking aghast. 'Please sit down. Don't go.'

'Where else would she run to? She came to me, and I've locked her in so she doesn't see anyone and no one sees her. No one will touch a hair on her head now she's in my house.'

'Why did you do that, aunt?' Zaki replied with difficulty, on the verge of tears.

'She came and asked for my help,' she replied. 'Shouldn't I rescue her? If Zainab had been alive and Zakiya had gone to her, do you think she would've turned her away?'

'The girl is in your house, which means she's our responsibility now,' he said quietly. 'What should we do, aunt?'

'What should we do?' she replied, as she struggled to heave herself up. 'You want me to tell you what to do, Zaki? Where's your mind, my love? You've truly saddened me, I swear to God. Help the girl, please.'

Since he was frozen to the spot and not even blinking, she leaned towards his hand to try and kiss it.

'Give me your hand to kiss, but just help her.'

Zaki pulled his hand away in annoyance. 'God forbid, aunt. I'll kiss your hand and feet, but please don't ask this of me.'

She stopped at the door to plead with him, calling on the companionship and love between them, but he appeared unmoved.

***

Now Zaki was caught in a trap. When Zakiya disappeared, he had been as relieved as everyone else, because it meant the problem would be limited to punishing Salama, and Salama could be handled. He would accept whatever punishment his uncle chose. But the old woman had gone and spoilt everything by taking the girl under her wing. Through her protection, she had turned her into something to be safeguarded, a burden on the shoulders of the Qassimis, and on his shoulders specifically. As if he didn't have enough problems and responsibilities already. The heaviest of his burdens was the feeling that everything was heading towards its demise, that the Qassimis no longer had the upper hand, that his power over the people was vanishing, and that he had become unable to fend off harm from himself, let alone from others. 'Where's your mind, Zaki?' True, where was his mind? His mind no longer obeyed him. The old woman thought he should marry Salama to Zakiya. She hadn't said it directly. But that was what she was hinting at, and that was what the opium-head Shabana thought, too. He'd been told that this was the solution that would've pleased Zainab, and that it was the solution that would please God and His prophet. But there was no way he could accept this. 'I'm sorry, aunt, sorry Zainab, sorry everyone. I can't, anything but this.' Shabana the opium-head - who quoted the words of the prophet about mating and breeding in his argument - deserved to be killed. He was a sinner who drank alcohol in Abu Kabir, according to the news that had reached him, who didn't abstain from committing sin, and who didn't care about anything except being high. He would gather the boys around him in the *jurn* to make them question everything, make fun of the Qassimis, and destroy everything they had built. And Radi had come to him, humbling himself, pleading and talking about community and brotherhood. But he was the greedy, arrogant man who didn't care about anything other than his own benefit. Not once did he hear of him helping someone in need or being generous to a guest or kind to the poor. Radi never opened up his purse to donate a piaster towards the maintenance of the mosque, and he didn't want to help refurbish the *seera*. 'The world has changed, Zaki,' Radi had said when asked for donations. 'The *seera's* time has passed. Who keeps their door wide open to every guest and passerby anymore?' This was despite the generosity of God, who had given him riches far and wide. He traded in cotton and wheat, his wife traded in chickens, eggs, and butter, and his son had a shop on the country road. They would sell the air if they could. And he tirelessly consumed all that belonged to the sons of Qassim. He had sought Zainab's friendship throughout her life because he was afraid of her might. But as soon as she passed into God's mercy, he dove deep into what she left behind and expanded his reach. He bought everything her sons owned, one by one. And that didn't sate him, so he turned to his youngest brother to tempt him into selling his share of the inheritance and to separate from his eldest brother. He continued to tempt Zaki's brother by increasing the offer until the fool fell in his trap. It wasn't enough for him to have a say in everything. Now he wanted to be related to the Qassimis by marriage in order to assimilate into their ranks. Salama was a naïve idiot. If he married one of them, he would forget his family. He would yield to his wife and his mother- and father-in-law, and his children would become the children of their maternal uncles, the Baharwa. And the Baharwa would become the indigenous population of the village, and the sons of Qassim would end up working for them. In the end, that was how it would all transpire. He would die and Radi would purchase his land from his children. And if Radi died before him - since he was older - his son Khalil would take on the task in his place, and that would be the outcome of all of this. 'Sorry, aunt, sorry, Zainab, sorry, everyone. I can't. *God burdens not a person beyond his scope.*'

He clenched his fist, as if trying to gather all his strength to reject what was being asked of him, when he heard a movement in the corner next to the door. When he raised his head and saw Zakiya, a shiver ran down his spine. How had she emerged from the shadows, pale-faced, her head unveiled and dressed in tattered clothes that barely covered her body? What did the girl want from him? 'What brought you here, Zakiya?' he shouted at her. 'Didn't you use my aunt as a go-between? Isn't that enough?' He saw Zakiya open her mouth to speak words he couldn't hear. So he shouted at her again. 'Young woman, what do you want?' The response finally reached him as she uttered a single sentence. '*Aba* Zaki, I need your protection'. She had spoken - with eyes locked on him - then disappeared as quickly as she had appeared. She walked away, withdrew, consumed by the darkness in that corner, just as it had opened to allow her to appear. He rubbed his eyes and became more exasperated. Was it Zakiya in the flesh and blood, or had he seen, God help us, a ghost? A hidden power had a tight grip on his heart, trying to crack and shatter it. So he knelt in prayer in the direction of the nearby corner, sobbing loudly. 'If this was your wish, let it be. But don't abandon me. We are all in your protection.'

It was midnight when he sent for Radi to come to him urgently. Radi showed up, looking perturbed, pale-faced, and anxious. He spoke in a barely audible voice.

'Is everything okay, God willing, Sheikh Zaki?'

'Sit down,' Zaki replied. 'I want to reassure you about Zakiya. The girl is well and she is safe and sound.'

'Where is she?' Radi asked him, fervently.

'Before I tell you where she is,' Zaki replied, 'I want you to please do me a favour.'

'Whatever you say Zaki, I'll agree.'

'Zakiya is my daughter and she is in my home, which is the same as being in your home.'

'Of course, Zaki, that goes without saying.'

'We are asking for Zakiya's hand in marriage for our son, Salama. What do you say?'

Sheikh Radi lowered his head to hide his tears.

'Give me your hand,' Zaki said. 'Let us read the *fatiha*.'

After they had read the first chapter of the Quran as a way of blessing the engagement, Zaki got down to business.

'The girl must have a dowry,' he said. 'That, as you know, is the rule according to Sharia law. And the dowry is my responsibility.'

'You've always been chivalrous, Zaki. May God prolong your life. But where is she?'

'I told you not to worry,' Zaki said, chuckling. 'She's as good as in her father's home. Tomorrow morning, she'll be at your house, having been treated like a queen. In the evening, after the *maghreb* prayer, you should bring a marriage registrar, and we'll perform the Islamic ceremony. The wedding feast will be held after the fasting month, God willing.'

Zaki smiled amiably, as a final thought crossed his mind.

'By the way Sheikh Radi,' he started. 'You are the oldest and the most educated among us. You're our eldest brother, and the village can't survive without you. I'd like you, please, to take care of the mosque.'

'Your wish is my command,' Radi replied immediately.

'The mosque needs money for its maintenance,' Zaki continued. 'God knows how much, but we will ask. What do you think?'

'I'm ready,' Radi replied.

A sense of contentment started to seep through Zaki, since he was now starting to grab hold of the problems one by one, so he resumed his confrontation.

'And you can't be happy with Sheikh Hamed's situation. That man and his sons have been in a pitiful state ever since Zainab died. She used to look after him, and you know that without him there would be no Quranic school or education for the young ones. How can that be? What do you think about us giving him a monthly salary? I mean a few piasters for him to live on until the wheat or corn harvest.'

'Whatever you say is fine by me, Sheikh Zaki,' Radi replied.

'So let's say a pound a month,' Zaki suggested. Then it seemed he had remembered one final concern. 'May God rest your soul, Zainab. She would always look after the *seera*. The *seera*, you wise man, needs furniture. And it should always be ready for guests, which means coffee and tea sets, bread, salt, and water. Otherwise, what would a stranger arriving at night, or the people staying there, eat and drink? And everything has its reward in God. We will split all this in half between us. What do you say?'

After Radi had agreed to this final request, he headed towards the door calmly and carefully, as if he didn't want to make any movement - any movement at all - that might jeopardize the beautiful agreement he had just reached with Zaki. God had written him a new future, and all he wanted now was to flee with it, to escape by the skin of his teeth. His daughter's honour was safe - *to you, God, we owe all thanks and gratitude*. And, for the first time in history, the wall between the Qassimis and the Baharwa would be demolished. Now he had to race home and announce the happy news to his wife and son. But he almost tripped at the door as he was putting on his sandals when he heard Sheikh Zaki bellow. 'Why did you let me down?' Just then, Zaki had seen a hole crack open in his belly, and it felt as though his heart was plunging into it, or that he himself was plummeting. Radi turned around. 'Let you down how, Zaki?' he began to say. 'I fulfilled your requests. I came as soon as you called.' But all he could see of Zaki was his back. He was curled up, facing the corner of the room. Who was he talking to? Something suggested evil was involved. But Radi decided to keep things moving. He had clinched a deal that he mustn't lose, no matter what, and he left hurriedly. What he had won was enough for him. He would come back tomorrow with the marriage registrar and the money.

***

There was a great deal of commotion inside and outside the *seera* on the day of the wedding. The place was sparkling clean like it hadn't been since its glory days, when Mansur and Zainab were still alive. It had been swept, and straw mats were laid out over the floor and the area outside. That morning, the celebratory rituals started early. Fahmi, the barber, appeared on his donkey. Following him was his brother Saeed, his assistant, and the demand for their services was high. There was a large crowd at the mosque's bathing basin, because many of the village men and teenagers wanted to bathe after having their hair cut, and it didn't matter to them that the bathing basin was 'inhabited'. In any case, they didn't care about its spirits, even in the darkness of early dawn, when one of them might need to remove traces of the impurity following intercourse or a wet dream before everyone woke up. Atiya, the vegetable seller, turned up with his usual chant, 'get your red tomatoes… radishes, soft and green-leaved' echoing through the village. Atiya would usually come just before noon, and on this glorious day he had completely sold out - of two full donkey loads - before the midday prayer was even called. Husniya the gypsy turned up in a bright orange outfit with her son, Ali the drummer, and his wife, Shahira, the gypsy dancer, and outside the homes of the Baharwa people, drums were beaten, tambourines thumped, and finger cymbals clanked. People said that day - and it was true - that Sheikh Radi had 'loosened the ties on his purse'. He brought a cook and several assistants over from Abu Kabir. Fires were lit in the bakeries and in the stoves in several homes as the cook circled between locations, handing out instructions and making sure that everything was carried out properly. The women preparing the food in their homes missed their aunt Nafisa - since she was a leader with whom no one could compete when it came to a celebration like this - but she wasn't in her usual spot. People asked about the secret behind her absence, since she was like a second mother to the bride.

Then came the big surprise, a little before sunset, as a large gathering of Salehis appeared, the likes of which had never been seen before. They seemed to tower in their loose *jilbabs*, their tall hats, and the scarves that dangled from their shoulders and grazed the ground. They stood frozen to the spot until the drums were hammered, when life beat into them and they arranged themselves into a circle. The dance started with a slow clapping that could barely be heard, but which then became louder and faster as the atmosphere heated up and a shiver passed through the audience, touching everyone. The Salehi dancers chanted in harmony to the beat of the clapping, '*Al Dah Yo…. Al Dah Yo*'. It was a phrase no one understood, but which had become the name of the dance passed down through generations of Salehis, who were now the best performers of the song in the whole district. The men's voices blended into one as they repeated the chant to that beat, and 'it tugged at the hearts,' as Shabana said. It seemed that the chant had seeped through the body of

Shahira, the gypsy woman, and without anyone realizing, she slipped past the men, took up a position in the centre of the circle, and wrapped one of the men's scarves around her hips. He didn't mind, and neither did the other men, even though the dance was traditionally the reserve of men. Her breasts and buttocks trembled and ignited the enthusiasm of the audience, some of whom added their voices to those of the dancers.

In the evening, the large brass dishes were carried, filled with copious amounts of food - particularly slabs of meat and a dish the village had never seen before called *thareed*, prepared by soaking bread in meat stock. Everyone ate until they were full. After dinner, the guests gathered in the *seera*, with a row for the women and children on one side, and a row for men on the other. It was exactly the way it had been in the past, when the poets would descend on the village to spend nights there, when feasts would be on offer, and the epics recited until past midnight. Just before midnight, Shabana couldn't stand the impact of Shahira's shaking anymore, so he snatched the drum from her husband's hand and took on the role of the drummer. Neither Shahira nor her husband seemed to mind, as the women laughed and clapped their hands. The hollers grew louder and the clapping more intense when the audience saw how the gypsy dancer responded to Shabana's drumming. She started to cross through the rows of the audience, dancing as she chinked her cymbals and flailed her hair like a filly showing off its brilliant youth.

Only Zaki's appearance spoiled the celebratory mood. The guests hadn't seen him except during the meal. He could have joined any table and eaten whatever he liked, but instead he kept hovering, jittery-eyed, moving from one tray to another to snatch a bit from here and a bit from there, which he would gobble while he stood or else shove in his pocket. Some of those eating lifted their hands from the food, while the morsels lodged in the throats of the others, out of shock and sadness. It distressed and pained them to see this man, renowned for being chivalrous and always in the service of his guests, acting in such a humiliating way. Zaki kept moving between the dishes until Shabana stood up, led his cousin to his house, and stayed with him until the dishes had all been removed.

Days later, the sons of Qassim went about repeating in anguish that bringing together Salama and Zakiya in a *halal* way was Zaki's last honourable task. After this achievement, Zaki had turned into someone they no longer recognised. Only two or three days after the marriage ceremonies in the *seera* were over, he started to act in a completely unprecedented way. The first sign was when he passed by a family gathered around the low table outside their home, preparing to break the Ramadan fast, and joined them without being invited and without uttering a greeting. Once he had recovered from the shock, the man of the house spoke. 'Why, hello and welcome, Sheikh Zaki,' but Zaki had started to wolf down the food without looking at anyone or even waiting for the sunset prayer call that sets off the meal. The rest of the family exchanged looks of surprise and annoyance until the father gestured to them to stay quiet. Zaki was gobbling down the food; this was the same man who was known for self-restraint and pride, the man who always waited until everyone else at the table had started eating, whether he was the guest or the host. And if he was the host, he would take the smallest share of food, since his duty and joy was to ensure that each guest ate what they deserved and more.

Then the signs of his collapse became apparent and the news spread. The once sober sheikh was seen eating and drinking in daylight during the fasting hours. People saw him lying down on his belly at the edge of the 'Gulf', drinking from the current. He stopped praying at the mosque, and he started to roam the streets and fields, always repeating the same phrase, 'Why did you let me down?' He wouldn't stop unless he saw a group of people eating, at which point he would join them and eat from their food, whether they allowed him or not. At first, people felt sorry for him. '*There is neither power nor strength but in God*,' they would say, or '*have mercy on an honourable person of a nation reduced to disgrace*', and would share their food with him. But when they grew tired of his greed and repulsed by his behaviour, they began to stop him and to throw him out. Some would even toss him some food as he approached, and he would catch whatever they graced him with like a dog and leave. That was the only way to get rid of him. Just after Ramadan ended and the celebrations of the festival of Eid ul Fitr were over, the boys would march behind him as they sang, '*Why did you let me down*?' Then he would become very agitated and repeat the phrase in time with the rhythm of their singing, which would speed up until he exhausted himself and his question turned into a whimpering and sobbing that would rouse even more laughter in the children.

The blow that struck Zaki extended to his aunt Nafisa, who was as good as finished in the village after that. She didn't go to the wedding, even though she was the one who had placed the bride under her protection and pushed Zaki to agree to the marriage. After that, she fell sick for a last time, an illness that led her to perish in sorrow over her nephew, one of the few who remained from the era of generosity. Even though she always insisted that everything was in God's hands, she kept saying that what had happened to Zaki was because of a marriage he never wanted, and that he had lost his mind from the severity of the defeat. 'Poor man,' she would say. 'He forced himself to take on more than he could handle.' People asked about the source of the phrase he muttered. Who was the poor man he addressed in his reproach? Sheikh Hamed and Sheikh Sayyid - the two jurisprudence experts - discussed the matter. Sheikh Hamed thought Zaki was reprimanding his brother, because he didn't heed his eldest brother's advice not to sell his share of the inheritance. But Sheikh Sayyid thought differently. 'What are you talking about, his brother and all that nonsense? I've been warning you all for a long time that 'The Enemy' is lurking between you, that he shines his torches at you, and crawls over you. Now he has dealt you the fatal blow. Zaki was the best man amongst you and, with his demise, you have fallen to the lowest levels of disgrace and abandonment. *There is no power nor strength save in God.*' Most people leaned towards Sheikh Hamed's opinion. Nearly all of them, in fact, apart from Sheikh Radi - who had seen Zaki utter the phrase for the very first time, folded over on his knees as he faced the corner of the room - and Shabana. But Radi didn't tell anyone what he had seen. And the 'stubborn' Shabana would only rebuff these ideas. 'I don't believe any of it. My cousin Zaki wouldn't go insane because his brother sold a measly piece of land.' 'So what does it mean then, Shabana?' the boys in the *jurn* would ask. 'God only knows,' he would reply, as he chewed on a piece of opium. But he did know.

***

The wedding celebrations were not limited to the *seera*; there were parties on the margins in several locations. For example, there was a room for smoking hashish and such things in Shabana's house. He'd hoped he could make Ali the drummer so high he would lose consciousness, clearing the way for Shabana and Ali's wife, the gypsy dancer. Unfortunately, Shahira was under the strict supervision of her mother-in-law, Husniya. A room was set up at the Baharwa house for women who preferred to celebrate away from the eyes of the men. Farid was positioned outside the door, wagging his tail, and looked both shocked and disappointed that he too wasn't allowed to enter. The only male in the room was Medhat, and he watched the goings on from the vantage point where Na'sa had left him, on top of the sacks of cotton lined up against the wall.

From his position, the boy couldn't stop staring at two strangers: the visiting foreign lady who was said to be an acquaintance of the Baharwa, and the girl from the *bandar* who came with her. What drew most of the child's attention and amazement were her curious features, like bright red hair and freckles sprinkled over her face, which left him dumbfounded. He switched between gazing at the two guests and ogling the red hair until sleep overcame him. Then it was Na'sa's turn to join the party. The girls who were drumming and singing insisted that she tie a scarf around her hips and dance, because she was a good dancer, but she kept refusing until the foreign lady leaned towards her and urged her. 'Please, do it for me,' she said. Na'sa couldn't refuse the guest's request, so she tied the scarf around her waist and began to sway to the beat of the drums and the singing. When Medhat woke up and saw his wet-nurse contorting her body and shimmying in a way he had never seen before, his eyes grew wide in shock. For some reason, he couldn't stand the sight and started to sob. Na'sa stopped dancing, and the girls stopped drumming and singing as she hurried to the child. He was weeping so feverishly that she thought he'd had a nightmare and picked him up to try to settle him down. But the boy carried on blubbering until she sat with him in a corner, whispering in his ear to make him feel better. When he finally surrendered to sleep, resting his head on her chest, she put him on top of the sacks of cotton once again, but her part in the celebration was over.

The presence of the visitor incited a great deal of interest and attention in the village the following day, because they had never seen anything like it. No foreigner had ever visited them - man or woman - let alone spent several days amongst them, sitting and eating with them, and speaking in their language. It was said that she was the wife of one of the bride's mother's relatives - a man called Salem from the Abu Hussein family - and that they lived in a large mansion between the forest and the town of Faqus. The next morning, a group of women and children found her sitting on a chair in the courtyard opposite Zainab's house and circled around her. She wore a blue dress with large white polka dots and a broad white belt around her waist that accentuated her full breasts, as well as nail polish and high-heeled shoes.

Shabana was squatting on the floor nearby, resting his back against the wall and monitoring the events with great interest. He had come over to thank the foreigner for the quarter of a pound she sent him as a tip for the drumming she had enjoyed. It was an amount that would secure him enough opium to keep him going for several days. But he couldn't get close to her. He had been hearing about her for years, through gossip going around in Abu Kabir about the daughter of the foreigner, Mr. Petros, who owned a bar that Salem Abu Hussein used to go to, and how the foreigner had refused to give his daughter's hand in marriage, so Salem stole her away. Shabana deeply regretted that he had never seen that bar or gone to drink there, because he had heard that only wealthy gentry, like Salem Abu Hussein, were welcome. How impressed he was that Salem had managed to snatch her!

Time passed, and she ended up here, sitting across from him while he, nailed to the spot, stared at her. Then he turned away to bury his face in his arms, feeling sorry for what he'd missed out on. 'See, kid,' he said to a boy who had come to sit beside him. 'Look how fair the foreign lady is, how soft her skin, and see how she's smiling? See how she's wearing shoes that show her heels, which are clean and as bright as crystal, not like our women's rough heels. God help us.' 'What's wrong, Uncle Shabana,' the boy replied. 'Why are you upset? The Christians have this world and we have the hereafter.' 'Shut up, you son of a bitch,' Shabana snapped at him. 'You think the foreigners are headed to hellfire and you'll go to heaven? Keep dreaming. I swear you won't reach it, and you'll have missed out on both this world and the hereafter.'

The foreigner was gazing at the faces of the many children who had gathered around her, dark-skinned, some of them naked or in dirty *jilbabs*. Then Medhat appeared from a distance, walking alongside his dog, hand-in-hand with the red-haired girl from the *bandar*. 'My name is Marika, what's yours?' the visitor asked him as he drew closer. 'And why were you crying yesterday?' she added. Medhat nodded but didn't respond, so she sat him on her lap and wiped his snot away with her napkin. 'How would you like to come with me to Ismailia?' she asked, managing to draw him out of his shell. 'Is Ismailia country or *bandar*?' he asked. 'It's proper *bandar*,' Marika replied.

Medhat hesitated for a long time. The temptation was strong, and what made it more intense was the girl - Salwa - who had approached him out of all the other children, perhaps because of his dog. Her red hair hung down to her waist, and she wore a dress with a decorated hem, embroidered all round with blossoms. Marika noticed his hesitation and interest in the girl. 'You'll be with Salwa,' she said. 'What do you think?' And with that the matter was settled. 'I'm with you, every step of the way,' Medhat replied, making the foreigner chuckle. She saw a strange being from a miserable background sitting on her lap. He clearly hadn't bathed for a while, his clothes were filthy, and he wasn't wearing any underwear. Yet he spoke in a way that made him appear much older than he really was. And she had seen him walking hand in hand with Salwa.

***

Shabana headed to Abu Kabir on market day. He left his donkey in the *wekala* - the donkey 'garage', as he called it - and hurried to the main café, al-Bursa, where both local and visiting traders and shoppers met. He took his time scanning the place, examining each face to see if he recognized anyone. His reason for coming wasn't to buy, sell, or broker any deals, and God knows that the money he had in his pocket barely covered the fee of the *wekala*, a cup of coffee, a bit of *muassel* smoke, and the tea and sugar he needed to buy for the house. Money was scarce. He had come for a 'change of scenery' and to find out something new about the foreign visitor. He scrutinised the faces of the people coming in and leaving, as well as the passersby, but he couldn't find a single person he knew. Just as he was starting to feel hopeless, his friends Musa and Bahaa, the mayor's sons, appeared. His face brightened. He stood up - let's hug then. How he loved these two young men! From time to time, he would visit them, and they would invite him to lunch. He would pretend to decline so they would insist, until finally they persuaded him to stay for lunch or dinner, according to the time of day. He didn't care about the meal itself, because he had a modest appetite by nature, but there were other reasons he enjoyed sticking around. First of all, he enjoyed their company by the grace of God because they were nice people, and they had a good sense of humour and enjoyed his company, too. And was there any objection, if you loved someone 'by the grace of God', of there being additional benefits? Why not?

Among these additional benefits were that, if it was market day when he bumped into Musa and Bahaa, they would cover his bill at the café, so he would save some of the coins in his pocket for opium. And there might be lunch and so on. That was exactly what happened. The three of them headed over to Shebrawy's kebab shop in the next street over from the café. It was a simple, small restaurant where Shebrawy barbecued his kebabs with two or three tables set out in the street, and the smoke from the barbecue and its tantalizing aromas would waft over to whoever was seated there. But for Shabana, the kebab wasn't the highlight, but 'what comes with it', the bottles of black 'stout' beer that would be brought out. Its bitterness delighted him and his body relaxed at its pleasing effect, at which point he would ask for more. He would ask, and his call would be answered.

The conversation outside the Shebrawy restaurant took its course until it became clear that Musa and Bahaa already knew about the foreigner and Salem Abu Hussein, because his family and the mayor's were related by marriage. As the black liquid flowed, so too did the story's details. The young men told Shabana that her father, Mr. Petro, or Petros as people called him, owned a bar that Salem used to frequent. That was where he saw Marika and fell for her, and the girl fell in love with him. It was said that he stole her away when Mr. Petros refused to let him marry her. But the truth, according to the young men, was that Salem married the girl with her mother and father's blessing. 'How is that even possible?' Shabana cried out. 'That doesn't make sense to me at all.' 'Be patient, you're about to hear more,' Musa replied. And more was coming: Grudgingly, the parents agreed, after they found out that Salem, the ladies' man, had seduced their daughter. 'But how?' Shabana asked again. 'He used to see her in the bar - understood. But how did he manage to reach her?' The answer was that only God knows. 'That guy is a tiger,' Shabana said. 'He's a real man! Order us some more beer, Bahaa, because the conversation's getting sweeter,' he continued before asking, 'Okay, so where's this bar?' 'The bar's gone,' Musa replied, pointing to where it used to be. 'If you pass the level crossing, with the station and the telegraph office to your right, then carry on walking, you'll find the siris trees to your left. That's where Petros's bar was'. 'I never knew there was a bar in Abu Kabir,' Shabana lamented. 'You mean to say I've been going back and forth between Abu Kabir and the village of the Qassimis my whole life, and I had no idea there was a bar? I must have been half-asleep. What a disaster! Okay, so Mr. Petros - where did he go? Did he die or what?' he asked, only to be told that Petros and his wife had moved to Ismailia to be close to their daughter.

So should he go to the place where the bar had once stood so he could inspect it himself? He hesitated for a while before settling the matter in his mind. He decided there was no point in feeling sorry for what had passed - *Glory be to the Eternal One* - and no point spoiling the serene state he had started to enjoy since he met his wonderful companions and enjoyed the ample lunch. 'We are the sons of today,' he said to himself. 'But how did Salem Abu Hussein get the girl? What a story!'

***

The donkey knew her way to the village. She took Shabana to the outskirts of Abu Kabir, from the direction of the forest, across the level crossing towards Kafr Saqr. And when she saw al-Sadi canal, she turned right with the road as she should, then sped up without being ordered and without being jabbed with a heel. He left her to follow her instinct, since she knew now that she'd nearly reached her destination. Six full bottles of stout descended upon his chest, cool and peaceful. All was well. If only he could find a constant source for this beer! But it would be impossible to bring it into the village, since it was both expensive and forbidden. What if his brother Sheikh Sayyid knew what he was doing and imposed the sharia punishment for those who drink alcohol? The Qassimis mainly drank water, either Nile water from the canal or groundwater from the pump. Most of the time, they wouldn't refer to alcohol by name but would call it 'water'. It would be clear what they meant from context, and when they wanted to hint that someone drank alcohol they would say 'he drinks water' to distinguish him from others.

It was a historic day when Khalil started selling 'Spatz' soda in his shop, keeping it cool in the water of the *zeer* - a large clay vat - since ice was only available in Abu Kabir. And what did the Christians drink in their nearby villages? Their religion permitted them to drink alcohol. So how much did they drink? It was unlikely that they could afford it, since most of them were penniless farmers, like most of the Muslims.

The point was that opium was Shabana's only refuge, unless he was lucky enough to meet Musa and Bahaa in Abu Kabir. And once again he asked himself: How had Salem Abu Hussein managed to get the foreigner's daughter? Everyone in Abu Kabir knew everyone else, and what they were doing at any point in time, and there was nowhere for lovers to hide. He had seen her in the bar, yes. But when she was in the bar, she had been under the watchful eye of her mother and father. So how had he managed to get her on her own and capture her like that? Shabana himself hadn't been able to get Shahira the gypsy woman on her own even though she was close to him, in the same room. From the beginning, he had felt something between them, ever since she'd danced to the beat of his drumming. He saw it in the wriggling of her buttocks and the quivering of her breasts, and there had been no room for doubt when he saw her in the hashish room on the night of the wedding. She was sitting behind her mother-in-law, stealing glances at him. If he caught her eye, she would look down. She'd glance at him then look away, glance at him then… and the water pipe would circulate around everyone but her. While Shahira's husband became intoxicated, overcome by fatigue until he leaned his head against the wall to surrender to sleep, his mother remained steadfast, eyes wide open like an owl, taking drag after drag without batting an eyelid. The hashish couldn't beat her - God forbid! - even though it was conquering him. He started to imagine that he had gone with Shahira to the fields behind the mosque and, when they reached that abandoned spot of land near the lake that the sons of Qassim believed was inhabited, he threw her to the ground and lifted himself onto her, unseen by human or jinn.

Overflowing with ecstasy, he loosened his turban and rested it on his shoulders. Then he pushed his hat to one side and crooned a folk song:

The beauty appeared, swaggering, flirtatious
Her gaze was low but oh, was fatal, - My friend,
Is killing in your law now permitted?

She laughed and said: love is not gifted
Love comes at a cost - of death - if granted

He addressed 'the beauty', saying: 'I'm dying from infatuation, Shahira. I swear by the One who raised the heavens without any pillars, that my mind won't rest until....' But his train of thought was suddenly cut short when he saw Zaki. He had spotted him from afar, near the canal, which immediately sullied his mood, and the effect of the beer dissipated. When Shabana approached his cousin, he climbed off the donkey and greeted him with a hug. Zaki was his main source of anguish, day and night. Although the man frequently criticized him because of the opium and the conversations he had with the boys in the *jurn*, Zaki was an honest and respectful man, and he was indispensable to the village. What had happened to him 'would make an infidel feel sorry'. Every time he saw him, he felt as though his heart would shatter. He wished, more than anything, that what had happened to Zaki would turn out to be just a phase, and that he'd come back to his senses. Shabana hadn't lost hope yet, since he knew his cousin had a mind as strong as that of ten men. Surely it was impossible to completely lose his mind?

'What do you think, Sheikh Zaki,' he asked him, 'about this thing with Medhat?'

The response was promising. 'What's wrong with Medhat?'

'He wants to go to Ismalia with the foreign lady.'

'Why does he want to go to Ismailia?' Zaki replied. 'We'll have to look into this. Drop in and see me at the *seera*.'

God is great! Now this was the wisdom Zaki was known for: 'look into this'. It seemed to Shabana that his cousin's brain still had some light left, so he grabbed his hand. 'Ok then, let's go to the *seera* so we can look into it.' But his excitement quickly turned into shock and sorrow when he saw Zaki's head lower to his chest.

'Are you happy now? How could he let me down?' Shabana heard him lament.

'Who abandoned you, Zaki?'

Zaki didn't reply. 'I did everything I could,' he said instead. 'Everything he said, I fulfilled, so why did he leave me like this?'

Then he started to sob.

***

In the *seera*, Shabana found his brother, Sheikh Sayyid - with a book tucked under his arm as usual - as well as Medhat's uncle, Sheikh Saeed, and Sheikh Hamed, along with his son who guided him. To his surprise, he also found a number of women present, including the foreign lady with the girl she had brought with her, Saeed's wife, Haniya, and Na'sa. They had all come to discuss whether to allow Medhat to go to Ismailia, but they were unsettled because they lacked the guidance of their 'wise elders'.

'If Sheikh Zaki was with us, we would accept whatever he decided,' Sheikh Hamed said. 'But what can we say about God's will?'

'I can't bear to let the boy go,' Na'sa said. 'I mean, if Hajja Zainab was here, she would have been the one to say whether he should go or not. Even if Nafisa was here, she would have....'

They asked her about Nafisa's health.

'May God help her,' she replied.

Haniya, who considered Medhat a son, was prepared. 'Saeed didn't want me to come,' she said, pointing to her husband. 'But I swore I would go and pitch in with my opinion. Listen everyone, I can't give up a son of mine. I might have three boys and two girls, but I wouldn't give up Medhat. How can he leave his family?'

After hesitating a little and stealing glances at the foreign lady, Sheikh Sayyid gathered up his courage.

'How can we let the boy go off with a Christian woman?' he asked, then back-tracked slightly as he addressed Marika. 'I mean, I'm not speaking ill of Christians. After all, the prophet urged us to be kind to the people of the book. But we want our son to be raised in the realm of Islam.'

'Of course, Sheikh Sayyid. You're quite right,' Marika replied. 'But see, my husband, Salem Abu Hussein, is a Muslim. He believes in one God, and he graduated from al-Azhar.'

Then she stopped to address Haniya, having figured out that she was the strongest character out of everyone there. 'I mean, Madame Haniya, in my opinion, we shouldn't turn this into something bigger than it is. The boy clung to Salwa and wants to come with us to Ismailia. So fine, let him go, for his own sake. He won't stay with us forever, it'll just be for two or three weeks and he'll come back to you.'

She pointed at Salwa, who was standing next to her. 'Here's Salwa, right in front of you. She insisted on coming with me, and her mother let her come along. There's nothing wrong with it. And honestly, I haven't got the strength to raise Medhat. What else can I say to you? I don't want him to stay with us forever. That would be impossible, and if you think he shouldn't come, then he shouldn't come.'

'I think he should go,' Shabana intervened, in support of Marika. 'As Madame Marika said, it will only be for two or three weeks and then he'll be back.'

Haniya softened a little. 'I swear I don't like to say no to Medhat. I don't like to upset him. He wants to see the *bandar*, so we'll let him go for two or three weeks and then come back after.' Then turning to her husband, she asked, 'What do you think, Saeed?'

Her husband agreed with her as always, and so the matter was settled.

As for Medhat, he had made his mind up without taking anyone else's view into account, and he started to go around the villages of the Qassimis and the Salehis to let everyone know - including Farida - that he was going to the *bandar* with the foreign lady, and that he was going to marry the 'red' girl. Farida didn't object to losing one of the members of her gang, and even willingly admitted defeat when she saw Salwa. 'Oh, my goodness! What a beauty!' she declared.

***

Medhat stood at the mosque entrance, watching with interest and awe as two men lifted the casket and carried it to the other side of the village to place outside Nafisa's house. He watched the many women flowing in and out, and he heard the sounds of howling and wailing that came from inside. The noise grew louder and the swelling crowd thronged towards the door. The howls intensified when Nafisa appeared, raised on the men's shoulders, wrapped up so tightly that none of her body showed. The strange thing was that she writhed inside the blanket that swaddled her as they tried to lower her into the rectangular wooden box. The two men were exhausted by the effort, and it seemed as though she was resisting the casket. Then Zakiya appeared. Here was the young woman - whose wedding had been only a couple of days ago - leading a procession of mourners all dressed in black, some of them unveiled. The scene filled the child with revulsion, and his skin tingled. Zakiya was slapping her cheeks and howling, and pressed forward towards the casket as she wailed with a deafening voice. 'Why are you leaving us, precious one? We are nothing without you.' A few people tried to calm down the mourners, who seemed out of control. 'Come on people,' they cried, 'Say: *There is no God but God*,' and 'We all have to die.' But it was to no avail.

'*Aba* Shabana,' Medhat asked his uncle. 'The people they carry in the casket - where do they take them?'

'They take them to the graveyard to bury them,' Shabana replied.

'And why do they bury them?'

'I know you want to drive me crazy,' Shabana yelled. 'But never mind. People must be buried when they die, and God will compensate.'

Shabana started singing: '*A hundred laments over the one who left us with no warning*.' But that didn't stop Medhat from persisting.

'So if someone's buried, they don't come back?'

'They don't come back, you stupid kid,' Shabana replied. 'Get it?'

'Then where do they go?

'What do you mean where do they go? Listen, Medhat don't drive me crazy. Why do you care about dead people?'

'I want to know,' Medhat replied.

'Okay, look. Whoever dies, goes to God.'

'And where is God?'

Shabana pointed to the sky. 'Up in the sky. And to cut a long story short, whoever dies will be looked after by God, and we have nothing more to do with them. Now get out of my face.'

But Medhat didn't budge, and it seemed as though an idea had just struck Shabana. 'How many mothers do you have, kid?' he asked.

Medhat looked at Shabana in confusion. '*Aba* Shabana, what's up with you today? You know exactly... one mother, and she died.'

But his response didn't satisfy Shabana. 'Count with me: your mother Fawziya died - may she rest in peace - that's one, and Na'sa who breastfed you, that's two, and your nana Zainab - may she rest in peace - that's three, and Haniya, your aunt, that's four. Four, you greedy and deluded child! Didn't you get your fill of mothers?'

'I guess you didn't take your dose of opium today,' Medhat grumbled.

'I'm completely sober,' Shabana replied. 'I want to tell you, you fool, that you were weaned a long time ago, isn't that right? And you clambered onto your feet a long time ago, when before you used to crawl, or am I wrong? Meaning it's high time for you to walk. Or are you going to keep clinging to the women and let the women cling to you until they cripple you? And here you are, going to Ismailia, meaning it's time to forget about who's dead and who isn't.... It's none of your business.'

Medhat was unconvinced. 'What do you mean it's none of my business? My aunt Haniya keeps saying: *Those who are not good to their family, are not good to anyone*.'

'Don't ever listen to women's talk,' Shabana said intently. 'They say it's only two or three weeks and you'll be back. No, that's not possible. Going to Ismailia means you'll go to school there, and become a human being, and you won't come back. School will be your mother and father.' Then he raised his voice. 'Why can't you get it, you ass? Don't come back.'

Medhat insisted on going to the graveyard to see his mother and grandmother - as he said - before he travelled, because he wouldn't leave without figuring things out. He walked down a long and winding road, together with his dog, ahead of Na'sa and Haniya. After travelling along the country road, they crossed a bridge that took them to the other side of the canal. Then the road began to twist between the fields, sometimes narrowing and other times diverging. The two heavyset women were panting as they tried to keep up with Medhat and the dog, who raced and leapt. The boy was growing annoyed with Na'sa because she hadn't given him a satisfying answer to the secret of his grandmother and mother's absence. Her explanations were nonsense. She claimed that his grandmother had gone to visit her relatives in Hussainia near Faqus, but when people go to visit their relatives, they usually come back after a few days. She also claimed that his mother had gone to the market to buy him sweets and special bread, but he had seen people go to the market in the morning and come back at the end of the day. And he didn't understand what Shabana was saying about the dead going to God and how He takes care of them. But now he was on his way to visit his mother and grandmother, where he thought he might finally find a definitive answer. 'I have to go to the graveyard,' he kept repeating. 'To see with my own eyes.'

They crossed another bridge that stretched over a water pipe full of putrid, stagnant water and walked in the direction of Nazlet Khayyal, where the mayor had his headquarters. When the village started to appear from afar with its white domes and dense palm trees, and they reached the end of the agricultural land, the area that extended ahead of them gradually became barren, except for a palm tree here or there. The number of graves increased. They stopped at a weak-looking palm tree, which had some dishevelled bunches of yellow dates that were 'not even fit for goats,' as Medhat said, after he inspected the sad fruits and compared them to the dates of the Sa'ida's palm trees. Na'sa and Haniya stopped at a square stone grave with a tombstone on it. 'Here's your ma,' Na'sa said. 'She's sleeping here next to your nana.' Nothing distinguished the grave from the others except its proximity to the dwarfed palm tree. Medhat wasn't convinced by what Na'sa had said because the dead, as he understood it, didn't sleep, wake up, or come back. Sheikh Hamed stepped in and offered a different explanation, which complicated matters further. He had been sitting nearby, waiting for them, with his son who had guided him there. He asked them to read the *fatiha* over the souls of the two women. Once they had said *amen*, he recited a few pages of the Quran and was offered the 'mercy' pastries Haniya had baked. At that moment, two other uninvited elderly sheikhs from the mayor's village appeared from between the graves. Haniya was not miserly with them, offering them some of the pastries before turning them away. But Sheikh Hamed felt that the two interfering sheikhs had been trying to usurp his role, when he had more right than they did, since he had come in response to an invitation, and since the two departed women were related to him. He stood up - as if he had decided to prove the importance of his role - and turned his head right and left then lowered it for a moment before delivering a sermon in which he talked about how, after they were buried and the mourners were gone, the dead wake up from the agonies of death and find themselves in the hands of their creator, 'the Living, the Self-subsisting, the Eternal, whom *neither drowsiness overtakes nor sleep*.' And that the deceased person then faced judgment - before Judgment Day - at the hands of two of God's angels, who descend into his grave. If they had been evil, then their grave would turn into a fragment of hell, God forbid. But if they had been kind, then their grave would become a piece of heaven. The sheikh's voice quavered as he spoke. 'Rejoice, my sisters. Zainab and her daughter were among the kind and they are, God willing, residents of paradise until Judgement Day, when the trumpet will be blown and all of creation will be brought forth, each will be brought to stand and carry his record in front of the Merciful, and the balance will be set. The day man shall flee from his mother and father, and from his wife and his children. And the disbeliever will say: Woe to me! Would that I were dust! And I advise you, my dear ones, to pray seven cycles of voluntary prayer every single day, following the *maghreb* prayer. These are good companions of the grave and they will light up its darkness - for the darkness of the grave is terrible - and lift the loneliness from the soul of the deceased. May God forgive us, Zainab, and her daughter, and rescue us from the torture of the grave, O, most Merciful most Gracious One. Amen.'

The sheikh looked venerable as he delivered his sermon. The image of the sheikh as he stood leaning against the old palm tree with a stick in his hand, with which he would strike the ground from time to time to emphasize what he said, would have a lasting impact on the boy. It was exactly what he would do during his Friday sermon when he would wave a wooden sword atop a pulpit, praying to God to bring victory to the 'Prince of the Believers' against the 'enemies of the Muslims'. Medhat went up to him and leaned over his hand to kiss it, prompting the sheikh to respond: 'God bless.' 'Does that mean, our Sheikh,' Medhat asked, 'that Nana and my ma can see us?' 'Of course,' the sheikh replied. 'They can see us and hear us and they are looking after you and me. Now you have understood.'

When Medhat returned from the graveyard, he didn't think twice before waking up his uncle Shabana from a tantalising nap.

'*Aba* Shabana.'

As Shabana opened his eyes, he heard Medhat conclude: 'This whole death thing is too much work. I don't understand anything anymore.'

Along the country road, a crowd gathered to bid Medhat farewell. The only men there were his uncle Saeed, Shabana, and Salama. The rest were all women - including Haniya and Na'sa - and a large group of boys. The excessive hugging and kissing annoyed Medhat. He wasn't sorry to be leaving his relatives or his birthplace. He was excited and couldn't wait to reach the *bandar*. Na'sa clasped him tightly as she cried, and it didn't reassure her to hear Haniya repeating how quickly he would return: 'It's just two or three weeks, my dear, and he'll be back', or that Marika had stuffed a bill in her palm. Hesitantly, Ismail came over to hug Medhat, and tried to wrestle with him in the usual friendly way, only letting go when his mother jabbed him in the shoulders and shouted at him. 'Now's not the time, Ismail. Let go of your brother.' He had only just freed himself from Ismail's grip when he started looking around him. 'Where's Farid?' Farid had lost patience with waiting his turn and was trying to cut through the crowds surrounding his owner, but to no avail. He leapt up here and there, barking louder so his way would be cleared. As his owner welcomed him eagerly, wrapping his arm around his neck and stroking his head, the dog surrendered to more of this tenderness. When he won a kiss on his mouth, he calmed down, reassured, his tongue dangling contentedly. But the joy wouldn't last, since he saw the child climb into a car, next to the *bandar* girl and the foreign lady, and the door slam shut. Then he went crazy. His protest yelps grew louder as he followed the car that was headed towards Abu Kabir, until he lost hope and his barking turned into a low howl and whine.

***

The Lost Sheep

Salem took off his fez, and a smile of contentment painted itself on his face. Past one o'clock in the morning, the European neighbourhood was calm, and, in this section of the neighbourhood where the post office was located, the square was clear of pedestrians, the lamppost lights were dreamy, and a cool breeze teased the leaves on the trees. The evening at Ahmed Safwat's house had been superb. More than superb. The hash had been soft and obedient to the fingers, so supple it wouldn't crumble if stretched over the palm, but almost oozed with oil. And when it grazed the flames, its pungent aroma diffused throughout the room. The most genial group of people had been there, and the singing had been wonderful, with Saleh al-Meqaty excelling as he performed some songs by Sheikh Zakariya Ahmed. His anticipation of what he would find at home made the early morning journey back all the more enjoyable. Some of the cafés on Thalatheeny Street were still brightly lit, and the backgammon players were tossing their dice. Marika must have returned from the countryside and would be waiting for him. He would get what he wanted from her, since this was the night before the blessed Friday. How sad the empty bed had been without her!

But the sight of a young stranger in his bed startled him. 'Who's this? What's this calamity you've brought us from the village?' Marika told him her version of the story as she helped him undress. 'Poor boy. He's an orphan and was desperate to come with me and Salwa.' She could clearly see how vexed he was as she helped him take off his clothes. 'It'll only be for two or three weeks, and then he'll go back to his family. He won't like living here and, to be honest, I don't have the energy to raise kids,' she said. He seemed reassured on that point. 'And why have you put him in the middle of the bed?' he asked her. She replied that, otherwise, she was afraid he might fall off the edge. She explained that this was only a temporary arrangement until she prepared a bed for him in the next room. 'And why can't he sleep on the edge of the bed that's against the wall?' he asked her. She answered quickly, as though she had already prepared the response. 'Because I want to be able to reach him if he wakes up,' she said. 'The boy's still a baby. Don't be fooled by the fact that he's five or even a bit older.' Eventually, he was somewhat convinced, mainly because the child was so puny and looked no older than three. And so he slept on the side of the bed against the wall and his wife on the outer edge. He felt frustrated at having his plan thwarted, but could think of nothing more to say. Yet it was odd that Marika was in a good mood and started chatting as though she wasn't troubled by this turn of events. She passed on greetings from Radi and his wife and began describing in detail what had happened at the wedding: how splendid the dinner was and all the singing and dancing - especially the *Al Dah Yoh* dance - and about Shabana the opium-head, and so on. But he didn't want to hear about it. He had only one thing on his mind, which was how that peasant boy had spoilt the night for him and squandered the effects of the hash on which he'd hung his hopes. And now here was his wife lying not far from him, but with this obstacle separating them. He had grown accustomed to drifting off only when she was in his arms, but now he couldn't even embrace her. If they couldn't make love, then at least he wanted to hold her in his arms, either facing one another or with her back pressed to his chest and their legs 'interlocked', as he always used to say to himself. That was how he wanted her, as though he wanted to be reassured that this Greek woman was his forever, and so he could sleep feeling gratified. She had given herself to him as a young woman, but he still desired her and couldn't bear to be apart from her. His mind was never at rest unless they were united. But sometimes he couldn't understand her actions. Why had she insisted on attending the wedding when she could have ignored the invitation? He hadn't wanted her to go, but she had insisted. *Who can understand a woman's logic?* He heard her suddenly become quiet and begin to breathe deeply. Here she was now dozing off. 'Goodnight,' she said as she drifted between wakefulness and sleep. As for him, he was incapable of sleep thanks to the presence of this strange body in his bed. He didn't start feeling drowsy until the dawn call to prayer had sounded. He extended an arm to pat the waist of his beloved before turning around to face the wall. The gesture had been his way of saying goodnight. His annoyance was starting to wear off and, as he prepared to sleep, he began to feel sorry for her. Poor Marika. No son or daughter. She adored children. She would gather the neighbours' children and feed them, take them on outings, and buy them whatever they wanted. She treated them more kindly than their own families. Even though she was European, her kindness surpassed that of local women, and she had more patience with children. Why had God not blessed them with children of their own? Exalted be His wisdom, but to be so in love and yet denied children was difficult to comprehend or endure. Sooner or later, the child would return to his family. He would have to put up with the next few days, even if he regretted - and what a shame it was! - that Marika hadn't offered him the night he'd expected. They could have gone to the room next door - as a token of love. It hadn't occurred to him to suggest that, and now she had fallen asleep and he needed to be patient. He closed his eyes. When they had lived in Port Said - where he struggled to earn his daily bread - they didn't have a bed, mattress, or bedcovers, so they used to lie down on his coat and keep each other warm. Despite all that, the lovemaking was exceptional. He would recall on those nights the reference to marriage in the Quran, '*They are your garments and ye are their garments*,' or, '*And among His Signs is this, that He created for you mates from among yourselves, that ye may dwell in tranquillity with them, and He has put love and mercy between your hearts*.' God Almighty has spoken the truth. Beautiful. Beautiful.

He must have been asleep for one or two hours before he felt a dampness seep onto his back. Touching his *jilbab*, he realised it was wet and so were the bedsheets. Suddenly he was wideawake. So the son of a bitch had done it. He woke Marika as he cursed, ranted, and raved, and she quickly realized what had happened. She started to laugh and made excuses for the young newcomer. 'The poor boy isn't used to being in a new place. I told you he's only a baby!' As for the child, he was fast asleep. Marika got up, switched the light on, then carried the boy to the bathroom and changed his clothes - all this while he carried on sleeping. She changed the sheets and brought her husband clean clothes. Everything took place calmly. Salem watched what was going on in astonishment. It seemed as though she had prepared for every emergency, otherwise how would she have found clean clothes for the child? She must have borrowed clothes from the neighbours. The cunning bitch. Then she slipped effortlessly back to sleep as if nothing had happened.

***

He waited anxiously for the day the child would say, 'I want to go back home.' But it seemed that he was finding life in

Ismailia agreeable. And he was sorry to see the boy had made some new friends. There was Salwa and her siblings, whose family lived on the ground floor of their building. He would go down to see them or they would go up looking for him. At first, Salwa's family didn't welcome him, because he was an uncivilised peasant and the grandmother disapproved of his dialect. She was worried he might have a bad influence on her grandchildren who were spending time with him, with his foul language and obscenely suggestive rural riddles. But Salwa took him under her wing. She included him in the games she played with her siblings and younger relatives, and they would sit on their own on the landing every day so she could teach him how to speak in an urban accent. They would also walk around town together, and she would take him along to visit the house of her married eldest sister. Barely two or three weeks had passed, and the country boy was starting to fit into his new society.

But then the summer holidays ended, the neighbourhood kids went back to their schools, and he was left all alone, a fact that delighted Salem. Now the peasant boy would ask to be sent back to his family. It was true that the boy had lost both mother and father, but Salem knew the village women were like mothers to all the local children, and the village men were like their uncles. Marika had also told him this particular child was a 'vagabond', passing from one home to another, eating and sleeping wherever he pleased. But Salem was disappointed when instead, the child requested that he be sent to school.

'Why do you want to go to school?' Salem asked, fuming.

'All the kids have gone to school and there's no one for me to play with.'

'And is school for playing, you little rascal?'

'I don't care. I want to go to school and that's that.'

It was disheartening that Marika supported the child.

'Let him go to school. Leave him be. He'll go for two or three weeks until he finds out that schools aren't for playing, then he'll get bored and go back to his family. And by the way, Medhat goes to the Quran school at the village, but his family says he's a failure and no good. All day long he either plays or falls asleep.'

It didn't take long for Salem to acquiesce. The idea seemed reasonable. Let the son of a bitch go to school. He looked mentally retarded. There was nothing to suggest that school would suit him or that he would be capable of exerting the effort required for studying. Marika informed him that Na'sa had told her how the boy had spent two years at the Quran school, but that he'd managed to learn only one section of the holy book. Apparently, some of his friends would carry him back at the end of the day after he fell asleep and hand him over to whoever would take him. This would be his grandmother, when she was alive, or Na'sa. Na'sa said that Zainab, the boy's grandmother, had indulged him until he was spoilt. She also said that Sheikh Hamed punished his students, including his own son, by beating them, but that he would never dare to punish 'Zainab's boy'. All this information encouraged Salem to agree to the idea, and he was confident that school would drive the peasant child out of the city.

One day, Salwa came to the shop, leading a delegation of her siblings and friends, to inform him that Medhat was the only one of them who could read. The boy had barely been going to school for a month.

'How did you do it, you son of a bitch?' Salem asked.

'I read the words written on the shop signs in the square.'

'Okay, so what does the sign on this shop say?'

'To be honest, I don't remember. Let me go and look,'

Medhat replied. He walked out then back in again before long.

'Here you go: "Salem Hussein Abderahman's shop for hardware and paints"'.

Salem was unconvinced and opened up the Quran.

'OK, show me how clever you are then.'

Medhat started reading. *'Read! In the name of your Lord, Who has created, Has created man from a clot. Read! And your Lord is the Most Generous. Who has taught by the pen.'*

He was reading with difficulty, but the words were comprehensible.

But Salem persisted. 'You must have learnt this chapter at Quran school. OK, read this,' he said as he pointed to a book he picked up from the shelf.

'The ABCs of Accounting, by Effendi Abdelaziz Mohammed Hanafy, a graduate of the Egyptian University.'

Three months later, Salem was extremely annoyed when the school headmaster passed by his shop to inform him that the boy was the 'cleverest' student in the first year, and that he wanted to move him up to the second. Salem asked why doing this would be better than waiting until the end of the school year, but the headmaster told him the boy was intelligent and keeping him in the first year was a waste of time. After some thought, Salem agreed. Let them move him up to the second year, so that he would struggle, discover that God is just, and then give up. Still, he was perplexed: How had the dim and idle boy suddenly awakened? Medhat didn't spend long in the second year before Salem received the news that the child was 'sailing' through. That was when Salem realised the boy was here to stay, a burden on his shoulders, and the only thing he could do was to pass this predicament into God's hands. But in his heart, he blamed the Greek woman.

And what saddened him was the realisation that Marika had been carefully planning the whole time to keep the child. He hadn't realised this at first, but her plotting had gradually become apparent. He remembered now how she had taken the necessary measures on the morning after the child wet the bed. She had immediately bought the material necessary for Salwa's mother to make several sets of pyjamas for the boy, and the sewing machine on the ground floor had roared into action. And so the country *jilbab* disappeared and was replaced by short trousers and a shirt with braces - even before the child had started to go to school. All this, he had noticed but not fully comprehended at the time. There were also things that happened behind his back. The boy's accent was starting to change. He had started to talk like Salwa and her siblings. But how? It wasn't possible that Marika had taught him, because she still spoke Arabic with a Greek accent. So who had taught him? Or had he just picked it up himself? And the mother of all catastrophes was that he had started to respond - with a word here and there - when Marika addressed him in Greek. So she had started to teach him her family's language. And it seemed that what he had learnt from Marika had become entrenched through playing with the neighbourhood's Greek children. Salem watched that 'peasant to the core' with resentment as he jabbered away in the language of the foreigners as though he were one of them, giving high fives.

Then there were the child's never-ending illnesses and the treatment plans that Marika diligently followed. First, there was the scabies that spread over the child's body like flames through firewood. Salem had to find someone to carry him, wrapped up in a blanket, to the military hospital to get the necessary ointments and then bring him back home. Another time, he needed treatment for bilharzia, since the son of a bitch liked to swim in the canal. Next, he suffered from a lack of calcium, followed by anaemia caused by an iron deficiency, and then it was malnutrition. The son of a bitch hated almost all types of food, apart from cheese and salty sardines. But, as Marika would say, he couldn't live on just cheese and sardines, so a suitable nutrition plan would need to be followed. When she served him veal liver, he turned up his nose in revulsion. His body was also in need of carbohydrates, but he hated rice, bread, and pasta. Let's try potatoes then. Impossible. Marika thought of serving him vine leaves stuffed with rice and minced meat. 'A Greek dish that your uncle Salem loves,' she said. But Medhat took a bite then pushed the plate to one side in disgust. 'Then what do you want, my dear?' Marika asked him. 'I want corn kofta like my auntie Haniya makes,' he replied. Marika laughed so hard she had tears in her eyes. 'Come on now, Medhat. Auntie Marika doesn't know how to make corn kofta.' 'I don't care. Figure something out,' Medhat replied, undeterred. And she had to figure something out. 'I can't get through to him,' she would say to herself as she used every ploy, unsuccessfully, to try and entice him. Then she would get angry at him and weep out of hopelessness. Looking after him was demanding. Her weeping would only intensify if someone asked her, 'Why don't you send him back to his family and be rid of him?' The disaster was that the peasant child - and Salem knew how cunning people from the countryside could be - was capable of appeasing her, despite everything, when he bantered with her in Greek. It would drive him crazy if he heard the two of them chattering away in total harmony, leaving him completely excluded.

As soon as Medhat arrived in Ismailia, all the illnesses that had been hiding under the surface throughout his life in the village began to emerge. The problem wasn't the cost of the treatments. What was truly painful was the cost of Marika's attention. The child's numerous complaints meant that she often left her marital bed to stay up late into the night in the child's bedroom or to sleep beside him. And if she went to bed in their room, she wouldn't settle or sleep deeply, nor would she switch off completely from what was going on in the room next door. If she heard the child crying - and he would often wake up bawling - she would hurry to him. The poor boy wet his bed, the poor boy had a nightmare, the poor boy's nose was bleeding, his temperature was high, his throat was sore. It was one thing after another. And strangely, she would never protest or complain, but would do whatever was necessary with infinite precision. Sex was no longer on her mind, as if she had lost the desire for it. As if she had started to accept a marriage without sex, apart from the rare occasion.

But Salem wanted it every night. He had married three times and had never known anything like this. He was shocked by how the woman had abandoned sex for the child, when he wasn't even her own. How had she forgotten the custom that had become established between them over all those years? She no longer showed signs that suggested desire or of being prepared to meet him halfway. It was always up to him to ask, persist, and to put pressure on her until she succumbed. If it so happened that she relented, she wouldn't surrender completely. Her ears would be fixed on the room next door, ready to detect any sign. Sometimes she wouldn't yield, but would drift off and leave him sleepless, tossing and turning in bed all night. How could she no longer feel his suffering? How could she ignore his needs?

She left him that night in this anxious state. He visualised himself travelling to her at night. The country road was quiet and only a frog's croaking could be heard from afar. His filly trotted along…just as he wanted her to go. And in the night, the aroma of mangoes wafted from the fruit groves to the left. He exulted when he saw the siris tree in front of her balcony. As for meeting her when she was dressed only in her nightgown: Oh, what joy!

***

Mr. Petros was standing behind the counter monitoring his daughter with concern, noticing her extended conversation with Salem as she served him. Why did she pay him more attention than the other customers? Salem was one of his best customers, and he was a local notable - his father was one of the biggest landowners, and they had a mansion that lay between the forest and the town of Faqus. But Petros didn't want his daughter to enter into a relationship with anyone right now, let alone a relationship with a Muslim 'Arab' who had been married three times already. She was still a young woman, and in any case she was on her way to Athens University once she finished her secondary education. The people of Abu Kabir accepted him completely and didn't object to him having a bar, even though they were Muslims and their religion considered drinking alcohol a sin. The minority who did drink, like Salem, were on excellent terms with him, and that was enough. 'We are guests here, even if we are permanent guests,' he would always say to his wife and daughter. No, he didn't want to ally himself with Muslims. Some of the Arab men drank alcohol, but not openly, and their orders were delivered to their homes. A few of them came by regularly to drink a sneaky glass of wine, claiming that their doctor had prescribed it to settle their stomach and there was nothing wrong with that. Everyone was welcome here, and Salem was one of the few who came to eat as well as drink, since he liked Greek mezze and would spend lavishly. Was it his generous tips that attracted Marika? That was what Petros hoped, and he prayed to God that the matter wouldn't exceed the desire for a tip. 'God protect us,' as the Muslims say. The man was handsome and stylish; he wore a suit and a fez and carried an ebony stick. Petros had seen his daughter greeting him warmly at the door as he tethered his horse.

'Haven't I told you again and again to keep away from Arab men?' Petros said to Marika, when Salem had gone. He was shocked at her reply. 'But I love that man.' 'What? When?!' he asked as he swallowed hard. He wanted to ask how long this had been going on. And why hadn't he heard anything about it before? But that wasn't important. The shock made him lose the ability to formulate any kind of logical response. The important thing was that Marika would travel to Greece for university, and he placed great hopes on her university education. He wanted to yell at her and remind her what was expected of her, but he saw Salem return because he had forgotten his stick on the table, and Marika took the opportunity to escape. Salem turned around and walked up to him before clearing his throat. 'I don't know how to begin,' he said. 'But we're friends. And I'd like to ask for your daughter's hand in marriage.' Petros placed his head between his hands, unable to utter a single word. 'In any case, think about it,' Salem said in an attempt to overcome the awkwardness, and then left.

Initially, Petros wouldn't allow Marika to serve customers, and he hadn't even wanted her to work in the bar. She used to live with his relatives in Mansura, where she went to the Greek school for girls. But during the summer holidays, she would offer to help her mother in the kitchen, which she enjoyed and which her mother encouraged so she could learn how to cook.

Sometimes, if there was too much pressure on him because the place was busy, she would bring the orders out from the kitchen. She would draw open the curtain that separated the restaurant and drinks area from the house's interior rooms and place the tray of orders on the counter, disappearing immediately. Then, during these last summer holidays, she started to serve the customers on a regular basis, as if she were a waitress. At the beginning, Petros reluctantly welcomed her help, but then began to express his reservations. The truth was he wasn't concerned about her learning to cook; that was something that worried her mother. As for him, he was proud of her academic achievements - especially in the natural sciences - and he wanted her to specialise in medicine, preferably dentistry. Marriage would come with time, and the same with cooking. If she earned a university degree, she would easily find a Greek husband - a doctor, a lawyer or a businessman - in Greece or in Egypt. He didn't understand why she would be interested in working in a bar in the first place. She started to linger at the counter, pretending to want something or other, which would allow the customers the opportunity to take a long look at the foreigner wearing a short-sleeved blouse and white apron over a skirt. They weren't used to a female waitress bringing their food and drinks to them. The Arab men weren't to blame. They considered alcohol sinful. So what if an eighteen-year-old girl carried it to them? This was especially true of the men of Abu Kabir, who only ever saw women wrapped up in the loose, black *thawb al-malass* robes, their heads covered in a black veil, a vision of total decency. The girl must have succumbed to the wiles of Salem the womaniser, and the real blow was that she loved him, as she'd said.

When Petros brought up the subject with his wife Doris, he realised she already knew. Mothers are always in the know, and fathers are always the last to find out. The mother and her daughter must have been hiding and plotting something intolerable together. What was even worse was the good woman's calm response. 'And why not?' she said. He objected as much as he could, sometimes calmly, other times raising his voice, arguing that the girl was on her way to university, the man was a Muslim and a womaniser, the age difference between them was huge, and so on. 'The girl doesn't want to go to university,' the mother said. 'And she loves him.' These two pieces of news were, for him, a cause of sudden shock and exhaustion. All night long, he raved between sleep and wakefulness. In the morning, his wife reminded him that parents cannot control the fate of their children and that he himself had married her against her family's will. 'Well, what did you expect would happen when we came to this town?' added Doris. 'Abu Kabir isn't Alexandria or Port Said or Ismailia. There aren't any other foreigners here. Your daughter can't possibly find a Greek or European husband here. Personally, I would've preferred to live in Alexandria, Mansura, or Ismailia, but you wanted Abu Kabir because we wouldn't have any competition.' 'Let him at least be a Copt,' Petros said. 'We share a church with the Copts.' 'And are there any Copts in Abu Kabir?' she asked. He seemed to have finally been defeated, yet he continued to protest. 'But we don't know this man. Will we marry our daughter to a stranger when we know nothing about him?' 'The answer is a six-month engagement period, and we'll keep an eye on him.' There was nothing left for him to say, and he passed the problem into the hands of God: It wasn't easy to win an argument against one woman, let alone two women in cahoots.

What was strange was how Doris had smiled throughout the conversation, as though she were happy with this turn of events, happy about her daughter putting an end to her education, and happy with the prospect of her marriage to a Muslim. He couldn't understand women any more. It seemed they had a unique logic that bore no relation to the logic of men. How could she accept this upheaval in her daughter's life and the life of the family? How could she have forgotten everything they had discussed and the dreams they had for their daughter to go to university and study medicine? It had all vanished into thin air. As the Arabs say in these situations, '*Late-night talk is smeared with butter that melts as soon as morning rises.*' Doris tried to appease him. 'The day you held her in your hands when she was born, did you ever expect that this beautiful child would one day grow up to challenge and disobey you?' she asked. 'No, I didn't expect that. But what do you mean? Am I supposed to be miserable or happy about this development?' Petros replied. 'The best thing for you and for everyone is to be happy,' his wife said. 'I wish she'd been born a boy,' he said. 'And would you have been happy if he'd married a Muslim girl?' she asked him. 'I wouldn't have been happy, but it is the lesser evil,' he replied. 'Girls only drag scandals along in their wake.'

Everyone agreed to the conditions set by the wife. Salem visited once or twice a week, and he would be invited to dinner from time to time with the family. The mother and daughter were delighted by how close the father and fiancé quickly became. Petros always softened after one or two glasses, and Salem was a cheerful and charming man who treated his fiancé's family with infinite kindness and courtesy. This was in addition to the gifts he started bringing Marika and her mother, or those he sent from his father's farm - the crates of fruit, jars of honey, ducks, pigeons, tomatoes, and lemons. How could Petros not love him? It was settled with Salem that the engagement wouldn't exceed six months, during which time he couldn't be alone with the girl or go out with her. Where could they even go together in Abu Kabir? Fortunately, there was nowhere for couples to go when they were married, let alone engaged. Everyone also agreed that Marika would no longer be seen in the bar, which pleased Salem greatly and which he would have called for in any case, since he didn't want his fiancé to be a waitress. The house became the only place he could see his fiancé, under the supervision of her parents.

Except that her parents were oblivious to the lovers' aptitude for deception. They didn't need to go out in order to escape detection. There was Marika's bedroom on the top floor, and there were the siris trees that faced the beloved's window, which would fit a ladder that allowed him to climb up to her discreetly. Which did happen. As soon as the official engagement had taken place, Salem started to visit the girl every night. After midnight, he would ride his filly, approaching Abu Kabir over the level crossing, then turning left until he reached the trees. He would tether the horse, climb the tree nearest to Marika's balcony, and stand on a branch to find his love waiting for him. Did her parents find out in the end about these nightly visits? It seemed that Petros had no idea about them. But did Doris know?

Salem didn't give the matter any thought, and it never occurred to him to ask Marika. Her love was enough for him, filling his entire life. But he was also prepared - if it came to it - to bow to the family's conditions and give up the nightly visits, spending the remaining months of the engagement period under observation, as long as she loved him. There were a thousand signs proving she did. She had given herself to him unconditionally.

But now, as he tossed and turned in his bed, suffering from

his deprivation of her, it pained him that she seemed to want him to clear the way for a child who was not his own and to be perfectly content to abandon him. God damn him and her. How could love begin this way, where the lover is given everything he wants, then end like this, with a gulf opening up between them?

He felt even more hopeless because he was in a weak position. He hadn't conceived with any of his previous three wives. And he had never dared suggest that Marika see a fertility specialist, so that no one could prove he was the source of the problem. Marika herself didn't mention the subject except from time to time, before pushing it aside. Maybe she suspected he was the problem and didn't want to embarrass him. She contented herself with his love and accepted this infertility even though she adored children. That was, until this strange child appeared out of the blue, and she found the perfect opportunity to become a mother and make a father out of him, whether he liked it or not. Why did God rain down this punishment on him?

***

Blue was Marika's favourite colour. Whenever she wore the skirt with white polka dots on a sea of blue, it reminded Medhat of the night she had nestled him in her lap. Now she was putting on a large straw hat and a pair of black sunglasses. He was mesmerised whenever he walked alongside her, *What a beauty*. She crossed Thalatheeny Street with him as they headed into the foreigners' neighbourhood. He became even more enthralled when he spotted a girl riding a bicycle. 'Look how that girl is showing her legs!' he cried. Marika explained to him that the girl might be French or Italian and that, in their culture, girls could wear shorts. He stopped at another astonishing sight. 'Oh my God! What about these women wearing trousers?' he asked, to which Marika replied that they were English recruits in the British army. 'Do women also join the army?' he asked. 'Then what have they left for the men?' He stopped when they reached a gate with a red brick building on the other side, which she told him was the Italian secondary school. 'I'd love to go to a school like that,' Medhat said. Marika assured him that if he continued to be as clever in his studies as he'd been so far, he would go to a good secondary school. And then he would be allowed to wear long trousers and his pocket money would increase from one piaster to two. He told her that some of the teachers at his school wanted him to join the scouts, where he would be given a whistle, a pocket knife, and a torch. He said he didn't want to join the scouts, but the whistle, the pocket knife, and torch.... She promised to buy the whistle and the torch if he came out top of his class at the end of the year. 'But forget about the pocket knife, because you might hurt yourself,' she added.

Marika always bought meat and some groceries from the foreigners' neighbourhood, and she would insist on bringing the child along in case he saw any food that might entice him. Though he wasn't tempted by the butcher's meat, he was impressed by the cleanliness and elegance of the shop. When she took him to her father's grocery store, he reacted differently to the food on offer. There he saw Petros sitting at a desk near the entrance: a grey-haired, fair-skinned, short man with a belly that he restrained with a tight belt. The man stood up from his desk to welcome him warmly and started showing him the products in the shop. Medhat was delighted by the variety on offer and the delicious aromas. He spent a long time in front of the different types of olives and pickles, and Marika was even able to convince him to try the pastrami. He left with a box of chewy sweets as a gift from Petros, who knew that Medhat liked them. Then they went to a café where he tried *cassata gelato* for the first time in his life, encased in a delicate layer of chocolate. It was there that he fell in love with chocolate, which pleased Marika, since she'd found something new to lure him with instead of cheese, salty sardines, and Turkish Delight.

One of his favourite pastimes was to sit in the cafés of the foreigners' neighbourhood and sip chilled soft drinks. He also loved to linger outside the bookshops, gazing at the foreign books and magazines in the display windows and staring at all the colour posters of foreign films. He would be baffled by the heavy make-up on some of the foreigners. And when he saw how many dogs the foreigners had, he would remember his own. 'We should've brought Farid,' he would say. 'He would've had fun here.' He hated the small dogs, some of which practically crawled and had to be carried by their owners, because he felt strongly that dogs should be large. He especially loathed small dogs with male owners. 'Look how big and tall that man is, carrying a dog as small as a pussy cat,' he remarked one day. 'What's wrong with that?' Marika asked, surprised. 'What a sissy!' he said.

He didn't know that the foreigners' neighbourhood was a window on Europe or a slice of Europe, as the idea of Europe wasn't clear in his mind. All he knew was that there were two groups: Egyptians on one side and foreigners on the other. But he couldn't distinguish between Armenians, Greeks, Italians, French or any other nationality. To him they were all just foreigners.

On Sham al-Nessim Day, Salwa took him and her siblings to 'the gardens'. They were carrying the snacks that Marika had prepared for the trip - painted eggs and sandwiches. But he wasn't interested in any of that, and was fascinated instead by the vast spaces of dense green vegetation, so different from the greenery of the flat rural fields, and the twisted paths that crisscrossed and would sometimes lead to bodies of water, thickets, or forests full of different types of trees. The only tree he recognised was the hummingbird tree, since there were no palm trees, camphor, or acacia. But the surroundings suited the boy who had grown up roaming the countryside. Whenever they played hide and seek here and he thought he was lost, he wouldn't be frightened and rush off to catch up with his friends - hearing their voices from afar was enough to reassure him. The density of the foliage also made him happy here. He could lean against a tree trunk and listen to the birds chirping or hide between the branches of the hummingbird tree that hung so low they nearly reached the ground. And it wouldn't have mattered if Salwa found his hiding place and caught him, except that the punishment she bestowed when she grabbed hold of him was to force him to take a bite of a sandwich or an egg, as per Marika's instructions. Nothing ever spoilt these outings apart from a tightening in his chest he sometimes felt whenever he remembered his dog. Who would look after Farid in his absence? Who would feed him regularly and bathe him in the canal, just like the water buffalos? It was the first thing he said when he returned home at the end of the day and saw Marika. 'It's such a shame we didn't bring the dog. He would've loved the gardens, and no dog in Ismailia could have challenged him.' It was also during this time that he got his first sight of the 'salty sea' in Lake Temsah, or Crocodile Lake.

Salem was watching the boy and his friends digging in the sand of the shallow water, searching for clams. So now the son of a bitch knew about clams and liked to eat them with *tahini*. He had integrated into city life as if he'd been born there, and he became a source of admiration among his friends, even though all of them - with the exception of Salwa - used to make fun of him at the beginning. He was excelling in his studies and had covered two years' curriculum in one and was set to move up to the third year of primary school after the summer holidays. Sometimes Salem would look at things objectively and see the child deserved care and encouragement, but this objectivity only ever lasted a few minutes because he knew deep down that he was incapable of loving this child. It was difficult to feel any empathy for the boy because, despite being so small, he was mature for his age, was often impertinent, and could always answer back. At the end of the day, this wasn't his son. Why had God afflicted him with infertility? And what was the point of being able to have sex if you couldn't also make someone pregnant?

People called him a womaniser because they didn't understand him. Had he been blessed with a child from the start, he wouldn't have divorced and moved from one woman to the next. His father didn't understand this problem when he'd first heard about Marika. 'You want to marry a Christian foreigner?' he had shouted in disbelief. He was even more furious when Salem replied that he loved her. If he had revealed his secret to his father and admitted that he still wanted to have children and to have an inheritor or inheritors like his father, then his father's response would've been ready to hand: 'Then why don't you marry an Egyptian Muslim woman?' The truth was his father was fed up with his multiple marriages and divorces. His father reminded him that, since he was still living under his father's roof, it was also his father who ended up shouldering the responsibility for each marriage and subsequent divorce. He was the one who paid the dowry each time, he was the one who would mediate whenever a conflict erupted, and he was the one who would end up paying the alimony and so on. 'And I'm very grateful to you,' Salem replied. 'But it's not like I'm sitting around at home like a layabout. I'm helping with the farming. And your every wish is obeyed.' But his father was already irritated by him, and deep down he felt that his son was a failure. He had hoped his son would earn a degree from al-Azhar University and become a respected human being - an Islamic scholar, a Sharia judge, or a teacher. But Salem left al-Azhar and took off the *jibba* gown and kaftan, replaced them with a suit and fez, and started to mimic the Europeans. News reached him - and this was the worst - that his son would often go to Petros's bar. Despite all that, the father calmed down a little. 'Sure, I appreciate that. I'm just tired of all the marriages and divorces. But Salem,' he continued. 'It still hurts me to see you on your own without getting married. We don't like anyone staying single like this.' He repeated the set refrain once again. 'Why don't you marry an Egyptian Muslim girl from an honest family? We can get you the best girl there is, instead of going off to marry the daughter of a Greek bar owner. Listen to yourself. What would people say about us?' The conclusion was obvious: If he insisted on being with Marika, he would have to leave.

And he had to insist on choosing her. He didn't explain - and he couldn't explain - the other side of the story to his father, which was that this marriage was the only one he'd chosen based on love. All the others had been grounded in choices made by his family and through arrangements conducted with the girl's family - as per tradition. As soon as he felt that Marika shared his desire, his heart leapt towards her. At first, he used to see her carrying orders over to her father in the bar. The beaded string curtains would separate to reveal her, before she quickly disappeared behind the threads once again, and his heart would throb - he wanted to feast on the sight of her. Things could have remained this way without any development. But one day, he noticed she paused and kept stealing glances at him. And when their eyes met, he smiled and she smiled back. That was when everything changed, and he knew then that she wanted him. She was the only girl who had ever loved him back, and that was the first time he understood the meaning of true love. There was no way his father could understand, and so he simply had to insist on her.

Before leaving his father's house, he managed to pilfer thirty gold pound coins that his father had been keeping safe, which Salem used to cover Marika's dowry. Then the couple travelled to Port Said, where he spent some of the money on accommodation and living expenses, and then lost the rest in a failed partnership in the textiles trade. Eventually, he ended up having to work as a day labourer on construction sites, as a dockworker at the port, and as a waiter in cafés and restaurants. Things started to look up once he received his share of inheritance and could move to Ismailia with his wife, where he opened up the hardware and paints shop he currently owned.

Financially, things were good now, thank God, and Marika had been supportive when times were tough and always accepted having to live on very little - next to nothing - over the years, but without having children. Had they been blessed with a child, he would have become very attached to him right from the start, and it would have been easy to love and spoil him. But for a five-year-old child to come along (who may even be older, since country people weren't necessarily scrupulous in registering children as soon as they were born, and might leave it weeks or months before getting around to it), and for him to be expected to coddle the boy like his own child.... That was beyond his capacity. If things had been different, and he had fathered several children before this unfamiliar child had been introduced to him, he might have found it easier to accept him in addition to the others, since he would have been swept up with the rest of the children. And Marika would have been over the moon if they'd had several children together. 'You can never have too much of a good thing,' as the saying goes. But he just couldn't bring himself to agree to adopt a child who would be the only one in his family. And in fact, no one had actually asked him to adopt a child. Marika monopolised the boy from the very beginning, and he monopolised her in turn, and she placed her husband on the shelf. It felt as though Marika wasn't that bothered about whether he was close to the child or not. She was happy to take charge of the boy, and the only thing Salem was asked to do was cover the costs. This was the culmination of a marriage based on love - mutual love - that should have resulted in procreation. But even though conception can happen at the drop of a hat, it hadn't for them. Where was God's wisdom in this? Why was He torturing him? Marika had nagged him until he managed to arrange membership through a friend of his - as an exceptional case - at the French beach that was under the management of the Suez Canal Company. She had never been interested in the beach until Medhat's arrival, but then started to take him there at least once a week. So he wouldn't be on his own, she would invite Salwa, her siblings, and any number of friends, all for his sake. She would cover the costs for everyone: the food, drinks, ice cream and sweets, all because of the country boy. Membership at the French beach required that he accompany them, even if only from time to time. But he didn't want to go because people there knew him, and he didn't like to be seen with this child whom everyone knew wasn't his son. 'We can't keep going to the beach without you,' Marika would chide. 'You have to come with us, even if it's only once every other week. Or do you want people to think I'm a widow?' Back at Lake Temsah, Marika was approaching. As soon as Medhat spotted her, he left the search for clams to his friends and rushed over to ask her for money to buy ice cream. Marika walked him to the buffet along with a group of children.

Medhat would dilly-dally so he could watch the 'naked' foreign women lying on the beach 'without a care in the world'. Marika tried in vain to convince him that wearing a swimming costume was not the same as being naked. 'Really?' he would ask. 'What else would you rather they wore?' she would reply. 'Do you want them to go into the sea wearing a *jilbab*? And by the way, they want to get tanned by the sun.' But the boy wasn't satisfied by this response. 'Those women are fools. Is there anything better than fair skin?' But it seemed that she had at least succeeded in convincing him that it was rude to stare at women.

Marika walked along barefoot in a delicate see-through cotton dress with a pattern of small, multi-coloured flowers. The sea breeze lifted the hem of her dress, revealing the striking beauty of her legs. The lake's gentle waves licked at her small feet. She wanted to be a mother at any cost, but Salem could see in her only the girl he had met in Abu Kabir. To him, she was a gift from God; He'd created them each for the other. She would rush into his arms whenever she saw him and, if his kiss landed on her neck, she would show him how it reverberated through the surface of her skin, her forearms chilly and covered with tiny bumps that quickly vanished, just like the ones that effervesce and float on the surface of wine to announce its awakening and revival. They were the scattered letters, which, if joined, would say, 'I love you. I want you.' She used to respond to any signal from him, however subtle. He would just need to touch her backside in bed for her to clasp him tightly. So what had happened? Everything - since they had shared that first smile - signalled that she was a gift from God, for him alone. So when would he ever get his Greek girl back?

***

How glorious it was at primary school! And it had so many advantages: it was a state school, which was an impressive and prestigious word. Since it wasn't a private school, being accepted was a great honour. A primary school student would walk to school on his own and cross Thalatheeny road on his own - and be transported to the world of the foreigners, since the school was located at the start of the foreigners' neighbourhood. There was also the fez, which meant that whoever wore it became an *effendi* like Uncle Salem. That's how it was with this student who carried his linen bag and walked to school in his new suit and a fez on his head. Surely it wouldn't be long before he carried an ebony stick, too? He was impressed by the school's morning routine, where the students would line up to salute the flag and sing the national anthem in adoration of the 'King of the Nation'. The supervisor would pass by each student, carrying out cleanliness checks. If a student was spotted whose hair hadn't been cut according to the requirements, or whose nails hadn't been clipped, or whose shoes weren't shined, the supervisor would drag them out of the line and send them home, and they would miss out on the rest of the school day. Medhat was never pulled out of the line and sent home because Marika went to great pains to ensure everything was in order: his hair was always cut on time and his nails, too. He always had a bath on school nights, his fez was always ironed, his shoes shined, his shirt spotless, and his tie knotted properly. 'See how elegant your uncle Salem is?' Marika would always say.

Missing a day of school was his greatest fear. If that happened, it would be a catastrophe. The same child who used to spend most of his time sleeping or dozing at the Quran school now refused to give up a day of school, even if he was sick, and Marika would have to force him to stay home and then face the consequences: ensuing misery and hysterical sobbing. It was as though the idea had become entrenched in the country boy's mind that school was his strongest weapon to propel him amongst the city kids. Hadn't Shabana instructed him that 'school is your mother and father'?

But his excitement about the fez would be short-lived. He was thin, scrawny, could hardly defend himself, and his accent still betrayed that he wasn't a local. After barely two days, he started to be teased for 'behaving like a peasant', and the fez turned into a makeshift football to be kicked around by the older students in the school playground during breaks. This came as a huge shock to him, and he went home that day in tears. Luckily, the school decided to abandon the fez from its uniform soon after.

Before long, he was called by a new nickname: 'the dead one,' chosen because he was quiet and often looked pale, lethargic, and sluggish. If he responded to a question or was asked to read aloud, his voice would be so frail it sounded like he was speaking from a distance. But soon a solution to this problem materialised when, one day, the headmaster came into the classroom and as usual asked the teacher and students to stand up. Once they had sat back down, the headmaster called him up by name. He patted his shoulder, shook his hand and congratulated him on passing his exams. 'Your classmate here received the highest grades in the first-term examinations and the highest in the second term, and I am confident that he will achieve excellent results in the end-of-year exams. So it gives me pleasure to present him with this modest award'. The award was a fountain pen and a selection of books. A fountain pen in one go! To him, owning a fountain pen had been a wild dream, and now it had come true.

As soon as the headmaster left, Mr. Shafiq, the Arabic teacher, called Medhat over once more and asked him to stand beside him as he addressed the rest of the students. 'I have received some complaints against students, and I know exactly who they are,' he said. 'I heard that they've been hassling Medhat and humiliating him.' He stopped for a moment to allow his voice to reverberate in the room. 'So I'm speaking to those scoundrels to say that Medhat here - this one standing next to me here - is the best of the lot of you. And from now on, he's under my protection. If anyone tries to attack him, either through something they say or something they do, then I'll consider it a personal attack against me. And if I hear one more complaint about any of you - and you know the people concerned - then I swear to God Almighty I will have no other recourse than lashings. Do you hear me? Do you hear me, you brutes? *Excused is he who gives advance warning.*'

Everyone understood what Mr. Shafiq meant about the lashings. This teacher had been allocated the task of supervising and disciplining students by the school administration, and he was allowed to punish whomever deserved punishment, with a whip if necessary. Everyone knew that he had exercised this power before. It had come to the attention of the school administrators that some of the students had created a gang they called 'the bats,' who would terrorise the rest of the students at school, or attack some of them outside it. Mr. Shafiq had been told they had committed some thefts and were catcalling girls as they walked to or from school. After carrying out the necessary investigations, Mr. Shafiq called in the relevant parents to the morning line-ups to watch as their children were whipped.

Medhat ran home from school, straight to his uncle Salem's shop. He announced the good news and showed off his prizes, particularly the fountain pen. Winning this pen wasn't something to be taken lightly, since a primary school student would normally use a quill pen and wouldn't be given a fountain pen until secondary school, and then only if he was lucky. 'What do you think, uncle?' he asked his uncle Salem. 'Good,' Salem replied flatly. 'Now run along home.' Medhat was stunned in the face of this apathy. He had felt proud of this success the headmaster had praised, which was confirmed by Mr. Shafiq, and he'd been expecting his uncle Salem to congratulate him warmly or to say some openly encouraging words. 'Is that all?' he asked Salem. Salem's response was decisive. 'What else do you want, you little rascal? He who succeeds should be doing it only for themselves.'

Marika felt annoyed and embarrassed whenever she saw the child's hopes dashed when he was clearly desperate for encouragement. But she tried to make excuses for her husband. 'Your uncle is a kind and generous man, but he's moody,' she would say, for example. 'Don't pay attention to what he says and don't be upset with him.' But experience had taught Medhat that Salem's generosity only ever encompassed him when a mediator was involved. If Medhat asked his uncle Salem for something, he would shout at him and tell him to 'get out of my face', but if he asked Marika to act as a go-between, then something odd would happen the following day: Salem would call him over. 'What were you saying last night?' Salem would ask. 'What is it you wanted?' 'Nothing,' Medhat would reply. 'I didn't want anything.' 'Tell me, you son of a bitch,' Salem would insist. 'What did you want?' Medhat would stutter when he replied, since stuttering was part of the act. 'I mean, I wanted to say… my shoes are too tight and I got a corn on my foot because of them…and….' 'So you want new shoes!' Salem would yell. 'Is that it? Then why don't you just say it? Or has the cat got your tongue?' By this point, there would be no need for any further clarification, since the message had been received and understood, and the new shoes would be bought or made.

Salwa also proved an excellent conduit if he took her to the shop. Salem would be thrilled and drop everything to hug the 'cute' girl and sit her on his lap, before sending someone out to buy enough sweets to feed three or four children. Medhat would naturally get some of the sweets but he would feel jealous of Salwa, at least until he thought things through and reminded himself that he was a boy and that only girls were indulged like that.

At the end of the day, there was no doubt the man was moody. How delightful he was when he was in a good mood! This was evident to anyone who saw the tremendous care he took in preparing the shisha after lunch. He would stand facing the window in his long-sleeved vest and baggy, white *sirwal* pants as he moistened the tobacco and crumbled it, lining it up deftly and with great care onto the coal. Then he'd go to the kitchen to bring the embers and line them up on the tobacco with precision. The smoke would rise through his nostrils and everything would point to joy and contentment. At that moment, it would seem to Medhat that if he asked his uncle Salem for anything, he would agree without hesitation. But he never dared to try, preferring instead to leave his requests to Marika's intervention while he happily watched what was going on in awe. The man was tall, handsome, always elegant and no one ever disobeyed him. His neighbours in Abbas Square were frightened of him, but they liked him. Some of them - especially the waiters who delivered his orders to the shop - would put up with his bad moods and accept his vulgar curses with a smile. The fruit or fish sellers on Misr Street always offered him their best products; no one would dare cheat him or give him second-rate produce. Sometimes he would decide to spend summer evenings at home and would take off his outdoor clothes, including the hat he always wore. He'd lie down on the bed beside Marika to talk to her or sing her one of the old songs by Sheikh Salama Hejazy or Sheikh Sayyid Darwish. He wasn't in awe of Abdelwahab or that enthused by Om Kolthoum, unless the song was composed by Sheikh Zakariya Ahmed. On those happy occasions, Medhat would be allowed to sit on the edge of the bed, amazed - since he'd be so close to his uncle Salem that he could almost touch his legs - by how gentle and charming he was. He'd wish that he could hold his hand or lie down next to him.

It felt as though Marika's love wasn't enough for him, and the fact that he'd started to love the city - in his own way - didn't make him any less miserable. Abbas Square was the centre and his starting point, with the Ismailia canal to his right, the railway fence to his left, Karnak Street behind him, and Sultan Hussein Street and the foreigners' neighbourhood ahead. That was the realm of his explorations and his 'getting lost'. This was then the territory he covered - a large square perimeter enclosing smaller built-up squares. He was happy to wander and get lost in whichever direction he headed - except on the morning journeys to school, when he would always walk straight there. But if he had finished school or was sent on an errand, he always found something to tempt him into deviating from the original destination or purpose. He would end up walking in zigzags, lag behind, sometimes even stop to join a group of boys playing football in the street or riding bicycles. Or he'd head to the foreigners' neighbourhood to gaze at the British army offices, the foreign books, or ogle the movie posters at the cinemas. He would stop and stare in awe at the wooden terraces, the red brick roofs, and the Italian secondary school, until he forgot where he was supposed to be going or the errand he had been sent on. Sometimes Marika would send him, for example, to his uncle Salem's shop, or his uncle would send him to the house for some reason, and he would wander here and there within the larger square perimeter before reaching the shop or home. It was never his intention to get lost, but the city would stand in the way with its many temptations, distracting him from his original destination. There was never a doubt in his mind that he would be able to find his way back eventually, and he would be mystified every time he saw someone calling out and asking anyone if they had seen a lost child. No one could get lost in this city as long as they remained within the domain of this square perimeter. His frequent disappearances were a source of great concern for Marika, but she would always forgive him and end up laughing it off. 'That's how the boy is,' she would say. Salem would get angry, fume, and curse the 'son of a bitch,' yet the 'son of a bitch' would never learn his lesson. He had grown accustomed to wandering around in the countryside and now here he was, wandering, almost instinctively, in the streets of the city. Even though it was a new experience, the city invited him to partake in it just as the fields had. At that point, he would forget Marika and Salem and surrender himself, in a dreamlike state, to the scenes around him that constantly found ways to renew themselves, despite their familiarity.

Abbas Square was the centre of the city, but it seemed like the centre of the entire world. That was where uncle Salem's shop was, and it was there he was first unfaithful to Salwa. He was in the second year at primary school when he saw her with a cousin called Ibtisam. It may have only been one meeting, but it was enough to make him fall for her. After that, he only ever saw her as she walked to school. Ibtisam was no more beautiful than Salwa, but she was older than the two of them. So, every morning, he would painstakingly wait for her to pass by, not moving an inch towards school until he had glimpsed her. But he never dared speak to her. Did she ever notice him? He would exert every effort to make sure she didn't. Perhaps the care he took in guaranteeing that she wouldn't see him made him feel - for some mysterious reason - that his waiting wasn't 'innocent'. But he was sure that his relationship with Ibtisam was different from his relationship with Salwa. He felt an irresistible draw to the girl, though he didn't understand what was happening. It wasn't the same feeling he had when he joined Salwa or any of the other children in playing 'house', where they would split up into pretend spouses and mimic grownups: the boy 'husband' would go to work and then, when he went back to their pretend house, he would find that the girl he had chosen, the 'wife', had prepared the food. After eating dinner, the two of them would go to bed and hide under the covers until it was morning, when 'married life' would resume its cycle. He would hug his 'wife' Salwa - since he always chose her - under the blanket as a man was supposed to, without feeling that strong attraction. But if he could hug Ibtisam now....

Then the perfume-seller appeared. She arrived at the square on Friday mornings before the prayer and circled around the café customers and shopkeepers, grazing each man's hand with an index finger moistened with perfume. One day, she passed by him near Salem's shop and didn't ignore him because he was young and would never be able to buy anything from her. He'd been busy reading an old Great War poster that showed a picture of a dragon and warned against the 'yellow peril' of those Eastern foreigners when she touched his shoulder. 'Give me your hand,' she said when he turned towards her. She touched his hand with her fingertips and, with that, she had him captured. After that, he would wait for her every Friday morning that he could. He didn't know her name, but she was now even with Ibtisam in terms of his interest and passion. The difference between the two was that the perfume seller would visit him in his dreams, and he would glimpse her between the branches of the hummingbird tree or in the shade of a thicket or in his bed. When both Ibtisam and the perfume seller approached to occupy the centre of his attention, Salwa's image faded, even though she was the one he saw almost every day.

Abbas Square was the location of the biggest occasion and the greatest celebration, as it was there he was first introduced to the circus. The city celebrated the arrival of the Helu Circus with drums, trumpets and horns, and a mass procession. A large marquee was set up in the square, where magnificent promotional processions set off, accompanied by brass music and traditional drumming, led by two jesters and midget entertainers. When Marika took him to the circus with Salwa and her siblings, he was astonished to see the wild animals: the lion, the tiger, and the elephant. But the scene with the most impact, and that made his heart race, was when Mahasen al-Helu leapt onto the back of a horse as it galloped. It had never occurred to him before that a woman could ride on horseback with all that power, lightness, and agility. Abbas Square was the place where Mahasen al-Helu soared to settle delicately atop her horse, as though she had wings!

Despite the fact that he loved Ismailia, a new feeling had started to take hold of him lately that he couldn't shake. He knew very well that he didn't really belong to anyone or any place in this beautiful city. The feeling wasn't new to him, in all fairness, since he also used to get 'disoriented' in the countryside, but it had intensified here. Was his disorientation in the city streets one of the symptoms of this realisation, or was it his way of escaping it? Marika wasn't his real mother. And Na'sa hadn't been his real mother. And did the tall, handsome man who ignored his existence play a role in that? Why would Salem not give him the chance to be loved?

***

When he grabbed Marika's hand, she turned to him and smiled. He was sitting to her left, following the circus scenes with intense concentration and responding like all the other children - he shouted, roared with laughter, or leapt up from his seat to get a clearer view of Mahasen al-Helu as she approached the horse. But he was the most excited among them, and he gripped Marika's hand the whole way through. She had hoped his decision to come with her to Ismailia wouldn't turn out to be a fleeting fancy and that he would prefer to stay rather than go back to his family, which is what she'd been planning all along. But she hadn't expected her plan to actually work. 'That child is a mountain boy,' Na'sa had warned her. 'He won't last with you.' Marika asked what she meant. 'I mean that he's a loner,' Na'sa replied. 'He doesn't get along with people.' But now here he was, still with her, and here he was, clinging to her. When he was feverish, the only thing that made him feel better was to lie down and rest his head on her lap. But whenever Salem got angry, the boy would be filled with fear, standing totally still while he received the beating. Medhat would wait until Salem finished slapping him and left before he broke down and cried, whimpering continuously. The thought of a different type of punishment would terrify him, and he would beg Marika to stop it from happening. 'Please, God bless you,' he would plead. 'Don't let him send me back to the village.' 'Don't worry,' she would reply. 'No one can take you back to the village as long as you're with me.' But it was those words, 'as long as', that were truly frightening. Everyone except this child tended to act as if things would last forever. She herself clung to Salem and for a long time didn't even contemplate the possibility of their separation. It never occurred to her that Salem - the womanizer - could abandon her for another woman or that he could take a second wife. She trusted their love implicitly. But these days, every now and then, she would recall that Salem was twenty or so years her senior. What would she do if he went and left her on her own? Then she would forget about this worry entirely, if only temporarily.

She had felt just as disconcerted when her parents decided to sell everything they owned in Abu Kabir and retire in Ismailia to live near her. The family may have been reunited, but their move to Ismailia had reminded her that they were all getting older. They would have lunch at her home every Friday, and Salem would come back after the Friday prayers carrying fruit to find them all waiting for him before they gathered around an ample buffet. But she began to feel anxious during this period of reunion and settled life as she thought of them separating from her one day. Then Medhat came along - he had sought refuge in her and she had somehow sheltered in him, too - but he was still young and needed long-term care. He was a huge responsibility that she would have to bear alone, since Salem didn't want him.

She was attached to both Salem and Egypt. She had fallen in love with Mansura and with Abu Kabir, even though life in the latter was very limited. Her parents would sometimes take her to Zagazig for the day. They would go shopping and have lunch in one of the restaurants there, but she never felt she needed any more. When once she'd gone back to Greece with her parents to visit an aunt in Mikonos, she hadn't been tempted to move there. It hadn't been a happy visit. She had caught a quick glimpse of Athens before they headed to Mikonos on a boat rocked by waves that leapt as high as her back, as if to drown her. She thought the seasickness would be the end of her. For two weeks, they stayed at her aunt's very modest house. Her father, Petros, felt the three of them were a heavy burden on the hosts' limited budget, so every day he would take everyone out to the seaside and treat them all to a simple lunch. The only food served there was sardines and octopus, and one or the other would be grilled on the beach in front of them before being brought out along with some salad, bread, and wine. The only thing she liked about Mikonos was the sea. And she wasn't sorry to leave Greece; she hadn't been very impressed by Athens, and when she later visited Alexandria and Cairo, she found the latter much more interesting than Athens. It was no wonder Egyptians called Cairo 'Egypt' in Arabic, since Cairo really was the crowning glory of Egypt, and it deserved its nickname, Mother of the World. At the end of the day, Egypt was her country - even though she'd had hopes during secondary school of going on to study at Athens University - and Salem, her parents, and this frightened child were her family. Where would she go if they left her?

As far as she could tell, Salem never thought about death, as if he considered the idea farfetched. He didn't like to get sick, and if he ever did fall ill, he hated going to a doctor or taking medicine.

He would have to be dragged to visit a patient in hospital, which is what happened when she had surgery to remove her appendix. Salem would also never attend funerals or march in a burial procession, unless it was for someone very close to him, as when his youngest and dearest sister Samira died. He acted as though he wanted to stay forever young. As soon as he began to get bored by the hardware shop, he decided to expand his business. He opened a textiles shop, a leather shop, and a shop for tailor-made clothes in the Arab style, because he said he'd discovered a market niche, targeting the Arabs of Sinai. They had come to Ismailia with large sums of money (it was rumoured that these were the fruits of their hashish smuggling operations across the Suez Canal), and would splurge on clothes (*jilbabs*, *abayas*, the *hattat* headdress and headdress cords, belts, and wallets), and sets for camels and horses (saddles and bridles). Salem would bring the saddlers and tailors and train them to make whatever the Arabs wanted, according to their specifications. She had no idea where the al-Azhar graduate had learnt these skills, but he had somehow managed to gain the Bedouins' trust until these very same people who refused to deal with banks started entrusting him with their money, never doubting his honesty.

It was thanks to his business expansion that he was able to convince her parents to leave Abu Kabir and move to Ismailia. They weren't there for long before he'd persuaded her father to become a partner in a grocery that Petros would manage in the foreigners' neighbourhood. As if that wasn't enough for Salem, he then extended his business activities into purchasing land to plant fruit in the countryside around Ismailia. He would spend abundantly, sparing no expense for himself or his family. When it came to his habits and pleasures, he held those sacred. He had an appetite for sex and tried to get his 'share' of it - as he would say - every night if he could. In the past, he would even want it - and often get it - after lunch. He was still full of energy, but she had started to reject his advances, either because she was tired or because she wanted to punish him for being so hard on Medhat. She knew that in Islam, a man could punish a woman by abandoning the marital bed, yet she was the one punishing Salem by deserting him without actually leaving the bed. If only he would get the hint!

She no longer understood him. He was one of the most forgiving people she knew, despite being a country boy and a former student of the Islamic university. He never tried to force her to convert to Islam, she could go to church whenever she wanted, and he would buy her all the alcohol she asked for, even though he had stopped drinking it as soon as he discovered it could cause cirrhosis. Even when he was told there was no danger of getting the disease as long as he drank in moderation, he would quote the popular proverb, '*If the wind passes through the open door, close it and worry no more.*' He spared no effort in pleasing people, and he loved children - all children. So why did he single out Medhat? This is what she couldn't understand, and it was the source of the child's constant anxiety. Once he'd been living in Ismailia for a few months and knew he was staying, he had stopped wetting the bed. But he became unsettled again when his relationship with Salem began to deteriorate and his nightmares became more frequent.

After the circus, they went to the foreigners' neighbourhood to buy sandwiches and ice cream. On their way there, Medhat stopped to greet all the people he knew - young and old - in several languages in addition to Arabic. Marika could hardly believe what she was seeing and hearing. She saw Sayyid the butcher standing on the other side of the road, waving at them, and Medhat rushed across the road to shake his hand. When he came back, she wrapped her arms around him in a spontaneous and impulsive gesture. At that moment, she felt as though she understood the boy implicitly. This was the child who had come from afar, overcoming numerous obstacles along the way, so he could end up sailing smoothly in this European neighbourhood with its multitudes of foreigners and languages. This was the child who used to fall asleep at the Quran school and refuse to learn - the child who hadn't learnt yet how to control his bladder - how could Salem's heart not soften towards him? Why did his generosity stop when it came to Medhat? Why could Salem not be moved by this captivating desire to blossom and flourish? How could he refuse this blessing?

***

Marika put a strict system in place, with an eight o'clock bedtime for the child. She would allow him one extra hour if he liked - on an exceptional basis - to look over the day's lessons (or to read without Salem finding out) before he had to go to sleep. But when Medhat was alone, he would quickly abandon his schoolbook to open up the pocket novel or children's comic book he had hidden inside. Sometimes Marika discovered his tricks, but she wouldn't object, since she was the one who bought him whatever he wanted to read outside the curriculum (behind Salem's back). What *did* worry her was when he stayed up late, since she believed children needed a good night's sleep to be healthy in mind and body. The problem was that Salem strictly prohibited any reading outside the school curriculum because he believed it distracted students from more important matters and cluttered their minds. In his opinion, a student shouldn't read anything outside schoolwork until they had completed their education. It was a foolish notion, in Marika's opinion, but she couldn't contradict her husband openly when it came to some of his more old-fashioned beliefs.

Sometimes Marika would excuse her husband because Salem thought his own interest in literature was the reason he didn't complete his university studies. She would often collude with Medhat, but she hadn't realised that the boy's ambitions, when it came to reading, had gone beyond the scope of the reasonable. He would always look longingly at the two bookcases in his room - floor-to-ceiling cases stacked with Salem's books. One held rows of large books left over from Salem's days as a student at al-Azhar, in addition to some religious books and general literature that he still bought on his trips to Cairo and arranged to have expensively bound. The other bookcase was full of contemporary literature by famous authors as well as novels translated from French and English. Initially, Medhat was content to just look at these books - especially the lavishly bound ones - or to touch them, because he thought he wouldn't be able to read them if he tried. But one night when he couldn't sleep, he overcame this hesitation. Getting out of bed, he stole a quick glimpse at the contents of the two bookcases and passed his hand over some of them before teasing out a small book with '*Thaïs*, by Anatole France' printed on the cover. He opened the book, read the first page without difficulty, then took the book back to bed with him and didn't switch his light off until it was almost dawn. And so began a phase - a new adventure - in his life.

No longer was there space for pocket novels or children's comics in his new world. '*Thaïs*' had unlocked the treasure trove within the two bookcases that included the large, bound books on Quranic interpretation, grammar, classic Arabic literature, and poetry collections - whether he understood them or not.

His greatest joy was to spend the final hours of the night - and in some cases the early hours of the morning - voyaging between the contents of the two bookcases. Marika would often wake up to check on him, and if she found him reading, would order him to turn the light off and go to sleep. 'That's enough now,' she would say. 'Leave some for tomorrow. Don't you know that children need sleep like they need to eat?' If Salem woke up and asked her what was going on in the next room, she would say, 'The boy won't stop studying. It's very strange.'

The novel '*Thaïs*' inflamed his imagination and raised thoughts and questions in his mind that he'd never before come across. The book was a detailed account of the story of a monk called Paphnutius - a hermit who was nearly a saint - following his journey from his isolation in the desert to Alexandria. His cause was a noble one: to find *Thaïs*, the beautiful Alexandrian woman who had seduced the people and made them stray from the rightful path, in order to return her to the folds of faith and virtue. Medhat read about how the monk managed to eventually drag *Thaïs* out of a life of evil and squalor and to guide her to the love of Christ, to whom she ended up dedicating her life, eventually becoming a saint. However, the journey that succeeded in achieving the noble goal ended with the fall of Paphnutius and his own rebellion against God. By the time Paphnutius's journey ended, he had repudiated everything he had once believed and felt a deep sense of remorse over not winning *Thaïs*. *What a crazy fool I was not to win over Thaïs when I had the opportunity! Oh, what madness! I thought of God, of my own salvation, and of eternal life as if these came close to the sight of Thaïs. How could I not realise that eternal joy lay in just one kiss from her, and that life without her means nothing?* Eternal joy in one kiss? What had caused this upheaval? The novel would need to be read one more time, word for word, for the answer to be revealed. And then it would become clear that his journey had been heading towards evil from the start, and that Paphnutius had been falling with every step, because of his vanity, victim to the devil's temptation, confusing good with evil and faith with lust. It even seemed that Paphnutius only went out on his journey because he was lusting after the Alexandrian beauty, even if it was a long time before he realised it. One incident in the journey of the misguided hermit was especially striking. Once, while he was sleeping, he'd felt his cheek settle onto a woman's breast. The woman disentangled herself a little and lifted her chest, yet he clung to it in the same way a despairing person would cling to a soft, warm, perfumed body. The man had been dreaming, but the dream was an expression of his underlying intent, and it was another one of the devil's ploys to drag him to his doom.

All this had become clear, or almost, since there was a great deal in the story that was difficult to understand. This included Christianity's position on how Paphnutius felt comforted by the woman's body in the dream and how he had clung to it - actions that would be considered a grave sin in Christianity. But these things could also happen to a Muslim during sleep, and all he would need to do when he woke up would be to call on God to protect him from the accursed Satan and that would be the end of the matter. Medhat realised that he had been through the same experience as the monk when the perfume seller visited him in his dreams and he had clung to her, but he hadn't felt he had sinned. And he wouldn't seek refuge in God from the accursed Satan, but instead wish he would be so lucky as to have her visit over and over again. Were Christians not overstating this sense of guilt? And what was lust anyway? What was a sin? They were two definitions he'd thought he understood, but it seemed they had deeper meanings he hadn't yet deciphered.

Another novel landed in his lap during this same period: 'The Pastoral Symphony' by André Gide. It soon became clear that it closely resembled the *Thaïs* novel. It told the story of a priest who helped a blind girl he had found so neglected, deprived of care, and unable to communicate with others that she had become mentally disabled, her life increasingly resembling that of an animal. The priest believed that his religious duty and love for Christ obligated him to rescue the girl from her wretched life and to educate her. His success was resounding: the girl bloomed, flourished, and started to talk, mastering the art of communicating with others. She loved her caretaker in a pure way, adored nature, and tried to savour its beauty, even though she couldn't see it, and she learned to play music and started to comprehend the lessons of Christ. In the end, she even regained her sight thanks to an operation, but matters become muddled for the caretaker as he began to confuse the girl's love for Christ with his desire for her. He and his son competed for her love and tried to usurp her affections, but she and her young love ended up choosing a life of monasticism. The priest in the 'The Pastoral Symphony' was Paphnutius in '*Thaïs*'. The two men were in essence the same, and both narratives portrayed what appeared to be an exaggerated belief in the personification of evil amongst Christians.

***

The desire to return the 'lost sheep' was the snare in both cases, and the start of the perilous journey towards evil. The subject had to be researched in the Bible, and there was a copy in Salem's library. The boy wouldn't rest until he'd read the large bound book in its entirety. This meant he finished reading the

Old Testament, then moved on to the New Testament and found the example of the lost sheep. However, he didn't stop there, as for a while he hadn't been able to resist the rush nor give up this delicious fever that had taken hold of him. So he finished reading the four gospels and the Acts of the Apostles, the Epistles and the Book of Revelation. When he reached the final page, he felt sorry to be closing the book. He had hoped the journey would continue - since there had been a journey - forever. Reading the New Testament hadn't taken long, but he spent nearly a year reading the Old Testament, which he mostly found boring and difficult to understand. There was much in it that turned him away, but also a great deal that impressed him. He enjoyed reading the psalms, the Book of Job, the Song of Songs and the Lamentations of Jeremiah, but he disapproved of those portrayals of the prophets that contradicted the narrative of the Holy Quran.

He turned back to the Gospels of Matthew to read the parable of the Lost Sheep. The disciples had come to Jesus and asked him: *who is the greatest in the Kingdom of Heaven? So Jesus called a young child up to him and placed him between them and said: 'Truly I tell you, unless you change and become like little children, you will never enter the Kingdom of Heaven. Therefore, whoever takes the lowly position of this child is the greatest in the Kingdom of Heaven,' he said. 'See that you do not despise one of these little ones. For I tell you that their angels in heaven always see the face of my Father in heaven. For the Son of Man has come to save that which was lost. What do you think? If a man owns a hundred sheep, and one of them wanders away, will he not leave the ninety-nine on the hills and go to look for the one that wandered off? And if he finds it, truly I tell you, he is happier about that one sheep than about the ninety-nine that did not wander off.'*

It both depressed and agonized him that the lost sheep was a child, and that children had angels to protect them in heaven. Then he stopped, bewildered: this was the same advice that Paphnutius the monk had followed in '*Thaïs*', as well as the priest in 'A Pastoral Symphony'. Then why had they both ended up with such a painful fate? Had God wanted to test the strength of their faith as He had tested the prophet Job? But that idea led to another question: Why had God allowed the friar and the priest to fail the test? At certain times, Paphnutius had known that the devil was luring him, and he sought refuge in God to rescue him from evil. But He didn't help him. Why didn't God rescue him when Paphnutius had turned to Him and instead abandoned him to become easy prey for the devil?

He paused for a while, considering the loneliness that tormented Jesus on the night of the last supper. *My soul is overwhelmed with sorrow to the point of death. The events took place at night in an atmosphere charged with signs and omens. Jesus informed his disciples, as they sat together at the dinner table, that one of them* (Judas Iscariot*) would hand him over to his enemies, they would doubt him that night, and some would betray him. When they moved to the Gardens of Gethsemane, he asked his disciples to stay up while he prayed (asking God to let the chalice pass from him), but when he returned he found them asleep.*

His heart pounded when he read about Jesus's signs and the specific and unequivocal prophecies. For when he informed his disciples that one of them would betray him and each started asking, '*Is it I?*' he left no room for doubt as to who he was referring, even though he hadn't mentioned him by name. Instead, he said: '*The one who has dipped his hand into the bowl with me will betray me.*' And when he informed them that they would all doubt him that night, Peter replied, '*Even if everyone else turns against you, I certainly won't!* his reply was: '*Before a rooster crows this very night, you will deny me three times.*' But the scene that brought tears to his eyes was the one narrated in the Gospel of John about how Jesus rose from the table, took off his clothes, picked up a towel, and fastened it round his waist. Then he poured water into a basin and began to wash the feet of his disciples and to dry them with the towel that was wrapped around his waist.

Were Jesus's actions at that moment an expression of total humility? As though he were saying to them, 'Here I am, your master, but I am your servant.' Or was he expressing a love that has no boundaries, as if saying, 'I sacrifice myself for you' or was it a kind of farewell, or did it hold another meaning? Whatever it was, these signs and acts had a breathtaking splendour he could find no way to describe. He was especially saddened to read that Jesus knew he was alone, without any supporters. This feeling was clear in the case of the disciples, since Jesus knew they would leave him one way or another.

It also became clear that the chalice he had to drink from (the crucifixion) was a bitter one, despite his knowledge that it was God's will and in accordance with His will, since he was praying to God to let this cup pass him by, '*Yet not as I will but as you will.*' This was logical since the weak body cannot withstand the ordeal and may be defeated or collapse - whereas the spirit is vigorous, as he said, steadfast, and surrendering to God's will. But it seemed that the spirit was defeated and collapsed when the crucified one screamed with a mighty voice, '*My God, my God, why have you forsaken me?*' Didn't that distressed scream prove that his spirit felt God had abandoned him? How could he despair of God after he was certain of His help? Jesus had said, '*Do you think I cannot call on my Father, and He will at once put at my disposal more than twelve legions of angels?'* Wouldn't it have been better for him to remain steadfast in his belief that he was being protected from above and that he would be resurrected from death?

During the break, he bumped into his friend Mr. Shafiq, the Arabic and Islamic Studies teacher, in the schoolyard. He told him about what he had read and posed the questions to him. But the teacher's answers didn't quench his curiosity. 'But that's the Christian narrative,' he said. 'And those are the problems that must perplex them, but why should it matter to us? We Muslims believe in what was revealed in the Holy Quran: '*But they killed him not, nor crucified him, but the resemblance of Jesus was put over another man.'* Christ was raised to the heavens without being afflicted by any harm. Isn't that so?' Medhat was strolling next to the teacher, who had his arms crossed behind his back as he walked on. The teacher repeated his question. 'Is that the case or not, Mr. Medhat?' 'It is,' Medhat replied. 'So then what's the problem?' the teacher asked. And with that, the discussion was over.

The teacher was right, but a problem persisted that he couldn't articulate. He exerted every effort to solve this conundrum the whole way home from school. By the time he arrived at Abbas Square, he thought he had reached a reasonable summary of the situation. How could the Bible attribute the following saying to Christ: '*My God, my God, why have you forsaken me?'* And how could Christ be described as the 'son of Man' - which was a description that pleased and reassured him - when on the other hand he was said to be the son of God? He was shocked when he read that God's spirit descended like a dove, and about a voice from heaven saying, '*this is my beloved Son, in whom I am well pleased.'*

He stopped in Abbas Square near Salem's shop. He could ask Salem, since he had studied at al-Azhar and must have considered these quandaries and found a solution to them. 'The Holy Quran teaches us that God always rescues the prophets in times of adversity. Isn't that right?' he asked him. 'Correct,' Salem replied, taking a drag on the shisha pipe. 'But what exactly are you talking about?' 'I mean, God rescued prophet Abraham from the fire: '*We said: O Fire, 'Be thou cool, and a means of safety for Abraham!"* and with prophet Moses, God parted the sea so that he could cross it with his people, and He drowned the Pharaoh and his army, isn't that right?' Medhat continued. Salem's face relaxed at Medhat's citation of the Quran. 'God bless you,' he said, which was the only time he'd expressed his admiration for one of the young stranger's feats. Medhat was encouraged and continued. 'So how did Jesus, according to the Bible, feel that God had abandoned him?' At that, the man's face clouded over, and he returned the mouthpiece of the shisha to its place. 'How do you know what it says in the Bible?' he asked sharply. Medhat started to stammer and his lips trembled. Salem immediately sensed that the child had been given some strange information that was intended to shake his faith. 'Get out of here!' he shouted. 'Get out of my face until I have time for you.'

In fact, he was trying to buy some time to think of a way to grasp what had happened and come up with an appropriate punishment for the son of a bitch. For now, he felt preyed on by dark thoughts and pursued by an imminent sense of danger. The boy had joined a Muslim Brotherhood school from the start, for which he was to blame, since he'd chosen it because of its proximity to the shop. He had chosen it - he the inveterate Wafdist who glorified Saad Pasha, loved al-Nahhas Pasha, and hated Hassan al-Banna. What a calamity! That was a huge mistake. He knew the school indoctrinated the students from the first day, and every single day, with the Muslim Brotherhood's principles, making them repeat their well-known slogans during the morning line-ups: '*God is our purpose, the Prophet our leader, the Quran our constitution, Jihad our way and dying for God's cause our supreme objective.*' Since its first year, the school had been a breeding ground for followers of the Supreme Leader whose authority they obeyed with blind allegiance. And with that, a state within the democratic state was being created to destroy it from the inside.

That was one side of the problem. But the boy was also being fed Christian ideas. Where was he getting them, if not from Marika, her parents, or all of them? That was another mistake that was no less dangerous than the disaster of the Muslim Brotherhood dogma. It pained him that he was the one who'd convinced Petros and Doris to move from Abu Kabir to Ismailia and helped them to settle in the city so that Marika could be amongst her family. This was his reward - he who did this out of love for her - that Christian principles would seep into the child from within the home? *Is there any reward for good other than good?* How could he face these calamities?

***

As soon as the boy walked through the door, Marika noticed he was upset. 'What's wrong, my darling?' But all he said was, 'Nothing. The heat is giving me a headache.' Then he went into his room. He knew now he had gotten himself into a tight corner that would be difficult to escape, and that he would pay dearly for it with Salem. When he was asked, 'What do you know about the Bible?' he could have lied and said anything convincing, like claiming he had heard about it from the religious studies teacher or one of the other teachers, or from his Coptic friend Husni. But the question had terrified him so much he'd become muddled.

Marika spotted the signs of sadness - was it sadness or anger? - on her husband's face when he returned. Normally, she would greet him at the door with a hug or a kiss on the cheek, but he turned his head away when she walked towards him. 'What's the matter?' she asked, but he didn't answer. She started to help him undress as usual, but this time he stopped her. 'Why are you teaching the boy about Christianity?' he asked. Marika denied the accusation fervently. She knew she was innocent. But Salem carried on angrily, taking her to task. 'We agreed from the start that you were free in your faith and we were free in ours, *to you be your religion, and to me my religion*. Isn't that right? Then why are you filling the boy's mind with these strange ideas? Why are you confusing him? Why?' Marika flew into a rage, and her husband only calmed down when she reminded him that he had a copy of the Bible in his library and that he was the one who had put it under the boy's nose. He then started to apologise to Marika and to try to appease her. The problem was no longer about Medhat reading the Christian narrative of Christ's story, but it was his disobedience to Salem's categorical orders. 'Didn't I tell you that you're not allowed to read anything apart from the schoolbooks?' he said. Before Medhat had a chance to reply - and anyhow, he didn't know what to say - a slap had landed on the side of his face that momentarily dazed him. Salem would have slapped him a second time if Marika hadn't stood between the two. 'If you want to hit anyone, then hit me. If you touch the boy once more I'll leave you,' she threatened. 'How can you tell him he can't read anything other than schoolbooks?' she asked Salem after he had returned to his senses. 'When the school wants to reward him, they give him books outside the curriculum to read. And anyway, how can you tell him not to read the books you put in his room?' In the end, Salem was forced to move his library to his bedroom, even though that didn't diffuse his anger.

Although peace returned between Salem and his wife, the row had left a deep mark inside him, as he now knew he was fighting a losing battle. The school was giving the boy books that were outside the scope of the curriculum, and Marika was buying him books and magazines that had no connection to what he was studying. Sometimes he even saw her reading to him from books that he couldn't imagine had anything to do with his schoolwork. And, at the end of the day, he wasn't particularly reassured by the Bible being the source, as she claimed, of the boy's Christian knowledge. Maybe he had read the Holy Bible, but how did he find that specific book from the hundreds of books in his room? And what made him stop at the torture of Christ, and why had the story raised these complex, thorny issues? Could it be that this boy, still fresh from the countryside, was able, without any help, to understand these matters? Something must have been going on behind his back. And the responsibility had to fall back on Marika, her father, and her mother. It pained him to feel that he couldn't implement his orders in his own home and that Marika - his love - was the source of the threat.

It wasn't long before the child found a way of bypassing this ban on non-academic reading. At first, he started borrowing novels from the students at school or buying them from the newspaper vendors, carrying them home tucked under his shirt and disposing of them once he'd read them. Then he found an even better trick, which was to distract Salem - and even to distract Marika herself - then raid the library in the couple's bedroom, take a book to his room, and put it back in its place once he had finished. It was thrilling to read by way of stealing, and a feverish ecstasy would overcome him, tinged with contradictory emotions of fear and the challenge that pushed him to devour the books.

He became addicted to reading; he couldn't sleep before reading for a period that often extended to hours. Marika would sometimes go into his room when she saw his light still on in the early hours of the morning, to find him still engrossed in a book or fast asleep with a book on his chest. Reading was his ultimate pleasure - his life was empty without it - and Salem wouldn't be able to come between him and reading. Unfortunately, he couldn't carry the large volumes back to his room anymore. Sometimes he would grow bored of reading novels, and he imagined some amongst those volumes contained lessons that dealt with the story of Christ and would respond to the Christian perspective. If only his uncle Salem liked him! Then he would have let him read those books and might have even given him lessons on the questions that occupied his mind. Why not? What was the harm in it, so long as the external reading didn't hinder a student's progress in his studies? In any case, the reading would continue, whether Salem liked it or not.

If Marika was responsible for what had happened, then her responsibility was confined to having encouraged the child to read, or to introducing him to extracts of Greek literature that were suitable for him. It had started with Aesop's fables, but he quickly lost interest in those -'They're for little kids, like the Kalila and Dimna stories' - so she moved him on to stories from the Iliad and the Odyssey. But she hadn't realised those stories would have a profound impact on him. The heroes of the two sagas - Priam and Hector, Paris and Helen, Agamemnon and Menelaus, Achilles and Ajax, Odysseus, and Penelope - quickly become familiar to him, and he wouldn't stop repeating their names and mentioning their feats. He even started to find echoes of some of them in Islamic history: Achilles resembled Khaled Ibn al-Waleed, the 'Drawn Sword of God' because, if he became enraged, he pounced on his opponents like a lion on its prey, and the legions collapsed before him. And Odysseus who opened the gates of Troy resembled Amr Ibn al-Aas who opened the gates of Egypt. They both were military commanders, resourceful and shrewd, and both - as he imagined them and drew them on paper - were heavyset men of an average build with large heads and muscular upper arms, unparalleled at archery and spear-throwing.

Marika didn't realise how much the boy's soul had been influenced by what she'd read to him or what he'd read himself in his bedroom, which pulled him away from all known realms. She didn't know he had read the Holy Bible and so didn't realise how this reading had inspired new feelings of stubbornness and a desire to challenge. He started to feel reading was a right that could never be snatched from him; he would read, whatever the outcome. Maybe the feelings had been sparked by the terrible slap he had received from Salem that had caused him to wet his trousers.

However, his transformation had actually started when he read '*Thaïs,*' and it must have crystallised when he approached the end of the Holy Bible and - more specifically - when he reached John's Revelation, when the sheep appears in a different guise. For there, he is no longer lost, but occupies a position near the One on the throne: '*Then I saw in the right hand of Him who was seated on the throne a scroll written within and on the back, sealed with seven seals. And I saw a mighty angel proclaiming with a loud voice, 'Who is worthy to open the scroll and break its seals?*

And no one in heaven or on earth or under the earth was able to open the scroll or to look into it.' And no one was able to open the scroll and break its seven seals, except a '*Lamb standing, as though it had been slain...And he went and took the scroll from the right hand of Him who was seated on the throne. And when he had taken the scroll, the four living creatures and the twenty-four elders fell down before the Lamb, each holding a harp, and golden bowls full of incense...*'

John's Revelation included much that he found difficult to accept or comprehend, but some of the scenes of the Revelation radiated, seeming to explode and launch flares across his imagination. His voyage, through reading, took on varied dimensions that unfolded ahead of him for around a year, a journey that immersed him in a sprawling historical and imaginative space. After the story of the lost sheep and the angels that cared for him in the heavens, Medhat found himself transported to the story of the slaughtered sheep and his position amongst the angels. Then both of the two stories carried him over vast distances to reach the story of Abraham, as it was narrated in the Holy Quran, and the command he received that he should sacrifice a son who had been chosen as a sacrificial lamb, that is until '*We ransomed him with a momentous sacrifice.*' Thus the first story, which advised us to treat children well, also suggested that amongst the children would be a lamb who would be chosen to redeem humans? And that this saviour of a lamb, found 'lost' and neglected in the cattle manger, would be the one who would establish God's kingdom on earth? And would he be the same child to be born, according to the Holy Quran, by the trunk of a palm tree, yet who spoke with authority and power when he was yet a newborn: '*But a voice cried to her from beneath the palm-tree, 'Grieve not! For thy Lord hath provided a rivulet beneath thee.*

And shake towards thyself the trunk of the palm-tree: It will let fall fresh ripe dates upon thee. So eat and drink and cool thine eye.' And where was all this in the story of Joseph the child, whose brothers claimed the wolf had eaten him (another lost sheep) - Joseph, whose shirt was thrown over his afflicted father's face, bringing back his sight, and who held a high position in the running of the Egyptian state?

Reading the Holy Bible awakened in Medhat what he knew of the Quran, which was plenty. He may have memorized only one section of the Quran at his village school, but the Quran maintained a strong presence throughout his life, despite his mind being sluggish back then. He used to hear the Quran being recited everywhere, and its quotations were on every tongue. And now here were the verses, in their revealed version, coming easily to his mind. He started to switch between the two books to compare the stories of the prophets in both, and found - and was frightened, enraptured, and moved - that the image of Mary and her son existed in both books. This story was the one he felt represented the greatest and most beautiful of all portrayals of motherhood. All these stories, in his opinion, struck a chord deep in people's hearts - just as they plucked at the strings of his soul - and responded to dreams, hopes, and sorrows that had and continued to preoccupy them. If only Salem would help him to crack these codes!

All this reading led him to feel he didn't belong in his bedroom, or the house, or even in the large square perimeter he loved in Ismailia, the one that enclosed Abbas Square. He belonged to the wide, open space that spread out ahead of him in whichever direction he faced, welcoming him without any obstacles, and where he never felt lonely. As if that vast space was his homeland, and his love of wandering and deliberately getting lost was nothing but a form of existence in that homeland. As if the freedom he enjoyed, as he moved from one book to another, was the flipside of living in this city.

He thought he knew the secret behind his choice of Odysseus as his favourite hero in the Iliad and the Odyssey: at the end of the day, Odysseus wasn't a shrewd military commander. He was the lost sailor who was bandied by the waves and attacked by horrors and temptations from every side on his journey back to his homeland. He thought that, had Odysseus been a real man, his son would have been the happiest person on earth. He decided right then and there that no-one - neither Salem nor anyone else - would ever be able to stand in his way or restrict his freedom.

***

Ismailia was a beautiful dream that was starting to vanish. Once upon a time, it was one united city and a wonderful homeland within the realm of a familiar square. He would cross the Thalatheeny Street to the foreigners' neighbourhood without feeling the separating road was a decisive limit. Most of the foreigners lived in that neighbourhood, whereas nearly all of the Egyptians lived in the Arab neighbourhood. However, the street wasn't an impenetrable wall between the two sects - or at least so he thought. The two neighbourhoods were intertwined: Greeks, Armenians, French, and Maltese also lived in the Arab neighbourhood, and some Egyptians lived or worked in the foreigners' neighbourhood. His school was located at the edge of the foreigners' neighbourhood. Greek families lived near the school, and it was said that some of the older students - who were repeating the fourth year after several attempts - befriended girls from those families. He himself wandered among the foreigners freely and communicated with them in fluent Greek or using nuggets of French, English, or Italian. When Marika was with him, there was total harmony. It also seemed that any divides - if any had existed - were erased by the time he moved up to secondary school when the Egyptian school moved into the beautiful red brick building that used to house the Italian secondary school, in the heart of the foreigners' neighbourhood.

Roughly around the same time, the cracks and fissures started to surface. Although he now wore long trousers instead of shorts and had started to take care of his overall appearance - moisturising and styling his thick, bushy hair with Vaseline or oil - for some reason he couldn't understand no one would greet him any longer when he was out walking. The waiters no longer welcomed him in their cafés, and some even threw him out, until gradually he realised these places were for foreigners only. At the French beach, the foreign mothers weren't keen on him befriending their children, especially their daughters.

One day, he was helping Marie-Francoise onto a rope swing when the girl - who had been enjoying his company - was called over by her mother and climbed down off the rope. 'Wait, I'll be back,' she said. But she didn't come back, and he kept waiting, to no avail. He could see her and her mother from where he was standing a short distance away, and she must have been able to see him, too, but she never did return. This was the same girl who used to swim with him in the shallow water or walk with him over to the buffet spread.

At that time, he hadn't quite fathomed the idea of discrimination against Egyptians. He knew the British army maintained a base outside the city and that some Egyptians worked at the base and supplied local goods needed by the army. But for a while he wasn't fully aware that there was a British occupation in Egypt, that the Suez Canal Company held special privileges in the canal, that foreigners in general had a privileged position in Egypt, and that Egyptians in Egypt were forbidden from certain places and some jobs. Only gradually did he start to realize these facts. It seemed as though he was clinging, out of some self-interest, to the idea that a prevailing harmony existed amongst everyone, despite the many omens. There was a game he used to play with his friends out in the street every year. They would fashion a doll out of cloth, sacking, and old rags, stuff it with straw and call it Allenby (after the famous English lord). Both Egyptians and foreigners would go around the houses with the effigy, begging for milliemes. Then one night, they would set fire to Allenby in a large celebration and sing, 'Allenby, son of *Allenbuha*, your mother's cunt is full of stinky *meluha*!' They would see the British soldiers on the trains that passed from behind the fence between the Arab neighbourhood and the railway and would trade obscene insults. He started to see the Egyptian police raid some of the homes or shops in that area as they searched for goods stolen from the British base and arrested Egyptians accused of robbing stores or helping to hide the loot. All this seemed normal.

There were days when he felt the city was united, and on those days he wouldn't be surprised by the differences between the two sides or driven to ask questions. There were certain signs he would notice but never really question, such as why there was no cinema in the Arab neighbourhood (all the cinemas were in the foreigners' neighbourhood, including the one that screened Egyptian movies), or bookshops (in the Arab neighbourhood there were only shops that sold stationery and schoolbooks), or cafés and restaurants of note. There were also no striking public parks (apart from some green areas in Abbas Square).

Medhat started to realize that the people of Ismailia (the locals of the Arab neighbourhood to which he belonged) in all their categories - from businessmen to labourers to employees and smugglers - were only interested in money and didn't care about reading or culture at all, and that there wasn't a single writer or artist amongst them. All of this was also quite normal.

His relationships with people in the foreigners' neighbourhood languished after the school moved out of the Italian building to a new one in the desert, on the edges of what was called Araisheyat Misr. It was a new Arab neighbourhood, recently constructed and separated from the foreigners' neighbourhood by the railway. The only sign of civilized culture out there was a summer cinema. He stopped interacting with foreigners, and Ismailia was no longer that one large, beautiful square that he knew from his childhood. He had finally started to realize the world wasn't homogenous but segregated, and that there were neighbourhoods on the fringes of the square where poor Arabs lived, confirming that the population really was classed into different categories.

That one beautiful square perimeter had been an idea of his own creation, a figment his rural imagination had detached from reality to create a haven for himself where he could wander. Had his imagination detached it, or had Marika? She was the one who made him feel unique: she taught him how to speak Greek, and she used to buy him comic books in Arabic, French, and English. She would read him Aesop's fables in simplified Greek and explain them in Arabic, and she read him stories from the Iliad and Odysseus. She was the one who wanted him to feel the city was his playground, which it was - until he realized he had been allowed into the foreigners' neighbourhood as a temporary visitor and that he wouldn't be permitted to stay for long.

News of guerrilla attacks against the British base began trickling through to him, either from other people or printed in newspapers. He heard the speech by Mustafa al-Nahhas Pasha where he cancelled the Anglo-Egyptian Treaty of 1936: '*For the sake of Egypt I signed the treaty of 1936, and for the sake of Egypt I call on you today to cancel the treaty.*' But it was when British forces stormed the governorate building and killed tens of Egyptian security forces that the decisive split occurred. That was in January. The following day, people went out in a demonstration that set off from the secondary school, which he joined, chanting with the others against the British occupation. The demonstration turned into a full-scale riot, and shops and homes were looted. This rapid descent into violence started before the demonstrators entered the foreigners' neighbourhood, when men suddenly appeared and stormed apartments that were unoccupied for various reasons, to emerge with refrigerators and pieces of furniture. In the foreigners' neighbourhood, a student tossed a lit match into the petrol tank of a Jeep (which might have belonged to a British soldier), setting the car alight before it exploded, which only encouraged the protestors to light more fires. The sound of bullets being fired echoed throughout the neighbourhood - which meant the British forces had come down into the square.

'Where were you?' Salem asked Medhat when he passed by the shop. 'I heard the students have gone on strike.'

'I was in a protest against the British,' he answered, triumphantly.

'What protest, you son of a bitch?' Salem replied, angrily.

Medhat was shocked. He had thought that his Wafdist-to-the-core uncle would congratulate him.

'It was a nationalist protest.'

But he was wrong.

'I won't have anyone under my roof go out demonstrating or getting involved in politics,' he heard Salem declare before adding, 'Fine. Go home and get ready to go back to your village.' Then Salem started shouting. 'Can't you hear the gunshots, you son of a bitch? You're going back to your family where you can protest as much as you want. But I'm not prepared to shoulder the responsibility.'

'Your uncle doesn't mean it,' Marika said, after she heard what had happened. 'He's just threatening you because he doesn't want you to put yourself in danger.' But Salem had meant what he said, and he confirmed it to Marika when he returned home. 'Medhat did something wrong, and he has to apologise to you and promise he'll never do anything like this again,' Marika said, before turning to Medhat. 'Apologise to your uncle, Medhat, and promise him that you…' Salem interrupted her. 'I don't want any apologies. This boy won't stay here. He has to go back to his family.' Marika was shocked and lowered her voice as she addressed him. 'The punishment should match the wrongdoing, Salem. He didn't commit a crime.' 'What do you mean he didn't commit a crime?' Salem shouted. 'I won't have anyone in my house who goes out demonstrating.' Marika continued to try to diffuse his anger. 'You're right. Medhat did something wrong, I agree with you. From now on, there won't be any demonstrations, but forgive him this one time. For my sake, forgive him this time,' she pleaded. 'Don't destroy his future because of a mistake like this.' But Salem stuck to his guns. 'I think you should pack his things so he can leave.' Marika started to cry. 'But where will he go? Who's going to look after him? He's still young.' 'Still young. Still young. You're the one who spoilt him,' Salem replied. 'Darling, I'm sorry if I was wrong, but don't throw him out. How can you throw your son out?' But this question only served to further ignite his fury. 'He's not my son. I don't have any children.' Then it was Marika's turn to get angry. 'When I brought him here, did you think I was trying to give him a mother? He had plenty of mothers there. I was trying to give him a father to look after him. Salem, where is your sense of chivalry?' Salem's eyes glistened with anger. 'I don't want to hear any more of this nonsense. If I say this boy's going back to his family, then he's going.' Marika managed to compose herself. 'Okay. Seeing as you're not going to compromise, then I'm leaving you and this house. I'm not staying here,' she said quietly. She went into the bedroom and came back a little later carrying a suitcase. She asked Medhat to go down and find her a taxi.

Salem had been sitting at the dining table waiting for his lunch, but when he saw Marika carrying her suitcase and ready to leave, he got up, changed into his outdoor clothes and went. He left her standing at the door with her suitcase beside her. It was a dreadful scene - where would Marika go? The only place left for her was her parents' home. It wasn't the first time this had happened. Marika would sometimes become so upset she would threaten to leave and would even pack her suitcase so she'd be ready to go. But each time, Salem would intervene at the critical moment and hug her, so she'd collapse into his arms and the couple would eventually make up after some reproach and plenty of tears. But this argument was different. There was no way Marika could accept Medhat being thrown out of the house. And Salem's angry departure meant he no longer cared whether she stayed or not. Medhat watched her wipe away her tears as she stood at the door flabbergasted, unable to comprehend what had just happened and not knowing what to do. Medhat walked up to her and took on Salem's role, hugging her until she lowered her head onto his shoulder. At that moment, they were united in solidarity, even if they couldn't help each other. They were strangers. In the end, Medhat offered the solution. 'Don't be upset. Don't worry,' he reassured her. 'Stay in your home. I'll leave.' She started weeping. 'But what will you do?' 'First, I'll go back to the village, then we'll see,' he said. He carried the suitcase to her bedroom where she sat, her head lowered, crushed.

As for Medhat, he spent the whole night shuddering in his bed, fearful of what awaited him. Going back to the village meant the end of his academic life. It meant returning to Na'sa - and what could poverty-stricken Na'sa do for him? And what would he be able to do for her? Or it meant seeking refuge with his uncle in the village of the Qassimis. He wouldn't turn him away, and Haniya would welcome him warmly, and with open arms, so that he could be stuffed in with the army of their other sons and daughters. But he wouldn't be able to become a farmer and work in the fields like his uncle's children. He wasn't familiar with that kind of life and wouldn't be fit for it. Then what would he do? Every door facing him was shut, and the future was dark and terrifying.

In the morning, when Salem called him to the shop, he felt certain Salem wanted to reiterate that he was standing firm on his verdict. He paused before reaching Abbas Square, when he spotted the shop sign from a distance. It was one of the signs Salem had made him read the day he had tested his reading skills. Could all that possibly end this way, as though none of it had ever happened? He considered going home to ask Salwa to accompany him to the shop, in the hope that Salem's heart might soften if she were there, but he carried on walking. No, Salwa wouldn't succeed where Marika had failed, and he had to face the dismal future alone. Or should he make one last attempt to appease Salem?

He started towards the shop, dragging his feet. But when he got there, he was sorry to find Salem decanting his anger on Henidaq, the coffee vendor. Henidaq had brought him a tepid cup of coffee when Salem only drank it boiling hot, and Henidaq, the 'ass and son of an ass' knew that, and his father, 'the permanent stoner' knew it, too. Was he fated - he, Salem - to have to deal with 'ignorant fools' for the rest of this life? Henidaq, the poor man, was apologising profusely. 'Yes, Uncle Salem. I'm sorry,' he kept repeating. 'Just don't get upset.' But his fury exploded into a full-on rage when Henidaq returned with a medium-sweet coffee. How could he do that when he knew that Salem only drank it without sugar? The curses rained down on Henidaq's head, this time extending to his mother and her honour.

Confronted by this scene, Medhat quickly ascertained that there was absolutely no possibility of appeasing Salem, so he stood with his head lowered like a condemned man, waiting for the sword to land on his neck. Then peace washed over Salem when he took a sip of the third coffee and a couple of drags on the shisha pipe. Signs of contentment flickered on his face. He finally noticed his presence - or had he been purposefully ignoring him to indulge in his torture? Salem asked him to sit down. 'You won't go back to the village,' he said. 'You'll go to Abu Kabir.' Medhat felt his heart pound. Was there hope? Did Salem want to extend a lifeline to him? It seemed so. Salem had another plan. Thank God. He told him that he would return to Abu Kabir to complete his secondary education there. Medhat broke down in tears when he heard Salem say he would take care of his expenses until the end of his university education. The boy bent over Salem's hand - there was still room for mercy in the heart of the tyrant - to kiss it and pray for his long life.

This was the solution everyone had reached during the reconciliation gathering that had taken place the evening before in Petros's house. Marika's father quickly came to the conclusion that the man was keen to keep his wife, but that he wouldn't budge a single inch when it came to Medhat's departure. Silence prevailed for a moment, during which it seemed there would be no way out of the crisis, until Doris spoke and addressed Salem. 'Okay. Medhat will leave as you wish, but you will take care of his expenses until he graduates from university.' Marika looked askance at her mother, objecting to her suggestion, but her mother responded with a look that said, 'Shut up'. Salem agreed without hesitation.

On the way to Abu Kabir, Medhat felt broken. Salem was as hard as nails when he argued and wouldn't settle for anything less than crushing his opponent. Salem's promise to take care of his expenses until he finished university meant that all he'd wanted was to get rid of him, and that joining the demonstration had simply been the perfect opportunity to achieve this goal. He'd been lying in wait so that, when the opportunity came, he could take advantage of it without worrying about Marika's objections. And she had to acquiesce in the end, especially after her parents mediated. 'The important thing is that you look to the future and succeed in your studies. Don't think about anything else,' she said as she bade him farewell. She had surrendered just as he had. There was nothing either of them could do. They had to accept the 'mercy' that Salem had offered once he'd gotten what he wanted. He was sad about leaving Ismailia and leaving Marika, but he had to follow the path Salem had paved for him. It was the best available option.

But before he reached Abu Kabir, he started to see the positive side of the situation. He was now fifteen years old and in the third year of secondary school, going back to his hometown healthier and stronger than he was when he left. Ismailia had given him the necessary push to become more ambitious and had granted him hope in the future. So now it seemed it was time to become independent. Abu Kabir wasn't the end of the world. It was freedom, or a launching point towards freedom. The road lay open before him. And he would move to Cairo within three years, 'the Mother of the World', the grand dream. Let him complete the rest of the journey, away from Salem, and without being forced to submit to his dominance. At least now he would be able to join in any demonstration that took place and read all the books he wanted. Maybe Salem had done him an unintentional favour by turning him out. And Salem must be defeated. This was a battle from which he would have to emerge victorious. He had to love this city that Salem had chosen as his place of exile.

***

As soon as he found a place to stay, he started to wander the whole of Abu Kabir, the length and breadth of it, so that he'd cover every inch of it in his own way. He walked at length along the country road adjacent to the canal and the railway line, and passed the cotton gin - the starting point from the forest end - then the girl's school, then the secondary school for boys, then the only café - 'al-Bursa' - then the only cinema, the ice factory, and the lemon fields. Then he retraced his steps back to 'al-Bursa'. This was the centre. The café had a wooden terrace that had deteriorated with age, but the beautiful yet worn shell was proof it had witnessed the good old days. It seemed that the naming of the café after the stock exchange proved that at one time or another, it had been a place where the biggest traders would meet - especially the foreign ones - as well as other eminent people to strike their deals. To the side of the café was what people dubbed the 'Big Road': an unpaved road, perpendicular to the country road that extended to the edges of the city.

He continued past the level crossing, then the railway station and the telegraph office, then turned left and saw a two-storey house. That was the building that had once been Petros's bar and home. Now it was abandoned, with no one left to restore it. It was more likely someone would knock it down to build an apartment block in its place. And here was the door that would lead firstly to the bar. It was locked with a chunky latch. If only he could go inside to see the counter that Petros used to stand behind and the place where Salem would sit, waiting for Marika to come by with the orders. Oh, if only he could go inside! Would the curtain with its coloured beads, which used to separate the residence from the bar and would part to reveal Marika, still be there? It was a crazy question. He stood underneath the siris trees opposite Marika's old balcony, the only thing that had stood the test of time, the colours of its leaves rotating between green, yellow, and red. That must have been the tree Salem used to climb at night to reach his beloved.

Within these borders, this was a city one could easily fall in love with. This was the aspect visitors would see upon arrival, an aspect that was heavy with the remnants of a historical heritage and which held its share of the landmarks of civilisation. The train from Mansura to Cairo would pass through here. And here, within eyeshot, the Delta train moved at a leisurely pace, heading towards Faqus in the east and Diyarb Najm in the west. Here, where the trains passed by, Cairo seemed close and would draw his yearning towards it. But first, he had to fall in love with this city.

Along the 'Big Road', there were no pavements, cafés, or shops with display windows, but there were - truth be told - some places that excited interest. There was the *sirja,* where they pressed oil and made oil cake, the *kusb,* to feed livestock, where a camel would circle round to turn the cogs. From either side of the Big Road, narrow paths and alleys branched out that bore no resemblance to civilisation and were mostly residential. He entered one on the left - which was muddy - and was shocked by the pungent smells. Here was the shop where they sold the fermented and salted *fiseekh* fish, as well as all the mud and dung. Facing it was a dimly lit shop where an old man with a trimmed white beard stood at the door in a white *jilbab*. And what was this man opposite the *fiseekh* vendor selling? Unbelievable! It was a used bookshop. Books? There were books in Abu Kabir then, as well as readers, when Ismailia - the modern city - didn't have a single Arabic bookshop. The old man greeted him, so he stepped inside, inhaling the pleasant aroma of incense and old books. There were dusty and, in some cases, tattered books, printed on stone in the nineteenth century. How had these books reached Abu Kabir but not Ismailia? And which of the residents of this rural town liked to read, let alone read books like these? If only he were well-off, he would have bought the entire contents of the shop. But to start with, he settled on the purchase of a strange book, entitled 'Shaking the *Quhoof* When Analysing the Poem of Sheikh Abu Shaduf' by Sheikh Youssef al-Shirbini. What were these *quhoof*? He knew that a singular *qahf* in the language of the Qassimis and Salehis was part of the bark of a palm tree, and that it also referred to a man who was rude, boorish, and coarse (like the bark of a palm tree) or gruff. So what did the author mean by shaking the *quhoof*? Did it refer to shaking a palm tree for it to drop its dates? The book had to be read.

He paused for a long time. Should he buy the book or not? His mind urged him to leave the book in its place on the shelf, since there were only a few piasters in his pocket. But he wanted to know what Sheikh al-Shirbini meant by the word *quhoof*, and what shaking it was all about. As far as he understood, the *quhoof* were not alien to him, and he had once been one of them. Didn't the people in Ismailia call him gruff? After a period of painful hesitation, he was able to resolve the problem when the sheikh with the white beard gestured to him. 'Don't worry, the money's not important,' he said. So he bought the book at a lower price.

That evening, he couldn't wait to get back to his room. As soon as he took off his jacket, he lay down on the bed, still dressed in his shirt and trousers, and didn't get to sleep before he had finished reading the book to the light of the kerosene lamp at three in the morning. He stopped for nothing but to laugh or take a bite of some halva, which constituted his dinner. It turned out that *quhoof* referred to peasants, about whom al-Shirbini had written his satirical analysis. In his introduction, the analyst wrote: '*'Now, let us explain what we promised we would and the occasion for all this song and dance …And before delving into the oceans of these words…we will mention what happened to some of the ordinary country folk and describe their personalities, their manners and their names. So we say: their bad manners and brutish nature is down to how much time they spend in the company of beasts and cows, their indifference to sophisticated people, and their tendency to mix with people of a coarse nature, their proximity to the plough and the shovel-sledge, shaking their quhoof around the threshing floors, and their manner of circling around crops and leaping into harvesting and reaping…'*

What did the sheikh mean about the peasants shaking their *quhoof* around the threshing floors? There must be another meaning to *quhoof*, and it wouldn't become clear without digging into the heart of the book. It then became clear that one of the definitions of the word *qahf* was no longer in common usage - at least not amongst the Salehis and Qassimis. The *qahf*, according to this definition, was a head covering 'made of wool or fur that is worn on the head...it is used by the poor...and they wear something they call a *tartur* and they throw the *qahf* over it...' So this definition had now been abandoned. Peasants, as he knew them, no longer wore the *qahf* or the *tartur*. They used to wear a *tartur* in the era of Abu Jad, whose *tartur* would scare the lads, but they were still *quhoof*, in the eyes of the sheikh, in the word's other sense.

***

Had it not been for the landmarks that greeted a visitor upon entering Abu Kabir, the town might have looked like a village, just like that of the Salehis or the Qassimis, although it was larger than both. But there was more to the town than those visible landmarks; it had a soul and a personality that was characterised by rigour. It wasn't a gentle city like Ismailia.

And during the first days of school, he witnessed a different style of student demonstration. The students gathered in the yard facing two people delivering speeches - one of them representing the Wafd party and the other representing the Muslim Brotherhood. Each speaker stood to one side of the steps, and they took turns talking. They were both eloquent, outspoken, and capable of mobilising crowds and igniting their audience's enthusiasm. After they'd each had a chance to speak, the entire rally - both the Muslim Brotherhood and Wafd supporters -

merged into one demonstration, setting off along the country road where the chants against the occupation and King Farouk grew louder. Despite his leanings towards the Wafd Party - just like his uncle Salem - he had been stirred by what he heard from the Muslim Brotherhood speaker, who, to tell the truth, had spoken skilfully. It pleased him to see how the two speakers gave each other the chance to talk without any interruptions. He was in awe of the eloquence of the speakers: Where had they learned these oratory skills? He had never seen the likes of it in Ismailia. A speech had never been delivered at a secondary school by someone who held any importance or a clear political awareness that divided people into parties, or by any kind of student leader, even though the city had been a stronghold for the Muslim Brotherhood. The group had a mosque and a primary school there, as well as an army of scouts and *jawwala* who were given military training. How could Abu Kabir, a rural town, achieve this miracle? Maybe the reason behind it was that life here was harsher. Ismailia was like a little piece of Europe, or a European island luxuriating in the Egyptian ocean. Perhaps the interaction with foreigners, and economic reliance on them, was the factor that led to the characteristic soft and gentle nature of the city's original residents and their reluctance to celebrate their culture. Other than in the foreigners' neighbourhood, which was full of foreign bookshops, there simply wasn't anywhere to purchase or borrow books, or even just to browse. Apart from Salem's bookcases, it seemed there really was no place in Arab Ismailia for books.

Then gradually, other miracles began to materialise before him. He found a library in the school with a small collection of books for loan, a library the likes of which he had never seen at the secondary school in Ismailia. It wasn't long before he became acquainted with some of the students who were interested in literature and who composed poetry. They were mostly from impoverished families or those whose parents were small-scale farmers and other peasants. For the first time, he felt that his move to Abu Kabir represented a return to his roots - since deep down he was a *qahf* - and that life in Ismailia had in fact been nothing more than a transitional and transient phase. A *qahf*, but moulded uniquely, he strutted around the school yard 'fanning his tail feathers' to the people of Abu Kabir, as if to say: 'Honestly, have you ever seen a *qahf* who could speak a foreign language?' But would he be able to love this town?

***

Though his room was very modest, its location was special as it was close to the mosque, the market, and the school, and it had a window that overlooked the main road. Right next door was a shop run by the landlord Amin and his wife, selling cigarettes, tea, sugar, and more, and they allowed customers to run a tab or pay in instalments. One of its only flaws was that the room was damp on the inside, which led to creeping rot in the wall by his bed. The other downside was that Amin would shut off the interior part of the house - where the bathroom was found - when he closed the shop at ten o'clock at night. So if a tenant wanted to do his business after that, he would have to use the latrines at the mosque. Why did Amin isolate the interior section of the house? Because that was where the married couple's bedroom was, as well as the other room where their son slept - 'Sheikh Khayrat' - who was nicknamed 'Sheikh' because they said he was blessed by his mental disability.

Thanks to that distinct location, the new tenant met his first friend in Abu Kabir. Emad lived near him with his married sister, and he started to pay visits to his room. More importantly, he would invite him for lunch or dinner from time to time at the sister's apartment - a generous meal that was a rare treat. The only drawback was that Emad ate so quickly that it was impossible to keep up with him, and then he would suddenly stop, announcing that he had finished by thanking God for the meal. And although the guest would not have had his fill, he would be forced to stop eating, too, out of politeness.

The truth was that he never knew what it meant to have a healthy appetite or to be hungry until he reached Abu Kabir. The food there was modest and very simple in comparison to what Marika used to serve, but he could never get enough, no matter how much his aunt Haniya sent over now and then. The speed at which the people eating with him wolfed down the food only made his hunger more intense. After getting to know Emad, he made two other friends: Bayumi, a poet from the countryside, and Hashem, a tough, broad-shouldered, muscular football player. Often the friends would lay out a meal on the floor of his room and eat together: salty 'Rashidi-style' sardines, *ful* beans, falafel, and grilled fish from the Wednesday market. But he wouldn't be able to glean much in the company of these savages. They would stuff the fish, either part or whole, into a piece of bread and eat the whole thing, bones and all. And they grabbed at the food - any food - oblivious to the fact that their friend had hardly eaten. It wasn't long before he learnt how to race and snatch what he wanted.

He noticed Bayumi because he would often be late to class, which would cause the teacher to pause his lecture. Bayumi would apologise. 'It's because I've come from Hahia, Sir.' The teacher would accept the apology, but Bayumi wouldn't move. Instead, he would look around the class with roving eyes, as if it was his first time there. Then he would slowly head over to his seat, his body as stiff as a statue. But when Bayumi got going, he turned into a first-rate comedian. The second the Arabic teacher, Mr. Ali Abdelazim, entered the classroom, life suddenly beat into Bayumi's rigid body, revealing a biting wit. The teacher liked him because of his excellent command of the Arabic language - for he was a poet - and because he supported the teacher in his prejudice against rural people. Bayumi was a peasant through and through, and he worked in his father's field with a plough, axe, and sickle after school. In fact, all the students at the school, including the locals from Abu Kabir, were country boys - at least in the eyes of the teacher. But Bayumi provided the teacher with a constantly replenished source of ammunition by way of peasant-related anecdotes that would either be gleaned from reality and flavoured with exaggeration or borrowed from the book 'Shaking the *Quhoof*' that he could recite from memory, as if he had memorised the whole thing.

Then one day, Bayumi brought along the footballer Hashem, a goalkeeper. His responsibility was to confront hooligans from the Muslim Brotherhood or others when they tried to harass his friends. Bayumi couldn't harm a fly, and Emad was tall but 'silly,' and Medhat from Ismailia was 'drowsy'. The school was teeming with hooligans: footballers, volleyball players, and parallel-bar gymnasts. There was a group of these hooligans in the class who were repeating the academic year. They sat in the back rows and traded signals through the window with the Police Commissioner's servant, or flirted with the prosecutor's wife whenever the teacher scribbled away on the blackboard. During the lesson, they would pass around erotic writings, including 'Eva's Diaries'.

And so a group was made: four friends who'd meet on

almost a daily basis and who ate many of their meals together on newspapers laid out on the floor. In this room that never saw sunlight, they would revise what they'd learnt that day and celebrations would ensue whenever Haniya sent one of her delicious meals. There would be other causes for celebration, too, like getting their shirts ironed. Suits would be taken to the presser once a year to be ironed using the foot-powered presser, but, since they couldn't afford to send their shirts for ironing, they would wrap the cuffs and dampened collars over the hot glass of the kerosene lamp. The rest of the shirt wouldn't need ironing, since it would be concealed beneath the jacket. Some of them might spend the night in the same room if they were too lazy to go back to their own homes. Straw mats would be laid out on the ground for them, whereas the person whose room it was would sleep on a single travel bed called a *sefary*, which was so hard it could almost fracture their ribs, since the base of the bed was made of wire. How happy the foreigner from Ismailia was with this band of friends around him! And how he would end up suffering with them! Before he met them, Abu Kabir would often shock and disgust him with its roads clogged with mud and faeces, both animal and human. And yet Abu Kabir never ceased to surprise him with happy discoveries.

One morning, at the beginning of the school year, a girl appeared, carrying her book bag tucked tightly against her chest and wearing - how incredible! - a beret. A green beret in Abu Kabir? A beret in Ismailia wasn't surprising, since there were English women recruits and foreign girls. One of the pictures that Salwa had given him as a present was a photo of her in her Girl Scouts uniform, which included a scarf tied around the neck and the beret. But in Abu Kabir…never in a million years. He would watch this new girl as she walked to school and he'd see her bright, radiant face, full chest, thick braid of black hair, and the way she sauntered, which was a sign of self-esteem. After that, he started to wait for her to pass by every morning - just as he used to wait for Ibtisam, except that this one was prettier. And he would revel in the privilege of being the only one to watch her walk past, until his friends arrived. If they had spent the night in his room, they would all end up waiting for her at the window, each claiming she had turned or smiled only at him - that's if she actually did smile or turn towards them, or if they believed she had. They called her The Lieutenant because of the way she walked. But they were oblivious to his sorrow, not realising that the beret-clad girl had lit up the darkness of his lonely existence and made him forget his feelings of disgust and victimisation in this vile exile.

He wouldn't get to dominate the view of her for long, before the number of her admirers gazing from the window multiplied. His morale reached rock bottom when he was struck by yellow fever. The disease was preceded by symptoms that included loss of appetite, exhaustion, and a yellowing of his face and eyes. The doctor explained to the patient that the cause of the illness might be food that was contaminated due to its proximity to human faeces. 'We have a lot of that,' the patient said. The mosque looked out - and released its sewers - onto low-lying fields of radish that grew and thrived and were sold in the nearby market. Even at home, Sheikh Khayrat would often fail to reach the bathroom quickly enough (hindered by his polio-affected foot), and so would drip faeces and urine on the way. This was Abu Kabir - the city of mud and faeces - which he had to love.

Luckily, from time to time and behind Salem's back, Marika had started to send him some extra money, so life became a little more comfortable and the friends came over more often to visit and spend the night. There was the *sefary* bed, a desk for studying, and the straw mats that the guests laid down on and covered with newspapers as a makeshift dining table. There was also Amin's shop, where a range of ways to pay made it easier to buy tea, sugar, and loose cigarettes, which they would share either by passing one around the group or by splitting the whole lot. From time to time, his aunt Haniya would send a messenger on a donkey carrying food such as eggs and *haseera* cheese and, in some rare cases, a pot of chicken cooked with rice. Then a feast would be held, and the friends would arrive in the blink of an eye, come rain or shine.

Without a doubt, the window overlooking the road was the highlight, since it was both a means of drawing in light and fresh air as well as a lookout point for watching the girls on their way to school. There were only a handful of places the young men could go. The most noteworthy was the country road where the friends would head in the mid-afternoon, when the temperature dropped. There, they would enjoy watching the teachers from the secondary school for girls as they stood on their balconies, or they'd even send them a flirtatious word or gesture. The teachers wouldn't be annoyed by this innocent fun or report the admirers to the headmaster. Sometimes they would even respond with a smile or wave to return the greeting. *Poor women*, the friends would often say. *Strangers living in this sorry town, prisoners in their own rooms after a full day's work, like nuns in a convent, with only these keen young men to pay them any attention.* The only people who would be irritated by this fervour were some Brotherhood students who opposed this 'vulgarity'. They would suddenly appear, armed with sticks and prepared for a fight. They would order the flirtatious young men to go to the mosque and pray instead of committing sins; that is, until Hashem confronted them. At this point, the round was over, although not the arguments among the friends over the outcome, as each claimed that the geniality of the beautiful women on the balcony - if they had been sweet to them - was directed at him.

There was also the Delta train, which stood permanently on tracks that extended beyond a sand dune. The friends would take their books there and lie down in the shade of one of the carriages, where they would study or watch the people going by. They might go alone or in pairs, and often he would go on his own to read, remember, or think, since Marika's balcony was nearby and the trees were tall and still resilient, having stood the test of time. If Bayumi went, he would make the most of the shade and quiet to compose poetry or to write his 'memoirs'.

The train station, with its facilities - the telegraph office, the railroad tracks, and the semaphore railway signal - held its own special magic. Here, trains would pass by, and he would see the passengers through the windows bound for Cairo, or those returning from there - people who seemed to be created of a different stuff than that of ordinary humans. The trains tossed newspapers, magazines, and pocket novels onto the street for sale - the latter for those lucky enough to afford them. As for Hashem, he would often go there at night to meet one of his girlfriends. The footballer was the most successful in the group at attracting girls - always the servants of rich families - and he lured them to that den. Even though the friends criticised him for his declining taste, they also benefited from his adventures, since he would bring back juicy stories and local sweets that his beloved would steal from her employers.

There were other places to wander on his own. Wednesday was market day, and the market was a huge celebration, as if it were Eid. Anyone walking along the country road in the direction of the 'forest' would first see the cotton gin and the traffic lights, and then farmers - men and women - laying mats on the ground and selling their produce of grains, chickens, and other food, which they would sell by container or by weight. They would also see crowds of people coming from hamlets and villages both near and far on the backs of jolly donkeys that trotted briskly and shook their tails and ears as if they couldn't wait to visit the market. The market was held in a large area where produce would be displayed, either shaded or uncovered. The Ismailia boy disliked the way the food was exposed to flies, but he was thrilled by the hustle and bustle of the people: their *jilbabs*, the cries of the market sellers, the yelling of the rural women, the clucking of the chickens, the clamour of the haggling, and the swearing, oaths, and curses. This was life! There was also another market that took place near the railway on the same day for livestock traders outside the city. Nothing could compare to that scene, where the place would be teeming with people and animals. Visiting that market meant having to wake up at dawn, which wasn't easy. But sometimes he would overcome his drowsiness to go and watch. That was the price he had to pay to see either worldly life and a semblance of Judgement Day in the same spot.

***

All the female students who passed by on their way to school were beautiful in the eyes of the beholders who stood at the window. But one was an outstanding beauty. Her face was radiant (especially the cheeks), her body slim, and her hair black and thick, tied into a single braid that hung down her back. All this one could just about bear. But what would truly blow your mind was the green beret she wore, tipped to one side. She knew she was special and would always march straight ahead without turning right or left. 'Officer Sir...Lieutenant Colonel Sir...,' one of them had said, and that military rank stuck until they discovered that her name was Amal. It developed into a morning ritual - after shaving and before having breakfast at the *ful* sandwich seller on the way to school - to wait for her to walk by, then greet her dutifully.

One morning, three of them - Emad, Bayoumi, and Hashem - rushed to the window as the Lieutenant Colonel was passing, and she turned around. She must've known she had admirers, and here she was, acknowledging their presence. But it seemed things didn't end there. Had she smiled? Opinions differed until they all settled on one, which was that the smile was mysterious and fleeting, since the girl quickly reverted to her proud and self-important swagger. In the evening, they disagreed again over who exactly had won the smile of the 'Officer Sir', each of them claiming the honour for themselves. The disagreement was full of laughter and mirth, but what was serious and certain was that the three young men were infatuated with her, even if they were sure there was no way of getting her. Medhat was besotted by her too, but he concealed his feelings. It was true she had looked over and maybe even smiled, but it was unlikely she had been glancing at him - that's if she'd glanced at any of them - since he was neither the best-looking nor the boldest. Reaching her would be impossible, just as reaching Ibtisam or the perfume seller had been. And anyway, how could he contact her? The Abu Kabir girls, as it was said, were known for their boldness and for making the first move - whoever managed to catch one was a lucky man. But there was tight security around each of these girls - from men of force and rifles, it was said - as if people realised how dangerous they were. Mr. Ali Abdelazim would always warn his students against approaching or harassing them in the streets: 'We're talking bullets here.' Bayumi would respond provocatively. 'Therefore, they are a form of temptation to the onlooker,' he would say. 'You must lower your gaze,' the teacher would reply. 'And pray. Prayer is the best protection from temptation.' So, with the exception of Hashem, they would pray as much as possible, yet none of them could free themselves from the devil's temptations.

They changed the subject when Hashem turned up and they noticed he was limping. 'Why are you limping, son of Sakina?' Bayumi asked him. This was how they addressed each other, using the names of their mothers in a gruff, playful manner. When he told them one of the players had kicked him in the shins, Bayumi asked to see the wound, then cried out when Hashem uncovered his leg. 'How could you fill the wound with dust, son of Sakina? Is that how they dress wounds in your village?' 'That's what happened, son of Aisha. It's not like there was an ambulance next to me on the pitch,' Hashem replied. 'What a loser… you remind me of how they do things in our village,' Bayumi replied. Thus the opportunity arose to practice his favourite hobby, to 'shake the *quhoof* of the countryside'. He told them how, when a child in their village had conjunctivitis, they would drip some of their brother's urine into the child's eye. If the kid fainted, an onion or dung pellet would be smashed over their head and this, in the villagers' opinion, was the most beneficial treatment. 'And here you are then, son of Sakina, treating the wound with spit and dirt. Have you ever seen anything as stupid as this?' Hashem changed the subject. 'Enough of this nonsense. Tell me, did you see the Lieutenant today?' 'What's the Lieutenant got to do with you? You just stick to your servants,' Emad said. Hashem was about to reply when he remembered he needed to use the toilet.

Then everyone suddenly remembered they needed to do the

same. Medhat checked his watch and cried out in annoyance. 'We're screwed!' He reminded them it was past ten o'clock, and that Abu Khayrat and Om Khayrat had closed the shop and the door leading to the toilet. 'The only place we can go is the mosque,' Bayumi said. 'Unless one of you wants to stand at the window and piss into the air or onto the patrol soldiers.' It was cold, and the mosque was empty and dark, with the only light emanating from a lantern that shook, its flame trembling in the breeze of the front foyer. The latrines were a long walk away in almost pitch-black darkness. Three of them headed there without hesitation, since they were familiar with the place, but the fourth lagged behind, trembling. This was the first time he had been forced to go to the mosque for that specific purpose. He had always made sure to do his business in the house before ten o'clock at night. 'May God curse you, Abu Khayrat. What would happen if you kept the door open?' He took care as he entered the toilets, feeling along the walls and searching with one of his feet for the grooves on either side of the hole. He breathed a sigh of relief when his feet found their rightful places. It was pitch black inside the toilet, and the putrid stench was suffocating. Then there was the matter of washing. To his right was a basin with a water supply running through for people to dip in and grab a handful. But suddenly, a shiver ran through his entire body like an electric shock. His hand had landed on a soft, furry creature and he shouted, calling his friends in panic. 'There are rats, you sons of bitches!' The rat he'd touched was as large as a cat… a predatory animal. 'Toughen up, Ismailia boy, you weakling,' someone said, possibly Hashem. The hairs on his head stood on end when he felt a rat scurrying underneath him and he screamed. But none of his friends were bothered by him or, it seemed, by the rats. 'What's the name of your mother, boy?'

Bayumi's voice came booming in. But he didn't tell them his mother's name so they wouldn't call him by it, as per their habit. He was too busy and troubled by what was happening. There were predatory animals in the latrines, and one of them might bite his testicles. What price did have to pay to love Abu Kabir?!

***

When Amal passed by that morning, his eyes got their fill of her and he breathed in deeply. He'd hoped she would at least smile or look over at him, but she hadn't. Even so, he'd discovered a new feeling of self-confidence. Why should he put himself down? Why should he be unfair to her? He was no longer as scrawny as he used to be: the sleeves of his shirt and jacket were now too short. This had happened all of a sudden, almost overnight. There was fiery blood pumping through his veins, and the mirror showed him that there was now thick, bushy, shiny hair on his head. He could now go out to the girl and follow her, and he might find something to say and the courage to pull it off, if he put himself to the test. She had to be shown that he was interested in her. She must have noticed him at the window whenever she passed, and he had to try. And what was the point of just standing at the window when she passed? Nothing would ever happen that way, not even if it carried on for another twenty years. He decided to wait for her in the street the next morning.

But that night Hashem stormed into the room, almost breaking the door. 'I love, therefore I am,' he declared. The friends shared looks of astonishment. What he'd said was a paraphrase of a quote their philosophy teacher, Mr. Abdelraziq, had attributed to the French philosopher called Descartes. The first one to bounce back with a correction was Bayumi. 'The man, you stupid fool, didn't mention anything to do with love.

He said, 'I think, therefore I am.' Meaning that, Hashem, the day you start to think, thanks to the will of God, you will be.' But Hashem stuck to his phrasing. 'I love, you sons of bitches. Therefore I am.' 'Who do you love now, kiddo?' Emad asked him. 'Which maid did you trick this time?' 'I love Amal,' Hashem replied. His audience traded looks of astonishment once again, and Emad threw down the biology book that was in his hand. 'And who is this Amal?' he asked. 'Lieutenant Sir,' Hashem replied quietly. Everyone was stunned, and the news struck their host like a thunderbolt. How had Hashem made contact with her? And how had he moved on from the company of servants to that of the one with the green beret, the proud rich girl?

Hashem told them that he had been following her for three months as she walked back from school, and that he'd started to send her fiery love notes with one of the maids. In the notes, he would swear he didn't sleep a wink at night and couldn't focus on his studies. He begged her to take pity on him, since his only sin was that he loved her, as God was his witness, sincerely and purely. In the final note, he invited her to have their first meeting on Tuesday evening at the Delta train. Hashem paused to whet their appetites before continuing. 'What do you think about this - she turned up last night at the set time. She came with her maid, can you believe it?' Bayumi was the first to emerge from the shock. 'We're done for. There won't be any more *baklava* or *basbusa*.' Everyone laughed apart from Medhat, whose heart ignited with jealousy, a tear poised to spring from his eye. Amal reminded him of Ibtisam and how he'd waited for her every morning at Abbas Square without daring to approach. She also reminded him of the Friday morning perfume seller who he only ever came near in his dreams. He was excused in those days because of his young age. Now, he had no excuse. Hashem was two years older than him, but this difference wasn't enough to justify his own weakness and failure. When would he possess the necessary courage? How would he ever succeed with someone from the opposite sex? When and how would his first adventure happen? He couldn't compete with Hashem - he wasn't a footballer and couldn't lift himself up on the parallel bars. How could he compete with muscles?

The next day, Bayumi turned up.

'What do you think?' he asked Medhat.

'About what?'

'About this love story business? So Amal's been snatched from our hands. What will we do?'

'Only God can help you - the guy with the muscles got her.'

'So we're not destined to come out with anything?'

'Wait till we go to Cairo. We'll meet girls at university and life will be sweet.'

'Look,' Bayumi said, after a moment of silence. 'There's no love for us in this city. We can only grasp at a few snatched moments.'

'What do you mean?'

'I mean… swear to God you won't tell anyone.'

'Tell me, don't worry.'

'Look, two weeks ago I was invited to a wedding in the suburbs of Zagazig. And at the end of the evening, the house was packed with guests who needed to spend the night there. The hosts were poor farmers who wanted to show me their generosity. They gave me a sofa to sleep on. The room was full of children, and bedding was laid down on the floor for them. The only other people there were me and a newlywed girl - she'd only been married six months - who was sleeping on the floor. It was deathly hot and I couldn't sleep. I put my leg out in the dark - I was stretching. My leg touched the girl's thigh, but I swear to God Almighty I didn't mean anything by it. Then I found her grabbing hold of my leg and pulling it. In the blink of an eye, I found myself tumbling from the sofa onto her, and then, listen to this, it was like I was riding a filly galloping as she pushed me up then pulled me down again, pushed me and pulled me. What can I say? It's driving me mad. It's enough to drive you out of your mind. But I swear to God almighty I didn't mean to do it. These are the fleeting moments you can snatch and nothing more. No "hello" or "how do you do". Just pouncing, right away, and then galloping - no love or anything. But since then, I haven't been able to sleep.'

'Why are you so upset? Who can find a girl to gallop with?'

'You don't get it. The girl's family are my relatives. They trust me. Can you imagine - the women there kiss my hands because they think I'm blessed, a man of learning. That's why they put me in the same room as the girl without a second thought. And then what do I do? But the other thing that's bothering me is that, the morning after, the girl acted as if she didn't even know me.'

'What else do you want? Do you want love and romance and friendship? The girl is married. Did you want her to bring shame on herself or what?'

'No. I understand her situation, and there was no chance for us to meet again. But I wanted...I mean, we were sitting having breakfast the next day. She was talking to everyone but me. Not even a single word, or a glance...as if I wasn't there. She should have at least said goodbye when I was leaving. Or am I just a....'

'Yep, you're just a...screw you.'

***

He smiled when he saw the welcome party that awaited him at the country road. The geese clapped their wings and the dogs barked, excited by the bike that was chasing them. A new generation of people he didn't know. The first question that popped into his mind was one he didn't dare ask - 'where's Farid?' - because he knew the answer. Two water buffalos were bathing in the canal with a child atop each. One of them was completely naked, which brought back memories of his childhood, since he used to love bathing with the buffalos. From afar, he spotted a man standing under the old sycamore that spread its branches over the waterwheel. Tall, thin, and dressed in a tattered jacket, he looked like a silhouette of a man. After lagging behind, the man approached, and he could see that it was his uncle Shabana. Shabana couldn't believe his teary eyes when he eventually recognised his nephew. 'Oh, God of the heavens! My, how you've grown, Medhat. I almost couldn't tell it was you. Don't mind me...there's a wasp buzzing around in my brain.' He understood what Shabana meant: either the opium dose hadn't yet arrived or he didn't have the money to pay for it. But Shabana's face brightened when he felt the piasters pressed into his palm. And when he asked Shabana to give him the highlights of what had happened during an absence that had stretched more than ten years, Shabana put his forefinger to his lips, signalling that talking wasn't allowed, which was also understood. But Shabana called out to his nephew before he got far. 'Hey, listen to this. Sheikh Radi bought a radio.' Then Shabana laughed. 'It's the first time the sons of Qassim have seen a radio...they've started to become civilised. But come and see me at the *jurn* before sunset and I'll tell you everything.'

Ismail, his milk-sibling, saw him approach on his bicycle and hurried into the house to tell his mother. When Na'sa came to the door and recognised her 'son,' she ululated with joy. It was his first visit since he left the village. 'Ismail has been blathering on and I couldn't make heads nor tails of it. What's going on, boy? No hope of any sense. And it turns out you've come to visit us. A thousand hellos and welcome. My darling, you've been away from us for too long.' She hugged him as she cried. 'We said it would be two or three weeks and you would come back, then you go and stay for ten years? Isn't that wrong of you, Medhat? And you stayed in Abu Kabir and didn't want to come and see us. You've had a heart of stone since the day you were born, Medhat.' As for Ismail, he hid himself away in a corner, not knowing what to do after he had completed his mission. In the past, he wouldn't have felt too intimidated to approach his 'brother' and would even have wrestled him, either out of affection or anger. But now it was clear he didn't know what to do when confronted by this stranger who wore a suit and rode a bicycle. He didn't budge from his corner until his mother told him off several times, and until Medhat went to him, shook his hand and kissed him. Ismail shook his head and smiled slyly as he punched Medhat in the shoulder to confirm that the water had returned to its original course and that everything was as it should be. 'You would really like Ismail now,' Na'sa said. 'He's a man now, as you can see, tall and broad-shouldered, and he goes out to the field.'

The village landmarks hadn't changed, except the *seera* had turned into a dump. And oh, how many of its residents had died. Nafisa had passed into God's mercy before he'd left the village. Zaki's collapse left her completely devastated. She was gone, the woman who had been a symbol of the village's heritage. He still remembered her tattoo with its three vertical lines between her bottom lip and her chin. And the golden ring that hung from her nose. And Sheikh Zaki had died - the keeper of the *seera* - after spending his last years humiliated and degraded, as Na'sa said. The older folk would throw him out if he descended on their dinner tables, and the children would march behind him, chanting and rousing his anger. He would wander and people would see him rushing about as if he had an appointment, repeating his famous phrase. '*Have mercy on an honourable person from a nation reduced to disgrace*,' they would say. In the end, they took action and had him transferred to the Abbasiya Mental Institute, the 'yellow palace'. He spent two years there among the insane, after which he returned in a devastated state to take his final breaths among family.

There was no one left to advise or preach to the people, since Sheikh Sayyid had also departed. People said that he spent his final days complaining about radiation shot at him by the gang leader, Ibrahim Abu Zaid, and this dealt the fatal blow. His death was followed closely by that of his friend and adversary, Sheikh Hamed, who was handicapped and completely blind in his final days. Luckily the Quran school was still standing, run by a young sheikh who had recently graduated from the Religious Institute of Zagazig.

'Sheikh Radi is still in good form and his trade is doing well,' Na'sa said. When Medhat asked about Salama and Zakiya, she told him they now had two 'perfect' boys. 'Medhat, pray that I live to see your children.' When Salama invited him over for dinner, Zakiya (how fat and flabby she'd become!) brought the dishes out onto the low table and everyone gathered around, including the two boys. The guest was just taking his first spoonful from the soup tureen when Salama surprised him with a question. 'So, mister, what exactly did you see in the cornfield?' His wife told him off, but then went back to say, 'You should thank him,' she said. 'If it weren't for him, you wouldn't have got me.'

As for where he would sleep, that would be at Na'sa's home. She had designated the room with the oven for him, and she and her son lay on mats on the floor in the room that faced the corral where the cow, the goat, and some chickens were kept. Staying in Na'sa's house meant that sleep would only be sporadic. Mice wandered freely, creating a racket as they raced about, nibbling and chewing. He was fully wrapped up to stop them from getting to him, yet they managed to break through his barriers. His head was exposed, and maybe they could find some kind of opening near his feet. Then there were other creatures - huge armies of fleas - which no obstacle could impede...they infiltrated his clothes and attacked every part of his body. He was astounded. Why hadn't fleas harassed him when he was a child? Or hadn't he noticed them back then? Or had he just forgotten? What had changed? Had the fleas found new and unfamiliar blood in him? Or had his luxurious life in Ismailia weakened his resistance? The mice must have been there, so how could he not remember that they'd bothered him once upon a time? Did their nightly fun get swept up into the general cacophony that seemed normal back then, like the frog's croaking that never ceased but no longer caught his attention? If he told Na'sa what had happened in the mosque of Abu Kabir, she would've laughed and no doubt responded: 'My God, you've become a true *bandar* guy, Medhat.'

His uncle Said had also died, but Haniya was still strong and full of life. How he cherished her soft and comfortable embrace when she greeted him, how he adored her large bosom. As usual, she never stopped laughing. Her two daughters had married and lived close by, and her sons were now men. Two of them had married and raised their children in the family home. 'There's nothing better than a crowd,' she would always say. When he thought about it, he realised that children in this environment were no source of worry for their families, since it wouldn't occur to anyone to send them to school. The Quran school was their academic limit, and the fields their professional domain when they were older. 'Children grow like weeds,' as Shabana would say.

In a show of generosity, Haniya had cooked corn kofta for him, but he wasn't keen on it and only took some to be polite. But she also served him something he didn't recognise at first, since she'd brought it out in a tureen filled with a white liquid that resembled milk. 'You're in luck, Medhat. Our buffalo gave birth. I hope you like the *sarsuub*.' The *sarsuub*! This was what Sheikh al-Shirbini had mentioned in his book about the shaking of the *quhoof*. The *sarsuub* met with his approval, so he finished off the tureen.

When he returned to the village of the Qassimis to spend the night in Na'sa's house again, he visited the mosque and noticed that it was in better condition than before. It had been rebuilt and refurbished in the last days of Sheikh Zaki. But the well was still there, as well as the screw pump and the bathing basin. He glanced at the casket. The carriage of the afterlife was still standing on its aging posts.

The wheels of time had turned, and the era of the corn *kofta* had lapsed. But God knows that he'd loved the *sarsuub*. In its description, Sheikh al-Shirbini had written, '*...it is milk that is combined with some of the milk released when the water buffalo gives birth which is called beestings...to which they would add some salt to adjust its taste and preserve it for their needs. So if they wanted sarsuub, they would place the milk in a large pot, pour the mismaar over it and boil the mixture on a flame, when it is* *called the mufawwar, and sarsuub'*. ...' He noticed with joy the abundance of reeds on the other side of the canal - the village children could still cross to that bank to invade the Sa'ida's land - and the hummingbird and acacia trees on this side of the canal. He visited his uncle Shabana and found him in an excellent merry mood. The man insisted that he sit and recall 'the old days' and tell him all about Marika and Salim Abu Hussein, but Medhat didn't stay long and didn't chat too freely. He was in a rush to return to Abu Kabir. And he didn't feel any desire to recall the past. Sorrow had started to sneak into his soul, and he knew no reason for it, except he had a feeling this visit to his birthplace would be his last.

He found the friends waiting impatiently for him to return. He didn't disappoint them when he turned up on his bicycle, since he told them a donkey would be there soon, bearing an ample feast of delicious food. They gathered over a bountiful dinner that Haniya had sent: a pot of stuffed cabbage topped with two chickens, as well as two pairs of pigeons. They said a prayer for Haniya. The enthusiasm showed on everyone's face apart from Hashem, who was trying to sit cross-legged on the floor, but couldn't because of the pain. 'I swear I didn't sleep a wink all night,' he groaned. Bayumi admonished him. 'Now's not the time, Sakina's son. Shut up and eat.' 'Stop playing football and focus on your studies,' Emad advised him. 'The girls are what's distracting him from his studies, not football,' Medhat said. Then silence prevailed when the lid was lifted from the pot and everyone charged in as usual. Hashem had barely finished his last mouthful when he spoke again. 'My leg hurts, you sons of bitches.' Bayumi changed the subject. 'Tell us, what's the latest with Amal.' Everything was going fine with the Lieutenant, according to Hashem. He would meet her whenever she found a plausible excuse to go out at night, for example to study with a school friend or to visit her married sister. And each time, they would profess their loyalty and devotion. 'Her sister, God bless her and prolong her life, covers for her.' 'That's what you always say to every girl at the beginning. Is the love still pure, or what?' Emad asked him. 'No, this time it's for real,' Hashem replied. 'I swear to God Almighty that I'm on my best behaviour with her.' 'Best behaviour? What a loser,' Medhat replied, critically. 'She'll end up hating you soon. She'll say to herself: "What's this sorry excuse for a man? He's not asking for a kiss or having a feel with his hand."'

***

Bayumi and Medhat lay in the shade of one of the Delta train compartments. 'There's something I didn't tell you about the Zagazig story,' Bayumi said. 'What Zagazig story?' Medhat asked him in surprise. 'The story of that damned night when I put my leg out in the dark,' Bayumi replied. He remembered what Bayumi had said and told his friend off for letting the story nest in his head. 'To be honest, my conscience is killing me, and I deserve to be beaten with a shoe,' Bayumi said. 'I mean the people putting me up are generous with me, and then I go and cheat the woman of the house and assault their daughter? That girl was their daughter after all.' His friend tried to lessen his load. 'Well, the girl was also in the wrong. She should take half the blame, or three quarters of it. You put your leg out, you didn't mean anything, and your intention was pure. So she goes and grabs it? And the family are also to blame. As if they've never heard of the sacred *hadith*: '*A man is never alone with a woman without the devil being their third.*' What if a young man and a young woman are alone in the dark? How could they let their daughter sleep in the same room as a young man like you? You said she was still a newlywed. And a young man of your age... that's a disaster waiting to happen. They basically put the fuel right next to the fire.' 'They're not to blame,' Bayumi said. 'The house was packed and they didn't know I was a criminal and a son of a bitch.' 'It was a mistake and it's happened,' the friend said, as he continued trying to make him feel better. 'I think you should ask God for forgiveness and forget the whole thing.' 'I can't forget,' Bayumi muttered.

His friends were always open about their desires and escapades. But he hid his secrets. None of them knew that he flirted with girls hesitantly and bashfully in the alleys of Abu Kabir. And what was he going to say? There was nothing for him to be proud about. Success always eluded him in any case, since his feelings were always unrequited. And he didn't tell anyone about the problem, or problems, that had preoccupied him ever since he'd heard Mr. Abdelraziq mention the man called Descartes. It was a problem related to the devil, who tricked him and made him doubt everything, including mathematics, and made him think our entire life was nothing but a dream. And it was also linked to the idea of God the Benevolent, who doesn't allow for His servants to stray and who rescues them from the grip of the evil one. So there was a struggle then between God and the devil...but God is the creator of the devil...is He responsible for evil? *One must seek refuge in God from this thought.*

Sheikh Sayyid believed the devil harassed him in the mosque. This was delusional nonsense that no one else in the village believed. But the Quran acknowledges the existence of the devil, as it acknowledges the existence of jinn, both the good kind and the evil. So when was the presence of the devil real and when was it an illusion? The devil must have interfered between Bayumi and the newlywed woman. And what was the difference between the two cases? Likewise, the subject of mathematics troubled him.... He couldn't stand doubt to be cast on the subject, which he had come to view as the most beautiful of the sciences and his favourite. In the past, he found it very difficult to understand algebra and could never come to grips with it. That was until he met Mr. Shaker, the mathematics teacher, in the arts room. The dark-skinned man from Upper Egypt became a friend because they both shared a hobby: painting. The teacher used oil paints while the student drew with gouache, and they would swap ideas and comments. One day, the student was emboldened. 'To be honest,' he said. 'I don't understand all this about x, y, and z, and how to add, subtract, multiply, or divide them.' The teacher started to explain, supporting his explanation using examples on the blackboard. From then on, he would be given some quick, extra lessons in the arts room that ended up untying the knots in his brain. And that's when he fell in love with algebra.

He never confided in his friends about other thoughts that preyed on his mind and in some cases chased away sleep, ideas that pulled him far from thoughts of girls and love and his friends - except maybe Bayumi. They were mysterious ideas that he couldn't express in any case. One day, he attracted the whole class's attention during the geography lesson and was tormented by shame. The geography teacher, Mr. Fadel, was a large man with a protruding belly and a booming voice. He never entered the classroom without a globe and a collection of maps. That day, instead of focusing the lesson on capital cities, population census records, crops, types of climates, and so on, he pushed the facts that required memorisation to one side and started to talk about the relationships between everything under the sun: the air and water currents, what happens in the subsoil, earthquakes and volcanoes. He put up a world map for the students and started to move the pointer around. Gradually, a complete image of the world began to form that was all-encompassing and explained everything. This image awed him, stirring in him a desire to name it, but he couldn't, and all he could do was shout. 'Oh God! Oh God!' Everyone turned to him and Mr. Fadel, the teacher, stopped to look at him disapprovingly. 'What happened, boy?' he asked. 'Are you going to be quiet or shall I kick you out?' 'I'm sorry, Sir,' the student said. 'I only just discovered today that geography is beautiful.' The giant smiled. 'You're right,' he said. That day he felt that true knowledge wasn't in all the details that could only be revealed if they were memorised, but it was.... What was it? An image? An idea? An equation?

What could he tell his friends? How could he explain to them how he was tormented by the constant wrestling between the lust that pulsed through his veins (which he felt in his chest and forearms) and which thrust him towards the opposite sex, and the attraction he felt to meanings and horizons that distanced him from his body and which he couldn't name? He had never experienced love in a pure form. But didn't love have to transcend the level of instinct? And how could that be? He didn't tell his friends that he'd learnt about carnal desires when he was a child. He knew about them when he used to wait for Ibtisam, and he also knew about them when he kept touching Marie Francoise on the beach (her mother was right when she prevented her from playing with him), or when he saw the British conscripts in their khaki uniforms, or when waiting for that friendly girl, the perfume seller. It felt as if she had taken him prisoner because she still often visited his dreams. Sometimes temptation seeks you and holds you captive, as in the experience of the hapless Bayumi. Or was Bayumi a fortunate fool who couldn't appreciate the blessing that had landed on him, that had pulled him towards her in the dark? Medhat felt no remorse. But he didn't understand his soul and didn't understand how to deal with it. What could he say to his friends? What could he say to anyone? Could he reveal to a single soul that he still wet his bed to this day? Could anyone understand him without telling him off or making fun?

***

After examining the x-ray, the doctor told Hashem the reason for the acute pain in his leg was that his wound hadn't been disinfected and hadn't healed properly, so part of the shin had rotted. He added that Hashem would need to be treated by cutting open the flesh and removing some of the bone (a coin-sized disk, he said), and a cast would need to be set around the leg for a month. Hashem asked if he'd be able to continue playing football afterwards, and the doctor said he had to stop playing football for at least six months after removing the cast. Hashem seemed downcast when he came to his friends with this news, but they all tried to reassure him by saying things along the lines of: 'Don't worry...forget about that damned football.' '*Every cloud has a silver lining*,' Emad said to him. 'Taking a six-month break from football so you're free to focus on your studies is wonderful and a blessing from the heavens.'

After the operation, the friends mostly gathered at the clinic around the bed where Hashem lay with his leg in the cast, and they would meet his father and siblings whenever they visited him. The man was happy because his son had such caring friends - 'Young and bright as flowers,' as he would say. 'I swear, I never had any intention to study or any of that,' the father told them once. 'We're farmers and don't know any work except the sickle, axe, and plough. Look at his siblings. These boys spend a year or two in the Quran school and then go out to the fields. Hashem is the only one who stuck with school, God bless him. And he wants to study medicine. My boy, I said to him, go to the military academy or the police academy. No way, it has to be medicine. But my boy, medicine needs good grades and lots of money. Seven years of study…that's a lifetime. But anyway, may God do what's best.' He turned to Hashem. 'But don't worry, my dear Hashem. And may God help us do what's right. Just take the cast off and forget about football. It's a dangerous sport.'

The cast was removed, and it was clear that the wound hadn't healed and was still festering. The doctor advised that the patient be sent to a hospital in Zagazig. There, they discovered the rotting had spread through the leg, and the doctors suspected the presence of cancer and suggested two solutions: either transfer the patient to a hospital in Cairo to carry out the necessary investigations and confirm the nature of the illness - which would take some time - or carry out an immediate procedure before it was too late, which was to amputate the whole leg and stop the disease from spreading. The choice was made to go with the latter. And it wasn't known who had made this decision, or whether Hashem was even consulted. But it came to his friends' knowledge that after he woke up and saw what had happened, he was filled with rage and wept for a long time.

But when they visited him after he returned from Zagazig, they found him looking revived, in good health (his cheeks were rosy), and high spirits. It seemed he'd accepted his new situation and was preparing to adapt. And he was now looking forward to university in Cairo. 'Listen,' he said. 'Promise me that when we go to Cairo, we'll live together in one apartment and we'll be brothers forever.' He was also looking forward to the resumption of his love affair in Cairo, since Amal would also go to university there and would live with her siblings in the Rawda neighbourhood.

Medhat stopped opening the window in the mornings because he no longer wanted to see the girl in the green beret. She was now his friend's girlfriend and would be his fiancé in the near future. He might see her in Cairo, but he would have to then consider her a sister. From now on, he had to learn to treat her and think about her from that perspective. Would he be able to do it? He had to try.

Then, one night, he heard a light tapping on the window. When he opened it, he found himself looking at the veiled face of a woman. All he could see were her eyes. Who could this woman be? His heart raced when she said his name. 'I need your help, Medhat,' she said. 'Can I come in?' So she knew him. He hurried to the door, feeling worried. When she lifted the veil from her face, he found Amal standing there in front of him.

She didn't look at the modest room and the chaos within it. 'Where's Hashem?' she asked. 'I haven't seen him for a while, and I'm really worried about him.' He was shocked. This was love. Here was one of the Abu Kabir girls who had the courage to search for her beloved and wasn't afraid to show it. She noticed that he wasn't about to budge, so she begged him, 'I want to see him, may God protect you.' Her wide, deep-set eyes were focused on him from beneath two large, arc-shaped eyebrows, urging him to move. This was the first time he'd ever seen her face-to-face and comprehended the extent of her feminine beauty.

They walked in silence and climbed the stairs leading to the clinic. He pointed to the room where his friend was staying, and she dashed towards it. When he went down to the street, a sadness that seemed to have been waiting for him at the building's entrance enveloped him. Amal didn't look at him, didn't utter a single word to him, and completely forgot he was there as soon as she found out where her beloved was. He'd felt pangs of jealousy when she surprised him with her visit, and now the envy burned and raged when she ignored him. It became clear that, to her, he was simply someone who could guide her to the one she loved, someone she could forget about as soon as she'd attained her goal. Here was Amal, forcefully commanding him to start taking on the role of the brother - now rather than in the future. But it was difficult for him. He still loved her, even if her visit made it clear as day she wasn't for him. Now he had to obey her orders and disappear. But he felt an overwhelming desire to weep. Why had Salem thrown him out? Why had he shown him no compassion? And would any girl ever knock on his door, which he would then open to hear her say she had come just to see him?

As soon as his friends visited him again, Hashem started hollering. 'Can you believe that Amal visited me yesterday.' He ordered 'the sons of bitches' to each find a place to sit down so they could listen to the full story. 'She was wearing a fancy *thawb al-malass* and said, 'Don't worry, Hashem,' and she held my hand....' He stopped to wipe away his tears. 'She held my hand and said, 'Don't worry, Hashem. I promise you, as God is my witness, that we'll be engaged as soon as you get your secondary certificate.' What do you think?' 'I think you need to focus all your energy on studying then,' Emad said. 'Amal will be your reward for passing your exams. Work hard,' Medhat said. 'This is a gift from the heavens,' Hashem said. 'Oh, if you'd seen her yesterday in her *thawb al-malass*....' 'Lieutenant Colonel Sir wearing a *thawb al-malass*? Wow. What a sight!' Bayumi exclaimed. 'I swear to God, I didn't recognise her when she came in,' Hashem said. 'I said, Who's this coming in? But when she lifted the veil - yes, she was wearing a face veil - what a girl! My heart took off…it turns out the school uniform is doing her an injustice. It makes her look like a little child, but when she walked in, I saw a tall and broad-shouldered woman. God is great! And when she reached out her hands to hold mine, the sleeve of the *thawb* slipped and I saw how fair her arms are… Oh, if you saw the whiteness of her arms…' He paused. 'But how did she know where I was? That's strange.' Then he sighed. 'What can I say? Ever since then, I feel like I'm dreaming. It was enough that she came and held my hand…. Tell me honestly, is there anyone in this world happier than I am? Nothing bothers me anymore. I swear, if they cut off both my legs I wouldn't care. As long as Amal's with me. I'm going to Cairo, whatever happens, and she's going to Cairo. She's going to the Faculty of Commerce and will live with her brothers, and we'll see each other…. Is there anything better than this? I swear to God Almighty that I'm going, even if they chop off both of my legs….' He stopped again. 'But this whole business with the artificial leg is annoying me…. Isn't it wrong for a pretty girl like Amal to have to take a guy with an artificial leg?' And he burst into tears.

Hashem didn't hang onto life for long after this visit. His friends would go to the clinic, and one would stay and help him study for the secondary school exam. But the deterioration began quickly: as it turned out, the cancer had broken through all the barriers and pervaded the body in such a way that no medicine could stop it. Bayumi, the poet, delivered the eulogy. 'Hashem was strong and quick-tempered, but he would be quick to offer an apology if he did wrong by someone. He didn't hold onto any bad feelings about anyone, he didn't like to hurt others, and he was loyal and compassionate towards his friends. And he was virtuous and loyal in his love for Amal. His final prosperity was nothing but one of death's deceptions in the twilight hours. The sun sends its brightest rays as it sets.'

***

Amal could no longer be seen from the window, and Emad brought them the news he'd heard from his sister: the girl had stopped her studies out of grief over Hashem. Then it was time to go to Ismailia to spend the summer holidays with Marika and uncle Salem while he waited for the results of the exam. He decided to say goodbye to Hajj Saleh and drink tea with him before he left. The man always insisted he have some tea with him. 'Mr. Medhat, you don't have to buy anything. Just come and say hello and drink tea with us.' A feeling akin to sadness overwhelmed him as he sipped the mint tea outside the *fiseekh* shop. He should have been celebrating leaving Abu Kabir and the exile Salem had chosen for him. Here he was, about to escape. Why did he find it so difficult to separate from this place of exile? Hajj Saleh was one of the best things about Abu Kabir. An undemanding man who was content with his lot in life, he might spend a day, or days even, without anyone going in his shop. He was delighted whenever he saw the student who spent a few piasters on a book now and then. They'd become friends, and now he had to say goodbye to the kind man - forever. He knew now that an image of Abu Kabir would last in his mind, wherever he ended up: al-Bursa café, the *sirja*, the train station, the telegraph office, and the Delta train. But he also knew that he would leave and never come back - just as he'd left his village. Didn't Amal tell him to withdraw, to disappear? Didn't she conceal from Hashem the fact that it was his friend who'd guided her to him?

For their final dinner together, the friends laid out a mat on the floor as usual. They ate silently, shrouded in the weight of their fourth member's absence. They were silent until Bayumi articulated what was preoccupying them: 'What a loss that Hashem isn't going to Cairo with us. What a tragedy!' They pulled their hands back from the food when Emad suddenly said he wasn't joining them in Cairo. His friends objected. 'Why, Emad?' they cried. 'I messed up the exam,' he said. 'And there's a ninety percent chance I've failed.' 'So what?' Bayumi replied. 'You can repeat the year.' 'I'm tired,' Emad replied, sounding hopeless. He was the oldest of them and the most diligent in his studies, even though that didn't stop him from stumbling repeatedly. No one knew why he'd chosen the difficult route of studying the sciences when physics and mathematics exhausted him.

Now here he was, taking his seat on the train with mixed feelings on his way to Ismailia. He was happy because he would see Marika and Salwa, but would his uncle Salem greet him any better now that he'd been gone for so long? He had vanished from sight for almost two and a half years. In her letters, Marika urged him to come back to Ismailia for the summer holidays, but he insisted on staying in Abu Kabir, preferring to suffer the boredom and the summer heat (with no parks, beaches, or any of the other benefits available in the civilised city) than to be near Salem. Was it time for reconciliation?

Bayumi suddenly appeared on the platform, panting.

'Didn't I tell you not to come?' Medhat said.

Bayumi laughed. 'Your friend has come to see you off. So what? Yes, we'll meet in Cairo, but God only knows how frightened I am.'

'Why are you afraid of Cairo?'

'I'm not afraid of Cairo. I told you about the Zagazig story.'

'Oh my God! Are we never going to hear the end of that? Do you think you're the first or last guy who's pounced on a girl? Forget about it, will you?'

'Man, you don't understand. I'm really hurt that the girl didn't give a damn about me the next day.'

'And so what?'

'You still don't understand. At night, it was like she'd handed me a glass of sweet melon juice. Then the next day she goes and pretends she doesn't even know me?'

'I think you need to forget it. Cairo will make you forget everything.'

'What can I say to you, Medhat? I've been so distraught I haven't been able to sleep. I'm frightened.'

The train started to move.

***

There was a book he'd bought from Hajj Saleh, entitled 'The Muqaddimah' by Ibn Khaldun, and it was this book that decided his fate at university. He'd wanted to join the history department until he realised from the book's first pages - which were all he read - that a knowledge of history relied on something else: the study of urbanism. He asked Mr. Abdelraziq, the philosophy teacher, what urbanism entailed, and he told him it was part of sociology. This led to him joining the sociology department in the faculty of Arts. As for Bayumi, he joined - reluctantly - the philosophy department in the same faculty. He had come from Abu Kabir with the dream of studying French literature. When he reached the university in Cairo, he discovered he wouldn't be able to join the French language department because he hadn't graduated from a French secondary school, such as a lycée. He asked which departments he could join to learn French, even as a minor subject, and was advised to join the philosophy department, so he did, out of love for the French language. The two friends would meet on an almost daily basis: either in the 'general' lectures for first-year students in the social sciences departments - sociology, philosophy, and psychology - or in the college cafeteria, or in the evening. And one evening a week, the two friends would visit one of Bayumi's colleagues, Saeed, where they would listen to classical music for the first time in their life.

On the way from Abbasiya, where they lived, to Sayyida Aisha, where Saeed lived, they discovered Cairo and classical music almost simultaneously, and became infatuated with both. During the long journey, they would gaze at the many impressive landmarks from Cairo's Islamic and modern history. They would set off from Abbasiya towards Bab al-Hadeed, then Ataba, then Bab al-Khalq, then Mohammed Ali Street with its porticoes, passing the Rifai and Sultan Hassan mosques, before reaching Sayyida Aisha. That was if they travelled in a straight line. Sometimes they would end up diverting from this route in Bab al-Khalq and would follow al-Khaleej al-Massry Street, which took them a different way towards al-Hussein. Then they would turn right into the Ghoria district, where they would find an extensive display of traditional crafts and industries: from Fez Street to Applique Street to Sugar Street to Leather-workers Street to Tentmaker Street - the roofed part of the street - then Grain Traders Street, Saddle-makers Street, and Mohammed Ali Street. From there, they would head towards the two old mosques that stood tall, like two giants guarding the entrance to Sayyida Aisha. One of the two friends knew nothing of life outside of what he'd seen in Hahia, Abu Kabir, and Zagazig, while the other knew nothing of Europe outside of what had been transplanted into a section of Ismailia, but they both found in Cairo things they'd never seen or heard. They found history present and pulsing with life. And, waiting for them at Saeed's home, they discovered Tchaikovsky, Rachmaninoff, Rimsky-Korsakov, and sounds they had never experienced but which leapt effortlessly to their hearts, as if they had known them since childhood. Whenever Bayumi listened to the opener of Rachmaninoff's Piano Concerto No. 2, he would exclaim, 'God is great!' or prostrate himself to God in gratitude, because He had honoured him with one of His miracles, allowing someone who had come from the heart of the countryside to understand the music of the Russians.

Three sources of infatuation - a passion for Cairo, for classical music, and for Najwa - made it seem that Bayumi had forgotten about the incident in Zagazig, that long and pitch-black night when he fell into the devil's snare - and the ensuing humiliation.

Najwa was the one who made the first move with him. The students in the philosophy department lecture hall were split into roughly three sections. In the front rows were the upper-class children who had graduated from French schools and some Lebanese students who spoke French. In the back rows were a minority who constituted, in Bayumi's opinion, some of the gruff country bumpkins, the *quhoof* like him, as well as some older students (some were married and had children) who had left al-Azhar, preferring a university education. These kept hailing questions down on the professors, either out of merit or pretension. And between the front and back rows were a mix of Cairo locals who belonged mainly to the middle and lower classes and who generally didn't like to attract attention. While the students in the front debated with the French professor about the set text, 'Carmen' by Prosper Merimee, the rest of the students would choose to stay silent. But as soon as the focus shifted to philosophy, the students in the back rows would emerge and steal the spotlight.

Towards the end of the academic year, one rural student, the poet, rose out of the back rows and entered discussions with the professor in French that was proficient, although not totally devoid of an obvious Arabic accent. Everyone's eyes turned to him when he suggested a comparison between Carmen the gypsy and Colomba the Corsican (a character who appears in another of the author's novellas), saying that he felt Merimee was drawn to strong female characters (in that they overshadowed the male characters) and rough, primitive environments where jealousy and vengeance prevailed. He claimed that these were all signs of the Arab influences that had then engulfed the Mediterranean world. When the professor asked what had prompted that theory, Bayumi went on to explain. 'Carmen is Spanish, isn't she? And the art of lamenting and listing the virtues of the dead in funerals, as it's described in 'Colomba,' is similar to what women do on these occasions in the countryside where we're from.' Bayumi didn't stop at Merimee, but turned to Shakespeare, since the English poet himself wasn't immune to these influences in his play, 'Othello'. 'Haven't you noticed that the soldier Don Jose, the hero of 'Carmen', murders the woman he loves out of love and jealousy?' he asked. 'And that Othello, the barbaric warrior from North Africa, kills his wife for the same reasons? Isn't it clear that Othello is from the same legacy as Tareq ibn Ziyad?'

Until then, the country boy had been isolated even from the people occupying the back rows, except from the al-Azhar graduates. He used to tease them for not being able to compose poetry, despite having studied the science of prosody and rhyme, and because they weren't proficient in grammar, even though they had studied Ibn Malik's rhymed book of Arabic grammar, al-Alfiya. They would enjoy his sarcastic remarks because they also liked to make fun of the institution of al-Azhar and its students. And it seemed that the rural boy's move to the forefront - through his command of French rather than in the physical sense - attracted Najwa, the upper-class girl and lycée graduate, prompting her to go over to where he was sitting, far at the back, and seek him out - 'a delicate butterfly that flutters in the Spring sun' as he used to say. She pursued him because he had a strong presence in the philosophy lessons (he would debate with the professors and they would praise what he had written in his coursework). More importantly, he used to jot down the lectures in shorthand, then copy them out word for word in such neat handwriting it looked as if it had been printed. Initially, the notebooks he lent to the 'butterfly' were the connecting link between them. Then their conversations developed and lengthened when she began to show him some of her prose poems and to ask his opinion. He would give her some of his poems as gifts - short pieces of virtuous flirtation that were suggestive but indirectly so - and she would praise them. And if she noticed that she was the object of the flirtation, she would blush and say, 'Merci.'

She became the star of his poetry, and she seemed pleased with his flattery. When they were in their second year at university, he suggested they meet in the 'Tea Island' inside the zoo near the university to discuss her whole 'collection', as he put it, and she accepted his invitation 'with great pleasure'. It seemed to him the perfect opportunity - since there were geese swimming on the lake and the hummingbird trees had lowered their branches into the water - to 'raise the relationship a notch', as he said.

He suggested they meet in the city centre and maybe catch an afternoon film. But oh, how his hopes were dashed when the girl rejected his invitation 'with many thanks' because her family, as she said, expected her to go back home as soon as her lectures were over. Yet this made him extol the girl's 'virtues' and the attention she paid to upholding 'good behaviour'. And he decided to be satisfied by the innocent conversations they had in the lecture hall or in the university cafeteria and to leave time for love 'to simmer slowly'. But after that rejected invitation, Najwa started to avoid him. She no longer went over to him to borrow his notebooks or to show him her prose poems. He would say hello to her when he saw her with her university friends, and she would either respond with a quick nod or not at all. One day, she looked the other way when he greeted her, and he saw her girlfriends laughing. On the last day of the academic year, he saw her sitting in a convertible car being driven by a Lebanese student with a gold chain around his neck.

Medhat laughed when his friend told him the news. 'So why are you upset? You don't have a car or a gold necklace.'

'But how can she go out with that milksop?' Bayumi said, disapprovingly.

'Don't take it so seriously. She's a spoilt, pretty girl who thinks a lot of herself.'

'So you think it's like when Shawqi said:

'By calling her beautiful they made her vain
since beautiful women are deceived by praise.'

'That's it. You nailed it. Maybe she's playing with him a little like she played with you.'

Bayumi's tone changed. 'But are people's hearts toys?'

Then he started to imagine that Najwa and her colleagues were whispering and making him the butt of their jokes whenever he walked by. He started to complain that the students he lived with knew what had happened and were also mocking him - as soon as he turned his back he would hear their malicious laughter. But he also claimed that they - he realised belatedly - were scheming and plotting against him. His grumbling would sometimes blend scorn and confrontation. 'Don't worry, you can see they're just a bunch of little kids,' he would jeer. He started to point and laugh at Najwa, calling her 'Madame Carmen'. His friend wasn't surprised when one day, on their way to Sayyida Aisha, Bayumi scornfully declared that Carmen was a bitch who tricked him after she had given herself to him. It was a passing comment, and his friend thought Bayumi was just joking. But Najwa and Carmen had become his main preoccupation, especially on the journey home from Sayyida Aisha to Abbasiya after midnight.

'Merimee really is an intelligent writer,' he would say, for example.

'Why, Bayumi?'

'Remember when the Corporal Don José saw Carmen for the first time?'

'Yes.'

'When the poor man saw the gypsy girl, you knew it was over. His fate had been decided.'

'Don't exaggerate, man. Be reasonable.'

The conversation stopped, but it was picked up again after a long leg of the journey.

'As for that Shakespeare! He was an English genius who understood it all.'

'How?'

'I mean, take the play 'Othello', for example. Othello is

a barbaric man from the Maghreb, a man who doesn't know anything but fighting, advancing, and retreating. So they go and marry him off to a beautiful white girl from Venetian high society. This marriage meant it was the end of him.'

'The man was crazy. Who kills their wife because of a handkerchief she loses?'

'You don't understand,' Bayumi shouted, angrily. 'If Othello had been a European man, he might not have cared, even if he was sure his wife was cheating on him. He could've swallowed the humiliation. Or said to himself: Sweet! She's cheating on me? I can cheat on her, too. But the poor guy who'd come over from North Africa - meaning he was an Arab with blood that boils like yours or mine or Tareq ibn Ziyad's and '*The enemy is in front of you and the sea behind*' - he couldn't cope. For him, this handkerchief is love and it's honour and it's the appearance of Carmen the gypsy in the life of the poor soldier.'

And he cited a verse of poetry by al-Mutanabbi.

'Honour isn't safe from harm
Until blood is shed on its sides.'

'Don't make a big deal of it, Bayumi. Desdemona didn't cheat on Othello so there would be honour and blood. He was a man who went mad from blind jealousy.'

But Bayumi would ignore his friend's objection and might continue until they reached the outskirts of Abbasiya.

'I mean, I never went near Najwa. She's the one who came to me. And she's the one who started talking and being friendly…'

And the associations might start rolling out. 'I mean, the girl I told you about, in Zagazig, she's the one who grabbed hold of my leg.'

'Bayumi, be honest now. You did touch her with the tips of your toes.'

'I swear to God Almighty I didn't mean a thing,' he said in protest. 'So what if I touched her with the tips of my toes? Does that mean she should grab my leg? She could've waited to see what was what. She could've pretended to be asleep and let the matter slide. She's the one who started. Okay, fine. Then the next day she goes and acts as if we don't know each other? That's why I'm afraid....'

'Come on, man, what are you afraid of? You're driving me mad. Of hellfire, you mean?'

'No, not just that.'

'Then what?'

'In case that simple movement that took place by chance in the dark is....'

His friend interrupted him, laughing. '...is Desdemona's handkerchief and is Carmen's appearance in the life of Don Jose. That'll be the end of us all.'

Bayumi woke up one day in the middle of the afternoon, agitated and aggressive. He attacked one of his flatmates and brandished a knife in the face of another who came to break up the fight. All four gathered and beat him until their hands grew weary. He was treated using electroshock therapy, and the treatment was more efficient than necessary. His agitation was over, replaced by absolute serenity and total inertia, so that Bayumi was no longer able to concentrate or continue his studies. It was as if his mind had decided to withdraw and fold into itself. He returned to Hahia to die amongst his family. They said he'd suffered a brain haemorrhage.

They had been four in Abu Kabir, all dreaming of going off to Cairo together. But Hashem left the world before leaving Abu

Kabir; Emad languished there after deciding to cut short his studies, once he'd lost hope in succeeding; and Bayumi wasn't in Cairo for long before he went back to Hahia and found his final resting place. So the beads of the necklace were scattered, with most of the members of the group falling to one side or another until none of the four dreamers were left but one, and that one continued to seek refuge in Tchaikovsky as if it were alcohol.

The Sign

In the absolute stillness of the night, a spaceship wades, soundlessly, its engines mute. Suddenly a telescope is lowered with eyes directed towards the planet called Earth. The spaceship wants to explore these terrestrial organisms called humans. What does it see? As soon as the first images appear, the engines roar and the red lights switch on. From the central processor, a husky voice emerges: 'I am incapable of handling this data.' The spaceship is you; its body swimming in space is your body; the eyes of the telescope are your eyes; and you are an alien, travelling from outer space, wanting to explore the conditions of Earth. The stillness is absolute, apart from the rustle of the wind over your metallic body. What do you see? I see a quiver in the night sky like the swift glow of lightning. And then look what happens. These naked bodies - some of them fall on top of others, then their thighs meet and then they attach. What's happening? And what's the news? I don't understand anything. The equipment will explode if this strange behaviour continues. It isn't familiar with these customs. Why are some of these beings riding the others? And what is the meaning of these sounds that are a jumble of meowing, barking, braying, neighing, clamour, hissing, cooing, and laughter that resembles weeping? Or is it weeping that resembles laughter? I can't be sure. After a while the images - the same images - begin to appear repulsive. Did I not tell you that the residents of this planet are nothing but dogs or despicable monkeys? Then the rumbling and whinnying intensifies. But the overwhelming uproar does not conceal the distant sound of a man whispering, 'Open up your flower's calyx to me because I am the lustful bee.'

Then signs of comprehension begin to materialize. Look how the cheek falls on the cheek and the lip grazes the lip and the leg twists around the leg and the body becomes intimate with the body. Who is the fool who refuses to join this gathering? If this is *tabazzuk* then take me with you, immerse me amongst you, thrust me between you…

Medhat woke up soaked in sweat and panting. He had been roused by his own cries, *'Take me with you…'*

Karima rushed over to check on him. 'Is everything okay, Dad? Do you need something?'

'It's all right, darling. I was just dreaming.'

'I was asleep. I thought I heard you screaming.'

'It was just a silly dream. Go back to sleep. Or bring me a glass of water.'

When Karima went back to her room beside her father's, she didn't drop off until she could hear him snoring.

The following morning was a Friday, and the family gathered around the breakfast table. The *ful*, falafel, white cheese, black olives, and pickles were all laid out just as they used to be when the 'dearly departed woman' was alive. And even though the eldest daughter, Fathiya, had married and was now living in her own home, she and her husband Ezzat still kept up the tradition of spending Fridays in her father's apartment. Sometimes the journey would begin on a Thursday night and the couple would spend the night there. But this time, Ezzat hadn't stayed over because he had gone to Qalyub and would be joining them for lunch after Friday prayers. Fathiya and Karima were determined to prepare a rich lunch - ducks and stuffed pigeons and more - so the father and his son-in-law would find a lavish buffet when they returned from their prayers.

They were dipping pieces of bread into the plate of *ful* when Medhat cleared his throat and dropped his bombshell.

'I've decided to travel.'

Their hands fell from their mouths and their mouths stopped chewing. Then Karima, the youngest daughter, spoke: 'Where to, exactly?'

Medhat started to talk, but Fathiya interrupted him.

'To Mecca, God willing. So you've finally decided to perform the *hajj*.'

'No,' Medhat replied firmly. 'I'm going to Vienna.'

Karima was about to speak but he gestured for her to stay quiet.

'The subject's closed. I couldn't consider travelling to Vienna when your mother was alive, but since she passed into God's mercy, I've been tired and depressed and in need of a change of scenery.'

'You'll travel and leave us on our own?' Karima asked.

'Leave you on your own? What do you mean? Are you still little children?' Medhat replied, bitterly. 'And you've got auntie Marika with you,' he said as he gestured toward Marika. 'What's the problem?' He turned to Marika and spoke to her in Greek. 'Isn't that so, my darling?'

Marika nodded in agreement.

'As you wish, Dad,' Karima said, grudgingly. 'How many days will you be gone?'

When he told them he would be gone for a month, the girl's eyes filled with tears, but she kept on repeating, 'As you wish, Dad.'

Medhat wouldn't let her tears weaken his resolve. Silence prevailed, so he thought the matter was settled, but Karima confronted him again.

'But why Vienna? Why don't you go to Alexandria for a change of scenery?'

'Or Ras al-Bar,' Fathiya added.

'That's a great idea,' Karima said, after she had seemed to relent. 'And Dad, what if we all came with you?'

Suddenly Medhat felt at a loss. He couldn't approach this argument until he'd thought of an ingenious idea. He cleared his throat and spoke meekly.

'You know, kids, your mother and I spent some time in Vienna....' He stopped so he could pray for God to house their late mother in His vast heavens, then he continued. 'I had just been recently employed as Third Secretary at the embassy. We were young. The four years we spent in Vienna were the most beautiful years of our lives. Now I want to go back to the country where we spent our finest days. I want to see the same places and the same streets....'

The meeting was adjourned, and Medhat sat on his own, congratulating himself on his shrewd performance. It was an inspired idea. Until Fathiya's voice drifted over to him from where she was sitting by the kitchen door, plucking the drake's feathers, as she parodied a song by Asmahan:

'Merry nights of Vienna...
Vienna, a garden of paradise.'

It was clear she hadn't been persuaded about her father's trip to the Austrian capital. He himself wasn't entirely sure of the secret behind choosing Vienna from all the cities where he'd lived, European or otherwise. The topic was raised again around the lunch table, and the debate raged, this time with Fathiya's husband Ezzat joining in, until Marika settled the discussion.

'Do you think you're still little kids? Let your father go relax for a bit, and I'll be here with you.'

***

There was a prolonged period of silence in the lounge after Karima withdrew to her bedroom. Marika was sitting in the corner near the window with her head lowered and her palms pressed together. She still tied a blue scarf around her head that slipped back a little to reveal a sliver of hair at the front - exactly as she'd done in the past, except that her hair was now grey. It seemed there was nothing left to say. The matter of travelling to Vienna had been settled, and he was waiting impatiently for morning so he could buy the plane ticket. He'd decided to grasp the opportunity and travel as soon as possible. Marika, who was past seventy, was still the strong woman he'd known as a child. If it hadn't been for her, he wouldn't have left his birthplace, and he might have lived and died without seeing Cairo, let alone visiting the European capitals. He felt as though he owed her everything. Thanks to her, he'd gone to school, then university. She was also the one who inspired his love of reading as a child, and she was the one who placed Salem's inheritance in his hands, enabling him to retire early and to free himself for the only work he loved and that suited him. And here she was, standing by him once again to ease the way for him to travel to Vienna. She'd colluded with him and stood firmly beside him, even though she knew he was being hypocritical when he claimed he was going to Vienna to reminisce about his happy days with the 'dearly departed woman'.

Finally, she broke the silence and addressed him in Greek. 'To be honest, I'm not happy about this trip.' Her voice flowed over from the corner in which she was sitting, and it left Medhat shocked. 'But this morning you backed me when I said I wanted to go abroad. What happened?' 'I supported you in front of your daughters. I was only hiding the fact that I disagreed temporarily…until I could see you on your own.' He asked why she was against it. 'Because I'm afraid you'll get lost there,' she replied. 'I'm worried you'll leave and you won't come back, or that you'll come back with a calamity.' He laughed as if he knew what she was hinting at, but he still asked her to elaborate. 'You need to know that I've never felt safe in the slightest when it came to you,' she said. 'I was always afraid of losing you.' Medhat laughed again. 'How can you say that, Marika?' 'At the end of the day,' she replied, 'you're not my son. I took you from your family, uprooted you, and I was always worried you wouldn't take to life in Ismailia in the house of a Greek woman, and that you'd decide to go back to your village. When I was raising you, I suffered in the same way a real mother would. As a child, you always came down with one illness or another - I stayed up late into the night so many times because of you. And I was always panicking that you would catch something fatal. Salem hated having you there in his home, and he hated how attached I was to you. In his eyes, you were an intruder. I was always frightened that he would throw you out, until he really did send you away. And the whole time you were with me, you'd get lost so easily. If you ever went out on an errand when you were young, you would always come back hours later, no matter how simple it was. Sometimes you wouldn't come back till the afternoon, or at the end of the day. Isn't that right? And I'd wait desperately for you to come home until it nearly drove me mad with worry. Do you understand me now?' 'I understand,' he replied. 'And I wanted you to marry Salwa,' she continued. 'Salwa was the one who chose you for me. She was the one who guided you to me. Don't you remember? I saw her walking over, and the two of you were holding hands. That's why my heart leaned towards you, and it was then that I got the idea of taking you back with me to Ismailia. And you know the rest.' She shook her head as she continued in what sounded like a lament. 'I wanted you to marry her. There was a long love affair between you - and don't think I didn't know what you were doing. She worshipped you. But you abandoned her and married Saniya against my wishes, and then Saniya captured you. She hated me because she knew I despised her - she crushed you for twenty years. Were they twenty years? I can't remember anymore. I was worried she would finish you off, and she nearly did finish you off, isn't that true?' 'Yes, you're absolutely right. But what's that got to do with travelling to Vienna?' 'I just explained it to you. Why won't you understand?' she said, sighing. 'You don't want to understand. Fine, do whatever you want. Who am I to stand in your way? But come back to us. Come back safe. I want you to be near me for the little time I have left.'

He asked what she meant about coming back safely. 'What could happen to me in Vienna?' She answered immediately, as though she'd already prepared the response. 'I'm worried you might go and never come back, or you might bring back an Austrian wife.' He laughed. 'I have no intention of marrying an Austrian woman or a woman from any other country. But what's wrong with marrying an Austrian, anyway?' 'I'm against mixed marriages,' Marika said, firmly. His laughter turned into a guffaw. 'How can you say that - you, the Greek woman who married Salem the Egyptian?' She raised her head proudly. 'I'm an exceptional case. I was born in Egypt, I was raised here, and I never dreamed - and in fact my parents never dreamed - of going back to Greece. Egypt was our homeland. We Greeks are closer to the Egyptians than any other nationality, apart from the Armenians. As for Western Europeans, they think they're the greatest people in the whole world, and they have no mercy in their hearts. If you come back with a wife from Austria or Western Europe, then you won't stay in Egypt. Sooner or later, she'll convince you to emigrate to her country, or she'll take the children with her and abandon you… trust me.'

She paused, and then it seemed as though she'd just remembered something important. 'Look at my marriage to Salem. It was also a disaster. I'll never forgive him for as long as I live for kicking you out and banishing you to Abu Kabir. And for what reason? Because you went out to protest against the British, just like the other students? How can that be?' 'That was a feeble excuse,' Medhat said. 'The real reason was that Salem….' He stopped abruptly, before continuing. 'The truth is I can understand why he did it. None of us are angels. At the end of the day, we're all human and I can put myself in his shoes. You were his final refuge after several failed marriages. Can you blame him for wanting you all to himself without anyone else in the picture? You came to him with a child from the country who'd monopolise all your attention when….' Marika interrupted. 'No, he was selfish and insensitive, so don't defend him. He couldn't understand just how much I wanted a child. There was a big age difference between us, and he'd married three women before me and didn't have any children. I was the fourth and I didn't have children. I accepted my fate, but I wanted us to have a family. And he didn't understand. As if he'd forgotten that women are born with a maternal instinct, just like a child is born ready to latch onto its mother's breast, before it even opens its eyes. So how could Salem deny my desire for a child?' 'But he only sent me away when I was in the third year of secondary school. Which means he only took me away from you for two and a half years before I would've gone to university in Cairo and left you anyway.' 'I would've preferred you to stay with me until the end of secondary school. You don't know how much I worried because you were on your own at that age, and how much I hated him for it.'

Marika paused before asking, 'And did you forget that he kicked me out of the house?' 'No, he didn't kick you out,' Medhat said. 'You got angry and decided to leave home.' 'No, he kicked me out,' she fumed. 'It was my right to get angry and threaten to leave. And he had to stop me. But he left me standing at the door, ready to go. Then he left, as if he couldn't care less whether I stayed or went. It was a kind of dismissal. I was completely content living with him when he had no money. His love was enough for me, and it was enough to be with him, no matter what the circumstances. So how could he allow himself to humiliate me to that extent?' 'You're exaggerating,' Medhat said. 'The man didn't try to humiliate you. There was a fight, and you were challenging him, so he confronted the challenge. It's normal in an argument when each side insists on their way.' 'But it wasn't a fair battle, and he knew it,' she said. 'He had the upper hand, and he knew my threats were baseless and I would have to stay and submit to his wishes. He knew I had no one and nowhere to turn. Where could I have gone?' The response was swift. 'How can you say that? You could've gone to your parents' home. And why not?' 'Do you think my parents could've stood by my side, even if they were just pretending to pressure him?" she replied. 'They couldn't do that. They relied on him for their livelihood. He brought them to Ismailia, he became my father's business partner, and he was the stronger partner. At the reconciliation gathering, my mother and father were both on Salem's side. What do you call that? 'I don't know what to say,' Medhat said, despairingly. 'You're confusing me, Marika.' 'That's called tyranny,' she said. 'That's called using all your power to defeat your opponent, no matter what the result. Do you want more proof of the tyranny?' She didn't wait for an answer. 'He agreed to keep supporting you after banishing you to Abu Kabir, so why was he tight-fisted when he could've helped you live comfortably over there? He was rich and could easily have been more generous. Isn't it shameful that he sent you only two pounds a month? Doesn't that mean he was humiliating you like he humiliated me? Isn't that tyranny? Didn't you know my heart was breaking during those two and a half years whenever I thought of how you must be living? I would think about it day and night.'

He couldn't find anything to say in defence of Salem when it came to the hardship he'd caused him in Abu Kabir. 'When he did what he did, he ruined everything,' Marika continued. 'Something inside me snapped. And, in this case, what broke couldn't be fixed again. I could've forgiven him if I'd felt secure with him. But when I saw what he was capable of, I didn't feel safe anymore. If he could abandon me once, then he could do it again. I started to live in fear of him, especially after my parents died, and a person can't be in love with a person they're scared of, even if they pretend to be content.' 'He was angry,' Medhat argued. 'Jealousy blinded him, but it was a lover's jealousy.' 'Love has its season, or seasons, that later vanish as if they'd never been,' she replied, bitterly. 'My love for Salem weakened when the maternal instinct took over my body. Then the love disappeared completely when he deprived me of you. And as if that wasn't enough for him, he pushed you into that miserable marriage. He was the one who landed you in Saniya's clutches, and the clutches of her sly father. The only thing that kept us together was the fact that we lived under one roof. I became lonelier when he fell ill. During those years, he started to act like a frightened child. I had to force him to take his medicine, and he would cry. I'd have to force open his jaws to give him his medicine. Do you know why he was scared?' Medhat shook his head. 'He knew I hated him,' she said. 'And he was afraid I would poison him. Can you imagine?!' 'How do you know that?' he asked her. 'One day, when he was sick, his family came to visit him. They gathered around his bed, and I left them to go to the kitchen. When I came back, I heard him complaining, just before I went in, that Marika wants to poison him. Even then, he clung to life and didn't want to die.' For a moment, she stopped talking. 'He's not the only man who was frightened that his wife would poison him,' he said. She asked him what he meant. 'Nothing,' he replied. She began to talk again in a low voice. 'His was a long and bitter battle with death. He started to try to appease me in various ways, as if he'd live longer if he kept me happy. Everything collapsed when he died. I found myself totally cut off, or 'torn from a tree,' as you say in Egypt. You were the only thing I had left in the entire world, so I came to you.' She lifted a handkerchief to her eyes as she spoke. 'And here you are now, wanting to leave.'

When the dawn prayer was called in the neighbourhood, Marika looked at her watch. 'It's time to sleep,' she said. 'What you said has stolen all the sleep from my eyes,' Medhat replied. 'Should I assume, from what you've been saying, that I have to cancel my trip?' 'I can't stop you from doing what you want. You do need a change of scenery, after the ordeal you suffered. So go to Vienna then.' Before she left, she stopped again. 'You know the story of Our Lady Mary. She had a fiancé - Joseph the carpenter - but she didn't marry him, and she fell pregnant with Jesus when she was a virgin…. She was destined to be a mother when she was still a virgin, but she was also destined to be a mother from the day she was born. So what is the significance of this story? I know your faith is weak.' He tried to protest, but she interrupted him. 'I'm not asking you to believe the story - believe it or don't believe it, that's your business - but you need to understand its significance.' She went to explain. 'It means that the role of the woman doesn't end with the sexual relationship. By nature, she's a woman first and foremost. That's what the story wants to say to the believers and the non-believers, and that's what Salem didn't understand, so do you understand now?'

She suddenly changed the subject. 'But why Vienna especially?' she asked. 'You've lived in plenty of cities, so why not go to Paris, or Munich, or Budapest, for example?' He didn't reply, because he didn't know the secret behind why he'd chosen Vienna. After Marika had left him on his own, he was smiling as he mused, 'Those Greeks! They're extremists. They haven't changed since Homeric times. They're ruthless when it comes to love or hatred. And everything has to have a tragic dimension.' Then another thought popped into his mind, which was that Salem and Marika's story would be a good topic for a novel.

***

He stood in Stefan Square, opposite the cathedral, contemplating the pigeons that peered out of the gaps in the church walls and swaggered on its ledges. The morning breeze rippled, and he sighed deeply. Here he was, safe and sound.... He had escaped. The square was almost empty of passersby this early in the morning. It was Saturday, and the locals were still asleep. He circled the cathedral twice. Marika was right to worry about him getting lost...and how easy it would be to lose one's way. Love is fleeting, like she'd said. It couldn't have been easy for her, when her feelings for her first and last love began to dissipate. Everything heads towards oblivion - this was a truth he recalled whenever he remembered his childhood in the village of the Qassimis. The signs of extinction could be seen back then, including the deterioration of the *seera*.... No longer would passing guests be hosted there, or travellers who found themselves there at nightfall, or the poets who recited the old epics. It had deteriorated with time because those who were responsible for its upkeep had died, the last of them being his grandmother Zainab and his 'uncle' Zaki.

Zaki was the last one to confront the signs of demise until he became insane. There was no one left in the village who had known people like Na'sa and Husniya the gypsy in their childhood, or Atiya the vegetable seller. The candy-floss seller didn't pass by anymore, and his uncle Shabana had died. They all vanished, and so too did their myths. It seemed that no one from the current generation of the sons of Qassim even remembered Saddina. 'Do you remember the story of Saddina?' he would ask whenever he met one of them in Cairo. 'Saddina who?' would be the response, and he would reply, 'Saddina who married Abu Jad.' The phrase wouldn't elicit a single reaction, which was a shame. When he was young, everyone in the village knew the story. Nafisa used to tell it sitting on her doorstep. She believed all the details of the tale as it had been passed down through successive generations. His uncle Shabana had memorised an entire song and would sing it in the neighbourhood *jurn* when he was captive to his intoxication, even if he did doubt some of the events recounted in the story. It seemed he was the only one from the village of the Qassimis who still clung to fragments of the story of the beautiful, oppressed woman who was forced to marry a man she didn't love. Maybe Saddina's plight remained rooted in his memory because he himself had married a woman he didn't love, even though he'd done it willingly. Few can understand what a tragedy it is for a person - or for anything found on the face of the Earth, and even for the Earth itself - to have a deadly stream of poison permeate one's entire being. A slow-acting poison but an effective one, a poison called Time. It is what runs through the joints of the cathedral's solid stones and in the rippling morning breeze. It is the shackle from which no being can break free. It is a current - is it a current? - that arrives in a wave with the tide dragging events. Then it recedes and casts them all out like refuse, into an abysmal pit called the past, from which nothing can be recovered. It retreats, collapses, and disappears forever, as if it never had been. The past is the rubbish tip, the void. Sadly, a great deal ends up in the heap: the majority of the events, and perhaps the most significant ones.

He contemplated the secrets people conceal in their hearts when they die, and how only fragments of past experiences survive to be recorded in history: some remnants (in the best cases), some documents, some memories and stories prone to doubt. It was a miserable form of knowledge, and he had to content himself with snippets of information, news, and ruins, and none of it came close to what was lost and tossed into the terrible black hole. Most people feel bitterness towards the end. Few are happy when death approaches. Most people feel, at that point, that they have been cheated and robbed of their rights. They know they will end up in that abyss, and that there will be nothing left of them. Only some hermits and saints welcome death calmly, because they solved the problem right from the start, when they chose to depart from worldly pleasures and adornments. They decided to die while they were still alive, out of love for God. As for him, he was intent on life and attached to it...like his uncle Salem.

He glanced at his watch. What was the reason for their objection to worldly pleasures and adornments? There was nothing wrong with those, apart from their fleeting nature. From here, the other life would seem to them an everlasting bliss, an infinite and improved extension to worldly life. But when would the cafés open so he could drink a cup of coffee that might drive out these bothersome thoughts? Wasn't it ironic that he would seek help from Time - begging it to speed up - after he had blamed it for everything, as though he didn't realise it was deducting from his life with every hour that passed? He told himself he couldn't take the route of the hermits and the saints. Since enjoyment or happiness was what everyone wanted, then he would be satisfied with living in the present, regardless of its disadvantages. Wasn't it better for him to live hour by hour and day after day, taking whatever pleasures were available to him, despite the slow-streaming poison? Marika claimed that sex wasn't everything...but she'd had her fill of sex, and plenty of opportunity for love. He knew nothing but deprivation....

All he knew of a woman's love was from Salwa's kisses. Saniya only ever offered him her lips grudgingly. She hated kissing and wasn't good at it, which eventually turned him off it. She made him forget that the mouth had functions beyond simply biting, chewing, and grinding, that the meeting of lip to lip could sometimes be a vow. She hadn't acknowledged him in the way a lover acknowledges another lover. So was it fair for him to leave this world empty-handed, bar a handful of kisses, some of them sweet and some bitter?

When the coffee was finally served, he continued to engage in contemplating how lucky he actually was. Despite everything, he had married and become a father. His eldest daughter was married and the younger one would be on her way to university soon. He had performed his duty towards the 'dearly departed' wife one way or another - free of any love or desire - and had practiced the patience of Job with his lot in life. He was very fortunate, because usually the woman ends up inheriting from the man after having destroyed him. But he was one of a few wondrous exceptions. Here he was, having escaped safe and sound. Without falling victim to diabetes, high blood pressure, or heart disease. How did that happen when he'd been susceptible to all these diseases throughout his married life? The only illnesses he'd caught since age seventeen were passing colds and a duodenal ulcer that he'd developed during his marriage to Saniya and was now cured of, forever he hoped. He'd also published a number of novels and enjoyed a certain amount of fame, despite everything, and could now enjoy early retirement, at the age of forty-five, since he had no manager or subordinates, and no promotions to wait for or regret when they passed, and that was all thanks to Marika.

The wave of contentment receded, to be followed by a surge of sadness and gloom, triggered by thoughts of how a woman inherits a man's fortune. When Marika came from Ismailia to live with him, she'd already arranged for him to inherit from Salem. But when she was sitting in the corner of the lounge before he went to Vienna, she had skipped certain details, making it seem as though Salem's inheritance had descended on him from the heavens, or had been handed to him willingly by Salem. She didn't mention how, during his final prolonged illness, Salem used to try to please her in any possible way so she wouldn't lace his food or drink with poison. And so he'd decided - whether of his own accord or urged by a suggestion from her? - to leave her everything, even though his siblings had rights over his inheritance since he never had children. She must have directed or pressured him, because he left everything to her in such a roundabout way that his siblings wouldn't be able to challenge in court, which was to 'sell' all his possessions to the intruder she'd dragged over from the countryside. The lawyers ensured that the sales contract was completely secure from a legal perspective. So was it Time that cheated people, or were they all cheating each other? Who would've believed that Salem's belongings would devolve to the young, orphaned stranger Marika had picked up from his village? It was as if Salem had predicted this on the day he returned to his house to find the young stranger in his bed and called out in annoyance, 'Who is this? What's this calamity you've brought back?' Smiling, he took a sip of coffee. Neither Salem nor his wife ever knew he'd heard him say this at the time, and that he still remembered it to this day, because he hadn't been sleeping deeply. It was true that his arrival at Salem's house was a great calamity that had befallen the man, since this intruding child would monopolise his wife's attention and eventually his possessions, in accordance to a deceitful sales contract, even if it was totally secure from a legal perspective. Could there ever be a more repulsive form of irony? Now, he found himself filthy rich without having made any effort towards that end. And Marika had come to live with him, and was now in his mercy, because he owned everything. She had wanted to run off with Salem's money, so she and the wealth ended up in the hands of the intruding child. Was this the reason she was worried he would go to Vienna and not come back, or that he would return with a wife who would compete with her over him, and who might take everything? He was now his own master, and there was no one to hold him to account. Wasn't his mere presence in front of these tall towers and the gentle, peaceful pigeons a blessing that no one could put a price on? It may be a blessing but a poisonous one.... Thanks to it, he had been able to retire early and to free himself for writing - which was a luxury not many people in Egypt could attain - and to spend the rest of his life independent, wealthy, and at leisure. But this blessing weighed on him. When he was asked to sign the 'sales' contract, he did it with a trembling hand - he couldn't believe what was happening because the inheritance had come to him in such a twisted manner that perhaps he didn't deserve it. May God bestow a good day upon you, Mr. Ali Abdelazim, wherever you are, and you've probably left this life and world already. The teacher, who was from Cairo, enjoyed degrading his students from the countryside, or those who resembled them, and he would sometimes conclude his lesson by chanting the famous verse of poetry:

'Lower your head, for you are a Numairi,
Neither Kaab nor Kilab have you attained.'

But the students didn't enjoy anything as much as they enjoyed the teacher's satire, and they looked forward to that moment when he would veer away from teaching and find some reason or other to practice his favourite hobby. He would often recite the first half of that verse and leave a choir of students to respond with the second. If only you could rise from your grave now, Sir, and see your student, Medhat, outside the St. Stephen's Cathedral in the heart of the Austrian capital, you wouldn't believe your eyes and might think you were dreaming. Your student miraculously escaped death and, to this day, he doesn't understand how he managed to slip away. All the circumstances surrounding his birth had pointed to his demise. Only God knows how Na'sa had managed to bring him out of his mother's belly. That must have been a miracle to top all miracles, in light of what he'd witnessed during one day of her work as a midwife. He remembered how he'd stood at the door of the birthing room, watching as Na'sa struggled to ease the foetus from its mother's womb. It was a difficult birth because the baby slithered and slipped from her hands whenever she tried to grab it. He'd seen her going to the stove when she was out of options and rubbing its black ashes over her palms to make them rougher. At the time, he had no idea what was going on, but he now believed that celebrating life was a duty. So why had he set his sights on Vienna, out of all the cities he'd come to know? Maybe there was a clue in the Asmahan song about Vienna. Love vanishes, as Marika said, and everything was headed towards oblivion, but the solution wasn't to depart from the world as the monks and saints do. Years of his life had been squandered on marriage, so now he had to spend what was left enjoying everything that life had to offer before he reached his end. He must have come to Vienna to eradicate the feeling of deprivation that had become ingrained in him. He must have come here in search of love and happiness. Filling his eyes with the sight of the girls of Vienna, with their skinny waists, would be his cure, and he would quench his thirst on their bodies. Saniya was slim when he first proposed to her. Their elderly neighbour used to always praise her when she saw her. 'Look how slender she is! Like a princess!' she would exclaim. But after barely three years of marriage, she started to put on weight and, as the years passed, she lost her former shape. But the crisis had begun right from the start, since bodies communicate in their own language…and, between their bodies, there was no communication. He had returned to battle the ghost of the 'dearly departed' and defeat it. He wanted to cheat on her and to take his revenge, since he'd failed at that when she was alive.

He ordered a second cup of coffee and a slice of gateau topped with a mountain of whipped cream. If the elderly people of Vienna devoured - as he was now seeing - such gateaux, then why should he deny himself this beautiful indulgence? Saniya had shunned all Austrian foods apart from desserts. Her favourite dessert was the Sachertorte. They were sitting in a café one day on the ground floor of an old hotel, famous for baking this traditional tart. When the waitress came to their table, he ordered two slices of Sachertorte and smiled as he asked her to be generous with the cream on the side, and to sprinkle some cocoa powder on the cappuccino. Though the requests may have responded to Saniya's desires, they resulted in her glancing askance at him. 'What's wrong, my darling?' he asked her. 'I know you've got wandering eyes,' she replied. He knew immediately what she meant. She was upset because he'd been friendly with the waitress. And what had added fuel to the fire, from her perspective, was that he'd spoken to the waitress in German, a language she hated him learning, even though he had lied and solemnly swore that German was essential to his work.

He lowered his head dutifully when he spoke: 'I swear that I'm honest and faithful.'

'Yes, honest and faithful because I'm watching you. Because I know you don't fear God.'

'May God forgive you. God knows I've done nothing wrong.'

'I can see you staring at them when we walk down the street. Or do you think I'm stupid?'

'God forbid I accuse you of stupidity, but you forget that you're the most beautiful woman in my eyes.'

She lowered her eyes as she took a bite of the delicious tart and yielded to the sweetness of flattery. But she quickly came out of her daze and widened her eyes. 'Stop it with the sweet talk, Medhat. I don't believe any of this.'

She was perceptive. It was true he was constantly cheating on her with his eyes. It was what they called adultery of the eyes. And now that she was gone, and it was time to be liberated from her constant monitoring, had he really escaped? His body was healthy, but what was the point of good health if you were crushed on the inside, if you could find no cure for yourself except through sexual intercourse? Wasn't that the very core of despair? While he was married, he'd managed to produce several literary works, but other projects of his had never materialized.

Did he have enough life left in him to make up for these losses before the privileges of youth were withdrawn? Would he be able to make up for lost time and write the great novel that would propel him to the top of the literary chain? Would he find someone to love, who would make him forget his prolonged deprivation? There were a multitude of questions that put him off the tart and the piles of cream. He stopped eating in disgust.

***

It was sunny, and the cathedral square was crowded and raucous, with a carnival underway. He was sitting in a café watching the magicians, dancers, clowns, and the men and women twirling hoops. A man was moving a dummy that looked like Louis Armstrong, and Louis was singing, 'Isn't This a Lovely Day?' It was a lovely day indeed. He was familiar with Vienna's biting cold, and how the icy nights penetrated the bones and the soul. If Time had generously provided a radiant day like this, then it was a priceless gift. There were also the male statues - Napoleon with his palm pressed to his chest, Charlie Chaplin with his hat and stick, and a musician whose hand held a bow over a violin, and so on - men standing on platforms in different costumes with painted faces, totally still and unblinking. They wouldn't move until someone from the audience gave them money, or if a child went up to them, at which point life would suddenly beat into the statue, who would move slowly and methodically. He would express his thanks one way or another, maybe by leaning towards the person who had given him the money and lifting his hat, or by allowing his photo to be taken with the child who had approached him in lieu of the parents.

The carnival came to an end for him when he walked off in search of a restaurant for lunch. But he stopped to join a crowd of people that had gathered around someone singing. He edged his way through the rows of people until he was facing the singer - a young woman singing in a language he didn't recognise and couldn't place on the map. It wasn't German of course, and it wasn't a language descended from Latin. Could it be Russian? Out of the question. He didn't know any Russian, but he'd be able to recognise it if he heard it. It was odd how the girl's voice, as she sang along to the accordion, made her audience deeply regret that they couldn't understand the lyrics. Her singing seemed to have drifted in from afar and was so sentimental, sorrowful, and piercing that it made people wish they knew what she was saying. Yet, despite their ignorance, they still responded and took off with her to that distant place. The girl stood facing a stand that held a musical score, but she wasn't looking at it. Instead, her eyes were directed towards the sky. Her voice emanated from the heart. He leaned towards one of the people listening and whispered, 'What language is that?' 'Serbo-Croatian,' the man replied. 'But she's not looking at the sheet music,' he said. 'She's blind,' the man replied. Blind? And singing this skilfully? Why not? Who says that eyes are necessary for music? Yet if a blind musician was as talented as this - if they were able to entertain people who could see - wouldn't they feel deprived? Wouldn't they feel that they were giving without receiving anything?

From that very moment - a moment of elation achieved through the singing - he couldn't bear his loneliness anymore. It was as if a force had shifted within him that had been dormant until it was roused by the girl's distant voice emanating from bottomless depths. Why was he feeling sad now when he'd been overwhelmed with joy as he listened to the blind singer?

And why did he feel that Vienna was aggravating him, and that he was aggravating it, even though just a short while ago the music had whet his appetite? He no longer knew what to do with himself or where to go. The evening brought with it a chill, as though the day hadn't known any sun, light, or joy, and as though the carnival had happened in an age gone by, as though Louis's celebration of the loveliness of the day had been a fleeting dream.

He hadn't walked down Kirtner Street for long when he came across a girl playing the *nay* flute, so he stopped for a moment before moving on. Around a hundred metres down from the *nay* player, he came across a man playing the clarinet. The tune was truly beautiful, but after listening to that 'crazy' clarinettist, he didn't want to surrender once again to the magic of music. When he finally passed by a bearded man playing the accordion, his resistance crumbled. He thought he recognised the melody. He joined a group of people out of curiosity and, after a while, a young man and woman stepped forward and started dancing to the music. They had been sitting with their arms wrapped around each other on a wooden bench in the middle of the street when suddenly they stood up, without warning, and started to dance to the melody. A tango tune. It was a tango then! He stood, flabbergasted. Tango music had plucked at his heartstrings as a child and awakened in him a new awareness of the world. But what he was seeing and hearing now was so different from the tango of the song 'Oh, Rose Of My Imagination' by Farid al-Atrash - a delicate and intimate address to the flower. This was a sharp dance, with a quick tempo, where the male dancer would become entangled with the female in an act that resembled sexual courtship. The female dancer either flirted with the male or rejected him, but he wrestled with her in a physical battle until he defeated her - he tamed her so that she loosened her chains - and she threw herself onto his chest and wrapped her leg around his, then leaned back on his forearm until it seemed that her hair would touch the ground, as though in that position she were saying: 'I am yours.' The music was stunning in both cases. The human race should thank Argentina for the tango, which had emerged from the underbelly of the city - carrying the music of its tramps and underdogs - and which had found him when he was still a child in Ismailia. It found him now in this spot in the heart of Vienna where the couple sat together in the middle of the street. The way couples interacted in Vienna was surprising. In every European country where he'd lived, he'd observed how people in love behaved, but it seemed that in the Austrian capital the public expression of passion was unique. In London, being passionate in public places seemed to be an overwhelmingly reckless and foolish act: 'A silly guy and a silly girl twisting and pulling at each other'. In Paris, it would carry a hint of exhibitionism: 'Hey, everyone, look how agile we are and see how we've made an art form out of kissing. But in Vienna, there was tenderness and a desire to communicate by touching hands. No one disturbed the lovers, and they in turn didn't want to provoke anyone or draw anyone's attention. As if they were a pair of doves on a cathedral facade, welcoming the morning with kisses. Here he was, wandering alone in the musical street, with the melodies transporting him to a different time, a different world. When Asmahan sang, '*What remains for you of bliss but its shadow?*' she wasn't saying anything different from what Verdi had in his 'The Drinking Song' from the opera 'La Traviata': '*Let us enjoy the delight / fleeting and swift / for joy is in love / a flower that blooms and dies.*' No, and neither of them expanded on what Abu Nawwas wanted to express in his wine poems; they all equally envisioned the danger of demise. Those were his family and clan, his companions and his closest friends. He remembered the sand of the beach, the blue lake, Salwa in her swimming costume, calling for him to leave the shallow water and to follow her, and he remembered the fluency of their first kiss. His loneliness wouldn't dissipate unless he slipped between these lovers and immersed himself within them. That would be the ultimate *tabazzuk*.

***

The truth had to be told. There was a time when he really did try to cheat on his wife. She'd gone to Egypt after announcing that her father's condition had worsened and he was on the brink of death. He grasped the opportunity and performed two foolish acts. The first was that he went to the opera to watch Beethoven's 'Fidelio'. But Beethoven was a disappointment and failed to make him fall in love with opera. As for the second foolish act, that was when he met a young woman on the street and invited her in for a cup of coffee. How shocked he was when she immediately accepted his invitation. This congruity thrilled him and made him want to prolong the conversation, to carry on chatting until he reached his objective, since it was clear that she was well-mannered and pretty - somewhat - and that she was from a 'good family'. But she cut him short when she looked at her watch.

'I'm sorry to interrupt you, but I'm a working girl.'

'I'm sorry if I've made you late for your meetings,' he began apologising. 'Never mind, we can meet another time and pick up where we left off.'

She repeated that she was a 'working girl,' but he didn't grasp what she meant, so she had to explain.

'I mean that I work with men and I charge them by the hour. If you like, we can go to your hotel or you can come to my apartment in return for a fee.'

He mumbled…the message had reached him.

They arranged to go to her apartment and fixed a fee. Her condition was that the payment would be made in advance, so he paid upfront. When they reached her apartment, she darted into the bathroom. He sat on his own, trying to control the trembling that had come over him, since he'd never known a 'working girl' before, and the apparition of his wife was floating in front of his eyes. The girl was haggling with him from the other side of the bathroom door while he struggled to keep up with her, in the hopes that going along with the situation would help him control his quivering knees. 'How do you want me?' she asked. 'If you want me naked then you should know that'll cost more.' 'It makes no difference to me,' he replied. 'As you like, my love.' 'Did you say 'my love'?' she shouted, scornfully. 'Don't confuse things. We're here to do a job - business, if you like - a relationship between a seller and a buyer. Do you understand? I hope you've understood. Anyway, since you don't have any specific requests, we can finish the job in fifteen minutes max.' 'Fifteen minutes,' he protested. 'That's impossible. What's the rush?' 'That's the condition,' she said. 'But you didn't mention that condition when we negotiated the deal.' 'So now I'm telling you,' she said. 'And you can take it or leave it but remember, there's no refund.' That was how the conversation progressed. She became furious when she walked out of the bathroom and found the client had decided to flee. He heard her scream and curse as he leapt down the stairs. 'Why don't you take what's yours? You feeble, lazy idiot. You wasted my time and lost your money.'

So let him try to avoid the 'working' girls and approach the ordinary ones instead. He headed immediately to the hotel. Charity begins at home, he told himself, and here was the receptionist. She wasn't very attractive - she wore glasses and seemed guileless. But despite his reservations, he didn't really mind. The important thing was to knock on another door in Vienna.

Initially, he felt his way along with caution. 'You know, I'll be leaving your hotel the day after tomorrow to move into a furnished apartment,' he said. 'But I enjoyed staying with you.'

'We were happy to have you,' she said. 'I hope you'll come back. We're at your service.'

'Great," he said. "So when will we have dinner together?'

She laughed nervously and mumbled, 'Thank you for your kindness.'

'When does your shift end?' he asked the woman.

She told him that her shift would end at eight o'clock.

'How about that's when you come up to my room?' he suggested. 'There are drinks in the mini bar, as you know, and….'

She interrupted him. 'That's absolutely forbidden, Sir.'

'Let's go out to a café or a restaurant then,' he said.

She didn't reply, turning her back to him to look at the pigeonholes where the keys were kept. Meanwhile, the door to the hotel accountant's office opened, and the face of a thin, pale and exhausted-looking man peered out. The woman turned to face him once again.

'I'm sorry,' she said. 'We don't have any letters for you.'

The bitch was trying to change the subject in front of the

accountant. He felt his throat grow dry, and the image of the accountant's eyes behind his glasses drained all his lust. The sight was enough to put anyone off. But he told himself that this scene couldn't possibly represent Vienna.

He rushed to the cafeteria of one of the large hotels. The head waitress caught his attention. She wasn't the most beautiful one there, but she was elegant and slim in her navy blue suit with a white silk handkerchief dangling from its breast pocket. She was smiling and friendly, flitting around the customers as she greeted them, asking if they were satisfied with the service.

'I hope you liked our tea,' she said to him.

'It was wonderful,' he said.

She started to leave, so he stopped her. 'By the way, these exquisite cups, where did you get them? I mean, can I buy similar ones to take back to Egypt?'

A lengthy conversation ensued between them about the cups, until she offered to place an order for him with the supplier for however many teacups he wanted. He just had to specify the quantity, then come back to the hotel at around the same time the following week to find the cups at his disposal. She also promised to ensure that they would be wrapped up securely so as not to break during his journey. She asked to be excused for a moment and then returned.

'I inquired about the price. One cup costs ninety shillings. It's not cheap, but the cups are really beautiful, and you won't be able to buy them anywhere else because they're produced especially for the hotel. So how many cups would you like?'

He pursed his lips. 'They are expensive, indeed,' he said. 'But they're beautiful, as you say. I have to think about it for a while, even though I doubt I'll be able to resist the temptation.'

'If I were you, I wouldn't hesitate,' the woman said. 'But it's your decision.'

'I'll think about it and let you know,' he said.

Then he fell silent. He felt plagued by a heavy burden and couldn't keep the charade up any longer, so he opened up to her.

'I'm really enjoying our conversation,' he said. 'And it's impressive how willing you are to help, but I don't want to stop you from your work. What do you think about having dinner together one day?'

The young woman grinned widely. 'Thank you very much. I would've loved to, if my boyfriend weren't the jealous type, the very jealous type.'

'Don't tell him then,' he said, smiling sweetly.

'That's impossible,' she said. 'I don't hide anything from him. One day, I told him that I had dinner - just dinner - with one of the customers. You can't imagine how furious he got. I nearly lost him. Would you be happy if I lost my only love?'

What a cunning woman! Look how flirtatious she acted when she said that final sentence, almost imploringly. Woe betide you, Medhat, when it comes to the women of Vienna! How can you possibly reply to that?

His throat was starting to feel dry again, so he started mumbling.

'The truth is... in fact...there's nothing that would call for jealousy...you know that...when a person likes talking to another person...then...then he wants the conversation to go on. Isn't that right? It's just about wanting to talk and exchange ideas, nothing more.'

'I know exactly what you mean,' the woman said, as she was leaving. 'But I'm sorry. Think about the teacups anyway, and let me know when you decide.'

He looked at his watch. It was three-thirty in the afternoon. There was still time to knock on more doors. He remembered that he had an old friend who worked in the United Nations building, so he rushed over there. But before reaching his friend's office, he stopped in front of a piece of paper stuck to a door that was slightly ajar. On the paper were a few lines of poetry written in the sarcastic, slang Halamantashi style.

'Who said I was tired
or that I'm worried?
I'm gonna get me a millionaire.
And when that fellow kicks the bucket
I'll inherit and smile,
since I'll find a prince to wed.'

He knocked on the door and walked in. 'Good morning,' he said.

The woman in the office returned the greeting without raising her eyes from the computer screen. Her hair was golden, dashed with subtle red highlights, and her lips were full. As for the roundness of her buttocks and the fullness of her thighs, he'd never seen the like, except in London. If she hadn't replied to him in German, and hadn't written her poetry in German, he would've said she was an English girl.

'I like that advertisement for marriage,' he said, causing her to look up briefly before she carried on tapping away on the keys.

'What can we do? We try to entertain ourselves.'

'Has the ad attracted any suitors?'

'Not at all. I haven't had luck.'

She was unlucky! She was beautiful, soft, and delightful. A slab of cream, a strawberry, or a combination of the two. Strawberries and cream. Oh, if you would be so kind as to sit on your uncle Medhat's lap!

'Is that even possible? This building must be full of young men who are marriage material. How can they not notice all this beauty?'

She sighed. 'If only you knew. Don't be fooled by appearances.... Everyone here is busy with promotions, levels, pay raises, benefits, savings funds, interest rates on mortgages, and personal loans. If only you could see what happens when the monthly wage slip is handed out - it's the only hour when everyone becomes excited, but what kind of excitement is this? You see them - including the young men - each one in a corner or behind their desk, armed with a calculator, engrossed in adding and subtracting, multiplying and dividing, to check that the company computer hasn't made a mistake with any detail. And the way their faces light up with pleasure is almost obscene.'

It was clear the girl was suffering from boredom and neglect in a society that cared only about money, so he cleared his throat and summoned up his courage.

'I'm a millionaire and I'm not married, or, to be precise, I'm a widower. And I'm over forty, meaning you don't have to wait long before the field is cleared for your patient prince. So what do you think?'

'What a deal!' she replied. 'Still, I hope you're not being serious.'

She looked up at his face, but she couldn't see any evidence that he was joking. Instead, she found his cross-eyed gaze focused so intently, as though he was undressing her with his eyes, that her face paled with anger, and she swore at him in English. 'Fuck off,' she spat. After that, he retraced his footsteps to the ground floor, no longer interested in seeing his friend. He had received the humiliation, and it was as cutting as a knife.

He was walking near The Augustinian Church in the early evening. As the rain started pouring, he took shelter inside the church where he spotted a young woman at the end of the entrance hall, sitting behind a small table. He greeted her as he approached, wishing her a good evening, and discovered she was selling tickets for a Mozart mass to be held in the church a week later, but no one was buying any tickets. The girl was skinny and slight, but she had delicate, sad features. Never mind! He enquired about the mass and the cost of the tickets. Then he bought a ticket to cheer up the poor girl, who he imagined would end up a spinster through her dedication to church service.

'It looks like you work long days,' he said, deciding to be kind to her.

The girl offered him a smile that he thought carried a hint of sorrow.

'I've only got half an hour left before I leave.'

'You must be tired,' he said. 'How about if I wait for you to finish work, and then we have a drink together?'

At that, terror filled the girl's face. Her lips trembled as though she'd been caught in a snowstorm. He thought she was about to cry, so he quickly left. All of a sudden, the curse that the English-looking girl had flung at him resurfaced. It jabbed deep inside him like a thorn he couldn't shift.

He slowed down when he reached the outer lobby of the metro station, trying to forget all the rejection and humiliation he'd received before going up to ground level. It seemed there could be capitalism in love, just as in economics, and that love was traded on a free market where people's prices were determined. Youthful men effortlessly attracted women, who flocked around them, and they took more love than they needed, while others suffered from romantic poverty and deprivation. The value of a person depreciated as he got older, or as his share of good looks diminished. Women flocked around the handsome young man - women either looking for marriage or temporary pleasure - and he didn't have to exert any effort, since the owner of assets received a return, and in greater measures. As for him, according to the laws of supply and demand, he couldn't expect to be treated well: an old man lacking in the looks department, who 'can rely on no one but God,' as they say in Egypt. These rules were reinforced for him when he saw a pretty girl handing out folded-up pieces of papers to passersby, printed with the words, 'An Invitation to Love'. Eager, he hurriedly unfolded the paper that had been pressed into his hands before he discovered that it carried an invitation to love Christ. That was all one gained after a day spent knocking on doors.

Scenes from his memory drifted through his mind, recalling his early childhood. He remembered how Farida had taken him, one morning, to the Sheikh Ashur sanctuary. His aunt Haniya's water buffalo was in her tenth month of pregnancy, and Haniya had sent her daughter Suaad with him and Farida to the sheikh's sanctuary, which was designated for the protection of animals, to seek the sheikh's help in protecting the pregnancy at this awkward stage. The two girls walked, and he and his dog followed them along the canal that Farida's house overlooked. They'd carried on walking for a long time and passed several villages (which in itself excited his interest and was a source of joy for his dog, since they had never been far from the village of the Salehis). The sanctuary was a mud hut encircling the sheikh's grave, lit only through a small gap in the middle of a cavity in the wall. The only thing there, apart from the square tomb, was a set of wedges hammered into the wall and a box for votive offerings that the shrine's guard was in charge of. Suaad placed a coin in the box while Farida hung the buffalo's rope on one of the wedges. With these rituals, the blessed buffalo Mabruka would, God willing, be passed into the protection of the sheikh. On their way home, they stopped to fish in the canal. Suaad was the most skilled of the three, since the fish wouldn't slip out of her hands, followed by Farida. As for him, he was distracted and a failure: he chased one fish until he saw another, at which point he would leave the first to chase the second until they both managed to slip away. Farida would laugh. 'Medhat, you silly kid. I swear you'll never catch a single fish.'

***

When he left the metro station, he didn't know where to go. Then his sight fell on a large column with hundreds of printed paper scraps stuck on it. At first, he thought they were romantic ads or invitations for fun, since there must be lonely hearts in this city. When he took a closer look at the printed scraps, he discovered that they were poems, all written by the same poet. What was curious was that they were called 'Airborne Poems,' which was a beautiful title, and many of the poems were lightweight. They were, indeed, airborne poems, and some of them drew his attention, including a poem of just a few lines.

'As you come and go, your face glows,
the smile never leaving your lips;

as if Spring were eternal and the sky knew no rain
Take then my poems - flowers
picked from the garden of my love.
My kisses, I lay on my palm and blow
so a petal may latch onto your hair
or land on your cheek.'

He shook his head. 'Never mind. This is better than what that English girl with the sharp tongue wrote.' Then the poet of the airborne poems came back to reaffirm his yearning.

'You've been passing me by since the start of Spring
and since the start of Spring I've been sending you songs.
Now, summer's approaching with its hot breath:
take care, these flowers may wilt of thirst.'

Could the poet be a shy young man, standing at the exit of the metro station, waiting for the girl he loves to walk by? Then he must be in that foyer, waiting for the right moment. Maybe the beloved would stand at the column of songs to read what he had written, and maybe then he would approach her and introduce himself. That was an odd way to get close to the person you love. But who said there had to be rigid rules to flirtation? He turned right and left to see if he could spot the love-struck poet, but the lobby had cleared, or almost cleared, of travellers, and no one appeared. Was he hiding behind one of the columns? Then let us draw him out of his hiding place. He started to peel off some of the poems - one by one - and placed them in his pocket in a way that would attract attention. But no one appeared to object to what he'd done.

How odd was the case of this poet who composed his verses, stuck them up carefully, then left them there and went, letting them dangle in the breeze. He hung them up so that passersby would read them, or take them, or trample on them, which made no difference to the poet. As though at the end of the day, it had nothing to do with him. The important thing was for the poems to be composed and available to people, and it didn't matter what happened afterwards. That is what creative artists did, one way or another; they produced their works and threw them to the wind. It's true that they hoped their work would become known and valued, but the desire for celebrity wasn't the main motivation for creativity. Creativity was a unique characteristic in a person, which formed part of their nature. Was creativity therefore an instinct, as in the case of bees, the producers of honey? That would be impossible, since creativity wasn't a blind force, and it didn't happen according to an inherited and prepared formula. The creative artist was fully aware when he produced his work, seeking its optimal form. The human being was the only animal who consciously produced works with which he transcended both his past and his present, while also transcending himself through them. In the old days, the Arabs said that the sweetest poetry was that which was most deceitful, and the saying was true. A skilful writer wasn't confined by his life experiences - even if he was writing his autobiography - but would need to lie in order to achieve the best or most splendid effect. And people would willingly accept these beautiful fibs, because creativity was part of human nature and varied according to the limits of each person's abilities. Only the greatest creative works overcame the inevitability of demise and slipped from the chains of time.

Whenever they came into existence they remained, for as long as human beings existed, and they would only vanish when the entire human race had been annihilated.

He wondered: when and how would he write the great novel? It was strange that, ever since he'd been liberated and freed himself for writing, the urge to write hadn't been powerful. Ideas and inspiration had been hailing down on him back when his nose was being pressed into the dirt, pushing him towards the pen and paper. Was he supposed to settle for just recording the things he saw and the various musings that Vienna was inspiring in him, that could potentially be turned into writing material one day? He would try.... But we don't need to rush. There was a cup that had to be drained to the dregs first.

***

The 'Airborne Poems' distracted him from his troubles momentarily, but thinking about the immortality of creative works made another sorrow surface. It reminded him of the period in which he'd written his first novel. It was during his first visit to Vienna. He'd given up Salwa's love and deserted her, but it was only a matter of weeks in Vienna before he began to feel remorse. At the time, he was living in a hotel while he looked for a suitable apartment, waiting impatiently to settle down. He thought the opportunity had come about when he found an apartment for rent in one of the nearby neighbourhoods, advertised at a reasonable rate. The landlord convinced him over the phone of its advantages, since it was only a few minutes away from the city by train and it was comfortable - the landlord's mother had lived there before she died - and the landlord offered to drive him in his car for a viewing. He immediately decided to leave the hotel, so he took his bag and settled the bill. Even though he hadn't yet visited the apartment and hadn't even wanted to live far from the city centre, he pushed his reservations aside because he wanted to settle down at any cost. But he grew anxious as soon as he saw what was being offered. The apartment consisted of a single room connected to a toilet, a shower, and a small kitchen. It was dark, and the furniture was worn. How could the owner have allowed his mother to live in such austerity? His eyes scanned the place: where was the bed? The owner pointed out that the bed wasn't actually on the floor, but attached in a vertical position, to be lowered when it was time to sleep, then be returned to its previous position. It was clear that, by doing this, the landlord was trying to create as much space as possible for sitting and moving around the apartment within the one constricted room. He decided to accept what was available, if only temporarily, but he prepared himself for a life in isolation and ended up spending the entire winter in the apartment.

After finishing work, he wouldn't go back to the apartment until he'd attended a German lesson and had an early dinner in the city. Sometimes, he would buy something to take home to eat and so he wouldn't go out again until the following morning. Darkness descended early and winter announced itself with severity as snow or rain fell from the sky. Reaching the train station, he would find three gypsy men on the platform playing the violin and singing. Though their melodies and songs were sad, they seemed to form a fitting conclusion to his time in the city and an apt prelude to the journey back to his home in the grey, dismal neighbourhood with no shop or restaurant lights to brighten his path - since there were no shops or restaurants. There was hardly a soul walking along the streets, except for an elderly person here or there leaning on a cane. The apartment was cold, the damp having settled in its walls and furniture, since the central heating was useless.

How had the old woman spent her last days in this place? He imagined her sitting in the middle of the room with a shawl over her head, using it to shield herself from the cold, fighting off sleep before it defeated her. She would just about lift her head when it would force her eyelids to droop. How had he found it in himself to isolate her in this fridge? She was obviously waiting for death. And why had he put himself in the mercy of these wretched circumstances? He now felt regret over how he had abandoned Salwa, and thought that he had must have agreed to this accommodation as a form of self-punishment. He also sensed that these surfacing feelings of remorse were merging with other emotions stirring deep inside him and propelling him towards writing.

Writing didn't call for a life of luxury, he told himself. But it might flourish with some discipline - gripping oneself firmly - and austerity. And maybe writing - writing his first novel, and what it necessitated of discipline - was part of the self-punishment. But that part of the punishment was also a door to hope. His first novel must be dedicated to Salwa. He felt implicitly, and for no clear reason, that he was writing it because of her, and for her, and he promised himself to preface the book with an honest dedication to her when it was finished. Writing the novel, in light of these circumstances, was nothing but an exaltation of her love. His walk home through the city in the early evening had been defined and designed for him; the music of the gypsies bid him farewell and handed him over to his work on the novel.

He was now sitting in the same chair the old woman had occupied, dressed in a robe, with a thick scarf around his shoulders. Sitting there all wrapped up, the white pages faced him, waiting for the work of the pen. He found himself meandering in a magnificent realm of thought. The obstacles that faced him in this space were literary ones. They were difficult but, at the same time, they acted as signs along the imaginary road that, in the end, guided him to literary solutions. They were solutions of his own invention, not inspired by any novel he'd read - or at least that was what he thought. Solutions imposed only by the necessities of the narration and aesthetic demands. Could any work better serve as atonement for his sins in wronging his sweetheart?

A novel doesn't separate from its author after its completion; it becomes independent of him during the writing of it. That's when he discovered 'the tricks of the trade,' as he laboured on, because it was the story that guided him. As he wrote the chapter or paragraph he'd stop, because the cycle he'd just completed, with which he'd initially been satisfied, now alerted him to the fact that the new addition wasn't working because it made for unexciting narrative, or read like a report that should only belong in an article. The novel spoke to him, asking: Where are the vivid scenes, the plurality of characters' perspectives, each carrying its own weight and demands? Where is the conflict, where is the drama? And how can you forget that the dialogue needs to excite interest or be evocative or revelatory? Thus it shouldn't be free of humour, paradox, or abrupt transformations that shock. As for the setting, doesn't that need to be romantic or dark or ominous? And don't forget the matter of language: the pace needs to be varied - sometimes it has to stick close to reality and use the prose of daily life, whereas other times it must be compressed, amplified, or it must soar into imaginary realms. And you must always keep the potential reader in mind, so much so that you try to invite them into the composition process. The author must leave gaps here and there that only the reader can fill.

True literary writing made use of reality, but didn't allow reality to constrain and subjugate it. It recalled the writer's remarks and observations, but it also had to bore through these into the comedic imaginary realms or hidden tragic dimensions. Reality, as it stood, beckoned beyond the visible, opening outlets to the writer that might contradict it. The skilful writer was the one who picked up on these signals or invented them.

As he writes, he experiences moments that are beyond Time itself, immortal. He loses interest in people's lives, content with the fate to which he'd finally been guided. Writing was his fate and his life's purpose. His destiny wasn't the search for adventures, whether with women or anything else, in Europe or elsewhere. He was assigned another mission that had to be carried out in the best possible way, and the task stemmed from within him and from the very essence of his life, ever since he was a child. And if his life was full of coincidences, then these coincidences were all leading to one outcome, which was not a coincidence: that he was a writer. It was by chance that he was even alive, by chance that he had gone to school, and it was chance that had led him to fall in love with reading. But writing was a necessity in his life. It was the expression of his permanent estrangement, the admission of the favour he'd been granted, and the celebration of all these happy coincidences. And he shouldn't suffer much because of his loneliness, nor should he search for any emotional or sexual fulfilment. Salwa was still there after all, and wouldn't reject him when he returned repentant, and would agree to accompany him and support him. The important thing was for him to go back with a completed novel. Indeed, the novel was dedicated from beginning to end to that red hair and velvet dress.

Some nights, a writing fever would seize him such that he wouldn't pull down his bed from its upright position until three or four in the morning. He would have to put a record on before curling up in bed. Music, as he used to say to himself, was his reward at the end of the day's work. The workday didn't end at getting into bed, because the process of composing might continue while he slept, since that was when he might add and delete elements. He might find a solution to a problem he'd faced when he was awake, or a new problem might present itself to him. He would visualise the lines and paragraphs and try to shift some of them, and they would either obey him or rebel. He was happy with his form of enslavement. Music would sometimes announce itself from behind the lines and pages - since it never left his consciousness - and an image might hover of Salwa in her swimsuit, standing between the sand, the blue sea and the sky, or sheltered in his arms from fear and sorrow. How could he have given her up?

Near the end of his university graduation year, she alerted him to the fact that it was high time he officially proposed to her. 'My family considers you my fiancé, they've never objected to us going out together, and they know we love each other. The only thing left is for the relationship to be formalised.' It was night, and they were sitting on the grass near the Ismailia Canal. 'But after the bachelor's degree, I want to leave to study at the Sorbonne,' he said. 'Great. I can go with you,' she said. 'What's the problem?' 'You know life in France isn't going to be easy for a student who has nothing,' he replied. 'I hope I'll be able to take a little money with me from my uncle Salem or from Marika. But after that, it'll all come down to how smoothly things go over there.' 'I'm prepared to live with you in France even if all we have to eat is plain bread,' she said, before she started crying. 'You're the one I love. Please don't leave me here alone.' 'Okay,' he said, trying to reassure her. 'Let's postpone it for a year. I'll travel on my own and get settled in my studies and accommodations, then I'll come back and we can get engaged and then we'll go back together.'

The idea of travelling to Paris had been brewing back when he lived in Cairo, which he found to be even grander and more beautiful than he'd ever imagined. Ismailia seemed small in comparison, let alone Abu Kabir. Its Islamic neighbourhood was magnificent, and so too were its modern quarters. In these latter parts, the capital resembled Europe, pointing to it persistently. Parts of Ismailia also resembled Europe, but Cairo was a city drenched in knowledge and culture. Cairo had a unique and individual soul that didn't try to mimic anywhere else, not even in its modern neighbourhoods. Everything was stamped with its own characteristics and it still enchanted people, as it always had, through its definition as the capital of the world, just as it had enchanted the historian Ibn Khaldun.

The high-achieving students in the sociology department believed that the greatest accolade was to be awarded a PhD in sociology from Sorbonne University, just as some of their professors had done in the past. Wasn't it natural for him to hold the same ambition when he'd been exposed to the European seduction since he was a child? Marika had raised him and taught him the language of her family. She had also taught him French at an early age, and he'd become familiar with the foreigners' neighbourhood in Ismailia and the French beach. Salem had given him access to - unbeknownst to him and in spite of himself - the many novels translated from English and French. But getting together with Salwa would pull him back to the past and close off the doors of the future. She hadn't studied at university, couldn't speak any foreign languages, and would be totally reliant on him until she adapted - that was, if she ever did adapt.

'Nonsense,' Marika said. 'You can't reject the girl because she didn't get a university degree. What's a university degree even worth? You know I stopped studying, when I'd originally planned to go to Athens University. But I pushed everything aside once your uncle Salem appeared on the horizon and was happy with the secondary school certificate.' 'My darling,' she continued, tenderly. 'When it comes to Salwa, you don't need degrees. That girl worships you, and she'll look after you and support you when you're abroad on your own, and she'll stand by you when times are tough. What's the value of a degree when compared to these qualifications? Forget about degrees, because that can be compensated for, and if it's not compensated, then love and fidelity will be enough for both of you.' But there was another consideration he was hiding and keeping quiet about, which was that having Salwa there would stop him from being able to immerse himself completely in the European adventure. The European adventure.... That was the ultimate seduction.

The strange thing was that he was aware the experience he was going through was similar to that of the main character in the novel 'Adib' by Taha Hussein, who faced the same temptation - having to choose between his wife or going on an educational mission to France. The character decided to sacrifice his life companion so he could enjoy total freedom and immerse himself in the European experience, unfettered by any obstacles. He imagined this main character had struck a deal with the devil, like Faust, and had to pay a high price. (Had Taha Hussein been thinking of the story of Faust when he wrote his novel?) Still, he'd decided to sacrifice Salwa. She had been in his arms, with her thick hair, surrendering to his embrace, warm and soft in her velvet dress, her breasts pressed against his forearms. In that position, she had felt completely at ease with him and in total surrender; she would have gladly done anything he asked. That night by the Ismailia Canal, he experienced a moment of deep conflict as he swung between the one who was resting in his arms, seeking his protection, and Europe. He was holding her close and kissing her hair while swaying slowly but steadily towards the latter option, so he decided to procrastinate. The matter was resolved when he passed the Foreign Ministry exam and joined the diplomatic college in preparation for travelling on one of the diplomatic missions. At that point, he abandoned the idea of studying at the Sorbonne. He told himself that he'd taken the wrong path when he joined the sociology department - he should have studied philosophy like his friend Bayumi - and that he wasn't suited for university in any case, but he didn't abandon the idea of giving up Salwa.

How could he have abandoned her? Her appearance was one of his life's wonderful, extraordinary coincidences. It amazed him now how everything that had taken place between them had paved the way for them to eventually come together. She was the one who'd guided him to his future, ever since she'd seen him in his village with a group of other boys, placed her hand in his, and led him to Marika. She was the one who he used to play 'house' with - that game that mimicked family life - and he would always choose her to be his wife, and she would lie in his arms. She was the one who remained in his life, even when he fell in love with others; she would fade away for a while, then re-emerge to remind him of herself and to beckon him. She was still a child, in her early teens, when she gave him a set of photos. In one of them, she was wearing her Girl Scouts uniform with the beret. In the second photo, she wore a black swimming costume, and the third photo was of her sitting on a window ledge in a loose black dress that highlighted her fair skin and the redness of her hair. She would beckon him and reaffirm her loyalty while he was oblivious, his attention always drawn to other girls. How could he have given up his childhood and boyhood sweetheart? Had the devil been with them that night by the Ismailia Canal?

***

At the end of metro line number one was a building that housed a swimming pool with all the usual facilities. He went there one Saturday and decided to benefit from all the available amenities, so he bought the most expensive ticket from the female attendant sitting behind a glass screen. After he undressed, he went down to a lower floor to find himself in a reception hall with corridors that led to each of the various facilities. Just as he opened the first door to enter that hall, he stopped, his mouth gaping wide, and then shut his crossed eye so he could focus with the good one. He passed his fingers over his eyebrows as if he were wiping off beads of sweat, even though he wasn't sweating. All the men were stark naked, and he was the only one in a swimming costume, which was in fact shorts.

He noticed immediately that he was the youngest one there. When he saw one of the men had an amputated leg and was leaning on a cane, a chill ran down his spine. Then he spotted another man dancing under the shower. The man was laughing, revealing his missing front teeth and shaking his hanging testes obscenely. He was short, had only a handful of hairs left on his head, and must have been close to eighty years old. He looked around him. Why did this beautiful place only attract the elderly? Where were the young men and women? Then he recanted: how could he ask himself these silly questions? The place was clearly only for men, and specifically men who didn't want to die. It must have been decided that no woman should have to see such things, even though that didn't solve his problem, since he hadn't come here to gaze at the animals of this forest. He started to wander around the place and to take comfort in its many advantages: a steam room, two saunas, a 'warm pool' where people could relax as they looked out at the plants that were set in the centre, a hot tub, and a cold room for those who preferred a climate that resembled the outdoors. It was a garden of paradise, but without the nymphs. So let him search for the swimming pool, where there was a chance he might find them.

From the swimming pool, he could see a row of young men and women to his right, lying down on pool loungers. None of them were swimming or talking to each other. Some of the young men were very handsome, but they paid no attention to the young women. And some of the young women were stunning, but they took no notice notice of the young men. So it seemed that people had come to this place in search of peace and relaxation. And how intriguing the Viennese people were to have created a dome of painted glass within the building, and constructed upon levels, with columns and balconies, as though it were a castle or cathedral. What was even more astonishing was the absolute silence. Where were the screams of children and the women shouting? Was it a place for exercise or for worship? He recalled an hour he'd once spent in one of Cairo's sporting clubs. The pool had been jam-packed, and there was nowhere for him to even sit since a human chain had been formed around the pool, consisting of families who had brought their lunch in the same pots in which they'd cooked the food.

When he entered the water, he found himself in the company of some children, some grey-haired elderly men, and two women of his grandmother's age. On his way back to the jungle, he opened a door and nearly bumped into a blonde woman as he walked in. She was also naked as the day she was born, so he sought refuge in God from the accursed Satan and stood flabbergasted as he faced her. Women were allowed to enter this place?! Oh, how mortifying! And they were allowed to be naked and to see these hideous bodies, both the ones who had been circumcised and the others who hadn't? She was around fifty years old and was holding a towel that didn't conceal an inch of her body, since she didn't even use it as a fig leaf. She also stopped to face him, looking him up and down, and he felt relieved that his genitals were covered. She smiled and offered him the common Viennese greeting, 'Peace and greetings to God', but he turned his head away and left.

He felt bewildered amongst the protruding bellies, the features distorted by old age, the legs that were no longer strong enough to carry their bodies, the truncated limbs, and the hands that trembled. Throwing himself into the hot tub, he closed his eyes and surrendered to the whirlpools of water that quivered over his muscles and tickled them. Oh, how ironic fate can be! When he was writing his first novel, blessed with the joy of creativity and of traversing the boundaries of time, he hadn't realised that a terrible earthquake was stirring within him, gathering its powers before it struck its sweeping blow. Because when he returned to Egypt he found Salwa had gotten married. He reeled inside from the horror of the shock, and his tears flowed between Marika's hands. 'I warned you, but you didn't listen,' she said. He told her how, in Vienna, he'd regretted deserting the girl, and how he'd promised himself to correct his mistake on his first visit back to Egypt, and now here he was, back again, but she wasn't there. 'Then you should have written to her to tell her your intentions. Why didn't you write to her? She waited a long time for you, until she lost hope. She waited for you to come back to your senses after you got a job and were in a position to marry. She waited for you to take the right step. But you left, without giving her any proof that you'd reconsidered your decision. One letter from you would have been enough to cure her of her misery. But you sheltered in silence, and she accepted the first young man to propose. You can't blame her, although I did. She should've seen this coming, but the poor girl lost hope.'

Salwa had remained in the background for many years, without taking up much of his attention. He always used to see her and, from time to time, she would remind him that she was there, one way or another. But other girls drew his focus away from her. It was as if she were a flower that grew slowly in the shadows, curling up around a femininity that developed gradually, before it revealed itself as fully bloomed. One day, she suddenly emerged from the shadows in her complete splendour. This happened at the French beach, when they were walking along the lakeshore, and he saw her jumping in and swimming in the deep waters - she was a strong swimmer - and signalling to him from a distance. She beckoned him to follow her, but he'd only dared to swim in the shallow water. She called out to him, but he stayed where he was, in his safe spot in the lake where the water only reached the lower part of his chest. So she went back to convince him to take matters firmly in hand and overcome his fear of the water. 'What's your problem, Medhat? You know how to swim, so there's nothing left but to be brave.' 'You know what swimming in the canals is like,' he replied. 'That's what I learnt in my village.' 'Do you call swimming in the canals real swimming?' she said. 'That's called splashing about. Come with me. Just give it a go.' She held his hand and saw that he was trembling, so she got out of the water and returned with an inflatable rubber ring that she carried to the deep end, and he followed her. 'I want you to let go of the ring and to float on your back,' she said. 'I want you to stay totally flat, with your arms stretched out on each side, and don't move. Don't be scared, I'm here with you.' After hesitating slightly, he obeyed her instructions and felt brave when he realised that he could float easily, so long as he stayed in that position. Then she told him to stand up in the water and hang on to the ring, which he did. 'Now, I want you to let go of the ring, but to move your legs and arms like I'm doing,' she said. He tried to copy her, but he lost his balance and was about to plunge. 'I told you to move your legs and arms and not to stop. And don't try to touch the ground with your tiptoes.' He noticed that her arm was wrapped around his waist, and found a Salwa beside him that he didn't recognise. She was no longer that thin, freckled child. He took the opportunity and planted a stolen kiss on her cheek. 'You rude boy!' she shouted at him. 'Should I complain about you to Auntie Marika?' He was forced to apologise, and they continued the swimming lesson. 'Now swim and don't be scared,' she said, when he managed to follow her instructions. 'I'm right here with you, and the ring is there if you need it.' As she started swimming, he swam alongside her unaided until they reached the shore.

There she was, having just come out of the water, a girl in the prime of her youth. They were walking, side by side, her shoulder touching his as she shook out her wet red hair. Like a filly galloping. Like she was saving her charm for him. And the black swimming costume - she liked the colour black - was stretched tight over her body. They strolled away from the shore, neither one uttering a single word, as if they knew there was something waiting for them out there. They walked along the paved path before their feet sank into the sand and they simultaneously stopped, both silent as they stood between the yellow sand, the sky, and the lake. What was waiting for them hung in the air like a bird hovering above them, swirling and eddying, until she was facing him. She moved closer and pressed against him, and it was their first kiss, and the first kiss was followed by another that was longer and deeper, to quench the thirst that erupted and intensified. He hadn't known that day that kissing could also mean a sipping of saliva and an admission of love through the path of the lips, so when and how had Salwa mastered this art? And why not? Hadn't Kierkegaard said that God granted men words, but gave women the eloquence of the kiss? And how eloquent she was! How had he abandoned her?

Salem's opinion had been different from Marika's. 'Don't let it bother you. We'll arrange for your engagement to Mr. Hussein Asaad's daughter,' he'd said. 'The girl is pretty, she's got a bachelor's degree in pharmacy, she's from a good family, and her father's a friend of mine.' 'I don't mind,' was the response. 'But you know I won't agree to get married in the traditional way. I have to know the girl before getting involved.' 'Don't worry,' Salem reassured him. 'We'll go and get to know the family. Then they'll visit us, and we'll visit them, and you can see the girl once and twice and so on. Gradually, we might be able to convince them to let you go out together, even if it's with a brother or sister of hers, to start off with at least. You know the Egyptian traditions. One step at a time. We'll take it slowly. And then God will facilitate the rest.'

They received an ostentatious welcome at Mr. Huseein Asaad's house, and an unmistakable celebratory mood immediately took hold. Saniya's mother and siblings came into the living room: two sisters and a brother. Then Saniya came in, wearing a long dress and carrying glasses of *sharbaat* rose cordial. It was obvious that the family knew the reason behind the visit and were in complete agreement. Mr. Hussein spoke first, addressing Salem. 'You know that your son, Mr. Medhat, is like our son, and you're very welcome here.' 'But shouldn't we read the *fatiha*?' the man said, after everyone had finished their *sharbaat.* As Mr. Asaad extended his hand to read the first chapter of the Quran, he glanced at Salem in surprise - didn't they agree that there wouldn't be any formal arrangement before reciprocating visits and so on? - but Salem leaned towards him and whispered, 'Put your hand out,' so there was nothing left for him to do but place his hand in Mr. Hussein's. The *fatiha* was read, and Saniya's mother stood up and let out a long, wavering ululation. Then Saniya's eldest brother brought out a camera, 'We need to take a photo.' He found himself standing in front of the camera and next to the bride, who had placed her arm on his shoulder, so he wrapped his arm around her waist out of politeness. 'Okay,' Salem said, 'May God grant a successful conclusion, but shouldn't we talk about the dowry?' Mr. Hussein's response was firm. 'What dowry are you talking about now? There shouldn't be any talk of money between respectable people. We'll get him all the furnishings for the girl, and take her right up to the house for him. Medhat is like our son.' Everything happened quickly, and he felt like he was sleepwalking through it all.

On the way home, he reminded his uncle Salem about their deal. 'Have you gone mad?' Salem replied. 'How could you go and ask for the girl's hand in marriage from her family, and base it on the condition that you go out on your own together? Would anyone agree to that?' He was stunned. Salem - who had captured Marika, whether her family liked it or not - was now accusing him of madness because he wanted to get to know - to simply get to know - the girl away from the family. He wanted to object, but he couldn't find the strength to do it. As for Marika, she objected, disapproved, and rejected the matter entirely. She said that reading the *fatiha* was nothing more than a declaration of intention, that it wasn't the final commitment, and that he could break this farcical agreement and easily withdraw. 'People change their minds after the *fatiha* - it's not a contract - and people are free.' But what she said had no impact on him. He felt both hopeless and powerless, as if he were committing suicide. If Salwa had despaired, then so had he.

He started wondering once again: had Faust, Goethe's hero, appeared to Taha Hussein when he wrote his novel? The story was an old one, but it kept renewing itself. The devil was always present and ready to strike deals. The devil had been there with Dostoyevsky in 'The Brothers Karamazov', and with Nietzsche, who constantly flirted with evil spirits despite his reclusiveness, and who lost his mind after contracting syphilis following his single visit to a brothel. And it was also there with Thomas Mann when he wrote 'Dr. Faustus', since the hero of the story, a great musician, was also a recluse, but he struck a deal with the devil and ended up infected with a similar disease and losing his mind. Had the devil been present when he and Salwa sat by the Ismailia Canal, and she begged him not to leave without her? Mephistopheles must have been there, murmuring to him and promising him everything his heart desired from the European women. If that was what had truly happened, then the devil never came through on his promise. He'd spent almost a year in Vienna without touching a single woman, and when he returned to Egypt empty-handed and didn't find his beloved awaiting him, he was struck by madness. He'd accepted an arranged marriage to an Egyptian woman in accordance to deep-rooted Egyptian traditions and to the conditions that her father imposed.

The water stopped bubbling, so he left the hot tub and moved to the sauna, where the tongues of heat lashed at the sweaty, naked bodies. It occurred to him that the image of the human body was vulgar in any form, and he remembered Sheikh Khayrat's journey from his room to the latrines and the nocturnal rats in the Abu Kabir mosque. It was a mercy from God towards humans that they - unlike monkeys - had discovered clothes. Would it be imaginable for a king to be naked while ruling his nation, or a leader running a country's affairs, or a judge sitting at a podium to implement justice, or an orator rousing people's zeal? Wouldn't seeing them coming or going like that be enough to raze all their plans? And could the naked members of the club be able to say anything of significance to each other like that? He thought of the mayhem that would erupt if these monkeys, who wandered around the place freely, suddenly started yelling and shoving each other, baring their teeth as they tussled over the blonde woman - despite how unattractive she was. And the fighting wouldn't stop until the strongest one of them emerged with flared nostrils, sharp fanged, sparks flying from his eyes. Then the opponents would scatter, and the female would succumb to the master of the herd. It would be a disgraceful sight indeed.

Saniya was the punishment handed down to him for a period of over twenty years. It was a life sentence. The first year of marriage passed relatively peacefully. He'd promised himself to sever his connections with the past, to forget Salwa, to ignore the circumstances and tricks that had surrounded his marriage, and to turn a blind eye to Mr. Hussein Asaad's scheming. At the reading of the *fatiha,* the man had completely refused to discuss the matter of the dowry. Other aspects of the story emerged after the father allowed him to go out with Saniya on their own. They'd spent an evening at an open-air restaurant near the port, drinking juice. He had placed his hand on her shoulder, and she'd quivered at his touch. The mother of the bride started to call for the period of engagement to be cut short and for the marriage contract to be signed. At that point, Mr. Hussein said he thought the dowry should be ten thousand pounds and that the groom should buy an apartment in Ismailia that would be registered in Saniya's name. His justification was that his daughter would be living in estrangement and that having an apartment in her name would guarantee her future if anything happened, 'God forbid'. So what could he do? He could cobble together the ten thousand pounds but, if he did that, he wouldn't be able to cover the cost of the flat. That's when the old fox suggested what he considered a simple solution, which was to buy a apartment that was under construction in a building whose contractor he knew. In that case, a quarter of the cost would be paid (only ten thousand pounds) with the rest to be paid in instalments over two and a half years, during which time the building would be completed. The suggestion left him perplexed. Where would he get the money? That was when Marika intervened. 'I'm against this marriage, and you have to reject the conditions that this sly man has introduced. This is your chance to pull out.' 'Why are you in a hurry?' she cried. 'You'll soon find a better bride than her. What's the problem?' Salem was opposed to this idea. 'We've already read the *fatiha*. Do you want us to go back on our word now?' Marika found this to be an opportune moment to 'back him into a corner' as she called it later. 'Then you cover the cost, Salem,' she said. 'Consider it a gift to Medhat.' Salem was at a loss and couldn't back out.

When the first child was born - a girl - Saniya started to show signs of depression, if not repulsion. What had happened? There had been preludes to this from the start. It seemed that the human body has a special sense, enabling it to distinguish the true mate from the false. It seemed that Saniya had discovered - without realising it at the start - that her husband's body was performing a role with her, while the husband's body discovered that his wife only surrendered to him grudgingly. Didn't she always object to kissing him unless he insisted? There could be no love without kissing. The first kiss Salwa had granted him near the Crocodile Lake guided one body to the other and one soul to the other, until the two bodies and souls surrendered.

Snippets of the conversation going on in the sauna floated past him, but he refused to listen. Should he blame Salem for what had happened, as Marika had? But he couldn't do that;

he couldn't accuse the man of harbouring bad intentions. He believed that Salem had changed his opinion of him once he'd sent him away and Marika was restored to him - or so it seemed. A true reconciliation had been struck between him and Salem. Salem was proud of him because he'd succeeded in his studies and had gone to university. Whenever he visited Ismailia, he would buy him the smartest clothes and shower him with money. 'Just don't tell Marika.' That was what he made him promise. And Marika would also give him money and she would say, 'But don't tell your uncle Salem.' So he became the spoilt child. The truth was that he'd loved Salem from the start, and he still loved him, even though the man had treated him harshly.

And if he did write Salem and Marika's story, he would make fear of poison the essential theme running through it, and a justifiable fear. Saniya used to always threaten him with poison. 'Don't forget that I'm a pharmaceuticals graduate,' she would often say, and he wouldn't eat anything she served him without feeling that whatever he was eating might be the last thing he ever consumed. He started to eat at home less frequently and to have his lunch anywhere near the office, contenting himself in the evening with a sandwich he prepared himself. He would pretend he wasn't really that hungry, but any sense of security completely evaporated. He began to live life constantly on edge. And now, these sons of bitches wouldn't stop making a racket. What was happening in the sauna? And what was behind all this bedlam?

As he began to tune into their conversation, he realised that this was a meeting point for veterans. There was a man dubbed 'Herr General' who was short, heavyset, and whose belly hung down over his thighs. Protruding blue veins spread over his legs, and swollen mounds protruded from his body. Even though he could barely carry himself, he was constantly restless. He would sit for two minutes before getting up to spray the heater with a scented liquid or leaving the room to fill a water bottle to spray over the hot metal because the furnace, as he would say, had cooled. He would roar, groan, and gesture with a hand that had been severed at the wrist. 'Look at this farce, Wilhelm. Have you seen this system in any other country in the world? They switch off the electricity every five minutes because they want the sauna to work according to a strict cycle. The heat starts gradually until it reaches its peak, when the faucet will open to sprinkle the blazing furnace with water, sending waves of blistering heat through the air. Then the electricity switches off and the sauna gradually cools and becomes unusable.' Then he started shouting. 'We came here to get warm, Wilhelm, not to suffer from the cold. We're too old for that, and we suffered enough of the cold in our youth on the Russian front. Is that not the case, Wilhelm? Then why do they use this silly system? And why doesn't the temperature stay stable? And what is the point of this faucet that reminds me of a dog urinating?' Wilhelm, whom the general was addressing, was a bald, skinny, and shrunken man, shaking in dread from the general's roaring, continuously uttering phrases to express his loyalty and obedience. 'You are right, Herr General. The cold is unbearable at our age, Herr General. The faucet is a farce, Herr General. Let me go out to fill the bottle and do not trouble yourself, Herr General.'

The atmosphere remained unsettled until the door opened to a young woman, wrapped in a white bath towel that extended from above her breasts to below her knees. He relaxed when he saw her. Finally, here was a woman who must be from a good family that had raised her well - a woman who respected her femininity and didn't place it on display for the villains. But what brought her to a place like this? How - when she seemed like a delicate young woman - did she bring herself among this lewd herd of animals? He was occupied with these thoughts, surrendering to the aroma of tangerines diffusing from the furnace, when he heard the voice of the general reprimanding him.

'And you, man, how could you come into the sauna wearing shorts? Do you not know that this is forbidden?'

'Is it really forbidden?' he replied, apprehensively.

The general raised his voice even louder. 'That is obvious.'

He started to take his shorts off - since he hadn't come to Vienna to argue with its people over their traditions - when the young woman challenged the general.

'Who said that being naked in the sauna was compulsory or obvious?' she asked, disapprovingly.

The general stammered a bit before responding. 'It's obvious, naturally, since clothes - any clothes - carry germs.'

The young woman replied immediately. 'Then why did you bring the towel you're sitting on? Doesn't that carry germs? And why don't you object to this towel I'm wearing? Isn't it carrying germs? Isn't it bigger than the shorts? Look.'

In the blink of an eye, she stood up and unwrapped the towel from her body. 'Look how it's crawling with germs.'

She had stripped off and oh, what a marvellous body! It was like a gleaming spark of lightning. He couldn't keep staring at her, so he lowered his gaze. Wilhelm's jaw dropped.

'Even so,' the young woman went on to say, 'I prefer to wear the bath towel, with all its germs.'

She calmly wrapped the towel around her body once again and sat down. After a period of silence, the general spoke up.

'All I wanted to say was that we came here to relax and leave everything behind and so, in that case, the sight of these shorts seems improper.'

'And was the towel improper?' the young woman asked.

The general fell silent, but the young woman wouldn't let him escape. 'This place is open to everyone, and it isn't a nudist colony, or do you think that people ought to act like a herd?'

She had spoken the truth! The general lowered his head. It seemed that Wilhelm wanted to lessen the impact of his leader's defeat, so he stood up to spray the heater with the scented liquid. Within a few seconds, the aroma of lavender dissipated into the air, but that didn't please the general, so he went back to roaring.

'I told you a million times, Wilhelm, that I do not like the smell of lavender!'

Medhat, however, liked the smell and succumbed to it, finding it relaxing after the sight of the naked young woman had ruffled him up. What was strange was that she sat down calmly and quietly after that astonishing scene, as if nothing had happened. And here he was, sitting on a higher level behind her. If he leaned over a little to the left, he would be able to see the surface of her beautiful cheek. He bent over cautiously. Her cheek looked as soft as a newborn baby's. Strands of auburn hair dangled over her delicate ear. Time's passing hadn't damaged her complexion. But let's leave Time aside and accept the blessings of the sight of the beauty still standing steadfast in the face of change. Why had she resorted to stripping naked in that discussion? What she'd said about bath towels and germs could have satisfied her. That would have been enough to refute the general and his assistant, Wilhelm. In any case, stripping bare had terrified Wilhelm. Still, the weapon to which she'd resorted had been fatal: hadn't the lethal blow defeated the general? With a weapon like that, a girl would be able to triumph in any discussion. Anyway, she'd used her weapon to defend him. And she deserved to be thanked. He was ready to greet her, with his head lowered and a suitable smile, but she - and what a shame it was! - didn't turn to him. It was as if she wanted to prove that she had supported him to defend a principle, rather than it being a gesture aimed at a specific person. May God create more people like her. She had done the right thing, even if he didn't understand why she'd stripped. And she was a nymph. So then there was a corner in this hell that was reserved for paradise. A similar nook had existed in Abu Kabir. Amal - the girl in the green beret - used to pass by his window every day, like a fresh breeze wafting through a muddy town, with its rising odours that bothered no one but him, it seemed. He used to call on the help of the Merciful to snatch him out of that sludge, until He'd relieved him in a way, sending him Amal to reduce his suffering, albeit temporarily. In Ismailia, there had also been a similar corner, but it was spacious and it had occupied the largest, greenest part of the city. And how plentiful were the nymphs there! There was always Salwa, and in the mornings Ibtisam, and the perfume seller on Fridays, Mahasen al-Helu once a year, and the foreign girls on their bicycles in their revealing shorts.

Maybe the girl with the bath towel had done the right thing, because it was only in defence of a principle. Had she turned to him, she would have deduced that he was destroyed from the inside. Saniya had wrecked him. She may have gone, but she left behind an enduring fear deep inside him. Why else would he have panicked in front of the general? He could have replied in adequate German, instead of starting to take off his shorts in unforgivable submissiveness. After Saniya, he had started to feel guilty for no clear reason. He had been subservient the whole time he'd lived with her, finding creative ways of being hypocritical in order to avoid her malice. He had become a coward and spinelessness set down deep roots in him. But in the end, he had escaped. He had bent his back against the storm until, finally, the winds had abated, and he was left standing.... He escaped thanks to his cowardice, and thanks to writing.

***

From the window, he watched as a white Mercedes pulled in and parked by the door to the building. Why was the landlord here when he should've received the monthly rent a few days ago? If he was here to give him a month's notice to leave the apartment - in accordance with their agreement - then that would be annoying and distressing. The apartment was cosy, exceptionally elegant, and it had everything he needed, including a television and music equipment. It was his, as long as he covered the maintenance costs and replaced anything that got damaged. When he first saw the apartment and liked it, Mr. Lopez, the landlord, told him that his daughter had lived there until she left to follow her boyfriend to Paris, and that she could come back at any time. That was what the father hoped would happen, because he didn't approve of their relationship. If it did happen, he'd ask him to leave the apartment, giving him enough notice to find alternative accommodation. In the meantime, they agreed on a suitable rent that he described as 'very comfortable' until that day would come. That was the basis of the agreement.

His fears were confirmed when he opened the door and Mr Lopez initiated the conversation. 'I'm sorry to disturb you, but I'm in a bit of a bind.' What bind? The man didn't seem down, and he was as elegant as always with his cashmere overcoat, his clean-shaven, scented face, and his bow tie. 'I don't want to be a burden on you,' he said. 'But I noticed that you're interested in music. So I wanted to ask whether you'd like to come to a few concerts with me.' Thank God! So there was no real problem, and there was no notice being given to leave the apartment. But what was the occasion that called for this invitation? Mr. Lopez sat down. 'I might've told you when we first met that I was once an opera singer. I studied music in Vienna and sang for a while, but then I stopped because of a throat problem. Now I'm happy to just practice for an hour a week and write reports about musical activities taking place in Vienna, which I send to the press in my country. I'm now a music journalist for some Spanish newspapers, which is why I receive lots of invitations and tickets for operas and concerts.'

'Wonderful. I'm jealous. So what's the problem?'

'I hate going to these events on my own. I used to take my wife or my daughter, but Christina moved to Paris and my wife doesn't like to go out at night anymore. But I've grown used to having someone with me. I've got to have a companion.' Then he laughed. 'For me, the evening isn't complete without dinner in a restaurant.... It's become a habit and I don't like eating alone. Is it a bad habit?'

'Not at all. It's a wonderful habit.'

Lopez rubbed his hands in rapture. 'Beautiful. So would it suit you to join me from time to time? Just to reassure you, as I said, the tickets are free. The problem is dinner.'

'I'd be happy to come with and it won't be a problem for me to pay for dinner. But my taste in music is limited, and my musical knowledge isn't as it should be.... I picked it all up in snatches.'

'In snatches? What do you mean?'

'I mean.... There's a long story behind that, and it's better that we leave it for now. All I'll say is I haven't been interested in the opera or ballet at all for several years, and I only like instrumental music, without any singing or dancing. My favourite is chamber music.'

'My dear man, how can you deny yourself the splendour of the symphony and the fireworks of the concerto? And how can you deprive yourself of the opera, where you can hear the sound of angels singing?'

'The truth is I haven't seen many operas, and I've only liked a few of them. I enjoyed 'La Traviata', for example. I also watched Beethoven's 'Fidelio', and I'm a fan of his, but I was bored. I'm sorry if you're offended by my opinion! But I can't help it. Mozart's 'Don Giovanni' was the only opera I really liked, and I've seen some of Wagner's operas, but none of them appealed to me. I'm sorry. His style just doesn't agree with me.'

'I don't blame you when it comes to 'Fidelio'. It's the only opera that Beethoven composed, and it was best that he stopped there. As for Wagner, let's put him aside, for now at least. Since you liked 'La Traviata', then in my opinion we should focus on Italian operas, the opera of splendid singing. On that note, I have some good news for you - next week, we'll go to watch Donizetti's opera, if you like, 'The Elixir of Love'. And tomorrow, Saturday, there's a chamber music concert being performed by a string quartet of amateur youth. I'm quite fond of them, and

I like to support them because they're excellent and deserve encouragement. What do you think?'

The concert started with a string quartet by Haydn followed by a quartet by Mozart. After the intermission, the band performed a third quartet, this time by Beethoven. 'What did you think?' Lopez asked him during the intermission. 'Don't they deserve to be admired? Don't forget that they're amateurs.' But Medhat couldn't respond, since he had become distracted and unable to focus ever since he'd noticed the second violinist. Where had he seen that face before? Once the musicians stood up on stage to bow to the audience and receive their applause, his distraction turned into agitation as he realised the musician was none other than the girl from the sauna. At first, he couldn't believe his eyes, but after some hesitation he was sure his eyes weren't deceiving him. Here she was, without a doubt, standing in front of him in a long black dress that revealed her shoulders, her auburn hair draped loosely over them. Her elegant black dress distracted him momentarily.

Now, his attention shifted from the music to the musician. How was her playing? How well did the orchestra play? What did he think of the music? They were questions he couldn't answer, because his attention was drawn to the movement of the arm holding the bow as it raised, lowered, tightened, and relaxed. He hoped he might get to sneak into her green room backstage at the end of the concert. But what would he say to her? And would she welcome him? Most likely, she would greet him tepidly, since she didn't know him and she hadn't turned to look at him in the sauna, even though she'd saved him from the general's grip.

He tried to wriggle out of the second invitation unsuccessfully, but Lopez wouldn't give him a chance to slip away. Yet after he'd watched 'The Elixir of Love', he was glad he went. Donizetti didn't disappoint him, and Lopez had indeed chosen well, since there were some marvellous songs in the opera, like the tenor about the furtive tear. Following that performance, he was sure he preferred the opera of beautiful songs, even if it was based on a tenuous story or was lacking in the drama of serious theatre, and the songs echoed within him for the rest of the evening. It truly was the singing of angels.

That night, they had dinner in a modest restaurant specialising in Argentinean beef. Despite its simplicity, the food was delicious: a thick steak, salad, bread, and a flask of red wine. More tantalising than the Argentinean food was Lopez's conversation about music. In fact, it was a lesson in musical appreciation on a broad scale. It seemed to him now that his long abstention from music, and how he had been restricted to one type of classical music - chamber music - was an expression of his own self shrinking and entering a state of mourning. His head was lowered as he listened to Lopez.

'Music, my dear man, is a human concern. Did you know that, in actual fact, the wonderful, varied music we hear is sound waves that cannot be seen or heard? What we hear, music in terms of melody, wouldn't exist without the existence of humans, not just because we create it, but because it needs our senses and abilities to come alive. Nature, independent of humans, is free of melody, even if it isn't free of its physical infrastructure. Therefore, we are responsible for music: it can't dispense with us, and we can't dispense with it. And if it's played, it invites us to participate in it.'

'But that applies to all types of art. The novel, for example, invites its reader to use their imagination to participate in its composition. The reader completes the work of an author by recalling the events, linking them, and filling in the gaps that the author sometimes leaves on purpose. An author doesn't reveal everything, and he relies on the reader's cooperation and complicity.'

'That's true. But music has a unique way of inviting the receiver to participate. It invites us to respond to it mainly through movement. We move towards it, or lean in, or tap with our fingers on something or other, or we hum, whistle, sing, or dance. Isn't that so? We move to its rhythm, with our hearts at least, as if we want to join it, so it might lead us, carry us, or - if it's great - soar with us. And we must prove, through movement, whether revealed or concealed, that music is an integral part of our existence, if it isn't a part of nature itself. How can anyone refuse - when we are the ones most responsible for its existence - the movement it calls for through song or dance? And how can you exclude singing and dancing from your life? You are not forced to sing or dance - that is left up to you - but, since you consider yourself a music appreciator, you must make room in your heart for those who sing and dance.'

At the end of the night, he said goodbye to his friend. 'You can count on me if your wife can't make it,' he said. 'I'll go to the opera with you or to any concert, whenever you like. You can cover the cost of the tickets, and I'll pay for dinner.' It seemed a profitable deal to him since, in addition to attending the performance, Lopez's dinner conversations about music were part of the package. It was a deal that had come to him purely through luck, effortlessly. The time had come, it seemed, to listen to someone who would talk to him about his passion. The time had come, it seemed, to understand this strange art form -

the peculiarity of existing in the world and journeying through its various locales - which fascinated him. And now he realised that, for some reason, a fascination with music had accompanied him throughout his life. He couldn't remember a time when he wasn't moved to listen to that strange language. He felt lucky because Vienna had been, and still was, the most musical of cities. There wasn't a spot in the city that wasn't influenced by music. This was a city where four of the greats had lived - Haydn, Mozart, Beethoven, and Schubert - in what resembled different rings of the same chain. Haydn - Papa Haydn - knew Mozart as a young boy and blessed him, and Mozart the man had met the young Beethoven and spotted the signs of genius in him, and it was said that when Beethoven was on his death bed, he was shown some of Schubert's pieces, and that he identified the divine spark to his music.

He began to wait for morning impatiently, so he could visit the record stores and the music bookshops. He had started to sense a bond that connected him with those four greats, because he found in their work a source of solace. The smile never left Haydn's lips, and his happiness didn't prevent the abundance of creativity. The other three knew misery like no one else, and yet they'd managed to create superior and unparalleled works. What was strange was that they'd created their greatest works near the end of their life. Rather than death's approach, and the intensity of misery, being reasons for their talents to waste away, they were an incentive for greater flourishing. When, for the first time in his life, he'd heard part of Schubert's string quintet, he felt so ecstatic he couldn't sleep a wink all night. The music had seeped through to him from the kitchen window that opened up onto the building's inner atrium, without him knowing to whom it belonged. When he investigated later, he discovered what he'd heard from the kitchen were snippets of the second movement (the slow one) and that the quintet was one of the works its composer produced only weeks before he died, whilst he was in the grip of the illness that eventually destroyed him. Despite that, along with its blazing protest and grievance, this sublime work included wonderful moments of calm, reassurance, and joy. How had Schubert done that? How did he find the language with which to defeat death? These four greats confirmed to him that outstanding artists exist on the horizon of a higher temporal state. They knew immortality, even before they died - they had attained it when they composed.

***

Music would arrive uninvited and force itself on him. What did music want from him? And what was it inviting him to? Where did the call come from: from the depths of his self, or from behind the solar array? When it played, he would forget his limited existence. That was his experience as a child, and the same thing was happening again now, when he had passed forty. Music still surprised him in every stage of his life. Yes, music had entered his life from the beginning. He recalled now how Haniya's daughters would sing to him as they carried him as an infant, coming and going between their mother in the village of the Salehis and his grandmother in the village of the Qassimis. And he recalled a night - or nights? - when he had heard the poets singing in the *seera* as he lay across Na'sa's chest, as he drifted in and out of sleep. 'That's impossible,' Na'sa had said, when he mentioned it once. 'You were on my chest breastfeeding.' Music had invaded him when he was at the French beach, in a house in Sayyida Aisha, at the train station on the outskirts of town, in the building where he lived with his wife, and on Kirtner Street. Each time, it had dragged him from his earthly existence and lifted him - then Mr. Lopez arrived to talk to him about his 'bind' and to give him lessons in classical music. Music followed him wherever he went. If it hadn't been beautiful and giving, he might have said it was pursuing him. What temptation did it see in him? And what was the truth behind this wine that outweighed the impact of any drug? Why did it travel with him as he wandered in his infinite space? What was the meaning behind the stupor that struck him whenever a melody seized him? And what was the significance of the girl from the sauna being transported to the string quartet? Why did music pay him this much attention, when he knew so little of it? Was he capable of responding to it by writing the novel? And how could that be? Writing fiction was concerned mainly with the prose of life. There were some poetic moments, true. But did the melody sometimes seep into the novel until it became a part of it? Could the novel mimic the symphony? Or could it be made of 'movements'?

This intoxication bound his life in Cairo to the beauty of the city. His long journey from Abbasiya to Sayyida Aisha with his friend Bayumi meant - as well as enjoying the sights of historic Cairo - listening to the Russian composers (especially Tchaikovsky) with their friend Saeed. It was a limited program that Saeed enforced on them, but it was perfect at the start. It was enough to seize his attention and captivate him during the entire journey from Sayyida Aisha back to Abbasiya, and he now realised it was an extension to his childhood elation with the world and his disorientation in it. That would be his lot in classical music, but that little amount was enough to last him until he travelled, for the first time, to Vienna.

In Vienna, he found music everywhere. It was there that, for the first time in his life, he acquired a record player, and there - in the first place he lived, in his cold and dreary room - that he bought his first records. Initially, they were Tchaikovsky and Rachmaninoff before he started to venture further afield. For a while, he wouldn't listen to anything but Tchaikovsky, until one day he gathered up the courage to buy a record with a violin concerto by Bach. He was amazed that the concerto - despite its strangeness, or because of its strangeness - was pleasant and beautiful in a way he didn't understand. That piece taught him he was capable of savouring more composers, so he set forth on his mission.

And it was in Vienna that he experienced - as no one else had - the evil of being denied music. One day, the wonderful sounds were silenced in his home. Saniya absolutely rejected foreign music. She refused to allow it to enter the apartment, refused even to let him have any contact with it outside, and a violent storm would erupt if he was ever seduced into approaching it himself. When their first daughter, Fathiya, started to crawl and to examine things with her fingers, her mother let her fiddle about with the record player, and that was the end of the device and some of the records. Thus, the marital nest cleared of music and its tools. No, it wasn't completely cleared, since music, as usual, found a way to reach him that the wife could neither foresee nor block. They had an elderly neighbour living on the upper floor of the building. One day, he found her gasping up the stairs, so he carried her shopping. When they reached the third-floor landing, she stopped to say, 'I think the years of our lives are like the steps of this staircase,' she said. 'After every ten steps, for example, there is a landing, and at each landing, or at the end of each decade, a person discovers - or let us say a person past middle age - they have lost one or more of their strengths, and that's how you find me after the end of my seventh decade of life. Thank you for your kindness.' He wished her a long life, so she laughed. 'I don't want to hurry up death, and I don't long for it.' She suddenly stopped laughing to add, 'But I've lost the ability to enjoy things. When I was young, I used to love men, food, and wine, in that order. But there is nothing left of that. Soup for lunch with a single glass of wine, and soup for dinner with another glass. That's all that's left.' 'And have you forgotten about music?' he asked her. She looked puzzled as she turned her head with difficulty to look at him. 'How did you know?' she asked. 'Because I hear your records,' he replied.

Every day, music travelled to him from her apartment until eight or nine in the evening. It would seep through to him from the building's inner atrium that the kitchen looked onto, and Saniya would be annoyed by this music that intruded as she cooked, or as they ate at the marble dining table in the kitchen. 'That deaf bitch,' she would complain. 'Does she have to make all that racket?' And if she saw he was listening attentively to the music, she would frown. Sometimes, she would tie a scarf around her head and complain of a headache.

The old woman wasn't deaf, but it was definitely lucky for him that her hearing worsened at each landing, since that meant she needed to turn up the volume. After the conversation on the staircase, she started to exchange greetings with him whenever they met, and she would stop to answer his questions about the music he'd heard. One day, he asked her about the music he'd heard the day before - an exceptional tune that made him stop eating as it descended from her apartment and invaded his soundscape. His soul clung to it and released itself as he grew dumbfounded and stood frozen to the spot. 'What's wrong with you?' Saniya kept asking him, but he didn't answer, as though he were suddenly deaf. He didn't stir until she screamed out. 'You obviously don't like the food!' Then the chiding began. 'I work myself to death all day in the kitchen and then you, Sir, come and tell me you don't like the food. You're like a spoilt little brat.' He would mumble, his ears still tuned to the window leading to the atrium. 'Not at all, my darling. Your cooking's delicious. Bless your hands.' The elderly neighbour told him what he'd heard the day before was Schubert's string quintet, and he timidly asked her if she could put that record on for him at ten thirty the following Sunday morning. The old woman smiled sweetly. 'Of course, Sir. You can ask for anything.' At ten thirty on Sunday mornings, Saniya always went out to the market on her own to buy Turkish and Arab food, and he stayed at home to look after their daughter. While she was gone, he could listen to the entire Schubert quintet, uninterrupted. The window to the atrium became the artery of happiness in his life.

Saniya wouldn't stop calling him a 'peasant' from a 'backwards' and 'uncivilised' culture. 'Don't your family still live in mud houses?' she would ask. 'And didn't they only recently live in tents made out of camel and goat hair?' 'You're right, my darling,' he would reply. 'But I don't know what type of hair they used.' It was best if he didn't rise to the bait. He had nothing to do with his ancestors' past practices, since he had left them, although he'd inherited their patience and perseverance. It was better if he was submissive, evasive, and existed just below the surface. It was important to maintain a clandestine resistance. She hated for the 'peasant' to be an avid reader - or writer -

and saw the acts of reading and writing as neglecting family life, a state of absence and a form of excessive selfishness. She would become furious if she found him engrossed in reading the newspaper or a book, or submerged in thought. 'How can you come back from work - meaning you're away for the entire day - and then when you're at home, you're still not here? You've got no presence here at all. Wouldn't it be better if you talked to your wife, who's been at home all day on her own?' She wanted to be his sole focus, and he would have to find creative ways to distract himself from her, even while he pretended to be interested. Her campaign to attract his attention would begin in the morning at the breakfast table, and it would pick up again as soon as the door was opened for him, when he came back from work. Saniya would be at the door, ready and waiting, and would launch her attack when he'd barely set foot inside the apartment. Was her hostility towards everything related to Western culture - apart from the Sachertorte - part of her desire to dominate him?

So there had to be an underlying layer of clandestine activity. He would wake up at three o'clock in the morning and wouldn't go back to bed until six, when he would enjoy a second burst of sleep before heading to the office. During that short wakeful period, he would sit at the dining table in the reception hall and set down on paper the ideas that had been pursuing him all day...quickly, before anyone got up. Oh, if Saniya woke up from her deep sleep and caught him red-handed, committing the crime of writing! It would be useless to protest against his fate and to curse it. This was just the turning of the wheels of time, with Saniya taking his uncle Salem's place. Salem used to forbid him from reading anything outside the academic curriculum, and now Saniya was banning him from reading, writing, and music. And once again, he was circumventing the ban, just liked he'd done when he lived with Salem, carrying out his passion in secret - stubbornly, passionately, and with an ardent hunger. He had to accept the few hours available, no matter what, and to 'be absent' whenever the opportunity for composing arose - whether he was in the office, in the metro, out in the street, or sitting beside his wife - but only in his mind, of course.

Saniya would sometimes surprise him with a question out of the blue, like, 'Why are you smiling?' He would reply with whatever came to mind, just to evade her question. Sometimes he would burst out laughing, so she would look askance at him or accuse him of madness. What could he say? Should he say, 'That's how novels are created?' He started to indulge in stealth and would publish his novels under a pseudonym, since he was sure that if a book was published with his name on the cover, it would be considered a provocative act.

He would only ever manage to listen to music through snatched opportunities in Saniya's absence - if she went out shopping, or if she was in hospital because of an illness. But the ultimate joy was when she travelled to Egypt to see her family. Life would pulse through the opera house and the music halls once again. They would call out to him, and he would hurry to them, oblivious to what he had taken or left behind. He wanted to devour everything that came his way before the jailor returned and closed the doors of mercy, bar an errant tune here or there. He rushed longingly towards music, hoping to quench his thirst. He would encourage his wife to travel. And he would just about say goodbye to her at the airport, or leave her in the hospital, before he withdrew to that forbidden pleasure. His enthusiasm for that string quintet by Schubert would never diminish, and he would travel to hear it whenever it was performed. Schubert was the decisive cure to his addiction to Tchaikovsky.

It might have been this quintet that led him to prefer chamber music to any other form of classical music. He wasn't sure about the secret of this transformation. It was restrictive, of course. Perhaps he'd discovered something in that quintet which would, to a certain extent, become a substitute for other types of music for him, since it contained protracted discourse (expansion and digression), splendid singing, and was of a clear symphonic form. Had his preference been out of some kind of mourning? Perhaps. Because within Schubert's quintet, there was a bitter grievance over the onrush of darkness, and it also contained a search for solace, and something that resembled the pursuit of a route to happiness. Why was this sorrowful music more agreeable to him than Tchaikovsky, which was also morose? And why did it lift him - despite the sadness and grievance - to a sort of reconciliation with the world, albeit momentarily? Tchaikovsky groaned and ached (the listener could almost hear him weep and wail). As for Schubert… as for Schubert.... What was the difference between one sorrow and another? He felt that Schubert's sorrows transformed, in his hands, into humanitarian and existential concerns. He would raise his grievances: the listener could almost see him lifting his face to the sky in complaint, and could almost see him, once he'd finished airing his grievances, feeling his way out of these worries, as though he were strolling or striding through the fields, wandering deep into a forest, contemplating the tops of mountains or imploring them to emerge from their silence. It was as if he were telling himself, after reaching the brink of despair, 'Let's go for a walk under the open sky, because there might be a cure in looking at the wild flowers or watching the clouds as they roam over the peaks.' Schubert reminded him of Job's grievances, reproaches, and search for solace.

***

It started to drizzle, so he opened up his umbrella and stood at the side of the road, not knowing where to go. Saniya had been edging closer to the truth when she described him as uncivilised and primitive. That was true since, in a way, he unconsciously worshipped his ancestors. He still felt the presence of his grandmother Zainab, even after she'd died, and she continued to influence his life for a long time after. He'd only known her in the first four years of his life, but for many years he had a mysterious feeling that being related to her had its advantages - of honour and privilege - that protected him and were inviolable. Any son of Zainab would come to no harm, no matter what happened. That was what he used to feel the whole time Zainab was still around. Then this immunity gradually weakened and, in the end, Zainab lifted her protection.

He walked into a music shop, greeted the young salesman, and started asking about the price of violins. He didn't intend to buy anything, but was 'flirting' with music in order to kill some time.

'Do you think someone like me could learn to play the violin?' he asked the young man.

'And why not? What's stopping you?'

'I'm past forty.'

'But you can learn. Nothing would stop you learning, so long as the motivation is there. You know the violin especially is extremely difficult, but it's possible, with hard work and perseverance.' The young man stopped momentarily, then continued, chuckling. ‘I hope you don’t get me wrong; I’m not trying to lure you into buying anything. But I have to tell you that you can learn to reach a certain level, a level where you’d be able to entertain yourself and maybe even some of your friends. Unless a miracle happens of course, since there’s room for exceptional cases. Personally, I learnt to play violin when I was a child, and I went to a music institute. But, after studying non-stop for a few years, I realised I wasn’t very talented and I couldn’t face an audience in Vienna, so I decided to quit. But I still enjoy playing, and my friends are happy with my performances. That’s enough for me.’

The young man started to show him the violins in stock, as well as the other string instruments, and he explained the advantages and difficulties of each until the customer interrupted his speech.

‘The truth is, I don’t know. I’ll think about it. But could you tell me where I can find a good Austrian restaurant to have dinner?’

The question came as a surprise to the young man, and he scratched his head in thought.

‘There’s actually an excellent restaurant near here. Its only drawback is that it’s a bit expensive.’

He started to describe how to find the restaurant. When he saw how confused his customer seemed to be, muddling up his left from his right, he took a piece of paper and wrote the name and address of the restaurant, then drew a simple map, complete with arrows. But he had barely taken a few steps towards the specific destination when he stopped in confusion at the first crossroads he reached. Did he really want to have dinner in a restaurant? That would mean sitting at a table on his own, when everyone else would be having dinner with their partners or in groups. It seemed it would be better to have dinner at home and to eat whatever he could find in the fridge. A boiled egg and a piece of cheese would suffice. But going home so early in the evening also meant confronting his loneliness. He needed a woman; it was as simple as that.

He remembered Mr. Ali Abdelazim's last lesson. The teacher was about to transfer to another school in a different town. During that final lesson, he kept teaching until the very last minute. As soon as the bell rang, he stopped and began gathering his papers as he prepared to leave.

'I would like to advise you to keep up your prayers,' he said. 'Even though I know my advice will fall on deaf ears with you country boys. Some of you don't pray at all, and the others just rush through the movements. Why? Because you're eager to get back to your abject life, a life of indulging in the fleeting pleasures of this world. I know you, country folk: a stubborn people. One of your lot would rather spend his life in the courts, battling out with his brother over two kirats of land, until they both end up bankrupt, having wasted all their money on lawyers' retainers and bribes for the bailiffs, court clerks, and orderlies. But I can't leave without advising you to care about the Arabic language, the language of the Quran, the language of the people of heaven. Most of all, I worry that Judgement Day will come and you will still be speaking ungrammatical Arabic and mixing the honourable classical language with vulgar slang. Then you won't be entitled to any intercession, because of your multitude of sins.'

He started to leave, then turned back. 'But there is one amongst you who rarely makes grammatical mistakes.'

He wandered between the rows until he stood next to him.

'The compositions you write are delightful,' he said. 'But it surprises me: how can a reprobate like you write well? But God is capable of anything.'

'I'm not a reprobate,' he said, his face flushed with embarrassment.

'Shut up. News of your scandals reaches me directly. Tell me, what happened when you saw the girl from Abdelrahim's family in the street last Friday?'

'Me, Sir? I'm innocent, I swear. They're all false accusations.'

'Tell me exactly what happened.'

One of his classmates intervened in an attempt to rescue him. 'It was the girl's fault. She was walking in the street shaking....'

'Shut up. Don't utter one more word.' The teacher turned towards the students. 'Do you see how these two reprobates try to justify disgraceful behaviour with an excuse that is even worse than the sin? The girl was walking and shaking....'

The teacher stopped, and then found no option but to use the pertinent word: 'Shaking her buttocks. So our friend couldn't resist the devil and followed her until she shouted at him and threatened to make a scene. Isn't that so?'

'I never touched her.'

'Shut up.'

He grabbed hold of his hair. 'If I weren't in a favourable position with Abdelrahim's family, because I deliver the Friday sermon and because I am the imam for the prayer, they would have killed you. So, I am warning you once and twice, never to do anything like that again. Now tell me, what makes you think God created girls to be harassed?'

The student who had tried to rescue his friend intervened again. 'If she's indecent, then she deserves everything that happens to her.'

'You have to understand something, you rural roughnecks,' the teacher said. 'Your duty is to protect girls. And you have to understand that the shaking of the bu...ttocks in the street is nothing more than a call, a call for marriage, meaning "whichever one of you is able to marry, then let him come forward to my family to ask for my hand". The call then is nothing to do with you, because your parents are still supporting you. Do you understand, Medhat?'

He nodded his head in agreement, but his eyes were tearing up, which made the teacher's heart lean a little and he patted his shoulder. 'Give me your hand and promise me.'

He had to place his hand on a copy of the Quran and swear not to harass girls and to protect them from any harm.

'You are talented, my son,' the teacher said, gently. 'Your proficiency in Arabic is a gift from God, so protect it, take good care of it, and do not obey your wretched nature.'

But he was still captive to his wretched nature. Writing made him forget his sexual obsessions and hallucinations, but only temporarily, when the shackles were loosened. If only he had married Salwa...she was suited to be the partner who would've kept him company in his deathly loneliness. As for Saniya's companionship, it fuelled his frenzy and opened the door wide to the absurd daydreams that haunted him. The strange thing was that, throughout his life, he had believed that calm conversation and gentle reproach would be useful, and that it was possible for a married couple to reconcile after arguing and exchanging cutting words, and to turn over a new leaf in their relationship. Even after an argument, he would continue addressing her - in his own mind - for a long time. He would continue the conversation in the street, at work, and in bed after she slept.

She disturbed him during the waking hours and the hours of sleep, until he would end up with a headache or feel nauseous. Why couldn't he get her out of his mind? Why couldn't he rid himself of her?

One night, she was sitting beside him, and the atmosphere was unusually calm and harmonious.

'My darling, how about we forget about what happened yesterday and the day before yesterday, and ten years ago?' he said. 'Are we going to carry on fighting for the rest of our lives? My dear, if I'm wrong, then forgive me. Give me your head and I'll kiss it. And let bygones be bygones.' Then he planted a kiss on her head.

'I swear to God, I'll never forgive you,' she said. 'Not even if it was the end of the world. You've made my life miserable. I haven't seen a single good day with you.'

Then she started crying. There was no use defending himself or explaining to her how she had wronged him or how false her accusations were. So let him try to discuss the nature of the crisis between them, since it might be possible, after some communication, for them to agree on a few solutions.

'Sometimes it seems to me that neither of us to blame,' he said. 'We should've extended the engagement period and become friends before we got married.'

She turned sharply towards him, and he noticed how her tears had disappeared as quickly as they came.

'And why didn't we do that? Whose fault was that?'

'The situation was to blame. My uncle Salem was in a hurry, and your father was in a hurry and so was your mother.'

'Are you accusing my family of chasing after you?' she shouted.

Sensing danger, he started to retreat. 'No, that's not what I meant. I meant to say that I was living abroad because of my work and everyone was in a rush, praying for God to draw the matter to a positive conclusion. That was the problem. I was to blame too, so I shouldn't clear myself of all responsibility.'

Her face paled and her lip trembled. 'Do you mean to say you regret choosing me?'

He took her hand. 'I also didn't mean that. Where else would I have found someone like you? Okay. Let's leave all this to one side. We have two beautiful girls, and we can learn from our mistakes and become friends. Why not? They're a treasure. Don't forget how long we've been together....'

Her eyes began to well up again. She accused him of being manipulative, devious, and of using all his cunning to lay the blame on her and make her feel guilty.... Then she stood up furiously and dashed into the bedroom. He began to feel guilty and to regret what he'd done. Why had he tried to open the door to calm conversation, reproach, and understanding when he knew from extensive previous experience that her anger peaked whenever he tried to explain the problem calmly? His calm voice infuriated her - as she said - and concealed his deception. It had the same conclusion every time, which was that he was trying to place the blame on her. So let him forget everything now, since she would no doubt calm down after a while. In recent years, she had become the master of the house. She had managed to completely dominate him and his role became restricted to avoiding arguments with her, and avoiding any discussion, however calm or important the topic. Sometimes he would excuse her - whenever he could find the strength - because he felt pity for the woman forced to love a man she didn't love, and whom she knew didn't love her.

But she emerged a little while later. 'Forget all that sweet talk, Medhat,' she said. 'I know your tricks. You want to destroy me.' He was so stunned by what she'd said that he forgot his promise to himself. 'How can I destroy you?' he asked. 'You're constantly insulting me. Did you forget that yesterday—' 'You're a liar,' she interrupted. 'I never insulted you. You're a liar….' She stopped to correct herself. 'And if I insulted you, then you deserved it.' It made him angry, how she had retracted her accusation, but he managed to control his temper and started to explain - calmly - how he didn't deserve to be insulted because he had come back from the fridge with lettuce instead of tomatoes, how that kind of mistake wasn't a crime, and that arguing over something as trivial as that wasn't fitting and was a waste of time. She seemed momentarily stunned, as though she couldn't think of a response. Then the answer came with the force of a storm. Had his reproach stirred her conscience and sparked a feeling of guilt that she despised, and which she expressed by pouring out all her anger on whomever awakened her moral sense? Was he making excuses for her because she didn't love him and because she knew he didn't love her, meaning that every time he made love to her, she felt she was being raped? Then suddenly she re-appeared. She had come back and stood facing him and smiling, carrying Karima in her arms (she had pulled her out of her crib, and the child was still half-asleep) and she gripped a pillow in her free hand. She carried on smiling as she walked into the kitchen and was still smiling when she walked back out. The pillow she threw at his face was on fire. That night was the breaking point. He felt then that the protection Zainab had swathed him in had been lifted and that he was now exposed to horrendous dangers.

'I never thought that a person's nature could be etched with malice until that moment,' he told Marika one day. 'I saw Evil setting a cotton-stuffed pillow on fire in an occupied apartment, and with children there.'

'Don't oversimplify the situation,' she replied. 'The girl deserves our pity, and you're being unfair. She's not well, that's all. Why don't you take her to a psychiatrist and try to help her?'

'A psychiatrist?' he replied. 'She can't stand to hear anything of the sort and will always accuse me of being the crazy one. And I know the first step towards being cured of a mental illness is the patient recognising that they're sick and need help. Isn't that right?' 'Why don't you divorce her?' Marika asked him, after giving it some thought. 'You shouldn't carry on like this. Situations like this could end up with one person becoming a murderer and the other the victim. And from what I know of you, you would never be the killer.' 'Divorce her?!' he said, incredulously. 'What about the girls?' He would have to live with the danger, the poison, and the fire.

Marika was disillusioned. She thought he was capable of escaping through the path of divorce. She didn't know Saniya very well. Around others, Saniya could appear all sweetness and light, and he didn't understand how she could burst into tears at the drop of a hat in order to come across as a victim. Her revenge would be dreadful if he divorced her. If she didn't kill him, then she would stop him from seeing Fathiya and Karima forever. Luckily, no one ended up as either murderer or victim. Cancer intervened and broke up the fight, after seven years of torturous chemotherapy and surgery. And she left him the two girls. He now regretted that he had left them and gone to Vienna, all because he still clung to the residue of youth. The eldest daughter lived with her husband and the youngest with Marika, but where was the paternal authority? He shouldn't leave her in this critical stage of secondary education. And had he truly escaped?

The protection around him had been lifted. And here he was, standing on his own, having been tossed to the side of the road. He had been liberated, but he was still a captive to his nightmares. The prison guard had departed, but how could he make up for the lost time spent serving this life sentence? It terrified him that he'd spent so many years coping through evasion, trickery, hypocrisy, and reproach. Especially reproach, the long conversation that would end in vain, or which would ignite the sparks of anger and violence. They were years he had spent without anyone to talk to. It had exhausted him until he stopped writing. His resistance, both furtive and open, was over, and he could no longer write. His freedom meant nothing any more. There was nothing more to say.

***

Here he was, standing under his umbrella, going nowhere and gripping his piece of paper. He'd already spent three days not speaking to anyone. He didn't feel hungry, but if he didn't go to the restaurant, any restaurant, then where would he go when it wasn't yet nine? And what would he do in his apartment? A smattering of people passed by in the street, each rushing to escape the rain, the flashes of lightening, the thunderclaps that followed and the sky that poured. In the dim light, he spotted three people approaching: a man and two women, so he strode off towards them.

'Excuse me, would it be possible for you to direct me to this address?'

He held out his hand, clutching the piece of paper with the address. The man walking slightly ahead of the others continued at the same pace without turning around. But one of the two women stopped to read the address.

'You want to go to that restaurant?' she said. 'That's where we're going, so just follow us.' Then she asked him, 'Where are you from?'

When he told her, she cried out, 'From Egypt? What a coincidence!' She called out to the man. 'Dad, you won't believe this. This man is from Egypt!'

At that, the man slowed down and greeted him with a nod of the head.

When they arrived at the restaurant, the head waiter welcomed them.

'Do you want to join us?' the girl asked him, whispering. 'Or would you prefer to sit on your own?'

He stammered for a bit before finally expressing his pleasure at joining them.

She whispered in his ear once again. 'Then don't mention that we met before.'

Taking a closer look, he could now see her properly and realised that he recognised her. She was the girl from the sauna; she was the violinist. He felt as though he had been dealt a dizzying blow to the head. Could she really appear to him three times, in a city as large as Vienna, in the space of a few weeks? It was very possible, because she was right there, talking to him. She was the one who had recognised him, even though she had never even looked at him in the sauna, and he hadn't recognised her when he saw her outside the restaurant in a red coat with a turned-up collar that concealed her whole face up to her cheek. Here she was now, in the flesh, standing in front of him. Someone came to take his coat and led him to a seat at a table near a fireplace, where he ended up sitting beside the young woman and opposite the father and the other daughter. He was still reeling from the shock when he heard her carrying out the introductions. 'This is my father, and his name is Carl. And this is my sister Salma. And I'm Nahed.' The woman repeated her name, which jolted him to introduce himself. His voice was hoarse when he asked, 'Salma and Nahed? They're both Arabic names, and Nahed at least is a genuine Egyptian name.'

Nahed raised her voice a little as she addressed her father. 'Mr. Medhat is surprised about our names. Why don't you explain it to him?'

'We're Muslims from Yugoslavia, from Bosnia.' the man said. 'I lived in Damascus and Cairo as a United Nations delegate. Salma was born in Damascus, and Nahed was born in Cairo. We chose a name from each city because we fell in love with them and wanted to keep the happy memories alive.'

He put an arm around Salma. 'Isn't that so, my darling?'

The young woman nodded in agreement. Her blue dress highlighted her pale complexion.

'We love Egypt,' Nahed said. 'I personally fell in love with Egypt when I visited it last year for the first time since I was a child. And what about you? Is this your first time in Vienna?'

'No, this is my second time; I came here for the first time around a quarter of a century ago.'

She leaned towards him and whispered. 'Please speak up a bit so my father can hear you. He's hard of hearing.'

He cleared his throat first to remove the huskiness in his voice. 'I was saying that I came to Vienna for the first time around a quarter of a century ago. At the time, I worked in the Egyptian consulate.'

Nahed laughed. 'I pale in comparison to all of you. My father was a senior employee in the United Nations, and you,

Mr. Medhat, used to work in the Egyptian diplomatic corps, and Salma is a communications engineer. As for poor old me, I work as a secretary in a company.'

'Don't believe her,' Salma said. 'She's a first-rate violinist.'

The waiter came to take their orders and asked what he wanted.

'I'll have whatever you're having,' he said.

'We came to have the boiled meat,' Nahed said.

'Then I'll have the same,' he said.

Warm currents flowed from the large fireplace that was packed with bulky, blazing lumps of wood, and his embarrassment quickly evaporated.

'I have to admit that I love Austrian cuisine. In my opinion, any cuisine that appreciates boiled meat, like you do, deserves respect.'

Carl leaned towards him so he could hear him better. 'What do you mean?'

'Boiled meat, if I'm not mistaken, is the food of country people, and I'm a countryman. I personally don't think anything can beat going back to the food of our ancestors. I've lived in many European capital cities, but I never found one where people like boiled meat as they do here. The English aren't interested in it, and the French and Italians are more advanced in the field of cuisine, and their tastes are more refined. But the French and Italians are no match for the Austrians. Boiled meat is a main dish here, served in the finest restaurants, and it's truly exquisite. What I like especially, and which you excel at here, even more than the country people of Egypt, is how they cook the spinach that's served with boiled meat.'

'But there are plenty of vegetables that can be served with boiled meat,' Salma said.

'In my opinion, spinach is the best,' he replied. 'Why? Because the chef who invented this type of meal made a discovery that was pure genius, which is that garlic - a little bit of garlic - raises spinach to the highest level.'

The two girls laughed.

'You should've told me this when we ordered the food,' Carl said. 'You said "I'll have whatever you're having," so I ordered the same thing for you that we ordered for ourselves: peas.'

Nahed didn't think they had missed the opportunity. She called for the waiter and asked him to bring Medhat a serving of spinach instead of peas.

'In my case, I liked the *molokhiya* in Egypt,' Nahed said. 'And that also shines with a little fried garlic paste.'

'*Molokhiya*!' he cried out. 'Europeans who visit Egypt either find it disgusting or it makes them ill.'

'I ate it wherever I was in Egypt,' Nahed said. 'I tried it in Cairo and in Sinai and in Aswan. I had the tastiest *molokhiya* in Aswan. And nothing happened to me.'

The conversation then progressed, through Nahed and her sister, to the Valley of the Kings, then Nefertiti's temple, the Edfu antiquities, the Mar Girgis church in the Old Cairo district, and then to the Ibn Tulun mosque. He was aghast, worrying a question might be directed at him about one of these subjects, and he would appear as ignorant of his country's antiquities as most Egyptians are - including the more cultured of them. He was about to say, 'We Egyptians don't spend much time looking at our antiquities, because of the abundance of treasure. Egypt is a huge museum from its northernmost tip to it southernmost point, but our tremendous riches have made us forget how wealthy we really are,' but he refrained from speaking, preferring to keep quiet on the topic. He didn't know anything about this history, apart from what he had learnt at primary school: about Menes, who united the two regions, Upper and Lower Egypt, and Khufu, who built the Great Pyramid. As for Khafre and Menkaure, he couldn't remember which one had built the medium pyramid and which the small. And the church in Old Cairo.... He'd heard it was there, but had never visited it. No, and he had never been inside the Ibn Tulun mosque, even though he had passed it. He was dismayed by his own ignorance. Though he had lived in Cairo and fallen in love with its relics, his wandering had been restricted to a few sections of the city. And he had never visited Upper Egypt, Alexandria, or Sinai. It pleased him when the conversation finally shifted away from Egyptian heritage with the arrival of the food. This took the form of a grand procession, presented by a head waiter and two assistants. As the fire raged, it shot out sparks, spreading cheer and joy in the air. The starter was a magnificent bowl of soup with marrowbones. May God bless you, Austrian people! He paused when he noticed that Salma was stealing glances at him. He hated it when people watched him. For a moment, he'd hoped he might end up sitting opposite Nahed, so he could revel in the beauty of her face, but now he thanked his lucky stars that hadn't happened. He didn't want anyone to discover just how much he lacked good looks. What he feared most was that someone could discern from his features that he was destroyed and terrified on the inside. During the great battle, his powers had been honed. But now that the war had laid down its burdens, he felt worn out, weary, and fragile. It was as though he'd exhausted his powers.

Nahed went back to talking about Egypt. 'We spent two nights in Sinai next to the St. Catherine monastery. Two of the most beautiful nights of my life. We would lie down on the ground - we'd each climb into our sleeping bag - and wouldn't shut our eyes until they had been filled with the sight of the sky with all its stars. And we would....'

He interrupted her. 'You said *we.* Were you part of a group?'

'There were only two of us: me and Salma. And in Sinai, I realised for the first time that we city people weren't just missing out on seeing the moon and the stars, we've also lost the ability to listen to silence.'

'That sounds like poetry,' he said glibly, since this was all part of an act. He felt a sweeping desire to direct the conversation towards music. 'I know that, in music, moments of silence are just as important as the melody,' he said.

'That's true,' Nahed said. 'Silence contains words we don't normally hear.'

He thought for a moment, then added, 'I discovered this when I fell in love with classical music.'

Salma changed the subject. 'What did you think of Vienna when you saw it for the second time?'

'I was seeing it from a distance the first time,' he replied. 'But now that I'm back, I wish I could kiss its walls and hug its people.'

Salma laughed, her face glowing as she spoke. 'Kiss the walls as much you like. But kissing its people...that's dangerous.'

All three of them laughed. Carl appeared to have somewhat withdrawn into himself, content with what he'd already heard. He drifted away from the conversation and looked as if he were masking himself behind his bushy white moustache and gentle smile.

Nahed asked him which composers he liked.

'I like all those who lived in Vienna, starting with Haydn, with the exception of Mahler and Schoenberg.'

'And why do you exclude Mahler?' Salma asked. 'I don't think you're doing him justice.'

'I don't hate him,' he replied. He stopped to think for a while before replying. 'It seems I'm not doing him justice, actually. The truth is I'm trying to appreciate him as much as he deserves, but unfortunately, I haven't been able to thus far. And I'm trying hard to like Wagner, but I can't....'

'How can that be,' Nahed asked, disapprovingly. 'I love Wagner. You don't know what you're missing.'

Should he express his opinions about Wagner in front of a professional musician, or play it safe and keep quiet? The best thing would be not to say anything, but Nahed nudged his shoulder with hers to spur him on.

'Tell us, then, why you don't like Wagner.'

He plucked up his courage and decided to take the risk after apologizing for his ignorance.

'Unfortunately, when I was young I didn't have the chance to learn music. No one where I grew up cared about teaching music. At secondary school, a music teacher came to teach us to play the oud, but he disappeared after two or three visits. He used to come along with his instrument, play it for a few minutes, and talk about the musical scale: do, re, mi, fa, so, la, ti. Then he disappeared forever. And my knowledge of music is limited. Now, when it comes to Wagner....'

Salma was still stealing glimpses at him to study his face. She must have noticed the crossed left eye, but now he'd forced himself to express his opinion of Wagner, come what may.

'As for Wagner, I've tried to like him, and I'm still trying, but I just can't fully appreciate him. First, I don't much care for the tales of northern European legends that inspire him. I come from the Mediterranean, or let's say I'm Greek in mind and heart. Second, I hate how he glorifies death. He believes love isn't crowned unless the loved ones are united by the darkness of death. Whereas I love light and the clarity of day, and believe that we can only lose ourselves in the beloved in this world of ours, and for a few moments, and in our human way. In other words, following separation and struggle. The rapture of uniting with a loved one is only available to those who have known separation and loneliness like we do in our life, this one. But when it comes to the ultimate extinction, there can be no uniting, euphoria, or love.'

'And why not, if this is his philosophy of love?' Nahed asked.

'It's difficult for me to accept this absurdity,' he replied, after some hesitation. 'I can understand the lover who wishes to die with the one he loves, in the hope they would meet in another life. But Wagner doesn't believe in another life. Death in his eyes is the complete dissolution. And third....'

Salma interrupted him playfully. 'Oh, and there's a third?'

He turned to her, laughing. 'And there's a third, Salma. To this day, I haven't seen a completely satisfying performance of 'Tristan and Isolde' - which is the closest of Wagner's operas to my soul. Why?' He laughed. 'Forgive me for what I'm about to say. To this day, I haven't seen a beautiful singer cast in the role of Isolde. Isolde has to be beautiful. It's not enough for her to have a beautiful voice. She has to be extremely attractive.'

'But that's not Wagner's fault,' Salma pointed out.

'That's true,' he said. 'It's my fault. I'm to blame. But you asked me why I didn't like Wagner, and these are my reasons. I'm waiting for the day when I'll watch an Isolde who has both a stunning voice and stunning beauty. Then I'll move a step closer to Wagner.'

'I hope you won't have to wait long,' Nahed said. 'The singing in Wagner's operas isn't easy.'

'I can't go to the opera if it isn't as pleasing to the eye as it is to the ear,' he said. 'And I think Wagner would agree with me on that. Wasn't he the one who proposed a theory of the opera as a comprehensive art that brings together poetry, music, singing, acting, and performance?'

He laughed, and Salma asked why he was laughing. 'I once saw an unforgettable production of Madame Butterfly,' he replied. 'I couldn't believe my eyes when I saw the singer playing the lead role. She was a huge mass of flesh and fat. Can you imagine! No one can convince me that this enormous singer - however fine her voice - can play the role of a young Japanese Geisha, delicate as a butterfly, as her name suggests. I had to close my eyes and force myself to be content with just listening - but it didn't work. Then the fatal blow came, destroying any chance of enjoyment, when I saw the butterfly's friends: a group of old crones. Lord, have mercy!'

Unfortunately, it was time for the bill, and they all prepared to leave. He'd hoped he would see Nahed's face as she laughed. But Salma looked like a child who was happy after a period of sorrow and pallor. Nahed noticed the signs of contemplation on his face. 'It seems you want to say something,' she said. There were indeed countless things he wanted to say. Time had passed quickly. He'd wanted the conversations about music to go on. Nahed was a girl of few words, and he'd hoped to hear her talk about music, and at length. That was what he needed. He was certain that a conversation like that would be capable of dispelling the remnants of darkness he felt were still perched in a corner deep inside him. And he didn't want to go back to his apartment. 'I'd hoped our get-together would continue for a little bit longer,' he said. 'Then here's to another one,' she said, smiling. The father was asked if he wanted a single bill for everyone or whether they wanted two separate bills. When Carl hesitated and looked at Nahed questioningly, she signalled to him with a nod, and he paid the whole bill.

'Tonight, you're our guest,' he said.

They agreed to meet again and exchanged telephone numbers, then the father and his daughters left. But Nahed turned back to kiss the guest on both cheeks the way friends exchange kisses when they separate. 'Goodbye,' she whispered. And the darkness immediately dissipated. He didn't move, not wanting the rapture to end. No one would believe him if he told them the whole story, but it had happened. Nahed's kisses were still imprinted on his cheeks. He struggled to leave the spot where they had left him, struggled to go back to his apartment, and to fall asleep when he went to bed. When he eventually closed his eyes, he found himself soaring above the towers of the cathedral. Was he one of the angels of the Merciful One, or Mephistopheles in the form of a bat, or a spaceship? His wings lowered him onto a dance floor and a girl approached, inviting him to dance with her. Was she Salwa? Had she returned to him? Or was she Nahed? 'But I'm not good at dancing,' he said. 'Follow me,' she said. 'Didn't I teach you how to swim one day?' She was Salwa then. But that was impossible - this girl didn't have red hair.

***

He closed the book, having given up on reading since he was too distracted. He would barely read one or two paragraphs before he'd have to tussle with drowsiness. In one of her letters, Marika had asked when he'd be back. At the end of the letter, there were a few words from Karima: 'We really miss you, Dad. But I hope you're happy there.' How could he reply? And how could he justify his long stay in Vienna? He put a Schubert record on without focusing on listening. But he perked up when 'The Singer's Possession' came on.

'Smash my joy into pieces,
Take from me everything I own,
Leave me just my cherished zither,
And I'll have bliss and riches known.'

He turned the telephone dial and called his friend Lopez: 'I want you to find me a music teacher.' 'You want to learn music?' Lopez replied. 'That's great, but I don't know anyone who can teach you. If Christina were here, I'd have asked her to take care of you. She teaches music to children.' 'I wish she were, because I want someone who can teach me the same way children are taught. Still, I'd prefer the teacher to be a man,' he replied. Lopez asked why he preferred a male teacher. 'I don't want us to be distracted by anything other than music,' he said. Lopez laughed. 'I know what you mean. Then give me some time to think. I might find a solution.' 'What about your friend who accompanies you on the piano every Friday,' he asked. 'Good idea,' Lopez replied. 'Why didn't I think of that? I'll suggest it to him, and I hope he says yes. In any case, I'll come back to you with an answer.' And the answer was that the teacher agreed to give him two lessons per week, so he asked Lopez if he could borrow the piano in the apartment. 'I know that it's Christina's piano. Please tell her I'm prepared to pay rent on it and also cover any maintenance costs that might come up.'

After everything had been settled the way he wanted, he started to feel regret. Was he being crazy? Was it possible for someone of his age to learn music? And did he have enough talent? People say those with the potential to pick up music are born with the talent, the musical ear, or vocal chords if they want to sing. And music is a challenging art, so did he have the capability, the time, and patience? And even though he'd found someone to teach him, he wouldn't be able to live in Vienna for long. He had to return to Egypt. The family had started asking him to come back. How would he reply to Marika's letter? It felt as though he'd acted rashly.

The doorbell rang, and he saw a short man with dishevelled grey hair facing him and smiling. 'This is a new and exciting experience for me. But let's give it a go,' the man said. 'Let's give it a go,' he said to Mr. Frederick. 'I can assure you from the start that I don't have lofty ambitions. I don't want to be a brilliant musician, since that's impossible. But I want to gain a good foundation in the language of music.' Frederick asked him to elaborate. 'I want to be able to understand its symbols, and how the composers can use it to express themselves through it. I want to reach a level of understanding that enables me to read the musical score of one of Beethoven's works, for example, and be able to follow it with its various fluctuations, while listening to the piece, and to work out its structure and the secrets of its craft. I want….' Frederick looked at him in astonishment. 'All that, and you claim that you don't have sweeping ambitions? So, in fact, you want to be capable of analysing a work of music, like a symphony or sonata by Beethoven, is that right? But in order to reach that level, you'd need to follow a planned course in music, music history, and the lives of its composers. It's a course of study that a young student would spend many years on. I propose that you satisfy yourself with taking lessons in music appreciation.' 'No, I don't like this impressionistic approach to understanding music,' he said. 'I don't believe it's possible to understand music the way I want to without learning how to play it and, at the same time, studying the theory. Let's put aside how many years would be needed. Let's start from the beginning - from scratch - and be content with that as a first step. I have a practical suggestion. How about we start with whatever a child would learn at primary school, with the first book in the curriculum? I think those initial lessons incorporate some practical teaching, or playing of instruments, as well as some theory, and I believe the two aspects are connected. You can sometimes stop to expand on one of the branches, or to open up parentheses, into which you can cram a historical fact: a note about harmony, for example, or about the origin of polyphony in western music, or about canon singing, or troubadour music, or whatever you like. In other words, I would like you to teach me as though I were a child, and I might be able to leap and skip some stages. That would do for me, and we can leave the rest for the future. What do you think?'

The teacher frowned and carried on shaking his head for a few moments, as if he wanted to turn the words over in his mind. It was clear he wasn't convinced by the proposed plan and was bewildered by this 'madman'. But in the end he sighed like someone who had surrendered his case to God, and agreed. And so the response to Marika was now clear; there was no need to search for excuses for his extended stay in Vienna. Let him act like an autocrat. 'My darling, Marika,' he wrote. 'Don't worry. I'm fine and I will return safely, without a European wife. But give me some time to have my fill of Vienna. I'm counting on your love and support.'

His view of music changed from the very first lesson. Quickly, he discovered that he didn't need to occupy himself with things like natural talent or the 'musical ear'. A much more basic and urgent issue had surfaced: finger control, since his fingers didn't function well. He couldn't place his index finger on one of the keys without another finger lifting or lowering. What was even worse was that his left thumb hung down of its own accord, below the level of the plank of keys, and it was unable to respond quickly or to coordinate with the other fingers. This always happened unconsciously and in spite of the teacher's repeated warnings. 'A musician needs to be prepared with all his fingers above the plank of keys, prepared to move the hands and fingers quickly to the right and left along the length of the plank. Don't you see how many octaves there are on the piano?' Frederick would then get up from his seat, his voice rising as if he were delivering a speech. 'Imagine you're gripping a billiard ball. Your fingers have to move from that position and then rush back to it. Imagine an eagle's claw. It's the eagle's crooked claws that enable it to grab onto its prey and not let it escape.' The student tried to carry out these simple instructions, but his rebellious thumb continued to betray him and to return to its wandering, dangling state. It would be surprised and disturbed if it were called to work, and the 'prey' would often 'escape'. Frederick was constantly shouting at him, 'The billiard ball, please!' to no avail. The student hadn't imagined that music started with the clasp of a hand, that controlling the fingers was no easy feat, and that some fingers rebelled and disappointed him (because they were deformed by old age and only ever used for activities that had nothing to do with music). This problem unfurled to reveal deeper challenges: the nervous system's ability to achieve harmony between the fingers of both hands and to respond quickly, as well as the brain's aptitude for memorising.... There were a multitude of problems he hadn't been aware of. Every time he thought of them, he started to despair. He'd go back to feeling indignant about time and its destructive role: he should have studied music at an early age, but time never stops turning, carrying our most valuable possessions along with it. He told himself that what he was trying to do now was a symptom of a mid-life crisis, and that it was trickier than finding a woman to love him.

'I noticed your fingers are shaking,' Frederick remarked one day. 'Why is that, when you're not yet at the age when your fingers should tremble? Have you had any traumatic experiences?' He stopped playing as a look of gloom passed over his face. Now the lid was being lifted from even worse problems. Here were even deeper layers of obsessions and fears. Why couldn't he learn music easily? Let's forget the billiard ball, his failing nervous system, and weak memory. There were other obstacles that gouged black holes in his concentration: the family in Egypt was calling for him, and Nahed hadn't telephoned him (every time the phone rang he thought it might be her, then he would be disappointed) and what was even worse was that Saniya's ghost loomed over him from time to time. She would be enveloped in shadows in a spot at the back of his mind before receding.

He complained to Lopez about his lack of control over his fingers, but his friend assured him he could overcome this deficiency through regular practice. 'Don't despair,' he said. 'You're still at the beginning. Music is a passion - that is, if you are passionate about it - and it's stubborn. You have to exert a great deal of effort to earn its love. But don't forget that patience and persistent hard work can achieve miracles.' He told him that Paul Wittgenstein - who was from Vienna - was a world-renowned pianist, even though he'd used only one hand - the left - after his right arm was amputated in the First World War. Frederick gave him a book with some finger exercises that he said Christina recommended. All that was splendid.

Now there were three people helping him to learn music, but he still needed someone for moral support; he needed a friend. How he wished Christina were there. The idea popped into his head, and quickly out again, when he remembered he was a substance that could combust if he ever came close to the opposite sex. How he wished he could meet a woman and enjoy her companionship without his obsessions. How could he get rid of these obsessive ideas? How could he escape his own skin? Was friendship with a woman even possible?

He realised now that he'd never known a single day of innocence in his whole life. Marika had asked him why he'd cried on the night of the wedding long ago, when he saw Na'sa dancing. He hadn't replied to the question, even though he knew the answer. He was afraid to tell her that he'd felt jealous. And why did he feel jealous at seeing his wet nurse dance? Because he saw a beauty in her that he had never seen before. He watched the body of a mother transform into a sensuous female one, and he watched as she separated from him to join the preserve of men. That's what he had witnessed with his own eyes. And he also hadn't forgotten the lessons Farida, who was a few years older than him, had taught him. She used to take him to the mosque to hide under the platform while everyone slept during the siesta hours, to reveal things to him that he hadn't known before. Then he remembered that music had also revealed itself to him at an early age. The angels arrived no later than the devils. Would music be his cure? Could music tame the beast that perched in his depths? Bach prays, Haydn smiles, Beethoven battles and defeats the challenges, and Schubert reproaches in order to reach reconciliation and joy. Would they be his physicians?

***

If his fingers worked the way they were supposed to, Frederick would congratulate him. 'Well done,' he'd say. 'You should've come to me thirty years ago, at least. Then you could've become a skilled musician or composer. No, more likely you would've become a composer. The great musicians normally start at age four or five.' But if the defect reared its head, he would complain and shout. 'Sir, control your fingers. And you must time the rhythm to the second.... Music is a good conductor of time. Count, tap your foot on the floor, or sing as you play. Or let me sing along with you.' And he would sing. If he despaired, he made it known. He would keep looking at his watch or stand near the window and whistle or hum, and he wouldn't leave any room for doubt that he'd lost interest or wanted to leave. Sometimes, he would leave in anger, and it would seem as though either he wouldn't come back, or he'd send a message through Lopez that he was stepping down from continuing the lessons. But he would always return, exultant. 'Did you practice? How long did you spend? What's the latest with your fingers?' He said that learning to play an instrument was like practising a physical sport, and that a great piano player was like a sporting champion with record scores, except that his strength was in his fingers, not in his muscles. 'You have to imagine how much effort and patience a championship requires. But don't lose hope. You should know that the greatest musicians put arduous effort into learning pieces. The greatest musicians suffered for music and the great composers constantly tortured themselves with difficulties and challenges. We decided from the start that you wouldn't ask for the impossible and would be satisfied with what you can achieve, as much as your energy permits. Isn't that so?'

One day, his teacher asked him for an update on the state of his fingers. 'Finger flexibility is a huge problem for someone of my age,' he said. 'I understand,' Frederick replied. 'But there's something that pleases me about your playing, which is that you don't look at the keyboard, but you look instead at the score. And sometimes you glance away from the score, which is a good sign. I think that you'll soon be able to ignore the score completely, for a relatively long period of time, and to even play with your eyes shut. You know, some blind people are very good at playing.' 'I've noticed that my fingers, despite their deficiency, do whatever is needed of them, sometimes of their own accord, even if I'm not focusing on them,' he replied. 'Am I right in thinking that fingers have their own memory?' Frederick asked him what he meant, so he continued, 'Some blind people, as you say, are skilled at playing music. And the great musicians don't need scores. They learn the tune and leave the rest to their fingers. Doesn't that mean that the melody seeps into the fingers and settles within them so that each finger knows when and where to land on the keyboard or strings? It's exactly the same way a person learns to type using their ten fingers on the typewriter, or learns to climb up or down the steps. At the end of the day, one has to let his fingers or feet take control and shouldn't interfere with their instinctive work, or else he will stumble. Isn't that so?' 'What also pleases me,' his teacher said, as though he had just remembered something important, 'is that sometimes you might stumble when playing a musical phrase, but after listening to me play it, it corrects itself. That's wonderful. That means the sentence has penetrated you unconsciously. That's how a child learns music. I also notice that you sometimes sway as you play, without realising it. I hope that's a sign that the melody has started to seize and move you. So let's continue. Show me what you'll do today.'

He'd started to understand some of the fundamental musical concepts that he used to encounter only through reading, and therefore would comprehend only in a vague, theoretical way. Thanks to the piano, he could now understand - in practice - the concept of pitch in sound, from raising by sharpening, to lowering by flattening, and what key and meter were. It occurred to him that poetry, like music, was organised according to certain moulds, described in Arabic poetry as scales, or *buhoor*. He could now read the most rudimentary essentials of music in the score.

Whenever he confronted music, he felt like the same child who had first learnt to read in Abbas Square. *Read, in the name of your Lord, Who has created.* Reading was one of life's greatest miracles. So too was the act of decoding the symbols of the musical score and transferring them through the fingers to the keys, or to the vocal chords through singing. Even if the happiness reached here was greater. The symbols of the musical score were precise and initially seemed impenetrable, as though part of an intractable puzzle. But when unraveled, they revealed a melody, or the melody broke through like rays of sunshine piercing thick clouds. Then the score would speak and express itself. The meaning revealed itself; we heard the singing of the composer, his message reached us. The rapture was unparalleled! That was what Schubert found in his lyre, a joy and richness that he sang and which contented him. Joy and wealth lived mainly in the five visible lines of the score, as well the other hypothetical ones and the spaces between the lines and the symbols, signs, and instructions that followed. Here, the composer lay down his poetry; here, an entire world existed. Music was an art form where only right would prevail, and the melody would emerge only after a long, arduous labour. But with the surfacing of a melody came the emergence of understanding, and this was the greater joy. If he could ease the tune out, then he would've placed one foot on the road to proper understanding, and he would become one of the champions.

But sometimes his ghosts would appear, blurring the lines and spaces, scattering the symbols, forcing his fingers to twist and cramp, and hollowing out black holes in his memory and attention. Only after suffering a great deal of hardship and hearing his tutor's grumbling and exasperation would he be able to control the chaos and disarray. It was true that his fingers rebelled against him and let him down, but his mind was controlling the fingers and nervous system, and it was his mind that was exposed to bouts of fear and worry. Karima, who he'd left behind in Cairo, was getting ready to finish her secondary education, and there was Nahed, who hadn't surfaced for about a month now, and so on. 'See you,' was the last thing she'd said to him. When would they meet again? Should he have asked her that question? Or was it better that he masked his eagerness? Nearly a whole month had passed, and she hadn't called. He started to flinch and jump at the phone whenever he heard it ring, before he realised that the caller wasn't the one he wanted.

Then there was the problem of his rebelling thumb: why did it withdraw and dangle? Had it been damaged when Saniya grabbed it, twisting it violently as he tried to grab the key to the apartment from her so he could go to work when she'd wanted him to stay imprisoned at home all day?

***

The final music lessons became a cause for ridicule, even though the teacher tried to hide his sarcasm. But Medhat could see it in his glances. So should he pack his suitcase, leave everything in Vienna, and go back to Egypt immediately? Should he summon all his strength and turn his back on Nahed, the music lessons, and the concerts in the company of Lopez? He could find a solution to the music problem in Egypt, even though Egypt could dent his resolve and drive him away from the things he wanted to do. As for Nahed…they'd spent a beautiful evening over a lovely dinner, but then what? 'See you,' she'd said, *Auf Wiedersehen*, but that's what people always say, whether there would be an occasion or not, and it wasn't necessarily a promise to meet. Yes, but she had turned back to say it. Let's say she meant what she said, what did he want from her? And what did she want from him? Yet…yet, he still faced a terrible challenge, which he had to overcome. The teacher had asked if he'd been traumatised. What could he have said? He couldn't have told him about marrying a destructive woman, about living in fear, a fear of being set alight and of venomous poison. Saniya had left her traces in his fingers, his nervous system, and his memory. If that was his greatest challenge, then he had to overcome it.

His interest in music distracted him from thinking about Nahed for a day or two, until he decided to call Salma to see whether he could glean any information about her sister. Salma greeted him warmly: 'Where have you been? Why did you disappear? Are you still in Vienna? When we didn't hear from you, I thought you might've gone back to Cairo.' 'I couldn't go back to Cairo without letting you know, after that wonderful dinner and the hospitality,' he said. And he was pleased when she replied, saying, 'Then you should've called. It's the man who should make the first move.' So there was no need for him to feel embarrassed. She was right. He was the one who should take charge and initiate contact. So that's what he did. 'Truth is, I want to invite the three of you to dinner, and dinner is nothing but an excuse to meet you and enjoy your company.' 'Oh, I wish we could, but my father has gone to visit his family in Bosnia, and Nahed is travelling on an assignment for work.'

Faced with this conundrum, he didn't know what to say or do next. How could he end the call tactfully? Salma's voice flowed over to him. 'Can we wait until they get back?' He didn't answer. 'Or what about we meet for lunch, you and me?' she suggested. He felt at a loss, since he hadn't anticipated her suggestion and hadn't wished for it. Still, he couldn't back out now. It would be rude to refuse. Luckily, she proposed they meet for lunch - in the daytime. 'I don't make a big thing of lunch,' she said, which pleased him. 'Or of eating in general. At least right now - managing my weight, you know.' Then she laughed. 'A sandwich or a slice of gateau with some coffee at a café would do. The main thing is to meet before you leave.'

They had lunch outside on the pavement at one of the cafés on Maria Hilfer Street. As he sat facing Salma, a question puzzled him - there were two sisters and their father, but there was no mention of a mother. Where was their mother? He was about to ask, but he overcame his curiosity and decided to avoid all personal matters. Instead, he asked how her father was. She said her father was well, although he sometimes became depressed because he lived on his own. After a short while, she ended up telling him what he wanted to know. She explained that her mother and father had divorced a long time ago. She and her sister had decided to live with their father until they completed their education, when each of them settled into their own space. He asked whether they saw their mother. 'From time to time, since she lives in Vienna, but actually she's the one who doesn't want to see anyone,' she replied, before adding, 'She's a difficult woman.'

He tried to change the course of conversation, but she asked if he was married, and he told her he was a widower. 'I'm divorced,' she said. 'I got married after a long love affair. Then, after we were married, I discovered my husband was having an affair with one of my friends - my best friend, in fact. Can you imagine! It happened after two years of happy marriage.' She stressed the word 'happy' in describing the marriage and laughed bitterly. He felt a desire to talk about his marriage - if only he could turn Salma into his keeper of secrets and a bandage to his wounds! - but he overcame the temptation. If he started that conversation, it would never end. Worse, he didn't know where the complaints and the bandaging of wounds would lead. It would be better to avoid that temptation and be satisfied by saying that marriage was a difficult social institution, but a necessary one. 'I don't think it's necessary,' she said. 'In my opinion, it's better that lovers stay lovers.' Then she added, 'and it would be best if they didn't live under one roof and only met by appointment. What do you think?' 'It's feasible, but only until we remember the social pressures,' he replied. 'There's also the desire to settle down or feel secure. Then there's the question of children, if they appear on the horizon.' It was better if he remained reserved and limited his contributions to generalities.

The important thing was that he'd finally achieved his goal. Throughout the lunch, he'd wanted to ask when Nahed would be back. He would take one step forward, then another one back, and then stop. But Salma finally volunteered the answer, as if she knew what was going on in his mind. 'I don't know when Nahed will be back. The company wants her to stay on in Sankt Pölten to supervise a training course for new employees, but she didn't want to take such a long break from her violin practice and from playing with the band. They're trying to tempt her with a promotion and a salary increase, and they're negotiating how big the pay rise would be. If it's significant, Nahed will accept the offer.' She asked him when he would go back to Egypt, and he told her he had to travel as soon as possible, even though he didn't know when that would be.

So he was still left dangling between the sky and the earth. Nahed was negotiating with the company, and things hadn't yet been settled. And he was negotiating with himself and couldn't settle things there either. He had to go back to Egypt sooner or later, and sooner rather than later. That was what he'd decided at lunch when he heard the news, and after he asked himself: Why didn't Nahed call him from wherever she was? There were telephones and there was the post. Why didn't she contact him directly? Then he would go back and say that the relationship was only superficial and didn't justify so much care and attention from her side. Maybe she wanted to see him, but she just left it to the circumstances. And he shouldn't ask for more from a superficial relationship. But if the relationship was superficial, wouldn't it better if he didn't place more importance on the matter than it could bear, and to pack his bags and leave instead? Then he remembered that Nahed had 'appeared' to him three times, which he felt was a miracle that shouldn't be downplayed. It was as if her appearance in that way had created a connection that should also be valued. And with that, his resolve would collapse.

And what about the music lessons? Should he stop them, when Frederick was a brilliant teacher who couldn't be rivalled in Egypt? He was obstinate, that was true, but he combined practical expertise in music with the mastery of music theory, as well as knowledge of the history of music. Great - but he couldn't live in Vienna for years just to benefit from this wonderful musical knowledge, and he had to leave. Inside this cloud of confusion, he decided to postpone his departure by two weeks. Why two weeks? Why was the grace period not one week or three? Because the decision was random, and he took it as it came. And because the truth was that he was torn and unable to take a sensible decision. And what was a sensible decision. anyway?

***

Frederick asked for an update on the progress he'd made since their last lesson. In between, the tutor had missed two lessons, giving his apologies each time. He replied that he'd taken the opportunity to practice all the pieces in the book several times over. 'In my own way, of course,' he added. 'There must be mistakes and faults. But I felt I needed to unleash myself.' 'How much time do you devote to practice?' the teacher asked him. 'Six hours,' he replied. 'Three hours in the morning from ten till one, and three hours after lunch from three until six.' Frederick thought that was too much time to spend practicing. After playing for some time, the teacher stopped him. 'Great. I don't want you to play the complete pieces. One or two phrases from each will be enough until we reach the end of the book.' 'That's enough for me,' Frederick said, when they'd finished the last piece. 'I want you to set this book aside, and let's start working from another one. Here it is.' 'In this book, you'll find extracts of the works of the greatest musicians,' he said as he handed it to him. 'The songs are simplified of course, but it raises us to a higher and more enjoyable level. It's over to you then. Show me how you'll deal with these.'

The first piece was an extract from Grieg's 'Morning Mood,' and he found it easy. So that one went well. As for the second, which was an extract of Beethoven ('Ode to Joy' in the Ninth Choral Symphony), he stumbled on the third line and found it difficult to cross this obstacle. After that, he came an extract from Tchaikovsky's Fifth Symphony, which was a familiar melody, having been stored in his memory from the days of Sayyida Aisha. It was one he particularly enjoyed, because he could hear Tchaikovsky's wails in it, and he played it from the heart, or so he thought. Frederick's feedback was encouraging. 'There are some flaws and lapses, but it's not bad… not bad?' The teacher paused. 'No, not bad isn't enough. I have to admit that throughout this lesson - this lesson specifically - I've been listening to you play in amazement - what can I say? There's been a leap. What happened during my absence?' 'I'm glad to hear you say that,' he replied. 'What happened in your absence? I don't know, but I know I was depressed all week.' 'It seems depression can sometimes be fruitful,' Frederick said. 'In any case, something like a miracle has happened for someone learning music at your age. But I don't want you to become vain. There's still a long, long journey ahead of you. Your fingers have become more flexible, and it pleases me to say that, when you make a mistake and play a wrong note, you realise it immediately. It's as if you know that music requires perfection. That's the business of music: perfection. The problem is, when you play, there's no chance to correct yourself. You can erase a word or sentence if you're writing, and carry on writing, but you can't do that when you play music. Music has no mercy, and there's no scope for correction. If you make a mistake in front of an audience, it's catastrophic and there's nothing you can do. There's also the problem of timing. I notice that you always speed… but I don't want to put down your efforts. There's a time for everything, and I'll be satisfied enough today to say: "Congratulations…I'm happy to be teaching you."' And he held out his hand to shake his.

He didn't want him to become vain? Vanity and ecstasy had risen to his head. He left, but couldn't bring himself to go straight home, so he circled the city restlessly until dawn. He had a long journey ahead of him. The extracts he was playing were meant for children, which he knew very well. But for him to be playing, at this stage, phrases by Beethoven? The 'Ode to Joy' in the Ninth would be the thread to guide him to the rest of the symphony. He would search for its original version, and he might ask the teacher to listen to longer and more difficult sections with him, and would ask him to explain the harmony and the sonata form that the classical music was set in. And the 'Ode to Joy' that came at the end of the symphony was the key, because he knew it carried harbingers and good tidings with it from the start.

But his rapturous dreams didn't completely protect him from earth's gravity. From time to time, the irritating question returned to him: when would he return to Egypt? He finally settled on a decision once he'd prepared for bed. He wouldn't leave before reaching the last extract in the book of classical pieces, come what may.

In the morning, he called Salma to let her know he'd decided to stay in Vienna for a little while longer, which she seemed happy to hear. 'In that case, there will be a chance for the three of us to meet before you go back to your country,' she said.

***

Whenever he recalled how the fingers of professional musicians - let alone the greatest of them - moved along the plank of keys, he realised that setting a goal of mastering music was like reaching for the stars. He didn't want to master music, since that would be a stroke of madness, but neither was playing music to a decent level an achievable goal. For example, when he went back to a song of a few phrases that he'd played the previous day, why did it seem as though he were playing it for the first time? What did that mean? That he was ignorant when it came to music? Or that his memory had weakened in middle age, or that his mind had become so packed, either forcefully or willingly, with knowledge or worries, that it became agitated when anything new presented itself? Or was it a mysterious feeling of guilt that caused him to become apprehensive in front of the piano? Did he dare enter the world of music? Was he an intruder or an aggressor because music was forbidden to him? Did someone deem this superior intellectual luxury excessive? He thought he was facing a power, or powers, that were trying to curb him whenever he wanted to launch himself. He had managed to overcome this power when he moved from the countryside to the city, and when Salem tried to suppress him, and when his wife exerted her utmost to restrict him, but he was no longer strong enough to resist. Or was it the lusts of the body? '*But the body, it is weak.*' Had the time come to sink and deteriorate?

That was what he was thinking as he wandered back and forth across the room and the telephone rang, so he charged towards it, yearning as usual. Salvation had finally come to him. Nahed was now coming to rescue him from his worries. He would describe to her - she, the musician - what he was going through, and maybe she would bring him some form of comfort. But the caller wasn't Nahed. He heard a female voice.

'Hello, Nahed,' he said.

Salma's reply came to him. 'It's Salma, Medhat. How are you?'

He was flustered, but replied, 'I'm fine. And how are you?'

'You were expecting a call from Nahed, is that right?'

'Your voices are indeed similar.'

'That doesn't surprise me,' she said.

'Medhat,' she said, after some silence. 'I'm really bored. I can't stand to just sit at home on my own. Can you take me out tonight?'

Embarrassed, he hesitated. He hadn't felt this way when he'd had lunch with Salma by the side of the road, when all they drank was mineral water. They'd met in broad daylight in a way that wouldn't raise any questions. As for meeting in the evening, and what dinner and drinks could lead to, that was another matter. But the idea of going out and escaping the piano and all the agitation it caused him was appealing. The strenuous daily practice had started to frustrate him - six hours of exhausting work every day - because it wasn't in his nature to do anything by halves. From what Salma was saying on the phone, it sounded like she was in some kind of psychological distress, and she was asking a favour from a friend or an older brother. Poor Salma... she was still in the prime of life, and it seemed she hadn't yet recovered from the tragedy of her marriage and divorce. He couldn't forget the paleness of her skin and the sadness that moved across her face from time to time, like a passing cloud. And he couldn't forget how the cloud would suddenly dissolve when she found a reason to laugh or to tease someone, as if she were still a teenage girl who'd never suffered a scratch. He overcame his embarrassment and agreed.

He saw her from afar as she swaggered along in a fur coat. When she saw him, she started to stride over, hunching down beneath the rain that had started to fall. 'I didn't bring an umbrella,' she said, gasping. 'Let me take cover under yours.' Then she looped her arm through his as she said, 'High heels are one of the world's biggest calamities. Men are lucky because they don't need any of these tiresome female wiles.' 'I've brought you to this Italian restaurant because I discovered they serve the best veal escalope in the world,' he said, as she read the menu. 'I didn't taste anything like it in Rome.' 'Good for you. As for me, I want to forget the diet tonight and being thin and all that. I'm fed up with denying myself food, and maybe that's the reason for my depression.' 'So what will you order?' he asked. A wide grin lit up her face and her eyes gleamed. 'I want osso buco and risotto, cooked with butter and marrow,' she said. 'And before either of those, a serving of grilled vegetables. And what will we drink?' 'As you like,' he replied. 'How about an Italian red wine?'

'Excellent,' she said. 'But I want a double shot of whisky with ice straight away.' She sighed as she drained her glass and relaxed.

'I was thinking about you yesterday,' she said. 'And it occurred to me…I mean, I feel sorry for you being so lonely after your wife's death. Don't you ever think about getting married again?' 'I think once was enough,' he said, then added, 'or that was my case. You're still in the prime of life, and you can easily—' 'On the contrary,' she interrupted him. 'You're wrong. A man can get married at almost any age. It's the woman who must succumb to strict restraints, restraints imposed by nature. Beauty as you know, fades quickly, since there's the weight that piles on and….' She stopped to laugh then continued, 'And the complexion that wrinkles, the hair that falls, and the hormones and so on. A woman doesn't get to enjoy her youth for long, and she spends most of it battling these threats. She's locked in a permanent battle to win the man's approval.' 'And have you forgotten about the dangers of high heels?' he asked. She was pleased by the mention of high heels. 'What you said is true, I swear,' she said enthusiastically. 'Thank you for reminding me about the nightmare of high heels.' Then she asked him to order her a second glass.

So now the awkward initial stage had passed, and it was no longer difficult to think of things to talk about. Actually, talking to Salma was easy, because she was open minded, brave, kind, and didn't hide anything. Should he tell her that his aversion to the idea of marriage stemmed from the failure of his first? He felt a strong urge to confide in her and vent, especially to this young woman who acted like a younger sister. But she distracted him with what she said next.

'Next time - I mean if a man looms on the horizon - I'll refuse marriage, and insist on being just a lover,' she said.

'Living under the same roof won't be allowed. We'll meet only by appointment.' She pursed her lips. 'That's my final decision.' 'Is faithfulness a condition in this relationship?' he asked. 'I mean, is cheating allowed?' She frowned. 'How would we know if we lived separately? Living separately means peace of mind. Anyway, he would be free to do whatever he wanted, as long as I don't know about it. As for me….' 'I think you would be loyal,' he said. 'That's true,' she said. 'You totally understand me. I can't be anything but loyal.' 'That's why,' he replied, 'I think after a month or two, or let's say six months into this arrangement, you'd pack your things and move into his apartment to live with him.' When she objected, he continued, 'If you're the loyal type, then you'd quickly start to depend on him and spend your time waiting for him. You wouldn't cope with his absence for long, and you might even follow him and insist on making plans to see each other. And maybe you'd feel jealous of his independence, or because you suspect he might be seeing another woman. Isn't that so?' 'You know me well. It's like you're reading an open book,' she replied. 'I'm incapable of cheating - that's my nature - and loyalty leads to emotional dependence, as you say, and, after that, permanent suffering. Why didn't I think of that?' After a while, she added, 'You're right. I'm easy prey to jealousy because I am, as they say, a one-man woman, and I want my man to be completely mine. My ex-husband used to complain that I was very clingy….'

She stopped talking, and the look of sadness that he'd spotted the first time he met her passed over her face. Then she looked up at him. Was she complaining to him? Was she pleading with him to guide her towards a solution to her problem of becoming too attached to a man? He wanted to make her feel better. 'You have a lot of time ahead of you and lots of opportunities,' he said. 'I'm sure of it. There's no need to exhaust yourself by overthinking it. Let's think about the osso buko and the risotto for now, since they've arrived.' The brightness returned to her face, and she raised her glass as she smiled. 'You're a wonderful person. You give me confidence in myself and in the future.... Cheers.'

She seemed obviously pleased with what she'd ordered. 'This butter and marrow risotto is irresistible. Oh, those devilish Italians! Look how they've added wild mushrooms - they must be wild, it would be enough....' She stopped to remember what she wanted to say, then it looked as though she'd changed her mind. 'I envy Nahed. We're two sisters, with the same parents, but different...totally.' He couldn't hide his eagerness at the mention of Nahed: 'How is she different from you?' he asked, keenly. 'She's much stronger than I am,' she replied. 'And she's often tough with those who get close to her. She thinks very highly of her beauty and musical talent. Even though she likes to attract male attention, she doesn't give much back.' Unhappy with this description, he started to feel depressed. He didn't want to eat anymore, although he carried on with a bite here and there.

'I don't know much about women,' he said. 'I got married, and I fell in love with plenty of women. In most cases it was unrequited.' 'Unrequited?' she cried in disbelief. 'You're just saying that.' She winked. 'Maybe this is one of the tricks you use with women.' 'Not at all,' he said. 'I won't lie, most of what I know about them is from reading and writing novels.' He'd only said this to steer the conversation towards novels, but it seemed she didn't notice his hint.

'But you've only drunk half a glass and left me to finish nearly the whole bottle.'

'I'm mainly interested in the food.'

'But you've only eaten a little. Look how I gobbled up everything I was served.'

'Don't worry about me. I eat slowly so you don't see my hideous country ways. If only you could see me when I eat on my own! That's when I return to my natural state and eat like a rapacious beast.'

'Don't exaggerate,' she said, laughing. 'I can't imagine you eating like a rapacious beast. In any case, I'm thirsty tonight and want to drink. I hope you don't mind.'

They ordered more wine, and she went back to talking about her sister.

'Our relationship is complicated. We're competitive and jealous of each other. And that has deep roots in our childhood. I was the first child and the star of the family until she arrived, when the spotlight turned to her. She became the spoilt one, since she was the youngest. And she's the more attractive one with the stronger personality, so don't blame me if I'm jealous.'

'And why is she jealous of you?'

'Honestly, I don't know. Maybe it's because I graduated with a university degree and she didn't. She struggled to finish secondary school. Ever since she was young, she's loved music, so she devoted herself to it and disliked all other academic subjects. She learnt about music purely through willpower and some private lessons. Basically, she doesn't like academic study, and hates studying and reading and exams, relying instead on her natural intelligence. That helped her get far in music, but now she regrets that she didn't study music at any college and didn't earn a degree. She should have....'

When the waiter arrived with the sweets menu, she ordered a dessert along with a glass of grappa and a coffee. Her face brightened when the waiter returned with a whole bottle of grappa and placed it on the table. 'You wouldn't hold me back from it,' she said coquettishly, pointing to the bottle. 'Or would you?' 'I couldn't hold you back from anything,' he replied. And he meant what he said. The young woman had a childish innocence about her, and it was difficult to keep a child away from sweets. They would hate you if you did. And how had this woman's husband found such coarseness in his heart to allow himself to cheat on her? If he'd married a girl like her, he would've spoilt her rotten and given her anything she wanted. But what could you say? The world was full of scoundrels.

During the taxi ride to her apartment, she asked him if he liked children, which made him laugh. 'I have two daughters. One of them is married, and I'm going to be a grandfather soon.' 'You're lucky,' she replied. 'I wanted a child from my Don Juan husband. Luckily, my wish wasn't granted, but women are restricted in another way, by the limits of fertility.' She continued, 'I don't understand infidelity or cruelty. Do you know that my parents have been divorced for around twenty years, and each of them lives in Vienna, but they don't meet and haven't spoken since they decided to separate? My mum hasn't found another man, but she still only sees us reluctantly.' Then she added, 'Why am I burdening you with these sad stories? It looks like I overdid it with the drinking. But I needed to drown my sorrows…forgive me. I'm dizzy.'

She leaned her head on his shoulder, but carried on speaking with a heavy tongue. 'When we met you on our way to the restaurant, I'd had an argument with Nahed, and my father wanted to bring us together over dinner to clear the air. Then Nahed forced you on us….' She stopped to apologise. 'I'm sorry

I used that expression. Don't be angry with me. We didn't know you. You were a strange man we met in the street. My father wasn't comfortable with what Nahed had done, and he wished you had chosen to sit at a table on your own. I'm sorry to admit that I agreed with him…but we appreciate you now. You passed the test.' 'Which test?' he asked her. She didn't answer. It seemed as though she'd fallen asleep. But after a while, she started talking again. 'Nahed took the initiative - as usual - when she invited you to join us. And it's a good thing she did, but that only makes me more jealous. She's quick-witted. She always manages to steal the limelight, and the men flock to her...even my father…what can I say? He's guided by her, even though she's the younger sister. I hate her….'

She asked him sweetly if he would go to the kitchen to make her a black coffee. 'My head's spinning, and I feel sick, Medhat. You'll find milk in the fridge, if you want coffee with milk. But I want it black.' And she climbed into her bed. He asked her if she was all right. 'Don't worry. Everything's fine,' she said. 'But please, you don't have to keep standing. Sit down here.' She pointed to the edge of the bed. She held his hand when he sat down, but as soon as she turned to lie down on her side, he took the opportunity to pull his hand away. He hadn't wanted to go up to the apartment, and the snow had been falling when they were in the taxi. But he couldn't leave her at the entrance to the building. It was obvious that she needed someone to help her up the first steps and into the elevator. She apologised for disturbing him. 'I should've been better company for you. That's the difference between me and her; she's always alert and doesn't seem to need anyone. But me…. You hit the nail on the head when you talked about my dependence on other people.' 'I enjoyed the evening,' he said. 'And I'm happy that I got to know you tonight.' 'You're just flattering me,' she said. 'Believe me,' he said. 'You're a wonderful person and you deserve all the best.'

He meant what he said, and he felt sorry for the girl because she had a capacity for love that was being wasted. That was, until she said, 'Take off your clothes and lie down beside me.' She'd mumbled it, so had he heard her properly? When she repeated it, he suddenly felt that disaster was imminent. Why did life expose him to challenges he couldn't handle? Was it fair that he should face a test like this? The prophet Joseph was able to resist the woman in whose house he'd lived when she tried to seduce him, and she did *desire him and and he would have inclined to her desire, had he not seen the sign of his Lord.* So he'd desired her.... He'd responded to her, he'd advanced one or two steps towards her, and he'd placed his hand on her. And if it hadn't been for the evidence, that clear sign, he would've fallen. Divine help supported him. He'd sensed the sign. But the sign was bright and cutting like a sword. As for him - Medhat from the village of the Qassimis in Sharqiya province, the son of his grandmother Zainab, and his wet nurse Na'sa, and Marika the Greek woman, and his aunt Haniya - what a multitude of mothers he had had! - he felt like an abandoned child. Medhat, who was obsessed with the opposite sex, and infatuated with this woman specifically. He was smitten with her, and he could see that clearly now. He wanted this vulnerable young woman, who was in need of some tenderness, who wanted to wrap her legs around him in this stormy weather. He was lonely and couldn't see any light; he was no prophet. His faith was weak, as Marika had said. And nobody would blame him if he answered the call. 'You can't go out in this weather,' he heard Salma say. 'They said in the weather report that there's going to be a blizzard.'

He got up from his place at the edge of the bed to look out the window and saw the snowflakes falling with terrifying intensity. He felt trapped between this accumulating snow and Salma. Was it fair to have to face this painful test? When he returned from the kitchen with the coffee, he could see her attractive figure and her soft legs through her short, transparent nightgown. Here she was, available. If his shirt had been torn from the back...*my dear, forget all the myths about being thin and dieting, you're attractive just the way you are, and you are flawless...I wish I could kiss every inch of you.* 'You can't leave in weather like this,' she repeated. 'Please don't leave me alone,' she begged him.

He'd experienced life in several cold cities and had become familiar with living below zero degrees, but the cold in Vienna was unique and could penetrate a body like a bullet, settling into the back and the feet, and here she was inviting him to the warmth. Finally, he would be capable of quenching his eternal thirst and achieving the goal of his journey. Didn't he come to this city in search of women? Now one of them was inviting him, and she was attractive, warm-hearted, and willing. *So approach her then*. He took two steps towards her bed, wanting to advance on this accessible female, when he heard her muttering. 'Nahed will be back before Christmas.' An idea or a whisper floated up from his depths. 'Triumph to joy,' he was told. Triumph to joy? For a moment that seemed to stretch out, he stood frozen to the spot, seized by this important idea. And what was joy? When he finally moved, he put his hand out and tucked the blanket around Salma as he mumbled. 'Go to sleep, you bitch. *Guten nacht.*' Then he put on his coat and left. So what was your sign?

***

He could now enjoy feeling safe and reassured, since the storm had passed. Except that his legs and feet still felt frozen, despite the apartment being warm. He got up to fetch a hot water bottle. The ice cold that had penetrated his extremities would melt only when he placed the hot water bottle directly between his feet. As he felt the warmth flow slowly through them, he relaxed, yawned, closed his eyes, and perhaps dozed off. Maybe he was writing, since he sometimes composed his writing when he was asleep or drunk.

Let's try then to look at this from another perspective. Imagine you're a spaceship and you have a telescope. Its lenses are directed towards this planet called Earth, so what do you see? I see it's better to look at the case of this spaceship. I often feel that Salem struck me a fatal blow when he threw me out. But my lifelong struggle with Saniya, which lasted for nearly a quarter century, was even tougher. Still, there was more to the story. The long journey started when I became attached to Salwa because she was a '*bandar* girl,' and then I moved to the '*bandar*', civilisation itself, and lived in many capital cities of the world, and now here I am, having ended up in Vienna, the mother of all *bandars*. Still, I have held within me, and continue to hold, the image of the camel that turns the cogs of the oil factory. Deep down, I am a peasant. I have the skin of a peasant, the patience of the parched land he farms, as it waits for the season of sowing. I have the steadfastness of the acacia, the sycamore, the cactus, and the crows during the dry season.

Here is a countryman returning from the Wednesday market, overcoming sleep on the back of his donkey. And suddenly a voice reaches him from afar, perhaps emanating from the depths of the canal. He opens his eyes, the voice drawing him in and tempting him, and here is the 'Summoner' calling him from the depths of the water. Woe betide he who answers her call. Foolish is the man who surrenders to the wonder of the voice, for the female jinn seduces him so she can marry him and lead him into her underground world. The intelligent man is the one who blocks his ears to the sound and doesn't stop, because another woman waits for him; she is his life companion and the mother of his children. Doesn't this remind you of the story of Odysseus on his way home to his own country after the wheels of war stopped turning? When he approached the sirens, he ordered the men to plug their ears with wax and keep out the singing of the seductive mermaids, and to tie him firmly to the ship's mast so the singing wouldn't lure them to their deaths. That was how Odysseus escaped, and there was a loyal wife still waiting for him after many years - she was his homeland. There is a place in the countryside, the image of which always follows me wherever I go, and it is the *seera*. The idea of hosting guests in a stand-alone place must've been established in the desert, from the arrival of the first Qassimis. I saw something that resembled it in Jordan, at the border of one of the towns - maybe Amman or Jarash - where travellers can alight at any time and be welcomed into a tent overlooking the road and invited for Arabic coffee, the pot constantly set on a low flame. At the Qassimis' *seera*, there was food for the vagabond, the poor, the wayfarer, the visitors, and the travelling poets. The pots of tea and coffee bubbled continuously, never resting. One of the stories from the Odyssey that Marika had told was that Odysseus had a similar place for hosting guests. It was there that the suitors, who were lusting after his wife, stayed while he was away. They stayed for years without ever leaving. They would eat from his bounty, devour the meat of his herds, and the dishes wouldn't be lifted unless others were being brought out. Each would try to win his loyal wife's heart. And when Odysseus returned, he killed the uninvited guests and wiped them all out. And hadn't Paris stolen Helen away, his host's wife, which prompted the grinding machine of war to turn for ten years? And I am a loyal man.

That's a lie. You cheated on Salwa and you tried to cheat on Saniya, but you couldn't. Yet I was loyal this time. Salma summoned me to drag me to her grotto, and I longed for her body, but still, I put on my coat and left in agony. She was available, and the weather outside was stormy. But see how I wished her a restful sleep and I left, anguished. So what was your sign? It wasn't bright or cutting - it was an idea or a whisper that hovered, but it was enough. Salma was sexy, lovely, and attractive. She had a childish sense about her, and she was sweet and in need of tenderness, and my soul was - and still is - keen for her. But I would've been opportunistic and vile if I'd jumped into bed with her as soon as Nahed had turned her back. And what was wrong with that? Maybe she would wish you both happiness when she returned. That was her problem, but my problem is that I love her. Yes, I love Nahed. When she stripped bare and dropped the bath towel in the sauna, I was blown away (she was like a flash of lightning that pierced the clouds), even if that act of hers was a bit flamboyant. But Nahed didn't truly 'appear' to me until she found me tossed on the side of the road. 'Follow us,' she'd said. That invitation seemed to harbour no ulterior motive. Was it truly free of any intent, from the desire to attract attention to herself? That's what Salma might have said. He noticed that Salma was jealous of her sister. Which one of them should we believe? Neither this one, nor the other…I believe myself. It was practically dark when

Nahed saw a man holding out an address in his hand that he was trying to find, so she said, 'Follow us.' And when she found out he was from a particular country, she invited him to join them for dinner, out of a love for that country - or so it seemed. 'Join us,' she'd said. It was unlikely there would be any ulterior motive.

But the assumption is enough for me. Because what Nahed did, whatever her intentions and motivations, abolished the evil of the foreigner's despair. I cannot deny that favour, no matter what Salma said. I don't know what lies inside people's hearts, but the care she offered me was enough. And see how she asked me not to reveal that we'd met before? Why had she done that? I don't know the reason. But what she did was enough to create a beautiful collusion between us, and that was enough. Therefore, I love her. And since that night, I have started to see her wherever I go in the city. Her image is with me day and night. I will triumph this time - to joy. When we separated, there was nothing between us but her words, 'See you.' It was a phrase that people usually say out of politeness and as a matter of courtesy. We hadn't promised anything, since there was no opportunity for that. She said it and disappeared. How can you claim you hadn't agreed on anything? Isn't there a vow between the guest and the host? A pact convened as soon as the guest accepts the invitation? Otherwise, why did Odysseus slaughter his burdensome guests? And why had the fierce war in Troy blazed and raged? But what was the use of keeping the vow if I knew with all certainty that I wouldn't get anything out of her? She was elusive, and I had nothing with which to tempt her. I'd go back to Egypt empty-handed, without her or her sister. And the prophecy that predicted I would emerge from the water with no catch would turn out to be true. The promise that was made between you meant that she would come back and find you just as she left you - her guest. Otherwise, she would've spoilt the unique moment of affection that shone in that night of despair. Admit she reduced your stumbling and lifted you from the abyss in which she found you. Admit that when you were tossed to the side of the road, you were on the brink of despair and losing faith in life. There was only pitch-black darkness and death. Then she came and said, 'Follow us.' That was joy. And that was your sign. You came to life by chance and moved to the city by chance and received an education by chance and loved reading by chance and escaped from Saniya's prison by chance and met Nahed by chance. And it was a happy chance, so cherish that moment and protect it, keep it in your focus, heed it, and don't aspire for anything else. Did you forget your promise to yourself when the rope was knotted around your neck, that if by a miracle the rope became unravelled, you would never again allow sorrow to enter your life? Now the rope has been released, and you are free. Triumph, then, to joy. You have the light of the sun, and the air, and the countries, the length and breadth of them, and your freedom, so celebrate. And you left Salma, and my heart was - and still is - full of agony.

When I'd almost reached the end of the journey back from the Summoner's grotto to my apartment, the snowflakes reminded me of the fireworks on carnival night. Nahed would return before Christmas. That was five weeks from now, and I'd wait for her no matter what happened, and she would find me the same way I was before she left, since I was nothing but the man she hosted. And I'd return to Egypt without getting anything more than she'd already given me, and what she'd given me wasn't insignificant. *Won't you feel deprived of her in*

Egypt? I will feel that. And will you be cured of your heartache? Won't you be beset by regret because you sacrificed Salma? And how can you imagine I'll be so easily cured? Salma could've been the woman I was searching for. Didn't she say she was a one-man woman? But that wouldn't change anything. I received Nahed's gift, and the matter was settled. And I wouldn't return to Egypt empty-handed. And why was I forgetting about music? Maybe some of it had seeped into my fingers. Then there was the tune that would need some work for it to emerge. The tune was your prize. I'd thought I had dried up, but I see now, at the end of the journey, that I had two projects for two novels, and I would flip the perspective in each. In the first novel, I would do justice to Salem, since Marika was unfair imposing a strange child on him who spoilt everything, because, if the child hadn't appeared, Salem would have revelled in his wife's love for the rest of his life. The collapse of the beautiful man horrified me. And then I would do justice to Marika, as Salem had been unfair when he didn't respect her need for a child. And could I deny her overwhelming motherhood? How to set the balance? The balance was there. This was the balance that the author set between two sides, each with their own perspective and rights. This novel was easy. In the second novel, I had to strip myself down in order to do justice to Saniya, because Medhat was unfair. Poor Saniya, she might be excused. She'd married a man who was impossible to access, a man who'd decided since early childhood to wander through an extensive, infinite space, and it had eluded him that being lost like this meant he'd be isolated from people of flesh and blood. The poor thing wasn't able to reach him. Maybe she would've responded to him and come to love him if he'd been a sure-footed man on the worldly land, if he'd made her feel free from fear. And that was absolution. And that wasn't easy. The problem, in this case, was that, when you hate someone in this way, you lose your faith in the whole world, and you hate everything. It seemed there was no solution to this problem, but you were wrong. It might be that Nahed's gift was the beginning of the solution, that it might purify your heart of hatred. Could it be the light at the end of the tunnel? You'd have to fight this battle on paper. The only hope was for the novel to become your guide during its writing, for it to lead you through this baffling labyrinth, and perhaps it would impose the necessity of forgiveness. Let us say that the trip to Vienna might have achieved its aim. Let us say that the two novels had become within reach. Let us say that they had dropped 'into the palm of your hand'.

My darling Marika. Don't worry. I will return safely, without a wife or a mistress. But I have to warn you, I will buy a piano, and you have to put up with the noise I will make. With my love and kisses. Yours faithfully, always, Medhat.

We would finish this page. *Gut Schlafen. Go to sleep, you bitch. Go to sleep, you son of a bitch.*

The phone rang, and Salma's voice filtered through. 'What's all this sleep? It's almost midday.' 'Good morning, beautiful,' he said. 'I hope you slept well.' 'You'll never believe this,' she said. 'I woke up at eight, and there was no trace of drink. I slept so deeply I felt reborn. That was all thanks to you. Thank you for looking after me so well. And how are you today?' she asked. 'By the way, why didn't I find you next to me when I woke up? Why did you leave the bed early?' He hadn't properly woken up until he heard her say that. 'But I didn't spend the night beside you,' he said. 'I left after I made the coffee.' She laughed. 'You don't have to be embarrassed or modest. You were amazing. You're an incredible man.' 'Amazing?' he said, annoyed. 'What do you mean? Aren't you joking, my darling?' 'You know what I mean,' she said. 'It's true I was drunk, but I was aware of everything that happened. It was an exceptional night of love, and you've risen even more in my estimation. I'm infatuated with you now. And I'm looking forward to the next time we meet. When will I see you? By the way, Nahed will be back soon, before Christmas….' Her laughter grew louder as she spoke. 'The sorceress has to know that you're mine now. So when will we meet? I miss you now; I want you. And I can't wait.' 'Salma, please,' he pleaded. 'You're dear to me…. You're like my little sister. Tell me that you….' Then he stopped and put the telephone receiver back in its place. He couldn't understand anything anymore, but he realised now he wouldn't be able to escape. There was no point in continuing the conversation. What would he do? Everything was over. It had all turned to dust. There was no point waiting for Nahed—he had to escape. He got up from the bed, trembling, and hurried to the kitchen for a drink, but the freezing cold water didn't put out the fire inside him. Collapsing at the edge of the bed, he gripped his head to stop it from exploding…*my darling Marika. I would've liked to come back safe.*

Glossary

al-Azhar al-Sharif University: A central Islamic university, known around the world

Asr: the afternoon prayer in Islam

Bandar: "the world of civilisation and luxury"

Basbusa: Middle Eastern semolina cake

Effendi: a Turkish title of respect

Esha: the nighttime prayer in Islam

Farquilla: a whip made of plaited rope and an iron handle

Fatiha: the first *surat* or chapter of the Quran, traditionally recited in Muslim families in Egypt to bless an engagement before it is formalised

Fatta: a dish prepared using bread soaked in soup with rice on top

Fiseekh: a salted, fermented fish

Ful: fava beans, or a dish made using fava beans

Ghazal poets: poets who write secular love poetry

Haseera cheese: cottage cheese made using a suspended straw mat

Hattat, plural of *hatta*: a form of headdress worn by some Arabs

Jawwala: higher ranks of Boy Scouts

Jilbab: a long garment worn by men in some Arab countries

Jibba: a gown worn by students and teachers at al-Azhar University

Jurn: a public space used for threshing and winnowing wheat

Kusb: oil cake used as livestock feed

Lycée: A school that follows the French curriculum through secondary level

Maghreb: sunset prayer in Islam

Muassel: a mixture made up of tobacco and molasses

Nay: an oriental flute

Sai'da: locals from Upper Egypt

Sakan: ash from a stove

Seera: a community guesthouse

Sefary bed: a single-person travel bed

Sharbaat: a cordial made from rose petal syrup usually served in Egypt during engagement or wedding celebrations

Sirja: a factory where oil is pressed

Sirwal: baggy, knee-length underwear worn by men and women

Suhur: the last meal consumed before starting the fast, typically during Ramadan

Thareed: a dish prepared by soaking bread in meat stock

Thawb: long dress-like garment

Thawb al-malass: a dressy thawb worn by women

Wafdist: a supporter of the Egyptian leftist Wafd party

Wekala: the place where villagers visiting their home town leave their donkeys

Zeer: a large clay vat